THE RISE OF
AURORA WEST

First Second

Copyright © 2014 by Paul Pope
Published by First Second
First Second is an imprint of Roaring Brook Press, a division of Holtzbrinck
Publishing Holdings Limited Partnership
175 Fifth Avenue, New York, New York 10010
All rights reserved

Cataloging-in-Publication Data is on file at the Library of Congress

Paperback ISBN: 978-1-62672-009-1
Hardcover ISBN: 978-1-62672-268-2

First Second books may be purchased for business or promotional use. For
information on bulk purchases please contact Macmillan Corporate and
Premium Sales Department at (800) 221-7945 x5442 or by email at
specialmarkets@macmillan.com.

First edition 2014

Art by David Rubín
Story by JT Petty and Paul Pope

Type set in "PPope," designed by John Martz
Book design by Colleen AF Venable and John Green
Printed in the United States of America

Paperback: 10 9 8 7 6 5 4 3 2
Hardcover: 10 9 8 7 6 5 4 3 2 1

THE RISE OF AURORA WEST

Written by JT Petty and Paul Pope
Art by David Rubín

:01
First Second
New York

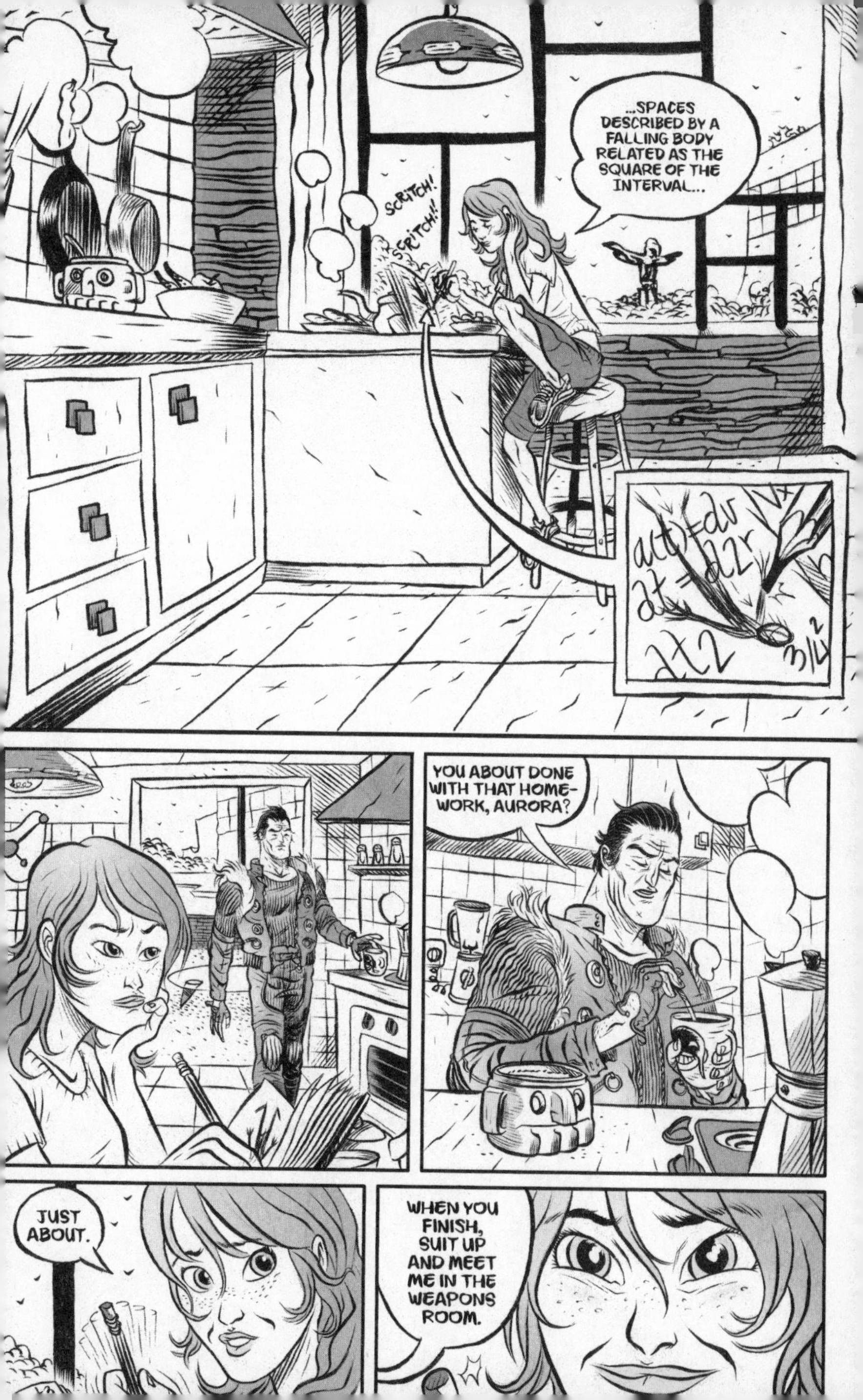
SCRITCH!
SCRITCH!!
...SPACES DESCRIBED BY A FALLING BODY RELATED AS THE SQUARE OF THE INTERVAL...
YOU ABOUT DONE WITH THAT HOME-WORK, AURORA?
JUST ABOUT.
WHEN YOU FINISH, SUIT UP AND MEET ME IN THE WEAPONS ROOM.

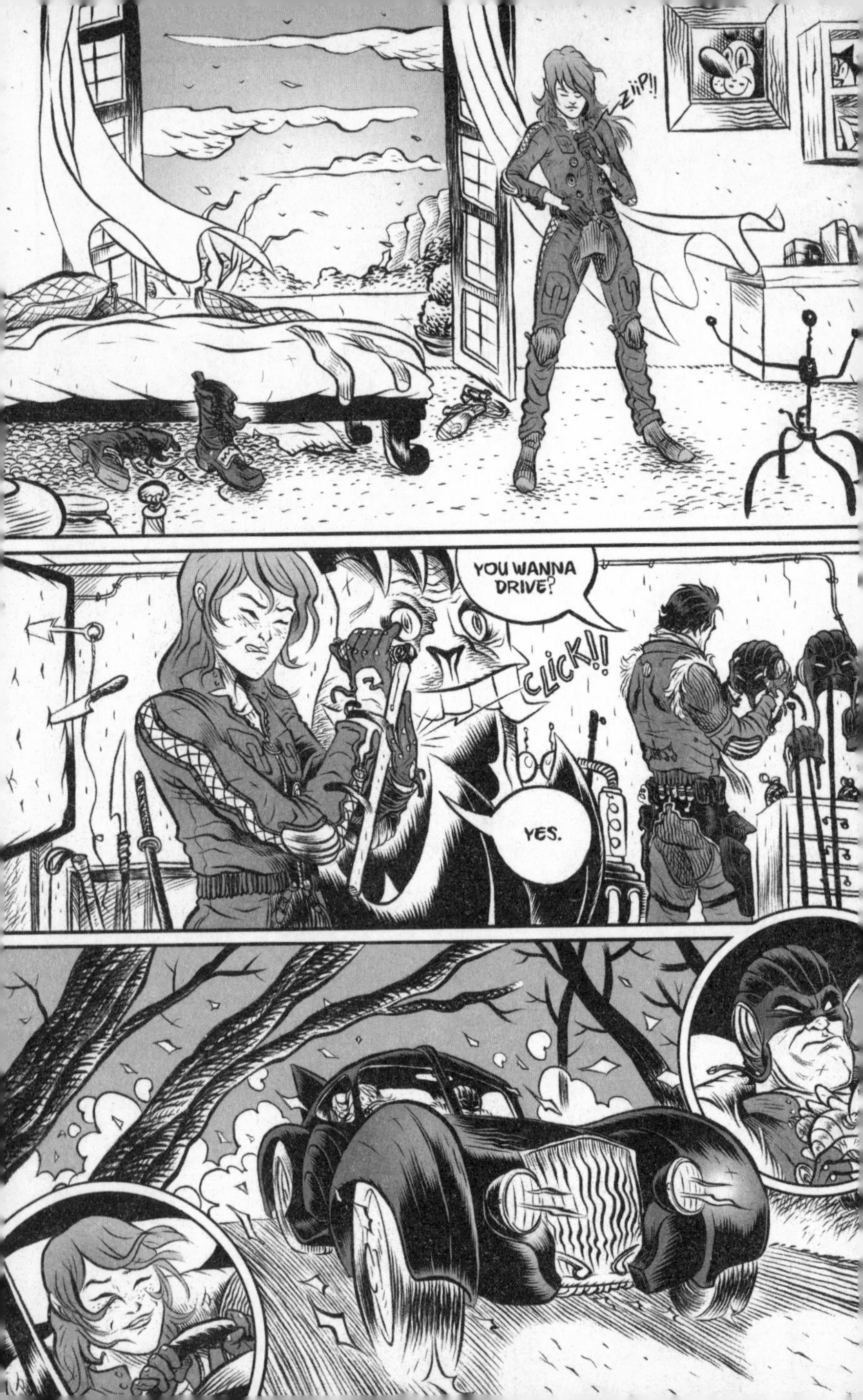
ZIIP!!
YOU WANNA DRIVE?
CLICK!!
YES.

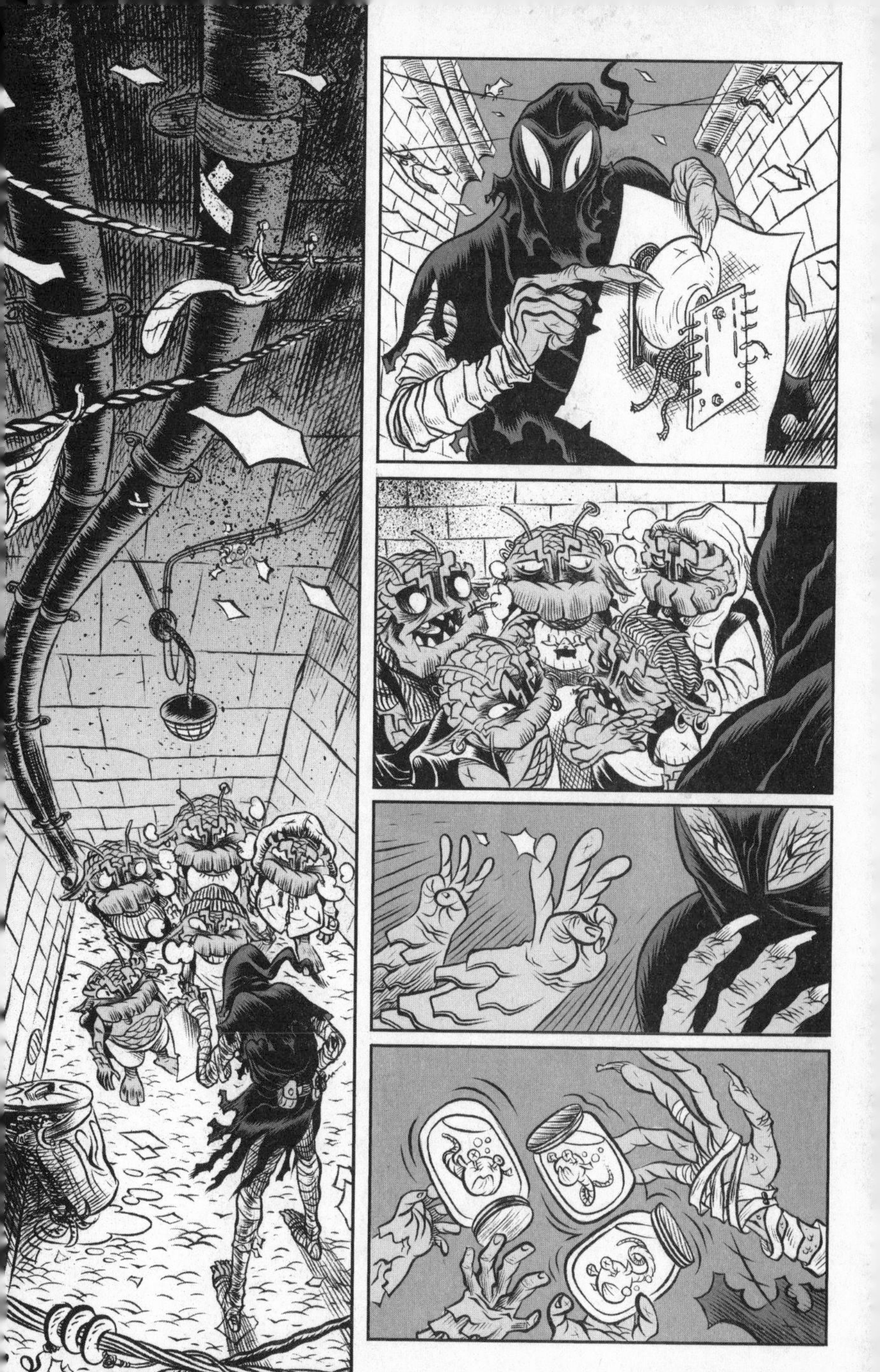

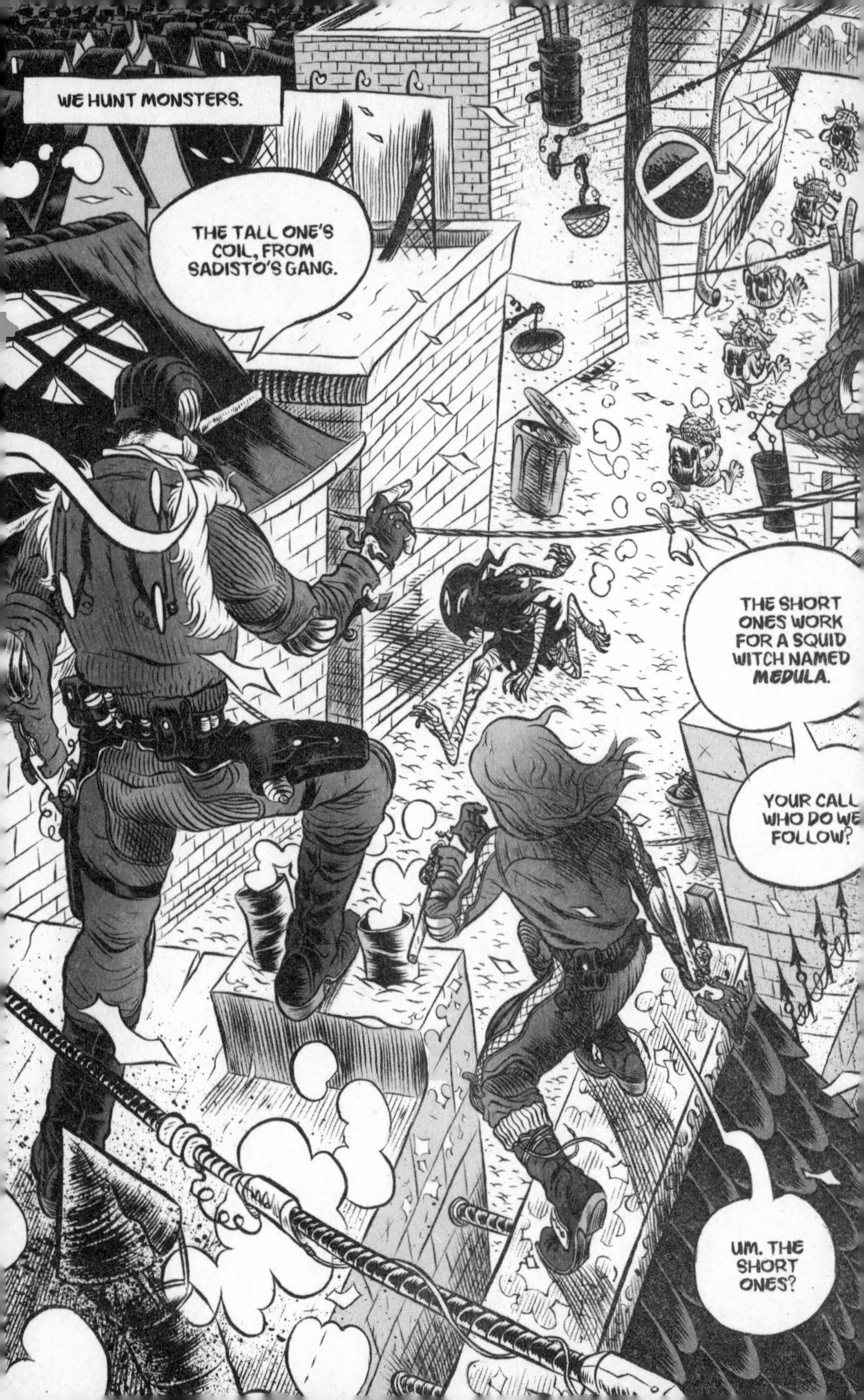
WE HUNT MONSTERS.
THE TALL ONE'S COIL, FROM SADISTO'S GANG.
THE SHORT ONES WORK FOR A SQUID WITCH NAMED **MEDULA**.
YOUR CALL WHO DO WE FOLLOW?
UM. THE SHORT ONES?

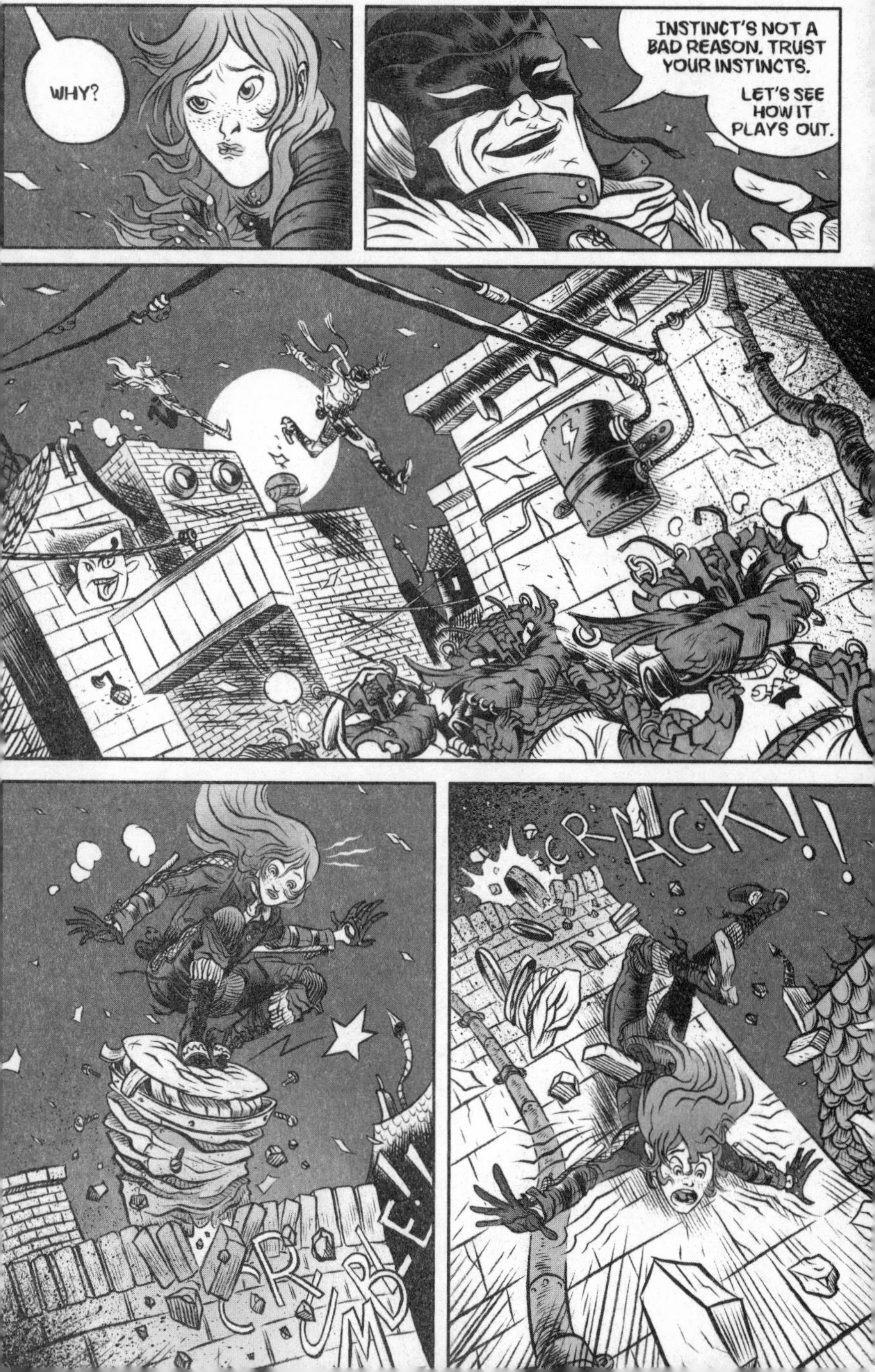
WHY?
INSTINCT'S NOT A BAD REASON. TRUST YOUR INSTINCTS.
LET'S SEE HOW IT PLAYS OUT.
CRUMBLE!
CRACK!!

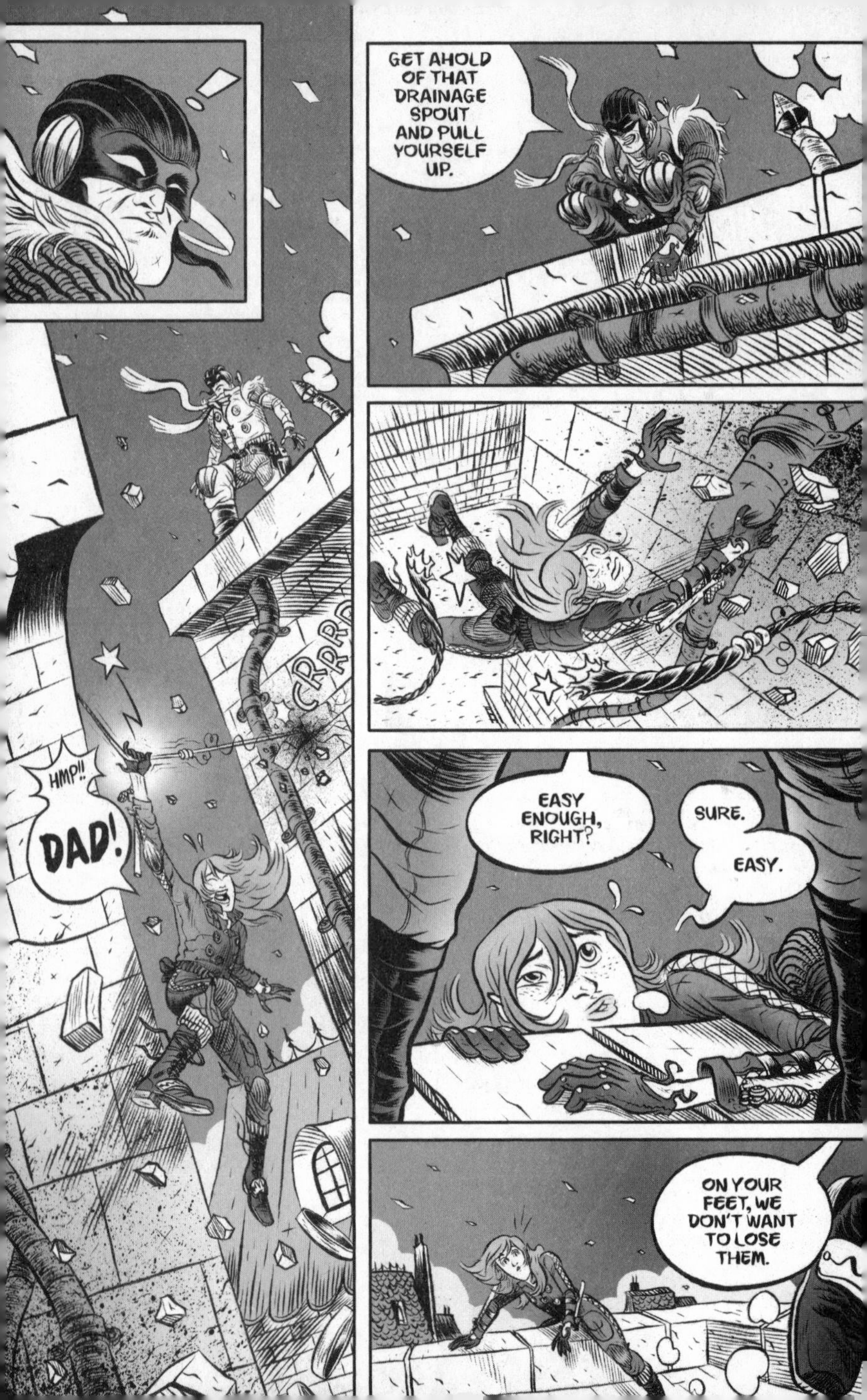
GET AHOLD OF THAT DRAINAGE SPOUT AND PULL YOURSELF UP.
CRRR
HMP!!
DAD!
EASY ENOUGH, RIGHT?
SURE.
EASY.
ON YOUR FEET, WE DON'T WANT TO LOSE THEM.

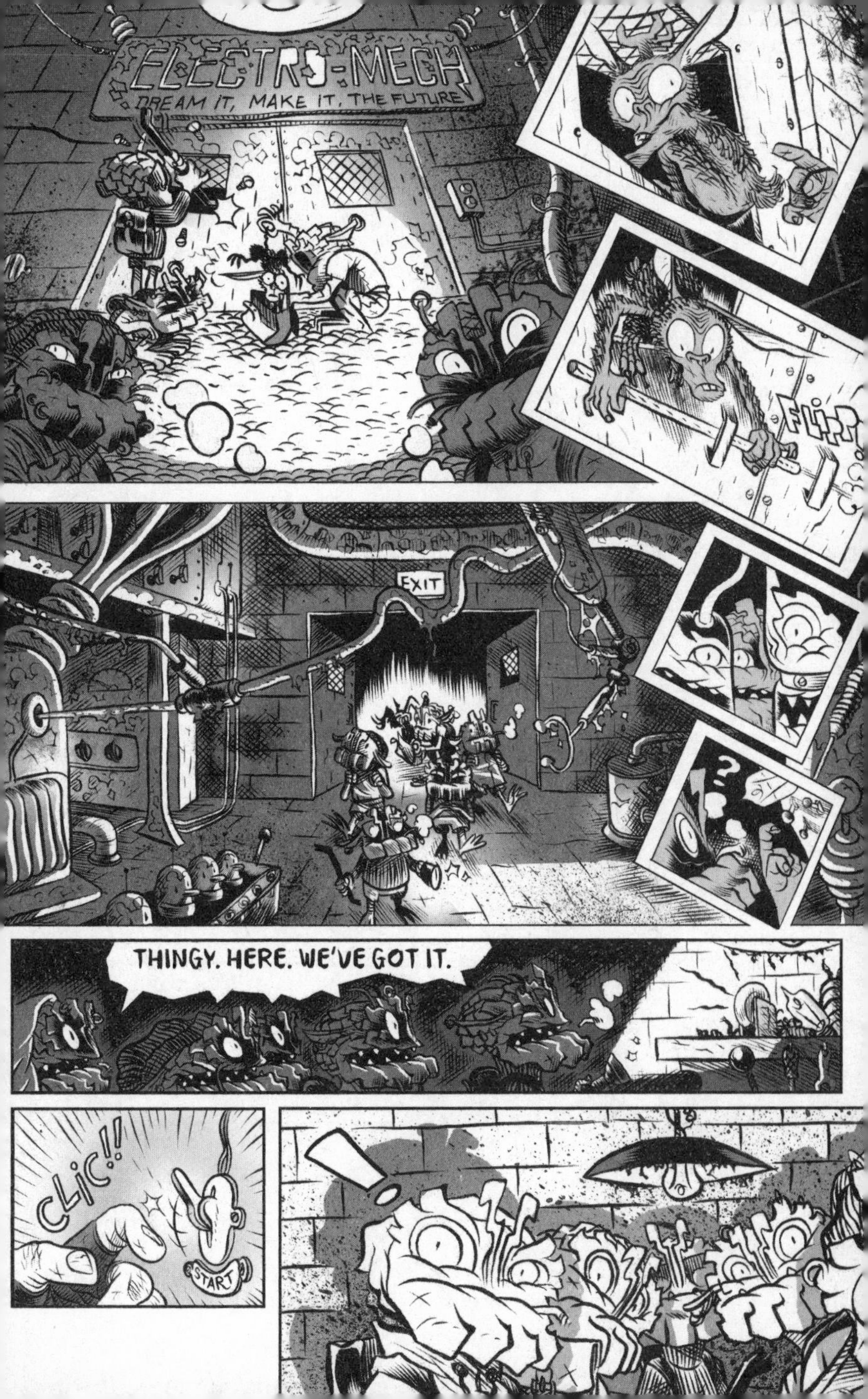

ELECTRO-MECH
DREAM IT, MAKE IT, THE FUTURE
FLIP
EXIT
?
THINGY. HERE. WE'VE GOT IT.
CLIC!!
START
!

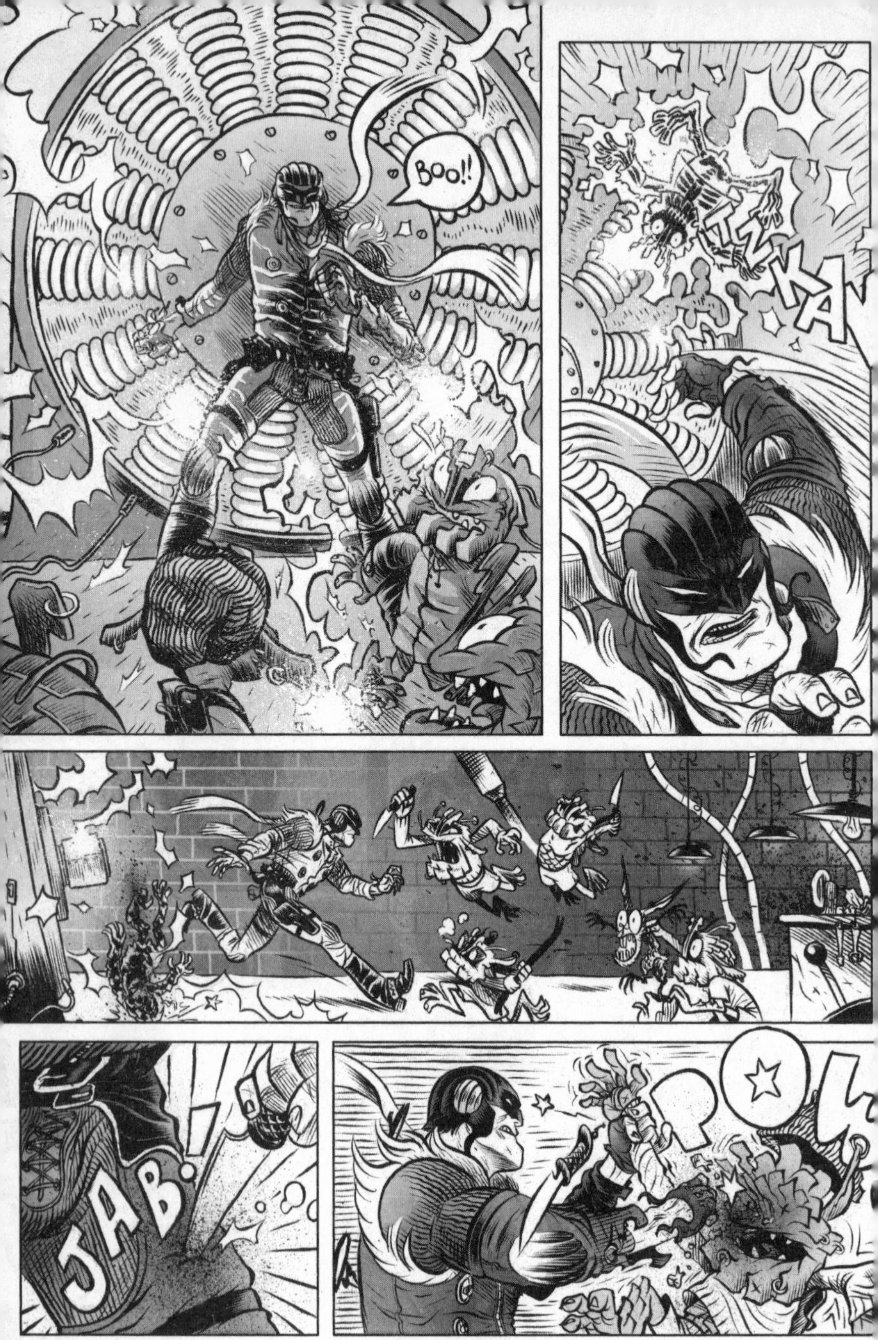
BOO!!
TZKA
JAB!
PO

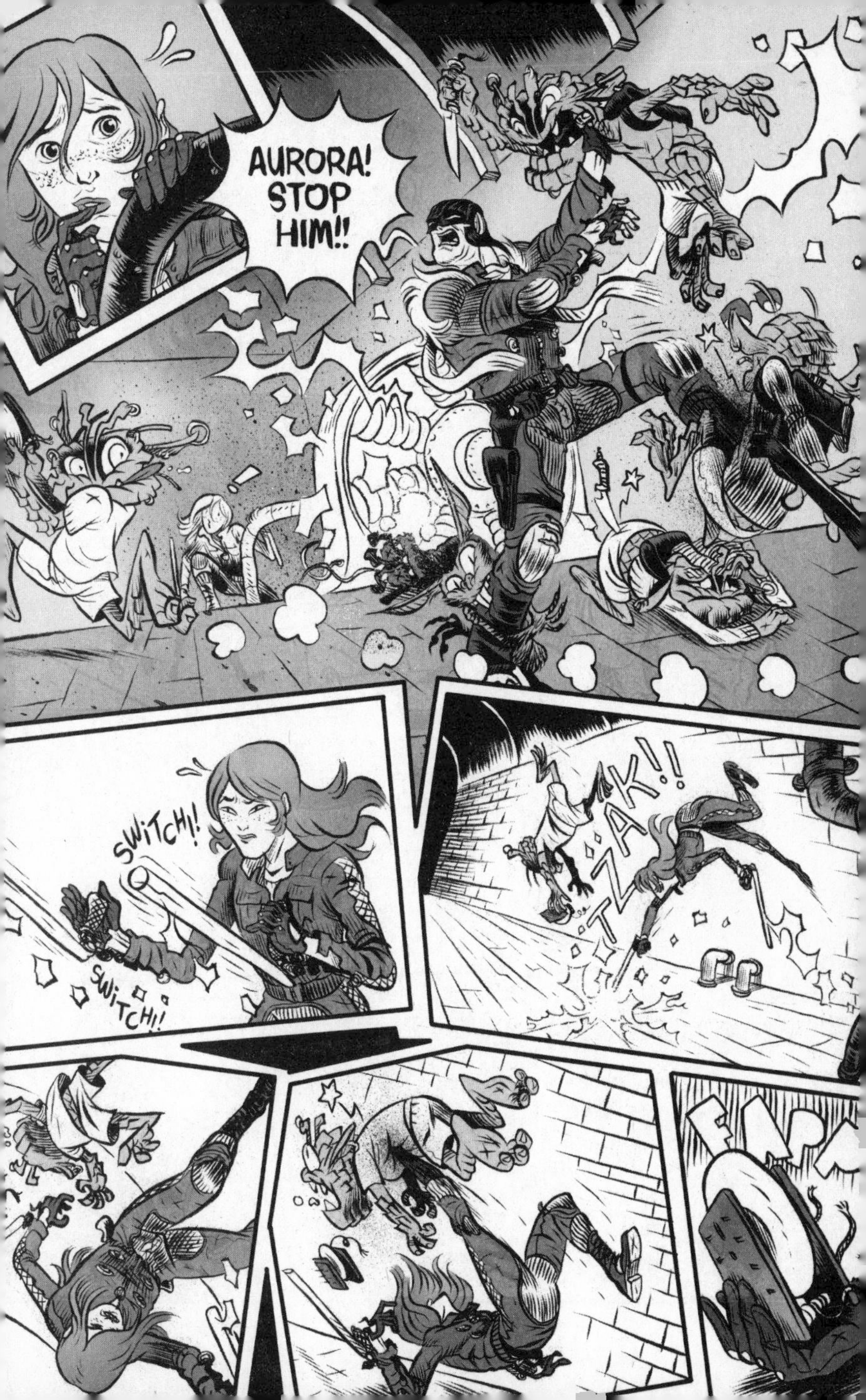
AURORA! STOP HIM!!
SWITCH!
SWITCH!!
TZAK!!

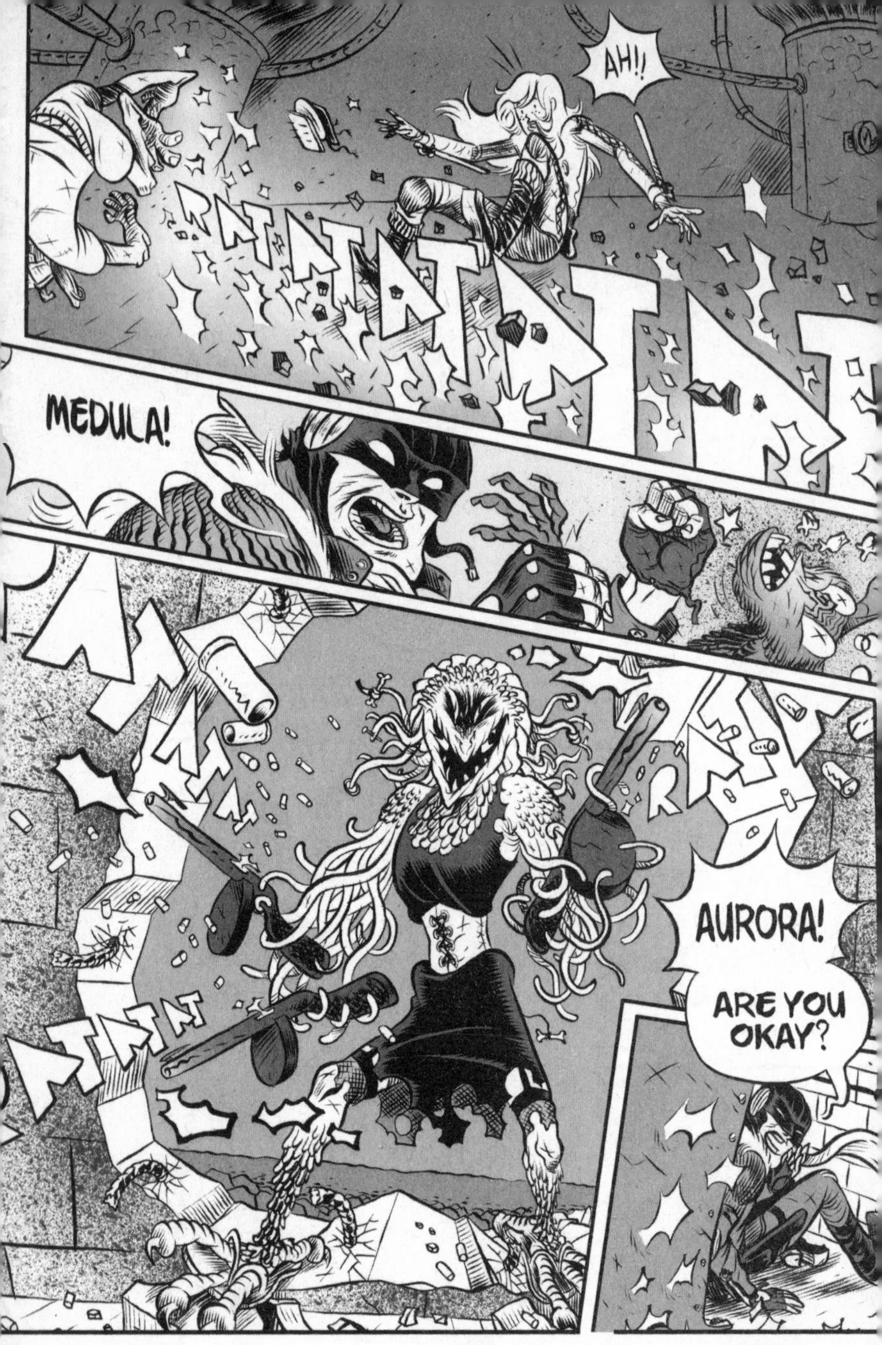
AH!!
RATATATAT
MEDULA!
AURORA!
ARE YOU OKAY?

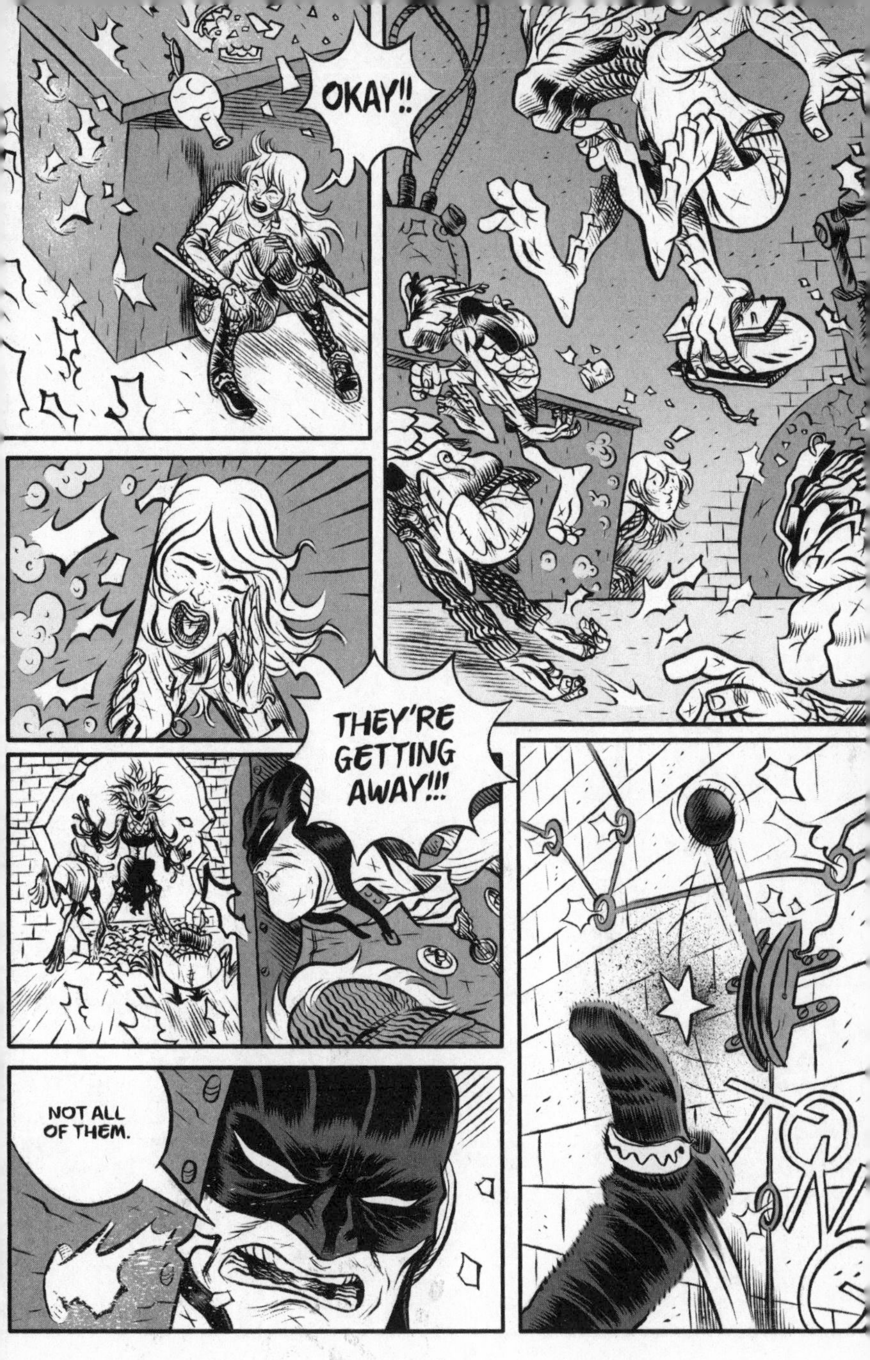
OKAY!!
THEY'RE GETTING AWAY!!!
NOT ALL OF THEM.

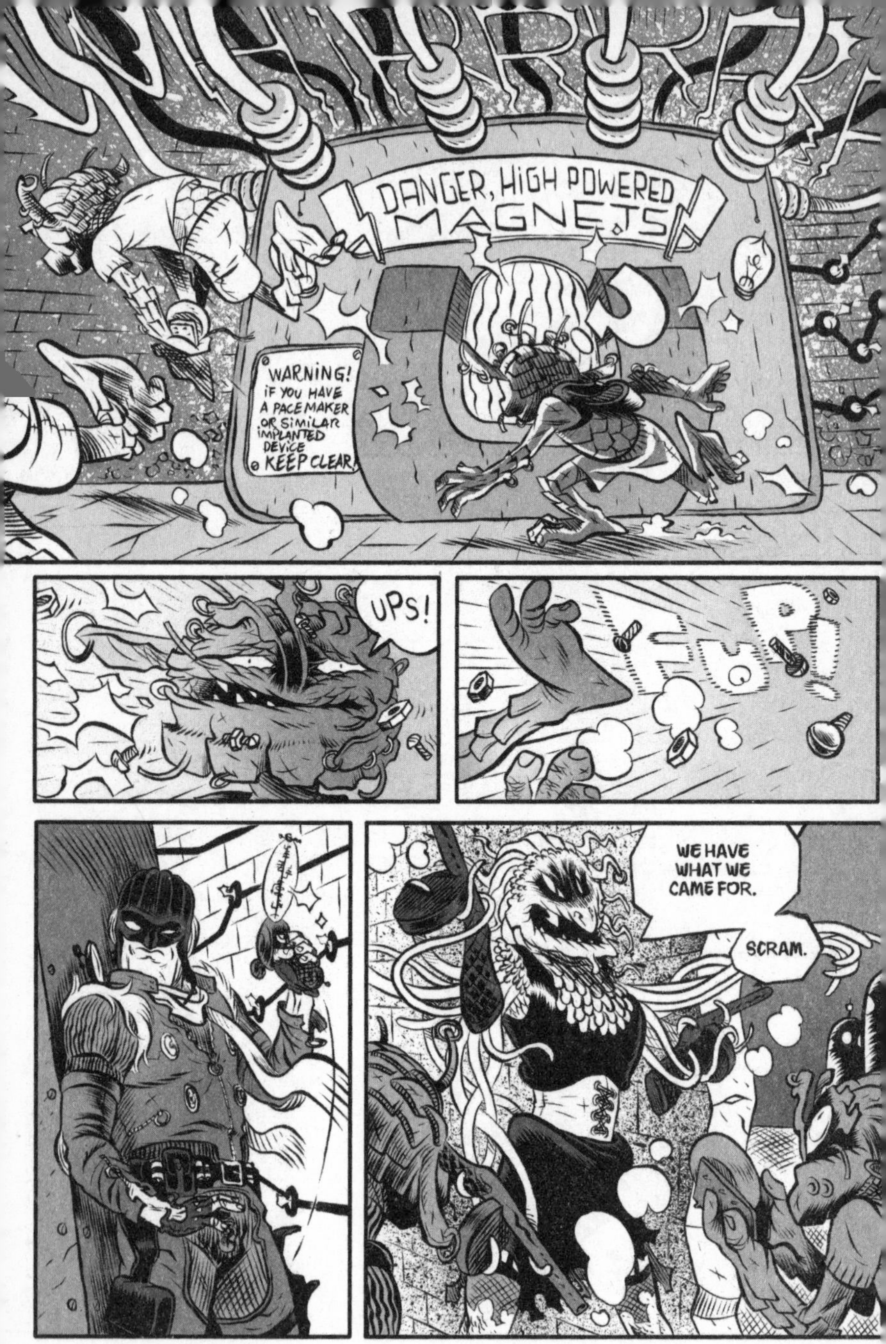
DANGER, HIGH POWERED MAGNETS
WARNING! IF YOU HAVE A PACEMAKER OR SIMILAR IMPLANTED DEVICE KEEP CLEAR!
UPS!
WE HAVE WHAT WE CAME FOR.
SCRAM.

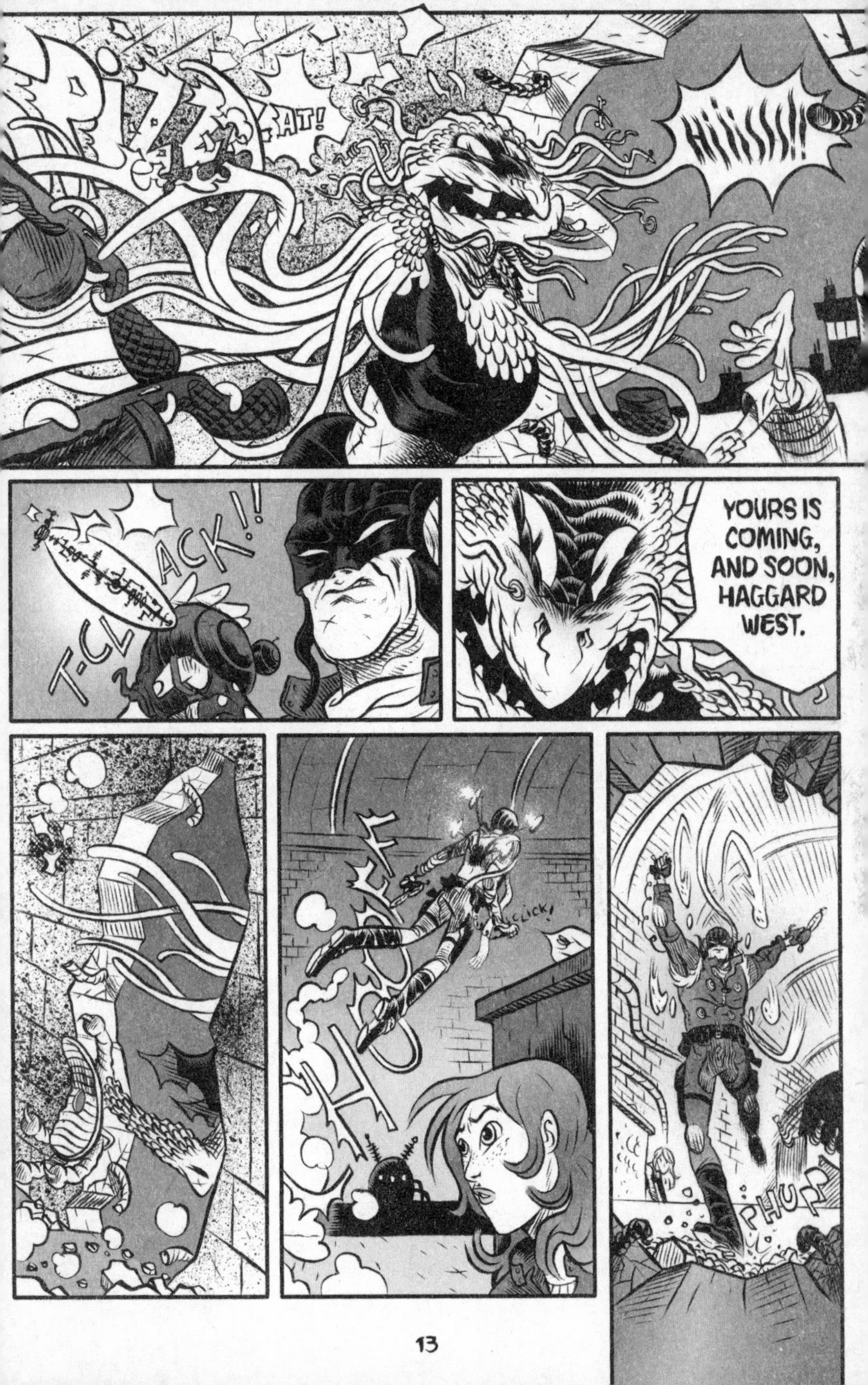
PIZZAT!
HIIIISSSS!!
T-CLACK!!
YOURS IS COMING, AND SOON, HAGGARD WEST.
CLICK!
PHUP

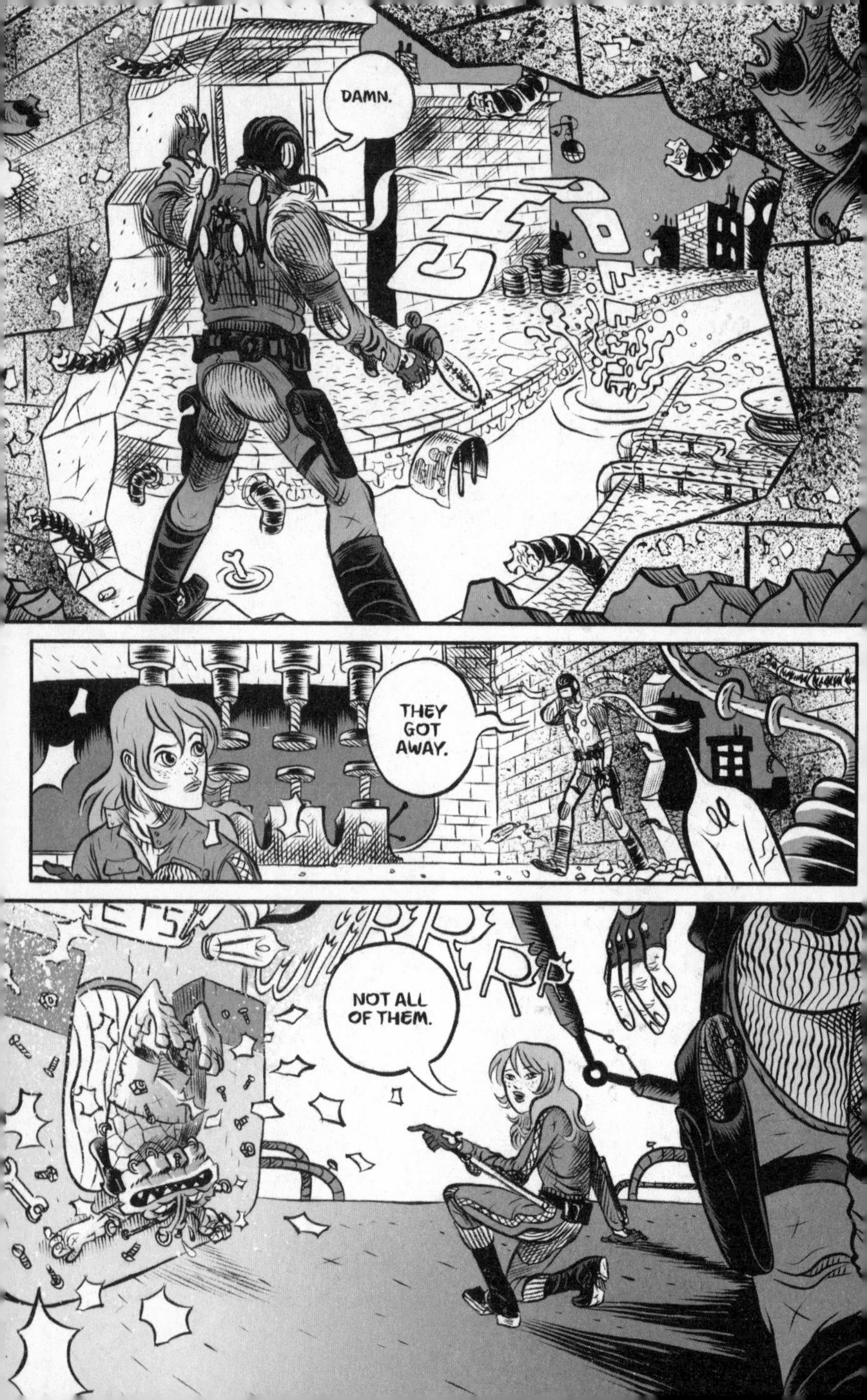
DAMN.
THEY GOT AWAY.
NOT ALL OF THEM.

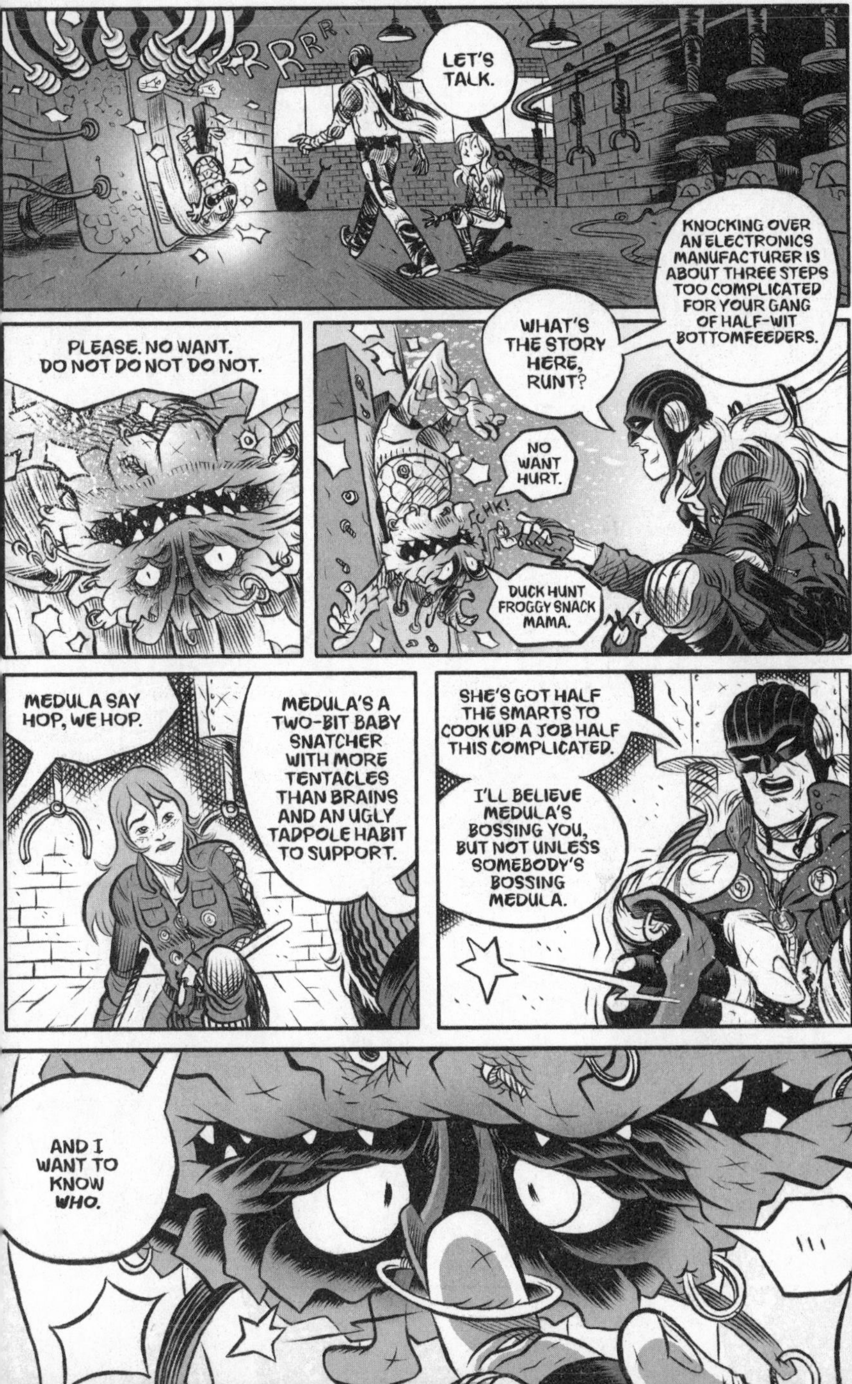
RRRRR
LET'S TALK.
KNOCKING OVER AN ELECTRONICS MANUFACTURER IS ABOUT THREE STEPS TOO COMPLICATED FOR YOUR GANG OF HALF-WIT BOTTOMFEEDERS.
WHAT'S THE STORY HERE, RUNT?
PLEASE. NO WANT. DO NOT DO NOT DO NOT.
NO WANT HURT.
CHK!
DUCK HUNT FROGGY SNACK MAMA.
MEDULA SAY HOP, WE HOP.
MEDULA'S A TWO-BIT BABY SNATCHER WITH MORE TENTACLES THAN BRAINS AND AN UGLY TADPOLE HABIT TO SUPPORT.
SHE'S GOT HALF THE SMARTS TO COOK UP A JOB HALF THIS COMPLICATED.
I'LL BELIEVE MEDULA'S BOSSING YOU, BUT NOT UNLESS SOMEBODY'S BOSSING MEDULA.
AND I WANT TO KNOW *WHO.*

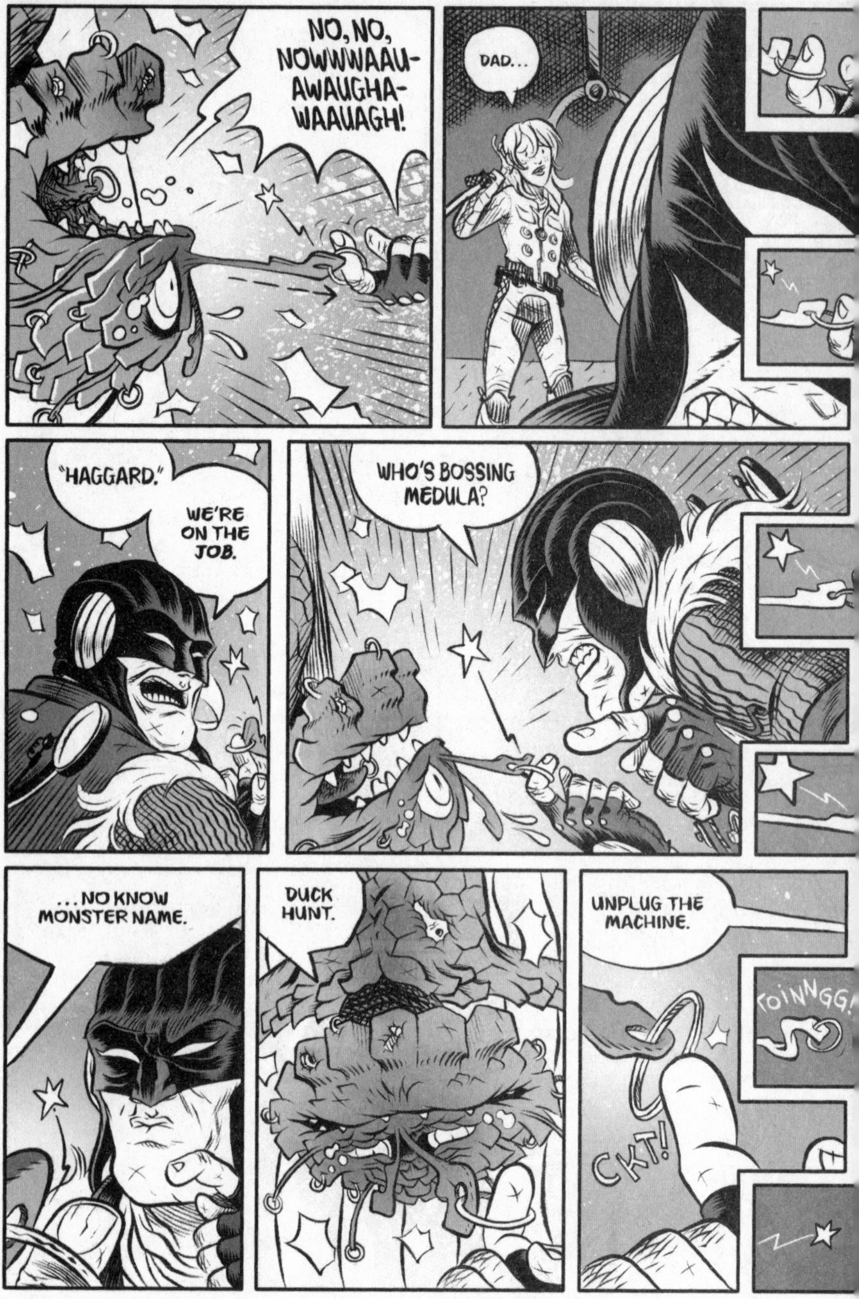
NO, NO, NOWWWAAU-AWAUGHA-WAAUAGH!
DAD...
"HAGGARD."
WE'RE ON THE JOB.
WHO'S BOSSING MEDULA?
...NO KNOW MONSTER NAME.
DUCK HUNT.
UNPLUG THE MACHINE.
TOINNGG!
CKT!

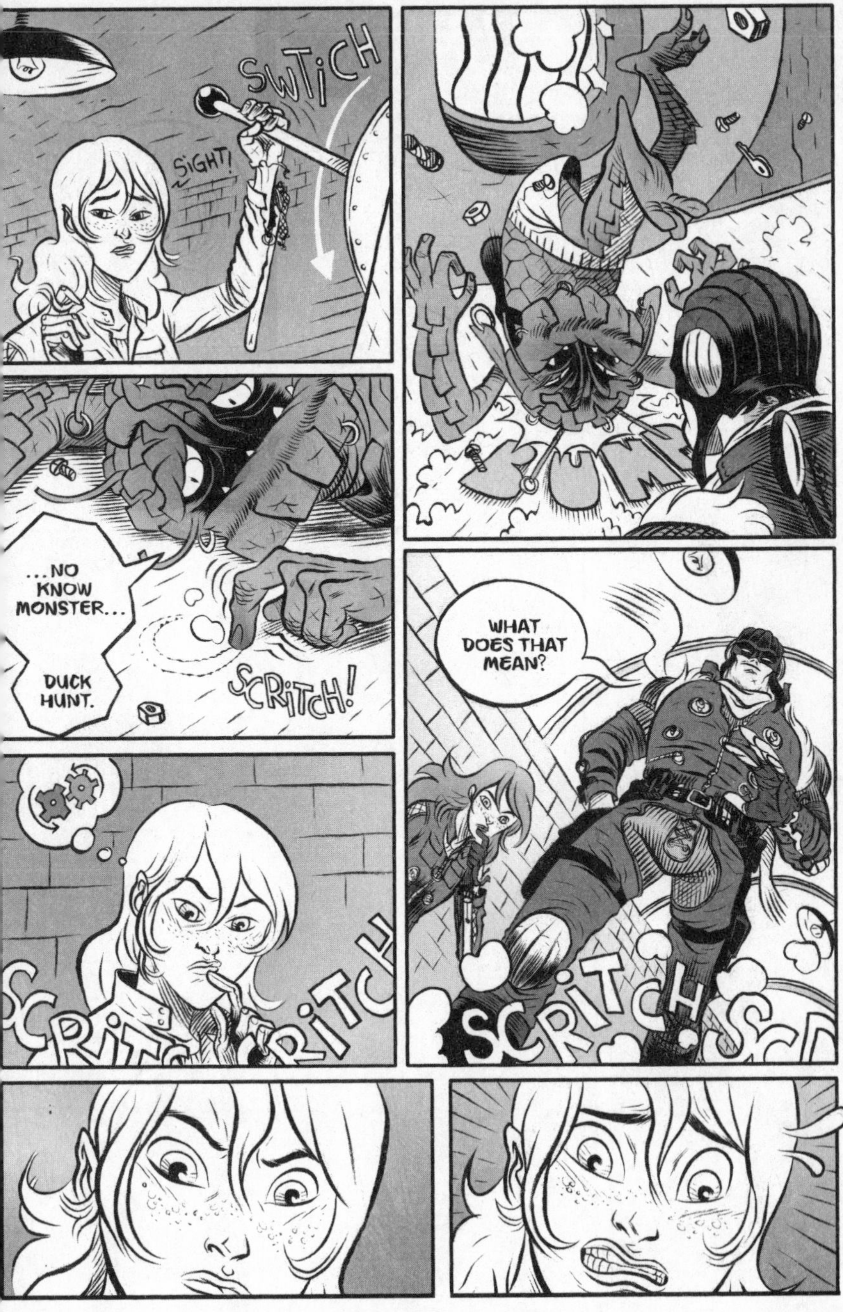
SWTICH
SIGHT!
BUMP
...NO KNOW MONSTER...
DUCK HUNT.
SCRITCH!
WHAT DOES THAT MEAN?
SCRITCH
SCRITCH

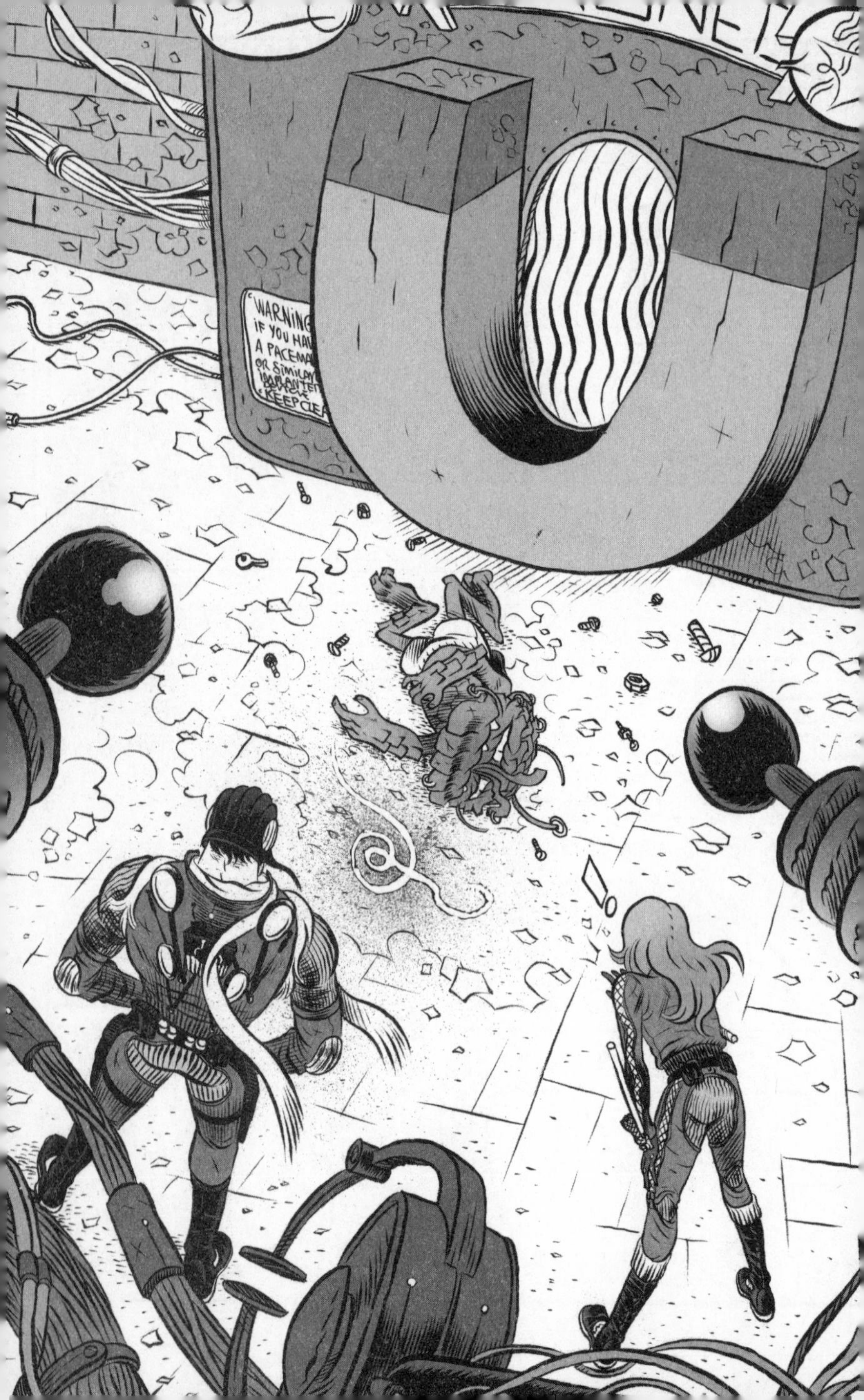
WARNING
IF YOU HAV
A PACEMA
OR SIMILA
IMPLANTE
DEVICE
KEEP CLEA

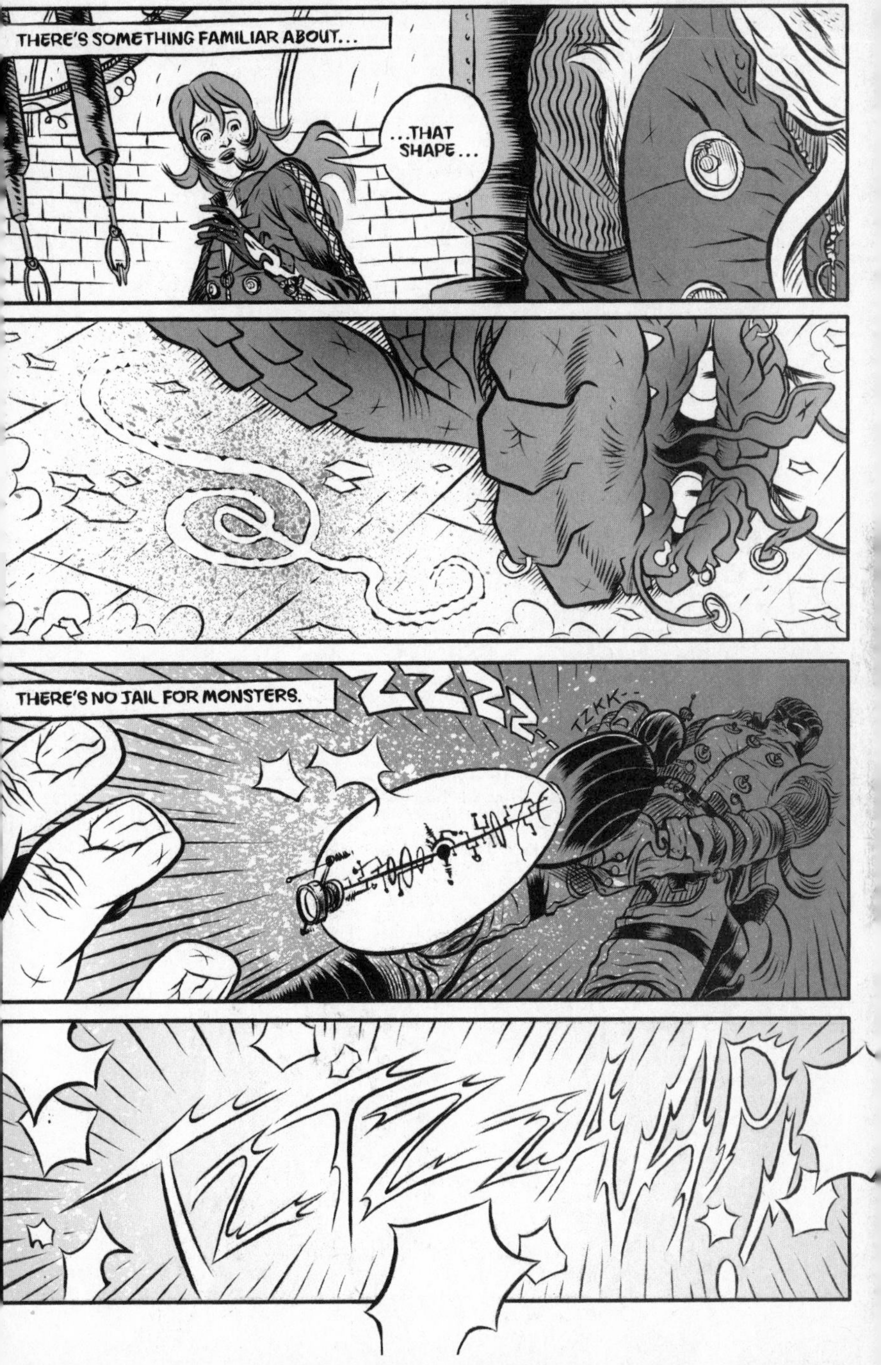
THERE'S SOMETHING FAMILIAR ABOUT...
...THAT SHAPE...
THERE'S NO JAIL FOR MONSTERS.
TZKK--

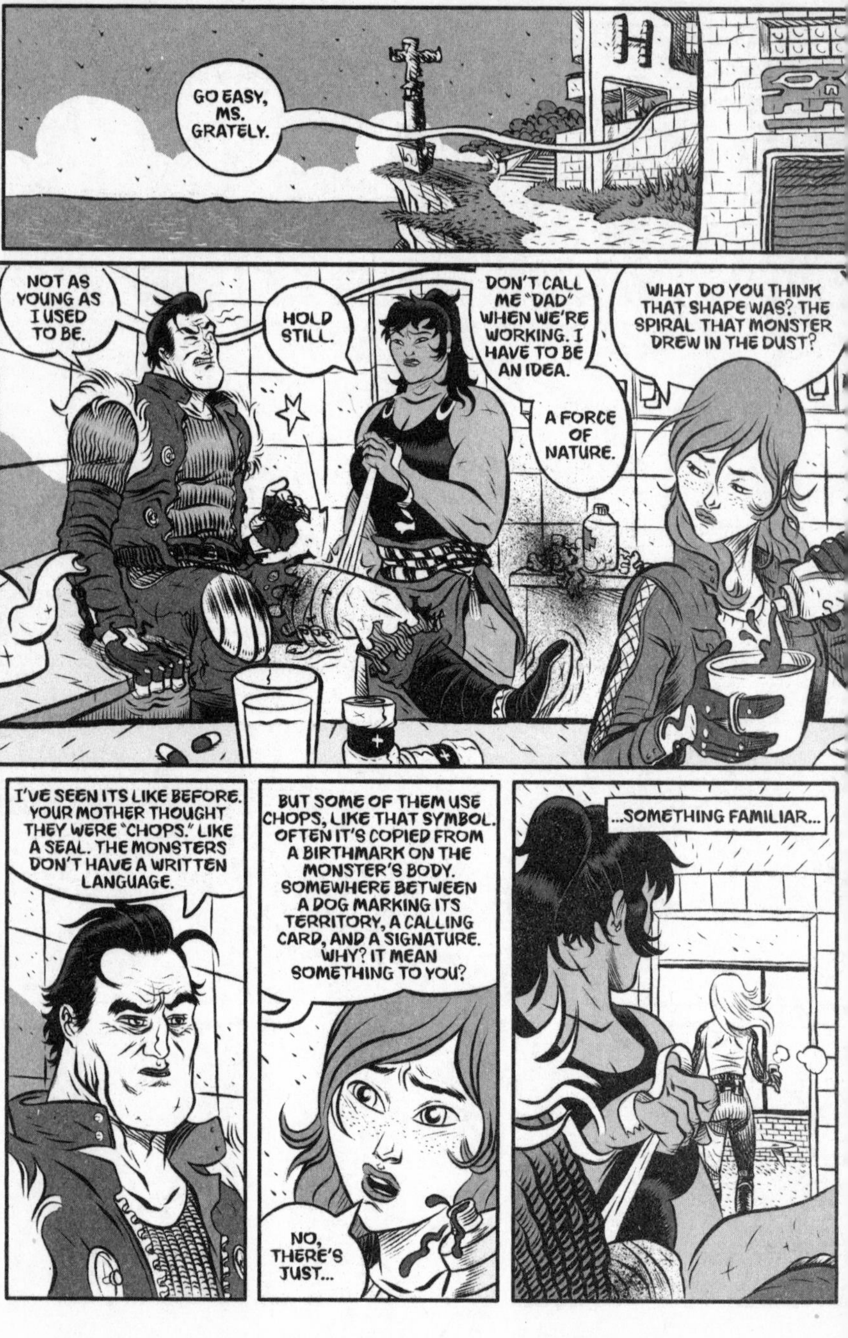
GO EASY, MS. GRATELY.
NOT AS YOUNG AS I USED TO BE.
HOLD STILL.
DON'T CALL ME "DAD" WHEN WE'RE WORKING. I HAVE TO BE AN IDEA.
A FORCE OF NATURE.
WHAT DO YOU THINK THAT SHAPE WAS? THE SPIRAL THAT MONSTER DREW IN THE DUST?
I'VE SEEN ITS LIKE BEFORE. YOUR MOTHER THOUGHT THEY WERE "CHOPS." LIKE A SEAL. THE MONSTERS DON'T HAVE A WRITTEN LANGUAGE.
BUT SOME OF THEM USE CHOPS, LIKE THAT SYMBOL. OFTEN IT'S COPIED FROM A BIRTHMARK ON THE MONSTER'S BODY. SOMEWHERE BETWEEN A DOG MARKING ITS TERRITORY, A CALLING CARD, AND A SIGNATURE. WHY? IT MEAN SOMETHING TO YOU?
NO, THERE'S JUST...
...SOMETHING FAMILIAR...

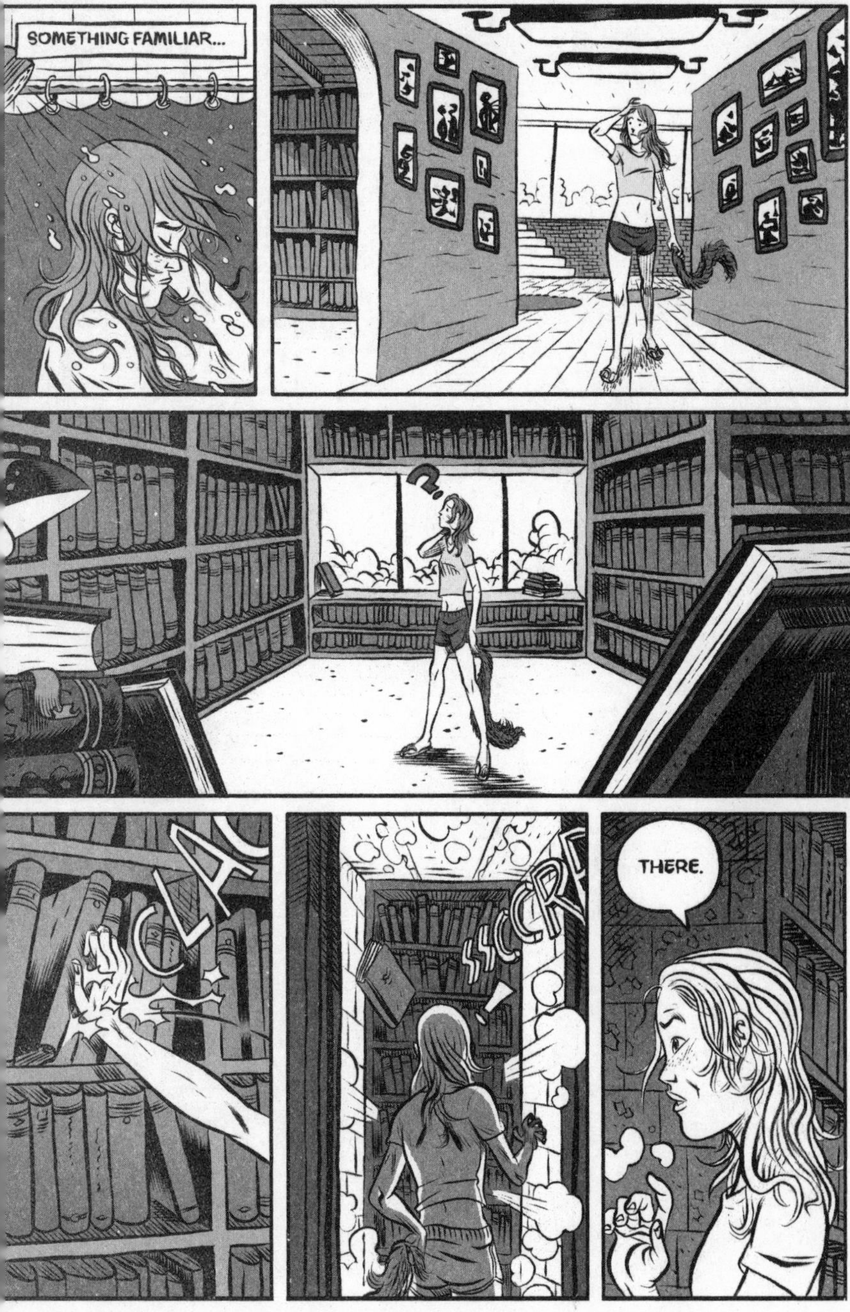
SOMETHING FAMILIAR...
?
CLA
SSCCR
!
THERE.

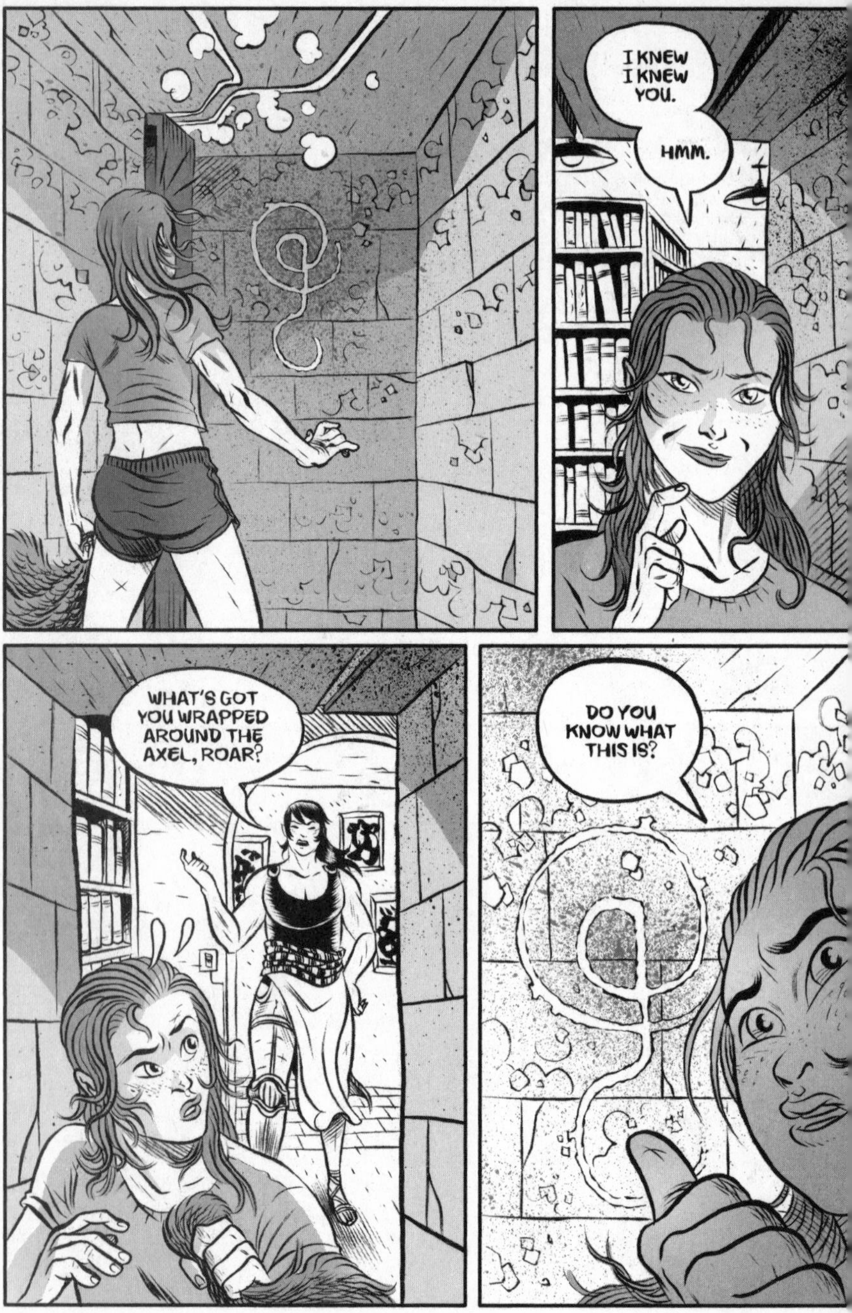
I KNEW I KNEW YOU.
HMM.
WHAT'S GOT YOU WRAPPED AROUND THE AXEL, ROAR?
DO YOU KNOW WHAT THIS IS?

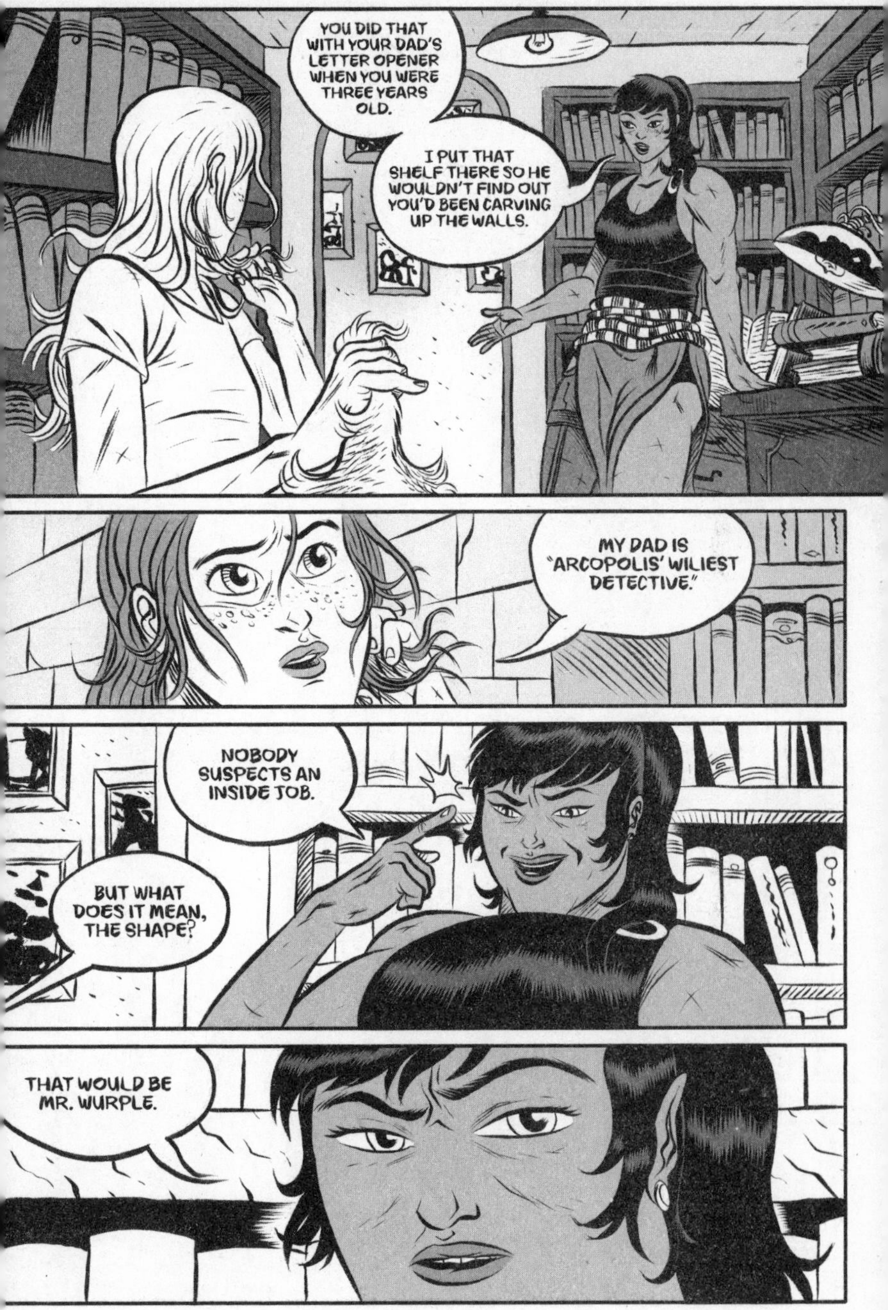
YOU DID THAT WITH YOUR DAD'S LETTER OPENER WHEN YOU WERE THREE YEARS OLD.
I PUT THAT SHELF THERE SO HE WOULDN'T FIND OUT YOU'D BEEN CARVING UP THE WALLS.
MY DAD IS "ARCOPOLIS' WILIEST DETECTIVE."
NOBODY SUSPECTS AN INSIDE JOB.
BUT WHAT DOES IT MEAN, THE SHAPE?
THAT WOULD BE MR. WURPLE.

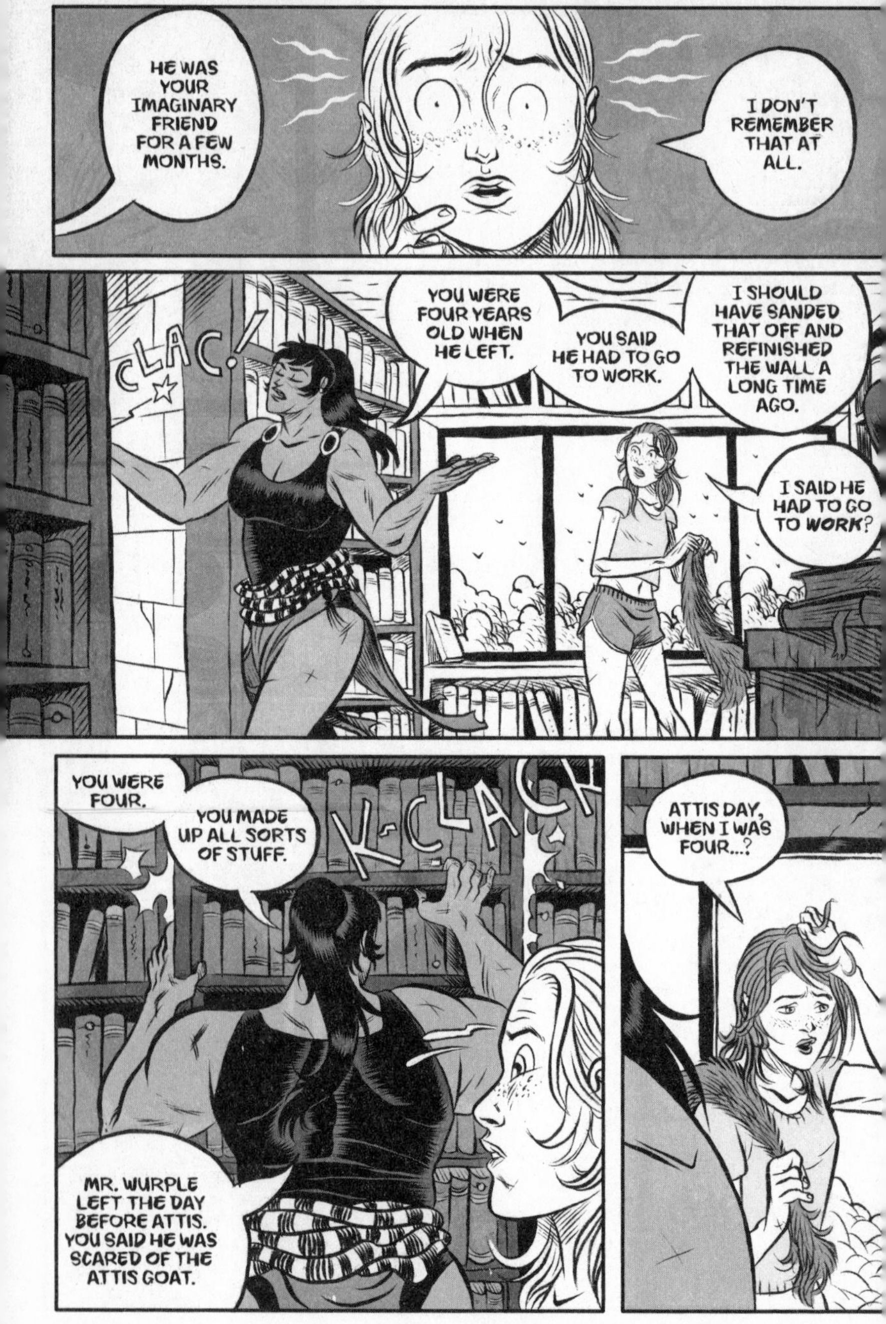
HE WAS YOUR IMAGINARY FRIEND FOR A FEW MONTHS.
I DON'T REMEMBER THAT AT ALL.
CLAC!
YOU WERE FOUR YEARS OLD WHEN HE LEFT.
YOU SAID HE HAD TO GO TO WORK.
I SHOULD HAVE SANDED THAT OFF AND REFINISHED THE WALL A LONG TIME AGO.
I SAID HE HAD TO GO TO **WORK**?
YOU WERE FOUR.
YOU MADE UP ALL SORTS OF STUFF.
K-CLACK
MR. WURPLE LEFT THE DAY BEFORE ATTIS. YOU SAID HE WAS SCARED OF THE ATTIS GOAT.
ATTIS DAY, WHEN I WAS FOUR...?

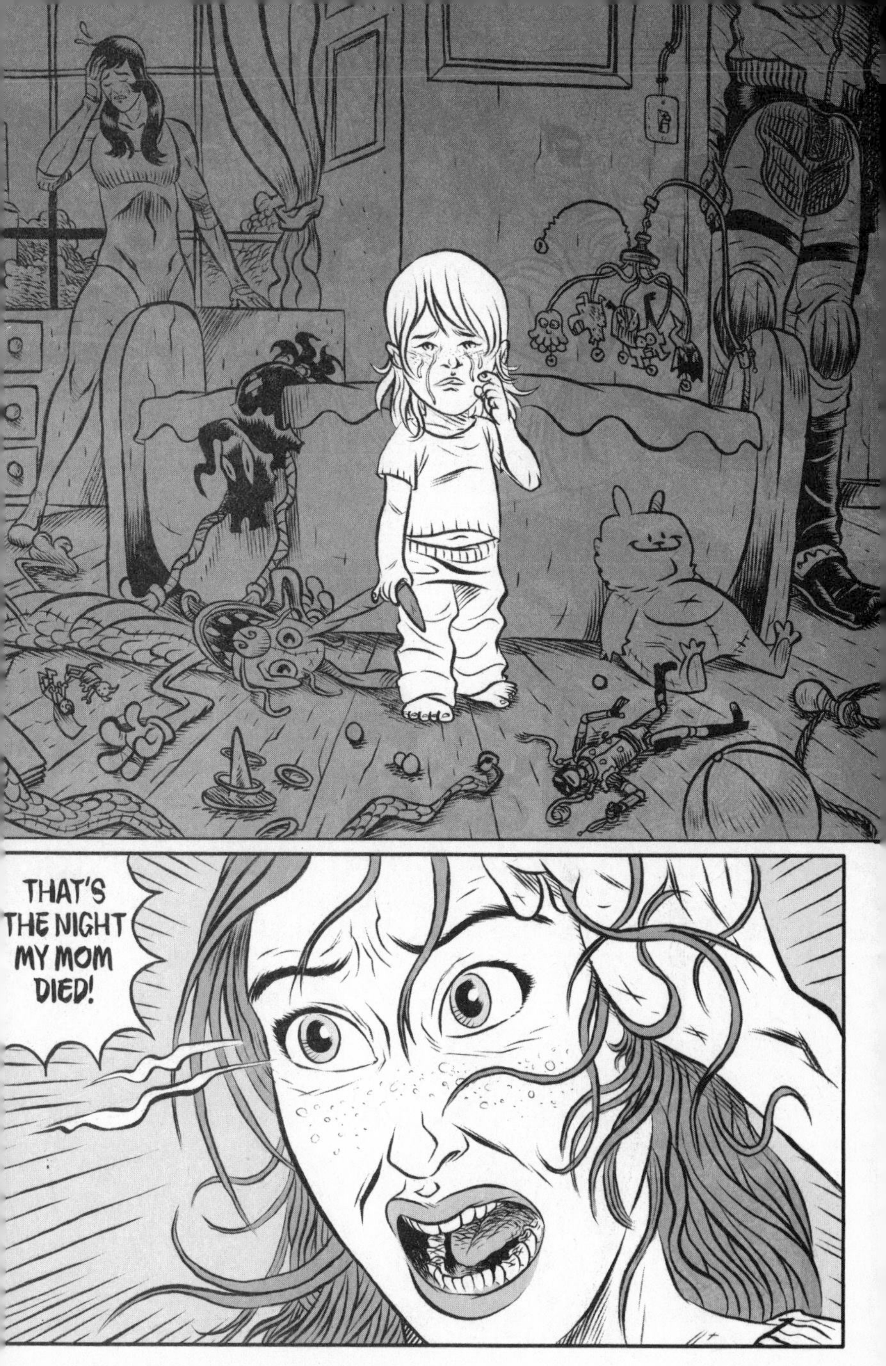
THAT'S THE NIGHT MY MOM DIED!

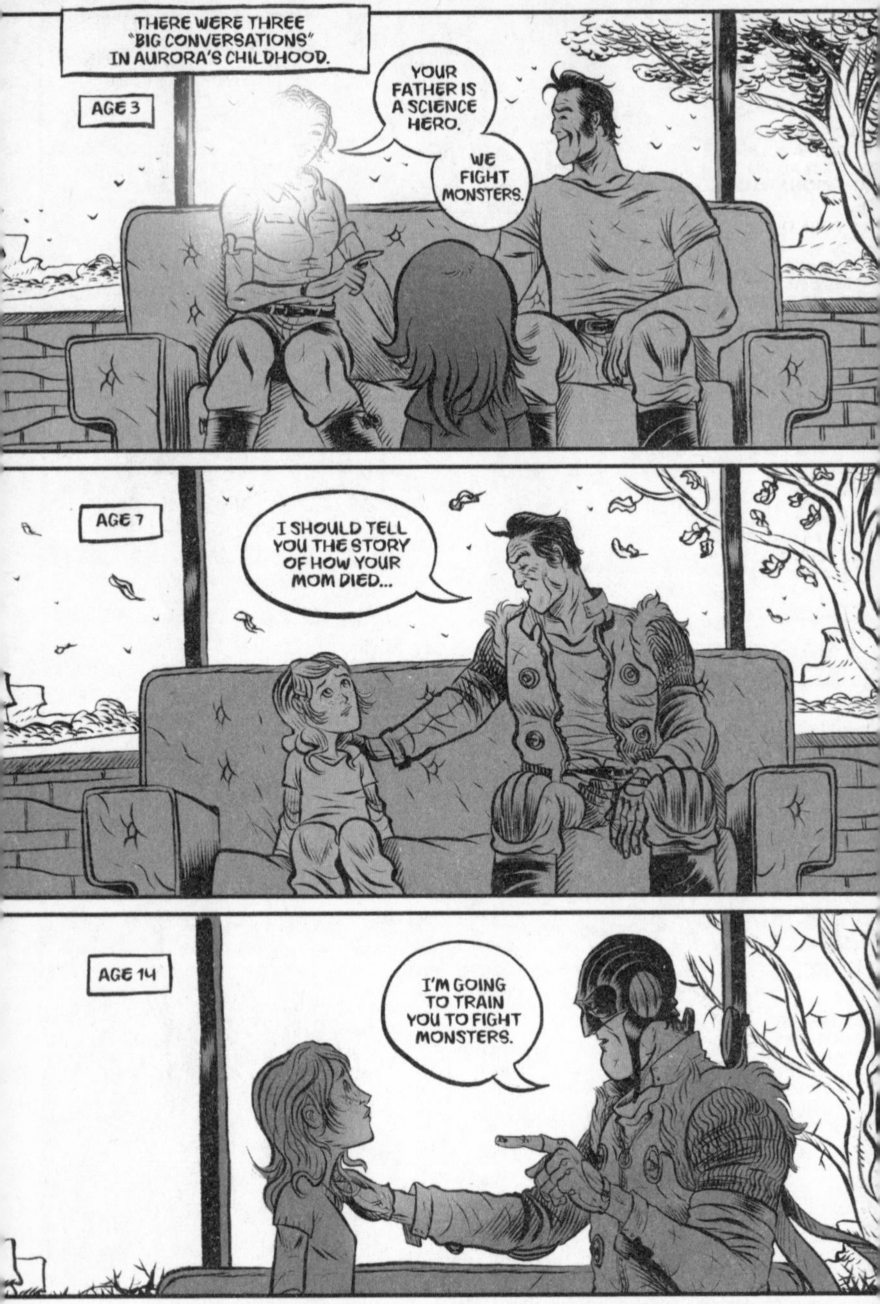
THERE WERE THREE "BIG CONVERSATIONS" IN AURORA'S CHILDHOOD.
AGE 3
YOUR FATHER IS A SCIENCE HERO.
WE FIGHT MONSTERS.
AGE 7
I SHOULD TELL YOU THE STORY OF HOW YOUR MOM DIED...
AGE 14
I'M GOING TO TRAIN YOU TO FIGHT MONSTERS.

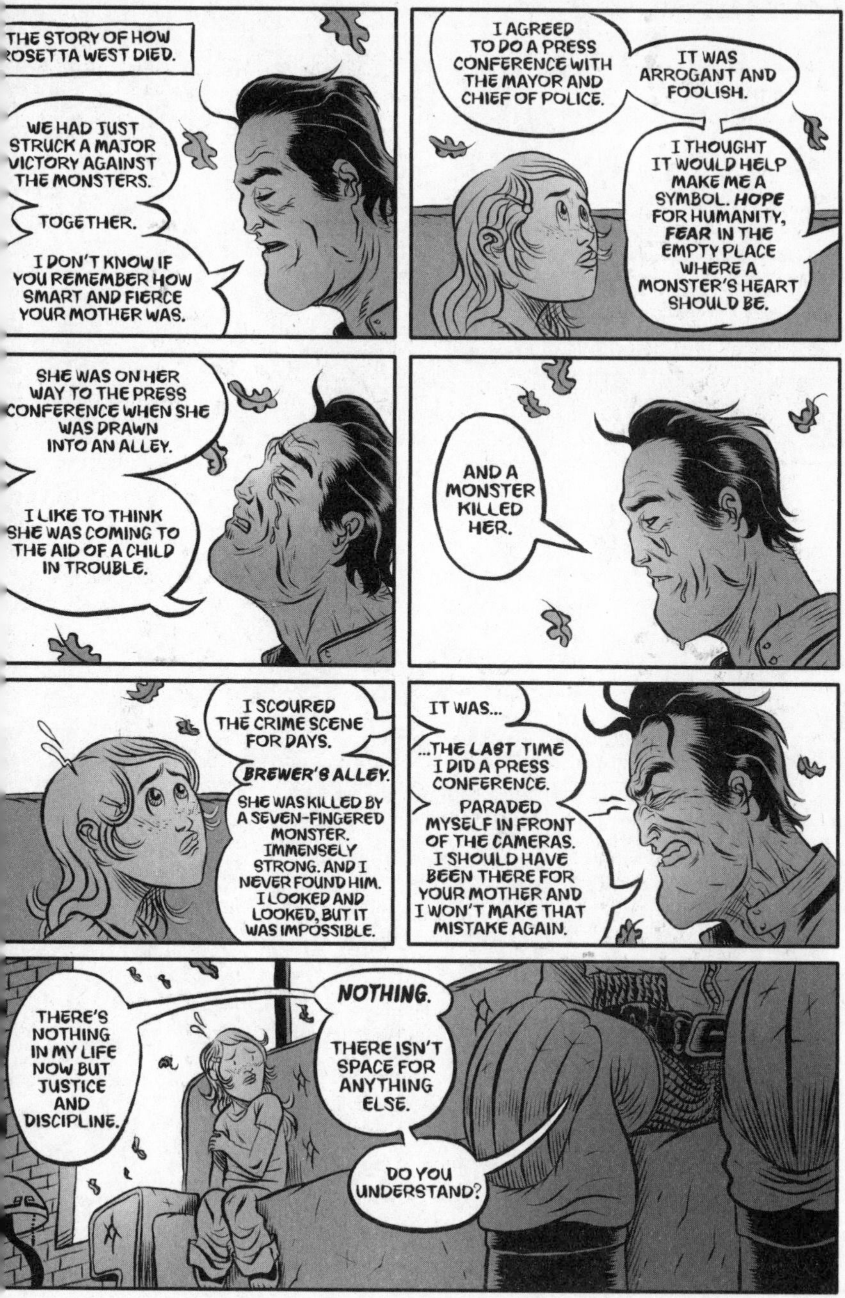
THE STORY OF HOW ROSETTA WEST DIED.
WE HAD JUST STRUCK A MAJOR VICTORY AGAINST THE MONSTERS.
TOGETHER.
I DON'T KNOW IF YOU REMEMBER HOW SMART AND FIERCE YOUR MOTHER WAS.
I AGREED TO DO A PRESS CONFERENCE WITH THE MAYOR AND CHIEF OF POLICE.
IT WAS ARROGANT AND FOOLISH.
I THOUGHT IT WOULD HELP MAKE ME A SYMBOL. HOPE FOR HUMANITY, FEAR IN THE EMPTY PLACE WHERE A MONSTER'S HEART SHOULD BE.
SHE WAS ON HER WAY TO THE PRESS CONFERENCE WHEN SHE WAS DRAWN INTO AN ALLEY.
I LIKE TO THINK SHE WAS COMING TO THE AID OF A CHILD IN TROUBLE.
AND A MONSTER KILLED HER.
I SCOURED THE CRIME SCENE FOR DAYS.
BREWER'S ALLEY.
SHE WAS KILLED BY A SEVEN-FINGERED MONSTER. IMMENSELY STRONG. AND I NEVER FOUND HIM. I LOOKED AND LOOKED, BUT IT WAS IMPOSSIBLE.
IT WAS...
...THE LAST TIME I DID A PRESS CONFERENCE.
PARADED MYSELF IN FRONT OF THE CAMERAS. I SHOULD HAVE BEEN THERE FOR YOUR MOTHER AND I WON'T MAKE THAT MISTAKE AGAIN.
THERE'S NOTHING IN MY LIFE NOW BUT JUSTICE AND DISCIPLINE.
NOTHING.
THERE ISN'T SPACE FOR ANYTHING ELSE.
DO YOU UNDERSTAND?

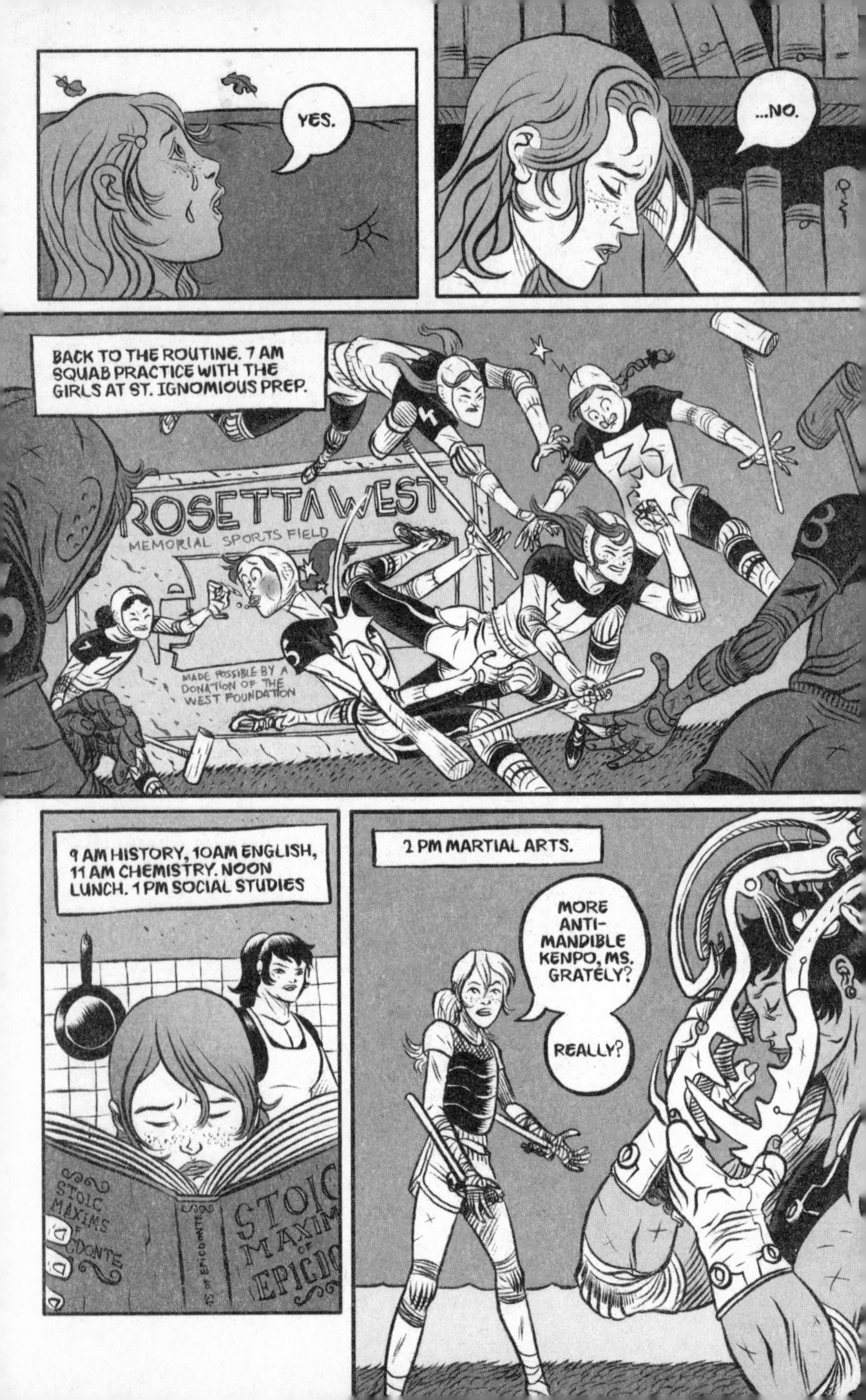
YES.
...NO.
BACK TO THE ROUTINE. 7 AM SQUAB PRACTICE WITH THE GIRLS AT ST. IGNOMIOUS PREP.
ROSETTA WEST
MEMORIAL SPORTS FIELD
MADE POSSIBLE BY A DONATION OF THE WEST FOUNDATION
9 AM HISTORY, 10AM ENGLISH, 11 AM CHEMISTRY. NOON LUNCH. 1 PM SOCIAL STUDIES
2 PM MARTIAL ARTS.
MORE ANTI-MANDIBLE KENPO, MS. GRATELY?
REALLY?

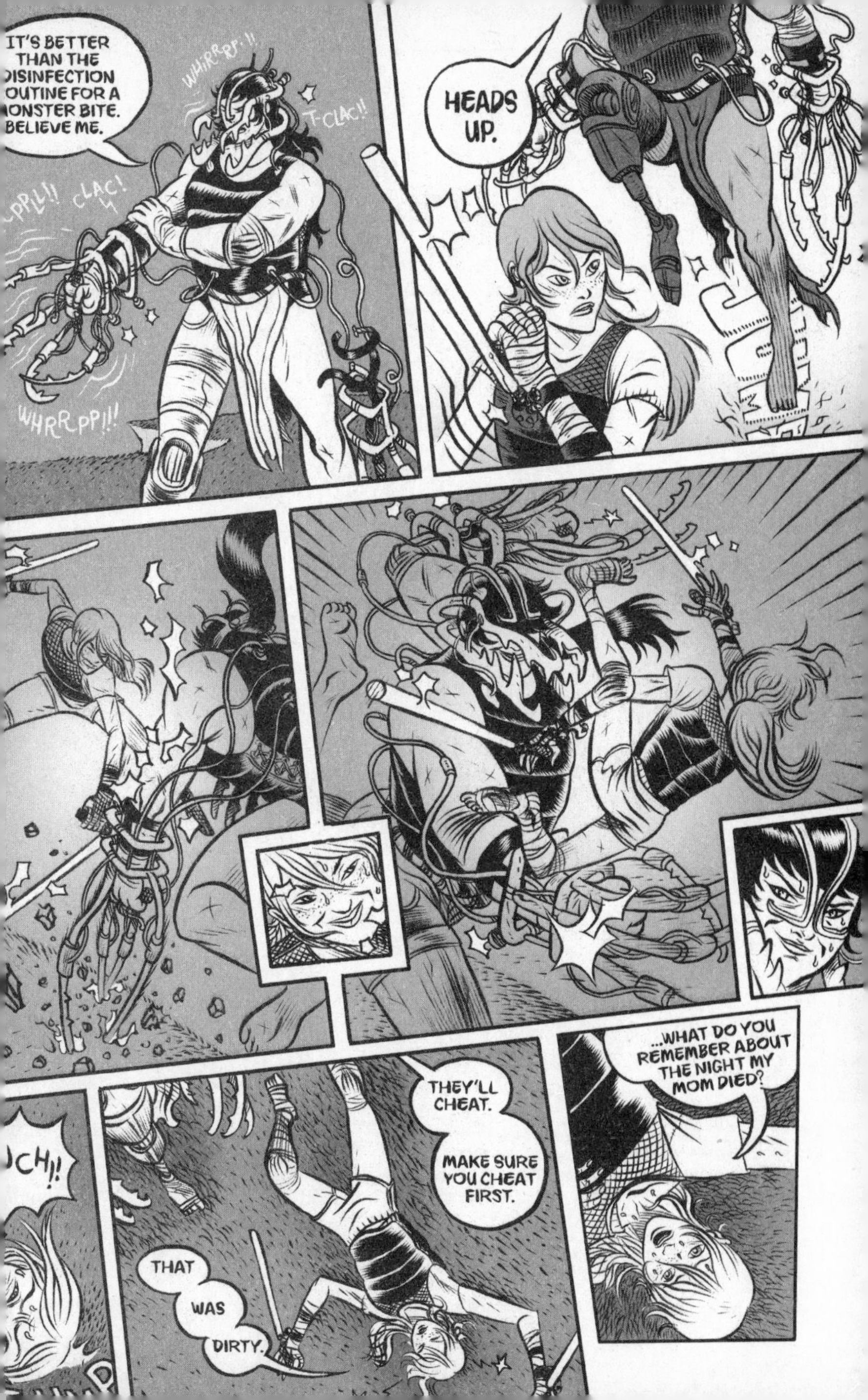
IT'S BETTER THAN THE DISINFECTION OUTINE FOR A ONSTER BITE. BELIEVE ME.
WHIRRRP!!
T-CLAC!!
CLAC!
WHRRPP!!
HEADS UP.
...WHAT DO YOU REMEMBER ABOUT THE NIGHT MY MOM DIED?
THEY'LL CHEAT.
MAKE SURE YOU CHEAT FIRST.
THAT WAS DIRTY.
UCH!!

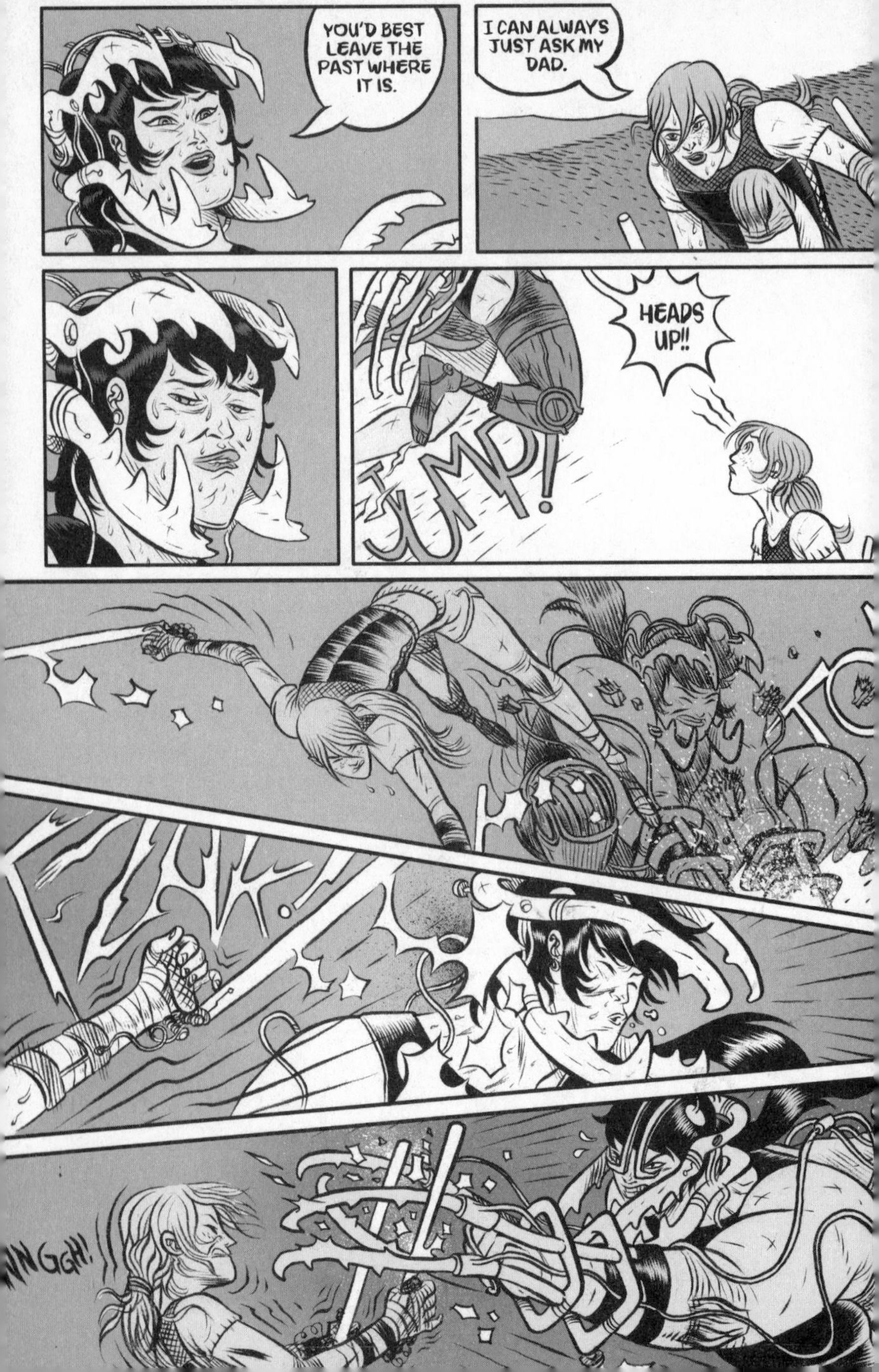
YOU'D BEST LEAVE THE PAST WHERE IT IS.
I CAN ALWAYS JUST ASK MY DAD.
HEADS UP!!
JUMP!
NNGGH!

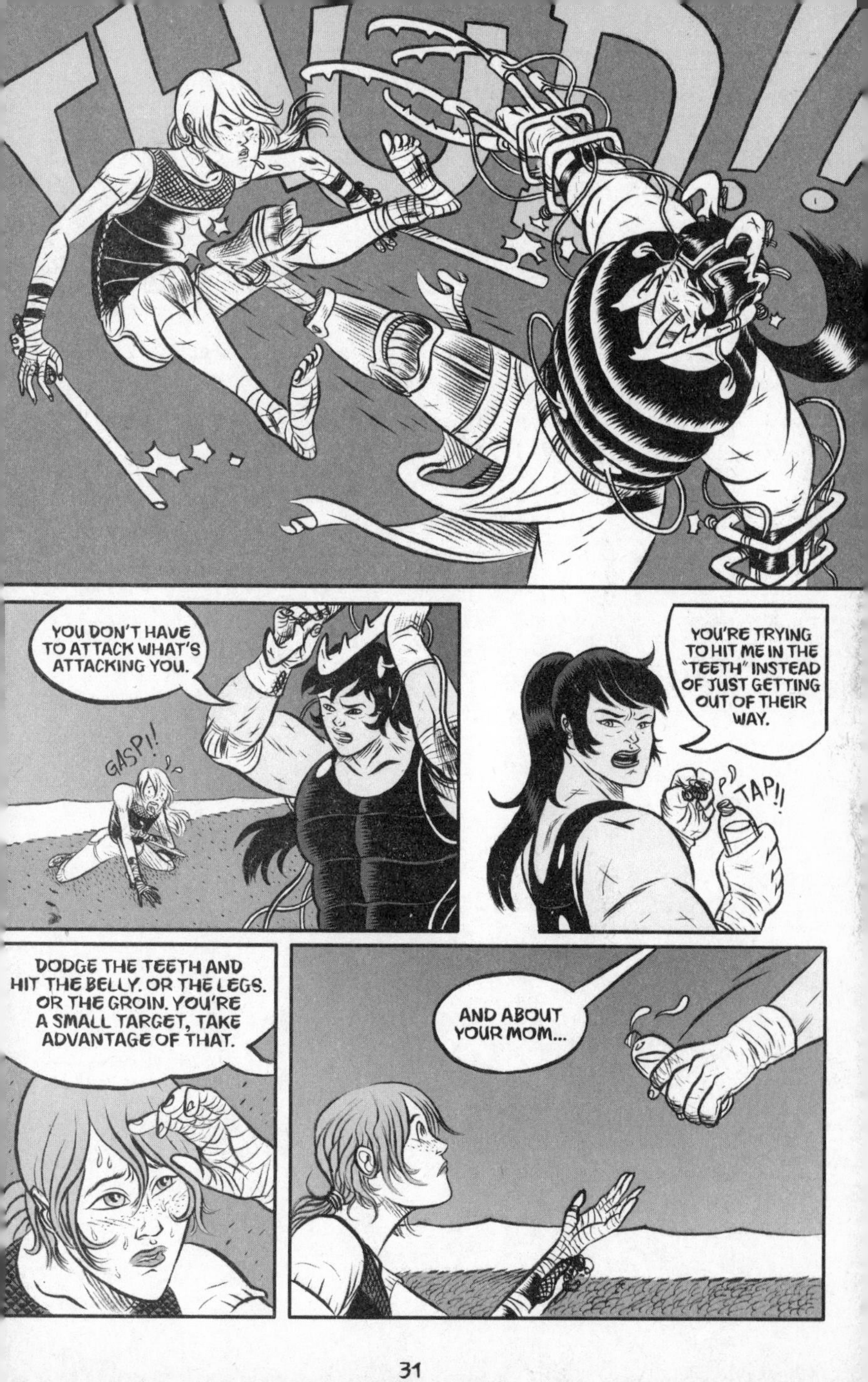
YOU DON'T HAVE TO ATTACK WHAT'S ATTACKING YOU.
GASP!
YOU'RE TRYING TO HIT ME IN THE "TEETH" INSTEAD OF JUST GETTING OUT OF THEIR WAY.
TAP!!
DODGE THE TEETH AND HIT THE BELLY. OR THE LEGS. OR THE GROIN. YOU'RE A SMALL TARGET, TAKE ADVANTAGE OF THAT.
AND ABOUT YOUR MOM...

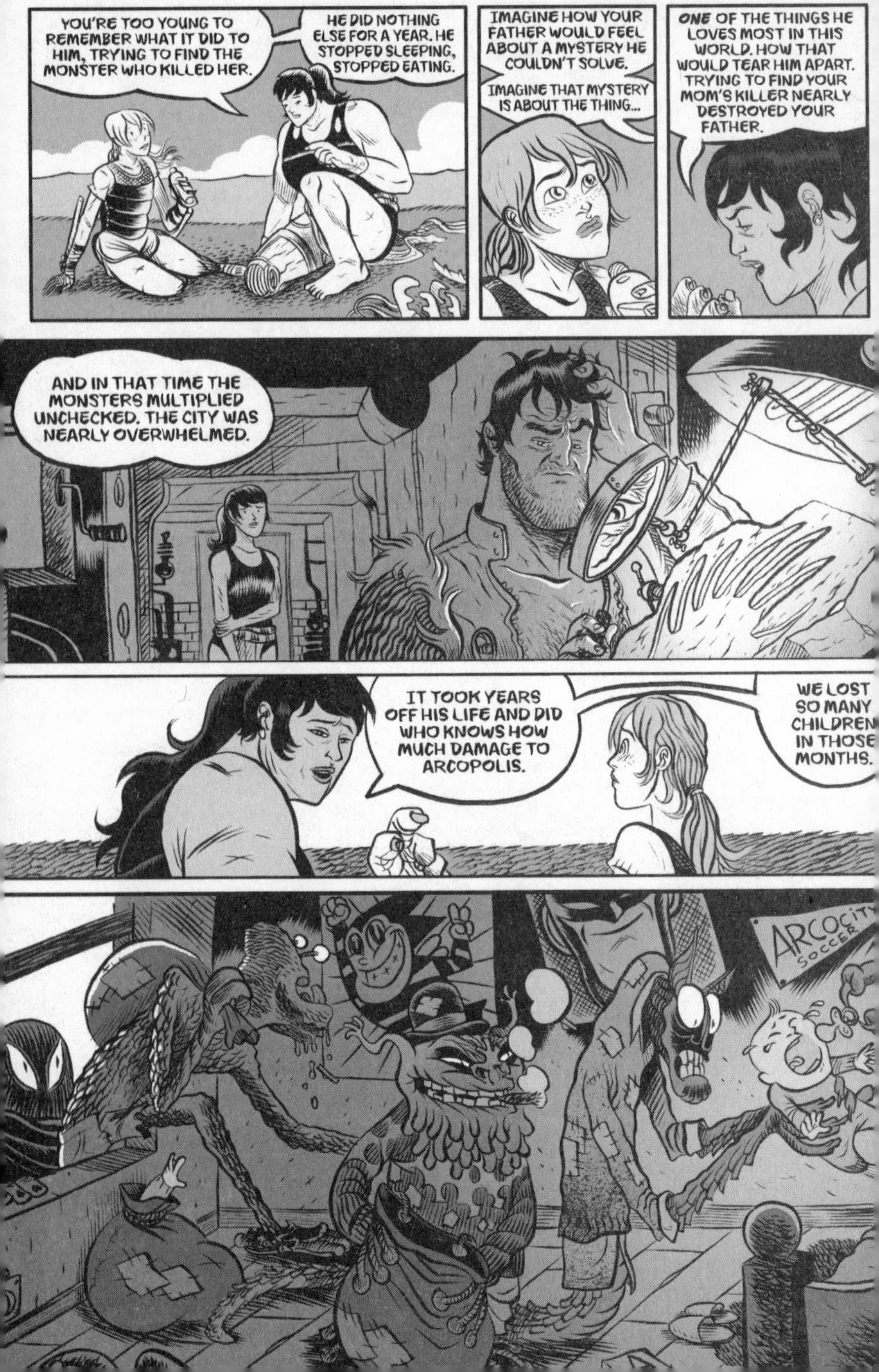
YOU'RE TOO YOUNG TO REMEMBER WHAT IT DID TO HIM, TRYING TO FIND THE MONSTER WHO KILLED HER.
HE DID NOTHING ELSE FOR A YEAR. HE STOPPED SLEEPING, STOPPED EATING.
IMAGINE HOW YOUR FATHER WOULD FEEL ABOUT A MYSTERY HE COULDN'T SOLVE.
IMAGINE THAT MYSTERY IS ABOUT THE THING...
ONE OF THE THINGS HE LOVES MOST IN THIS WORLD. HOW THAT WOULD TEAR HIM APART. TRYING TO FIND YOUR MOM'S KILLER NEARLY DESTROYED YOUR FATHER.
AND IN THAT TIME THE MONSTERS MULTIPLIED UNCHECKED. THE CITY WAS NEARLY OVERWHELMED.
IT TOOK YEARS OFF HIS LIFE AND DID WHO KNOWS HOW MUCH DAMAGE TO ARCOPOLIS.
WE LOST SO MANY CHILDREN IN THOSE MONTHS.
ARCOCITY SOCCER

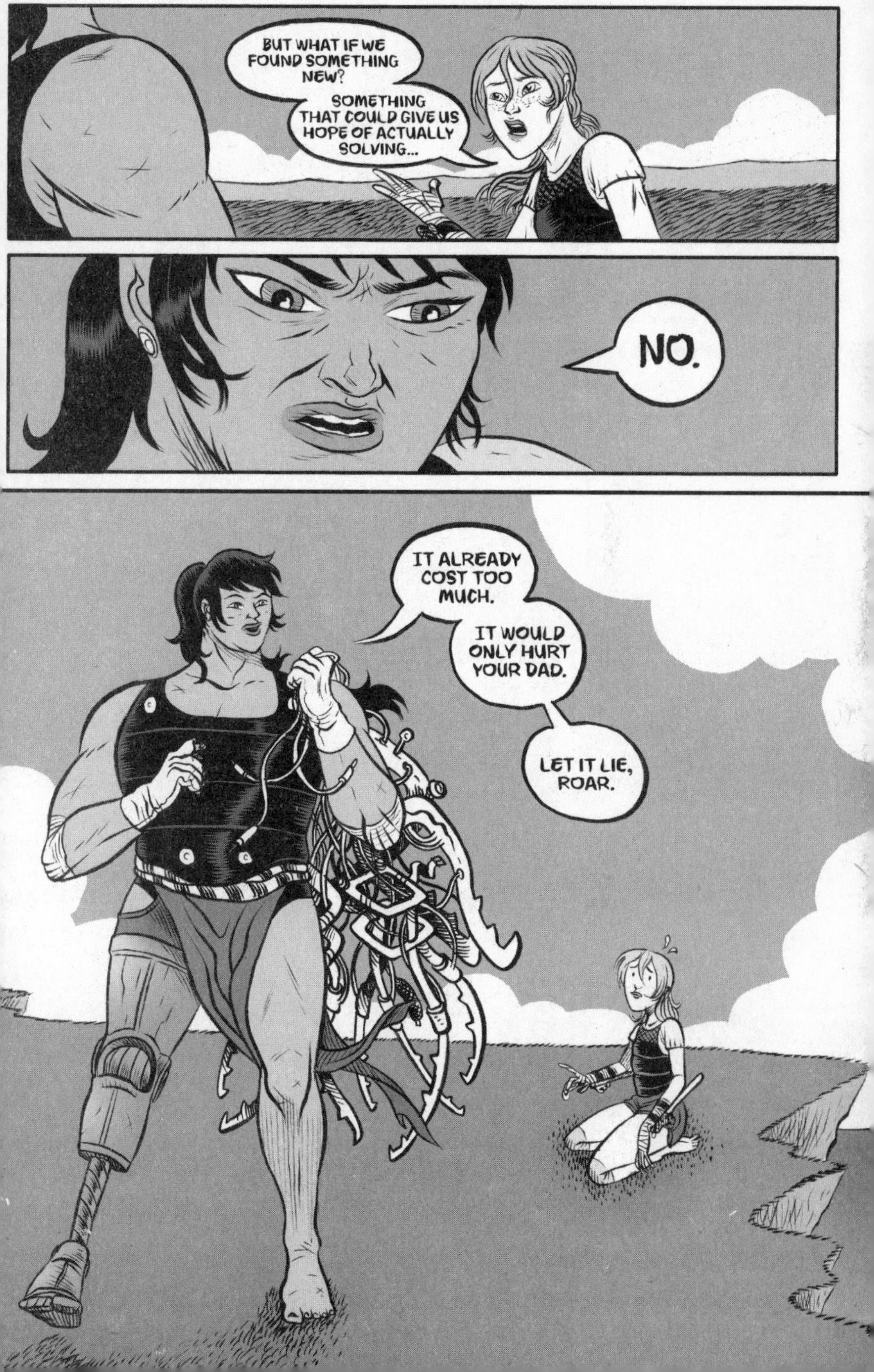
BUT WHAT IF WE FOUND SOMETHING NEW?
SOMETHING THAT COULD GIVE US HOPE OF ACTUALLY SOLVING...
NO.
IT ALREADY COST TOO MUCH.
IT WOULD ONLY HURT YOUR DAD.
LET IT LIE, ROAR.

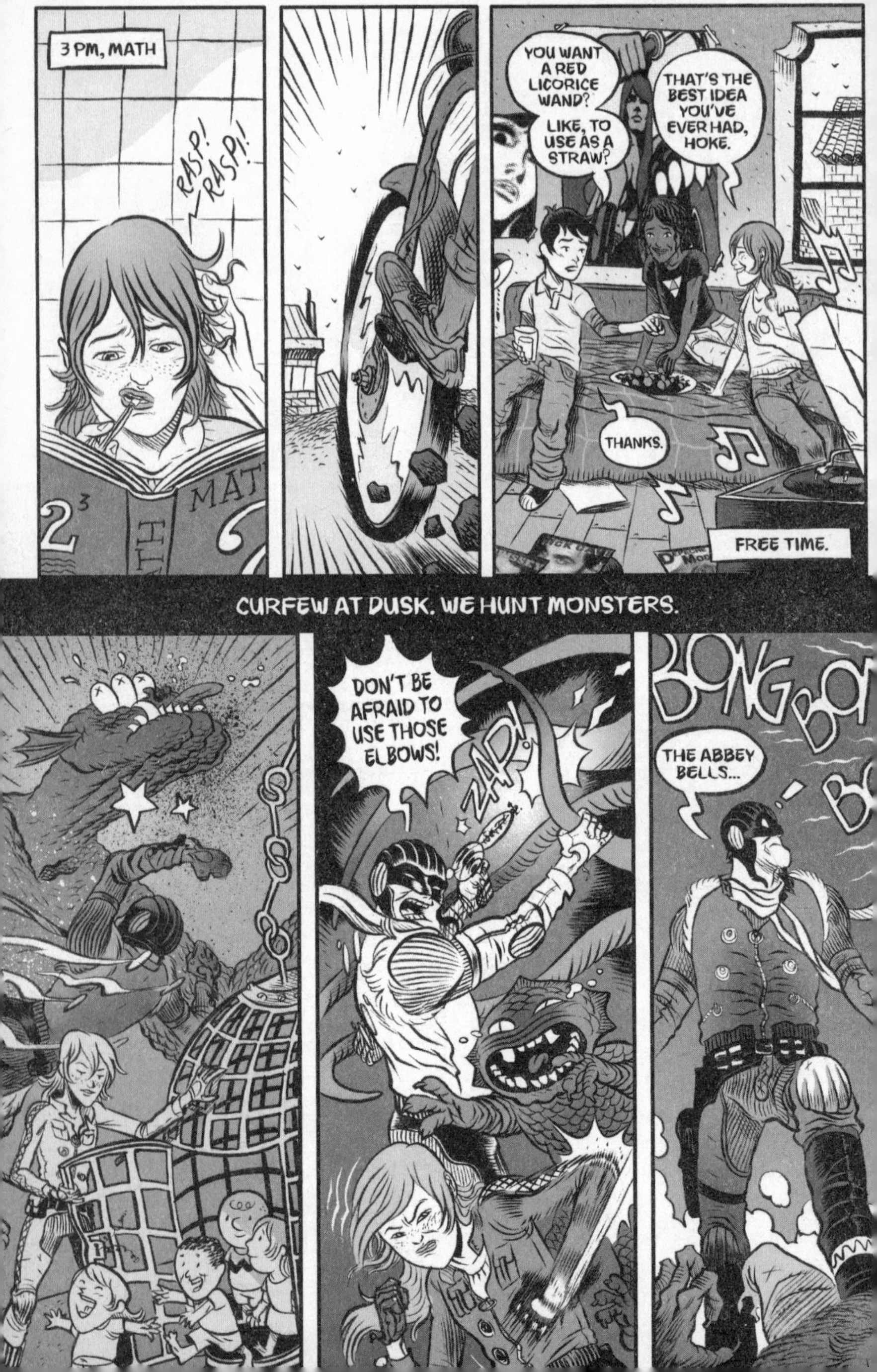
3 PM, MATH
RASP! RASP!
YOU WANT A RED LICORICE WAND?
LIKE, TO USE AS A STRAW?
THAT'S THE BEST IDEA YOU'VE EVER HAD, HOKE.
THANKS.
FREE TIME.
CURFEW AT DUSK. WE HUNT MONSTERS.
DON'T BE AFRAID TO USE THOSE ELBOWS!
ZAP!
BONG
THE ABBEY BELLS...

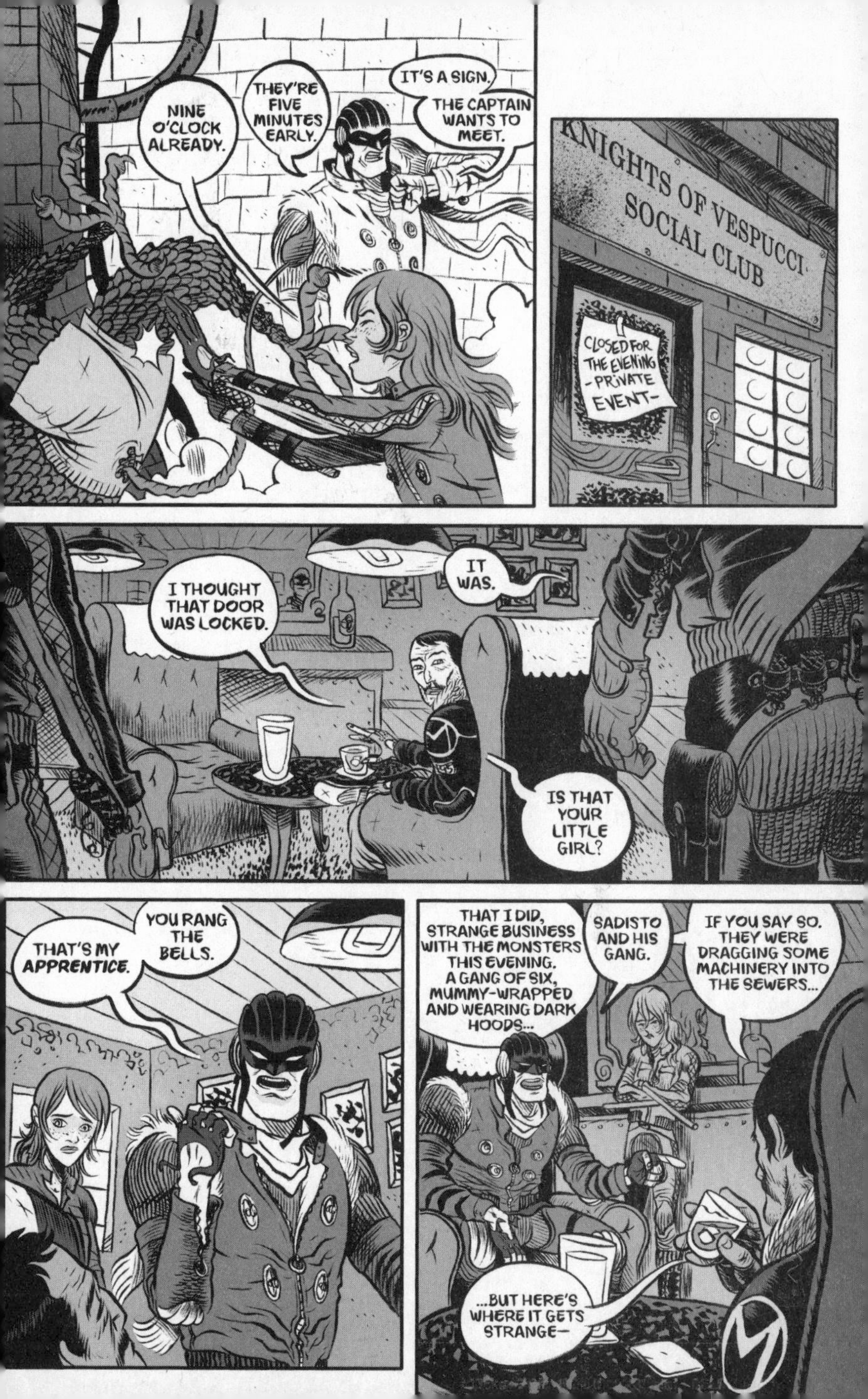
NINE O'CLOCK ALREADY.
THEY'RE FIVE MINUTES EARLY.
IT'S A SIGN.
THE CAPTAIN WANTS TO MEET.
KNIGHTS OF VESPUCCI SOCIAL CLUB
CLOSED FOR THE EVENING -PRIVATE EVENT-
I THOUGHT THAT DOOR WAS LOCKED.
IT WAS.
IS THAT YOUR LITTLE GIRL?
THAT'S MY APPRENTICE.
YOU RANG THE BELLS.
THAT I DID, STRANGE BUSINESS WITH THE MONSTERS THIS EVENING. A GANG OF SIX, MUMMY-WRAPPED AND WEARING DARK HOODS...
SADISTO AND HIS GANG.
IF YOU SAY SO. THEY WERE DRAGGING SOME MACHINERY INTO THE SEWERS...
...BUT HERE'S WHERE IT GETS STRANGE—

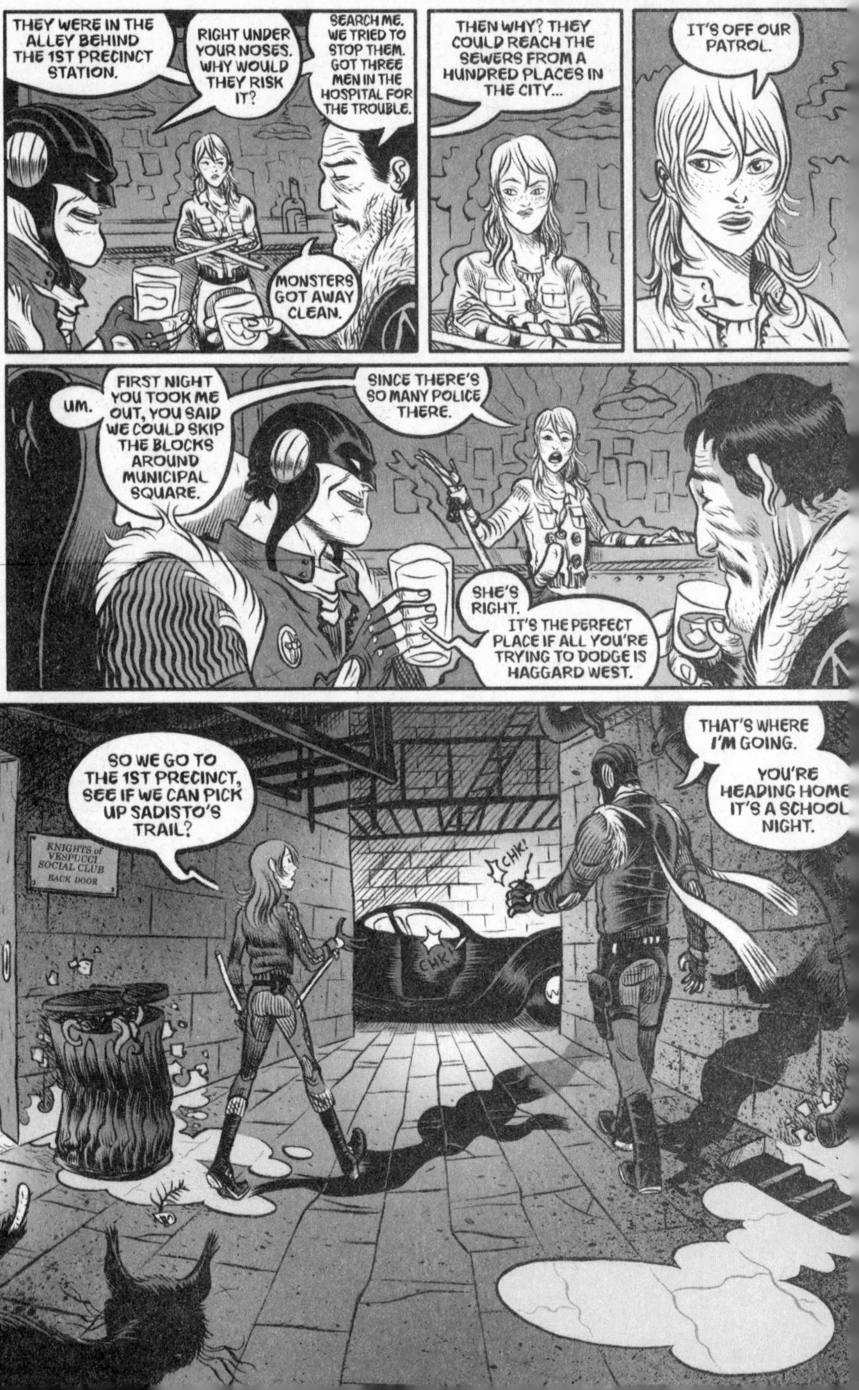
THEY WERE IN THE ALLEY BEHIND THE 1ST PRECINCT STATION.
RIGHT UNDER YOUR NOSES. WHY WOULD THEY RISK IT?
SEARCH ME. WE TRIED TO STOP THEM. GOT THREE MEN IN THE HOSPITAL FOR THE TROUBLE.
MONSTERS GOT AWAY CLEAN.
THEN WHY? THEY COULD REACH THE SEWERS FROM A HUNDRED PLACES IN THE CITY...
IT'S OFF OUR PATROL.
UM.
FIRST NIGHT YOU TOOK ME OUT, YOU SAID WE COULD SKIP THE BLOCKS AROUND MUNICIPAL SQUARE.
SINCE THERE'S SO MANY POLICE THERE.
SHE'S RIGHT.
IT'S THE PERFECT PLACE IF ALL YOU'RE TRYING TO DODGE IS HAGGARD WEST.
KNIGHTS of VESPUCCI SOCIAL CLUB BACK DOOR
SO WE GO TO THE 1ST PRECINCT, SEE IF WE CAN PICK UP SADISTO'S TRAIL?
CHK!
CHK!
THAT'S WHERE I'M GOING.
YOU'RE HEADING HOME IT'S A SCHOOL NIGHT.

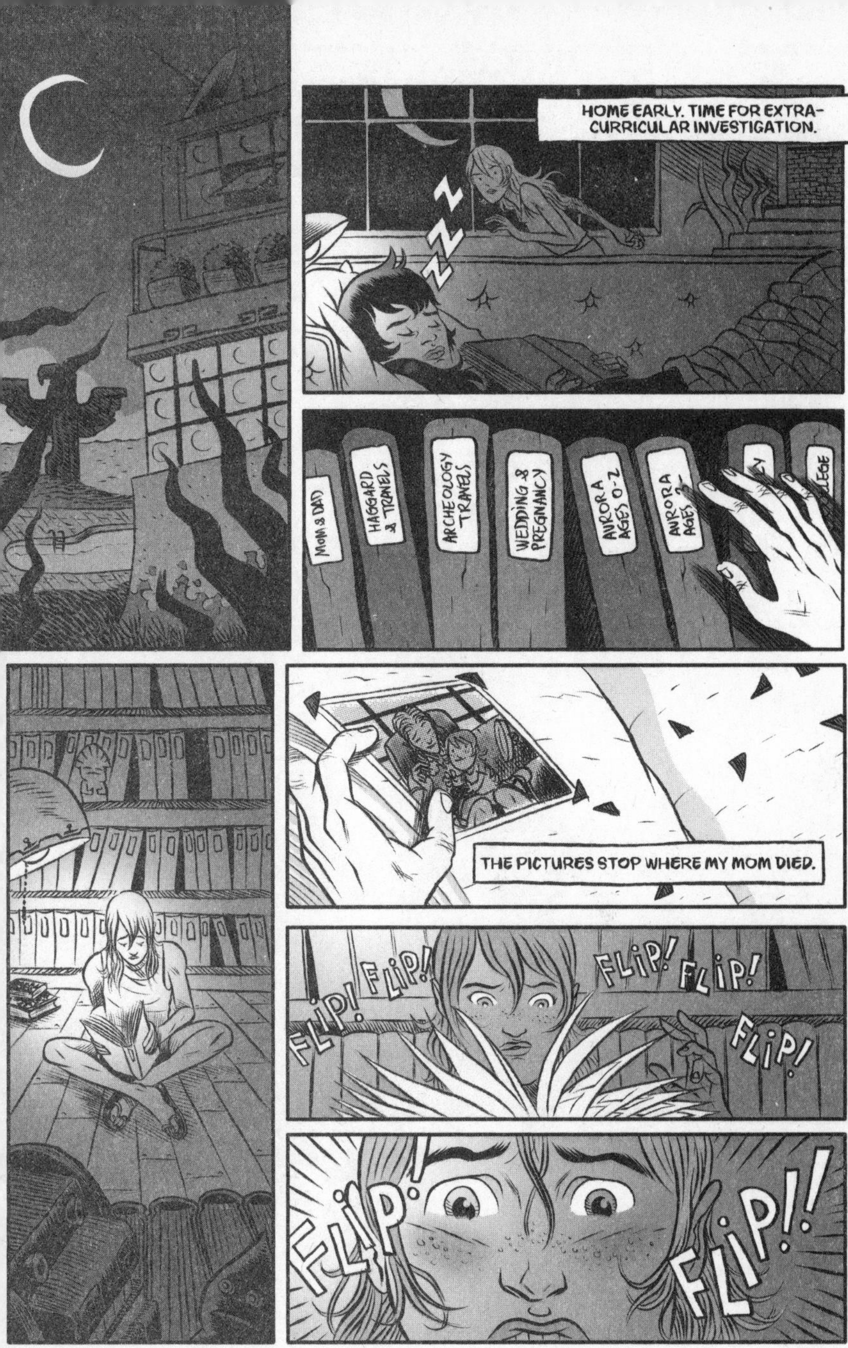
HOME EARLY. TIME FOR EXTRA-CURRICULAR INVESTIGATION.
Z Z Z
MOM & DAD
HAGGARD & TRAVELS
ARCHEOLOGY TRAVELS
WEDDING & PREGNANCY
AURORA AGES 0-2
AURORA AGES 2
THE PICTURES STOP WHERE MY MOM DIED.
FLIP! FLIP! FLIP! FLIP! FLIP! FLIP!
FLIP! FLIP!!

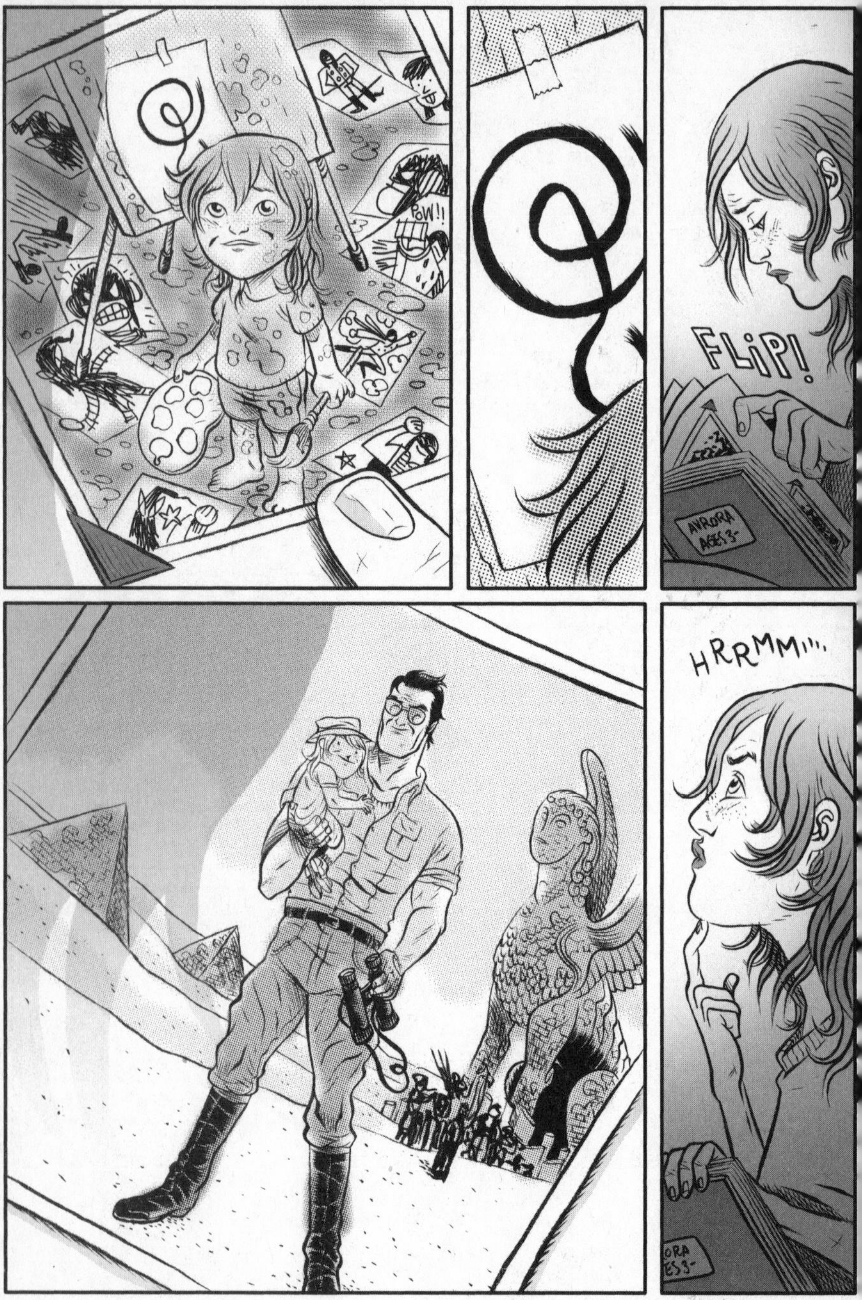
POW!!
FLIP!
AVRORA AGES 3-
HRRMM!!..

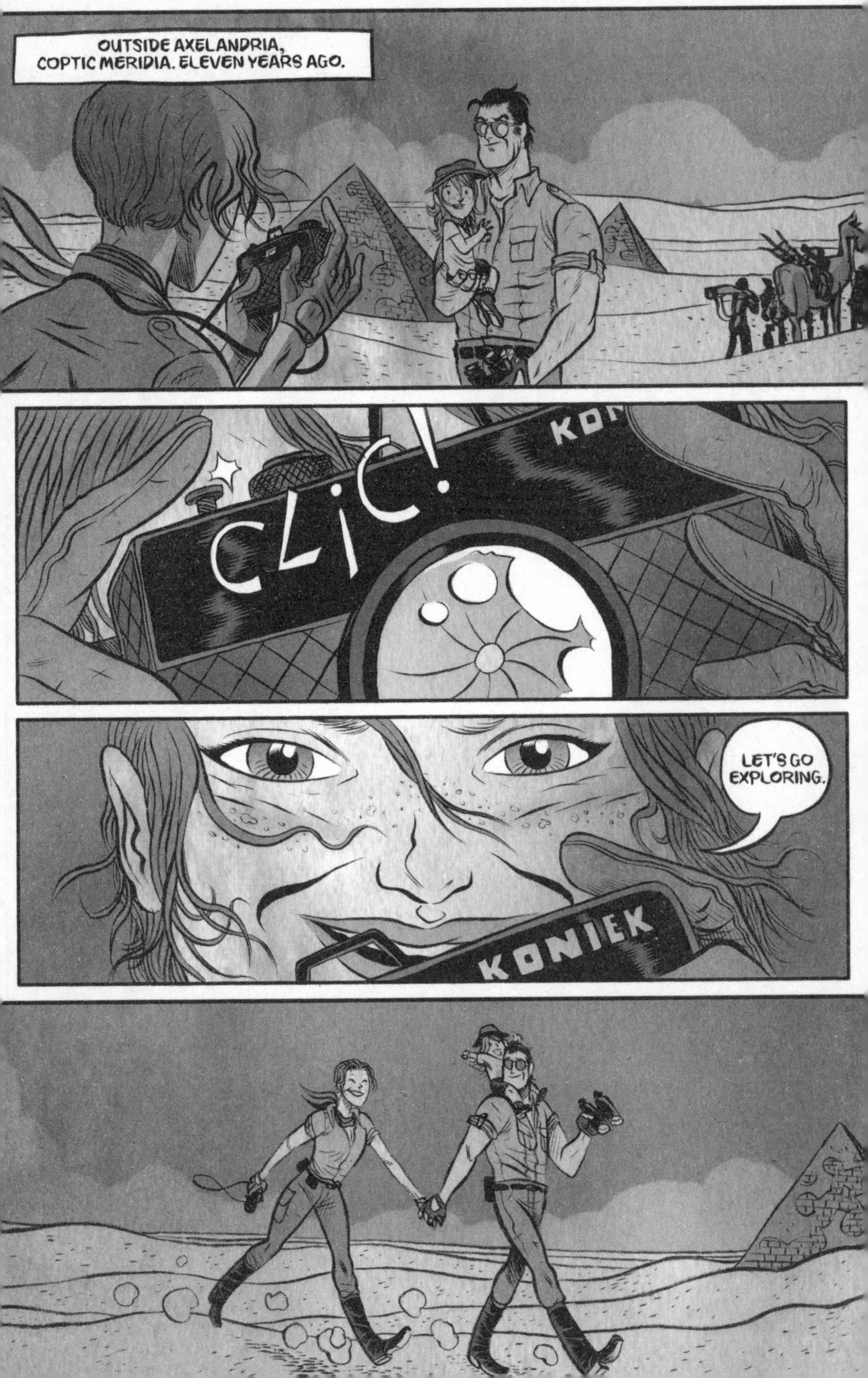
OUTSIDE AXELANDRIA, COPTIC MERIDIA. ELEVEN YEARS AGO.
KON
CLIC!
LET'S GO EXPLORING.
KONIEK

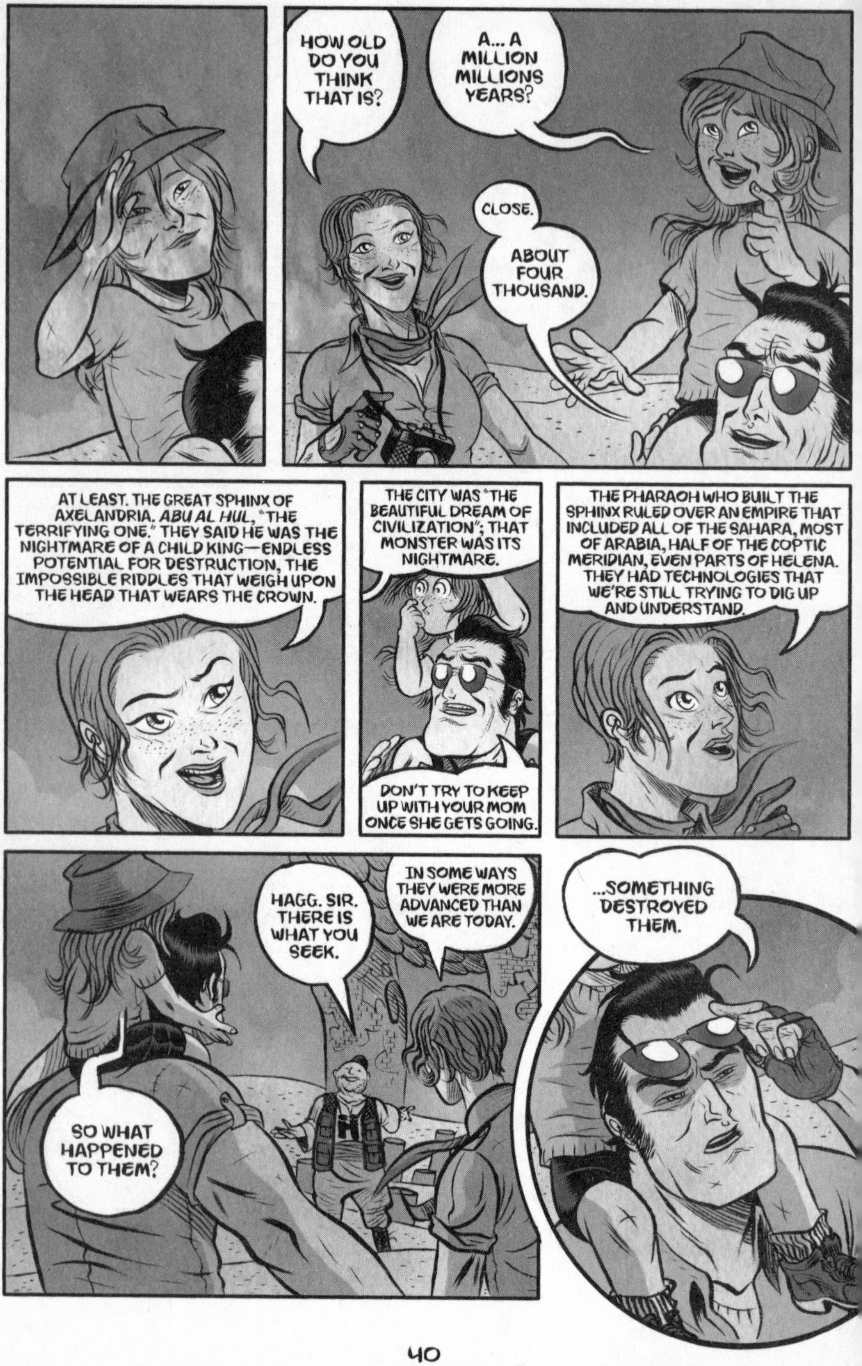
HOW OLD DO YOU THINK THAT IS?
A... A MILLION MILLIONS YEARS?
CLOSE.
ABOUT FOUR THOUSAND.
AT LEAST. THE GREAT SPHINX OF AXELANDRIA. *ABU AL HUL*, "THE TERRIFYING ONE." THEY SAID HE WAS THE NIGHTMARE OF A CHILD KING—ENDLESS POTENTIAL FOR DESTRUCTION, THE IMPOSSIBLE RIDDLES THAT WEIGH UPON THE HEAD THAT WEARS THE CROWN.
THE CITY WAS "THE BEAUTIFUL DREAM OF CIVILIZATION"; THAT MONSTER WAS ITS NIGHTMARE.
DON'T TRY TO KEEP UP WITH YOUR MOM ONCE SHE GETS GOING.
THE PHARAOH WHO BUILT THE SPHINX RULED OVER AN EMPIRE THAT INCLUDED ALL OF THE SAHARA, MOST OF ARABIA, HALF OF THE COPTIC MERIDIAN, EVEN PARTS OF HELENA. THEY HAD TECHNOLOGIES THAT WE'RE STILL TRYING TO DIG UP AND UNDERSTAND.
HAGG. SIR. THERE IS WHAT YOU SEEK.
IN SOME WAYS THEY WERE MORE ADVANCED THAN WE ARE TODAY.
SO WHAT HAPPENED TO THEM?
...SOMETHING DESTROYED THEM.

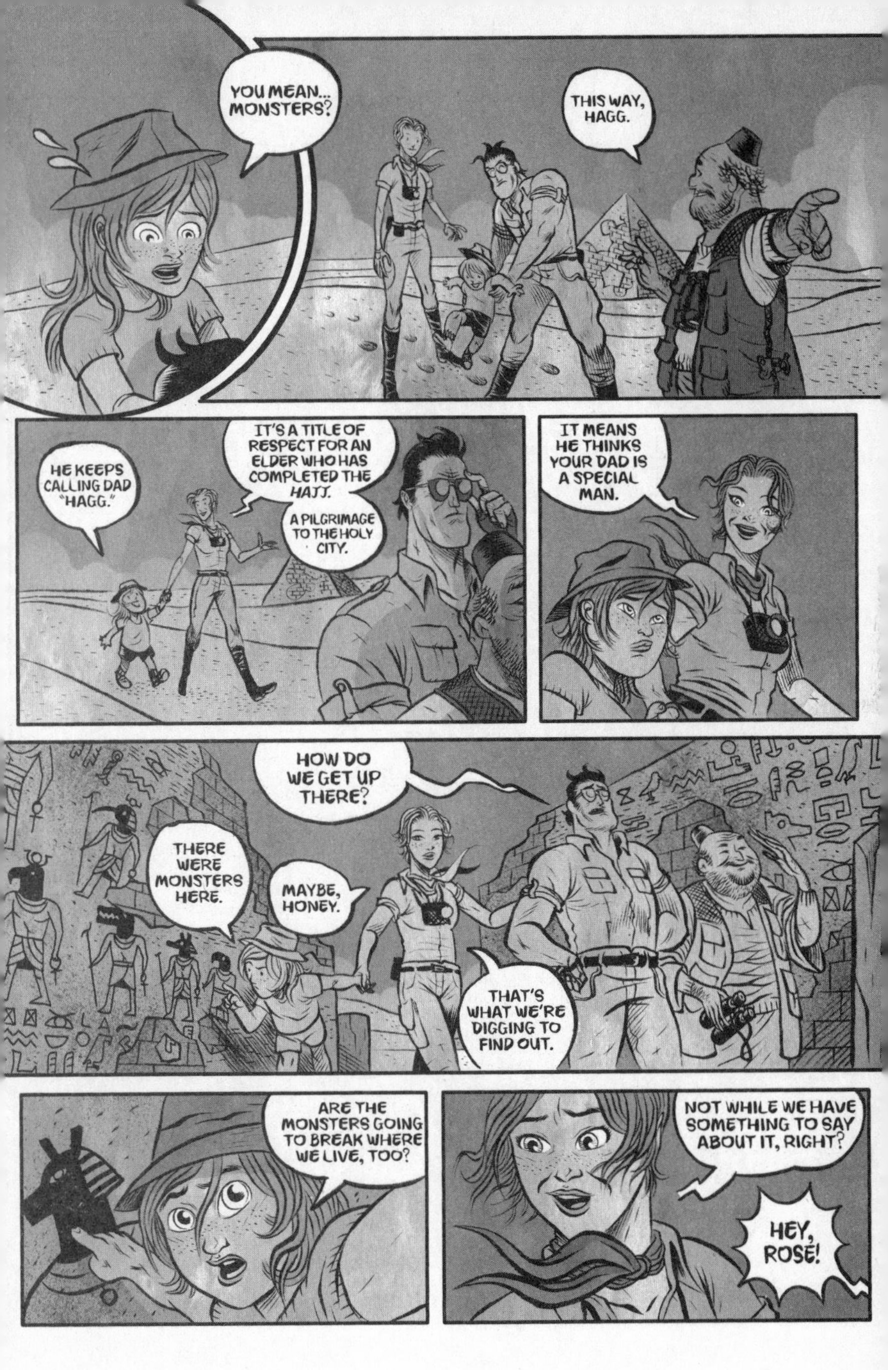
YOU MEAN... MONSTERS?
THIS WAY, HAGG.
HE KEEPS CALLING DAD "HAGG."
IT'S A TITLE OF RESPECT FOR AN ELDER WHO HAS COMPLETED THE HAJJ.
A PILGRIMAGE TO THE HOLY CITY.
IT MEANS HE THINKS YOUR DAD IS A SPECIAL MAN.
HOW DO WE GET UP THERE?
THERE WERE MONSTERS HERE.
MAYBE, HONEY.
THAT'S WHAT WE'RE DIGGING TO FIND OUT.
ARE THE MONSTERS GOING TO BREAK WHERE WE LIVE, TOO?
NOT WHILE WE HAVE SOMETHING TO SAY ABOUT IT, RIGHT?
HEY, ROSE!

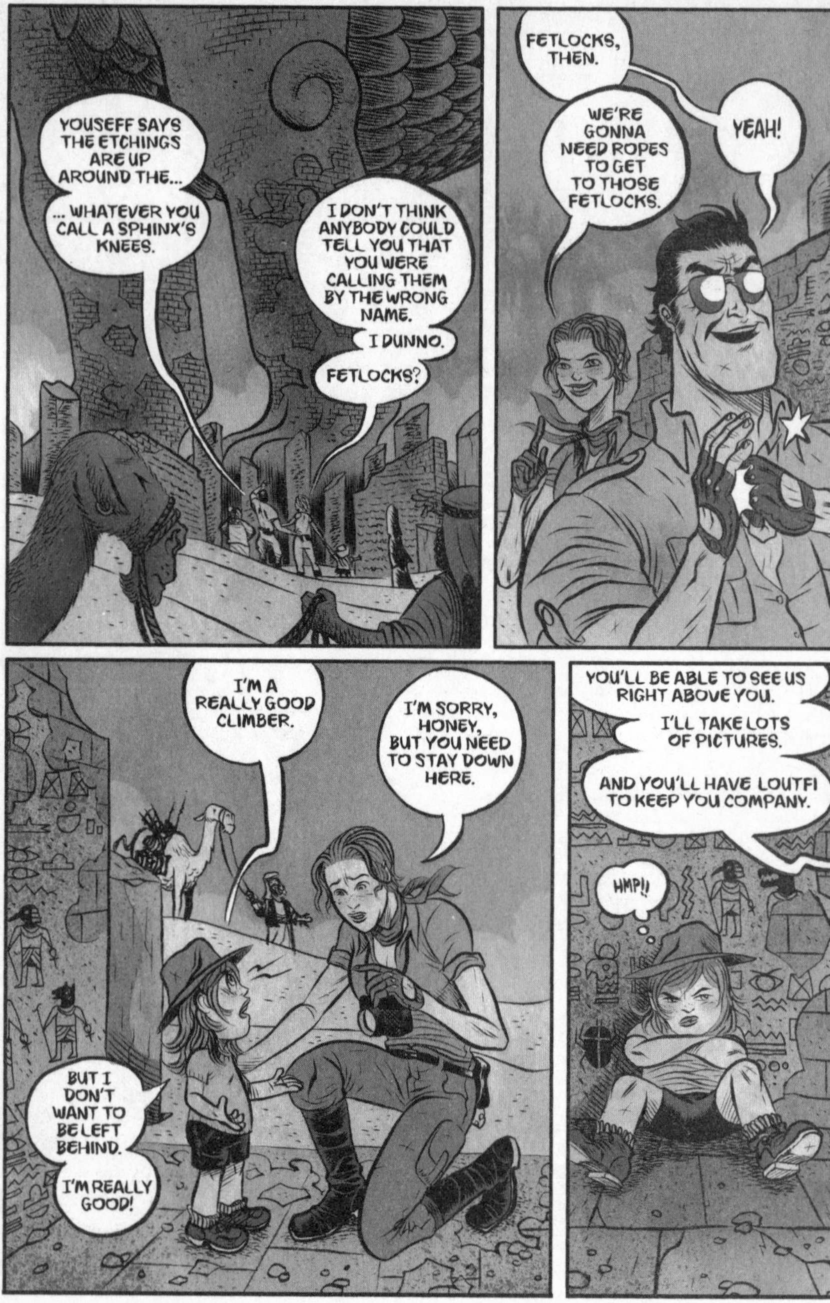
YOUSEFF SAYS THE ETCHINGS ARE UP AROUND THE...
... WHATEVER YOU CALL A SPHINX'S KNEES.
I DON'T THINK ANYBODY COULD TELL YOU THAT YOU WERE CALLING THEM BY THE WRONG NAME.
I DUNNO.
FETLOCKS?
FETLOCKS, THEN.
WE'RE GONNA NEED ROPES TO GET TO THOSE FETLOCKS.
YEAH!
I'M A REALLY GOOD CLIMBER.
I'M SORRY, HONEY, BUT YOU NEED TO STAY DOWN HERE.
BUT I DON'T WANT TO BE LEFT BEHIND.
I'M REALLY GOOD!
YOU'LL BE ABLE TO SEE US RIGHT ABOVE YOU.
I'LL TAKE LOTS OF PICTURES.
AND YOU'LL HAVE LOUTFI TO KEEP YOU COMPANY.
HMP!!

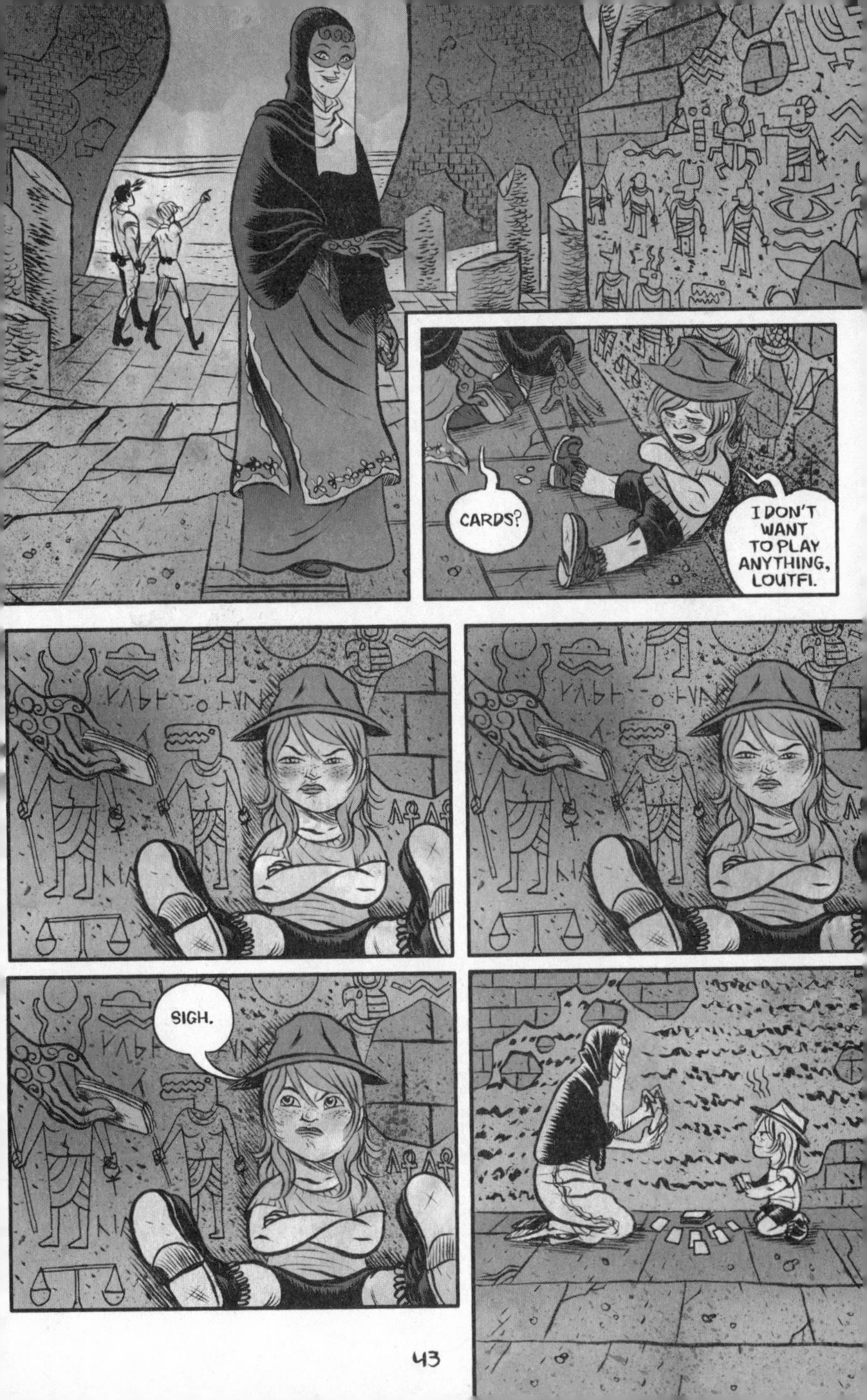
CARDS?
I DON'T WANT TO PLAY ANYTHING, LOUTFI.
SIGH.

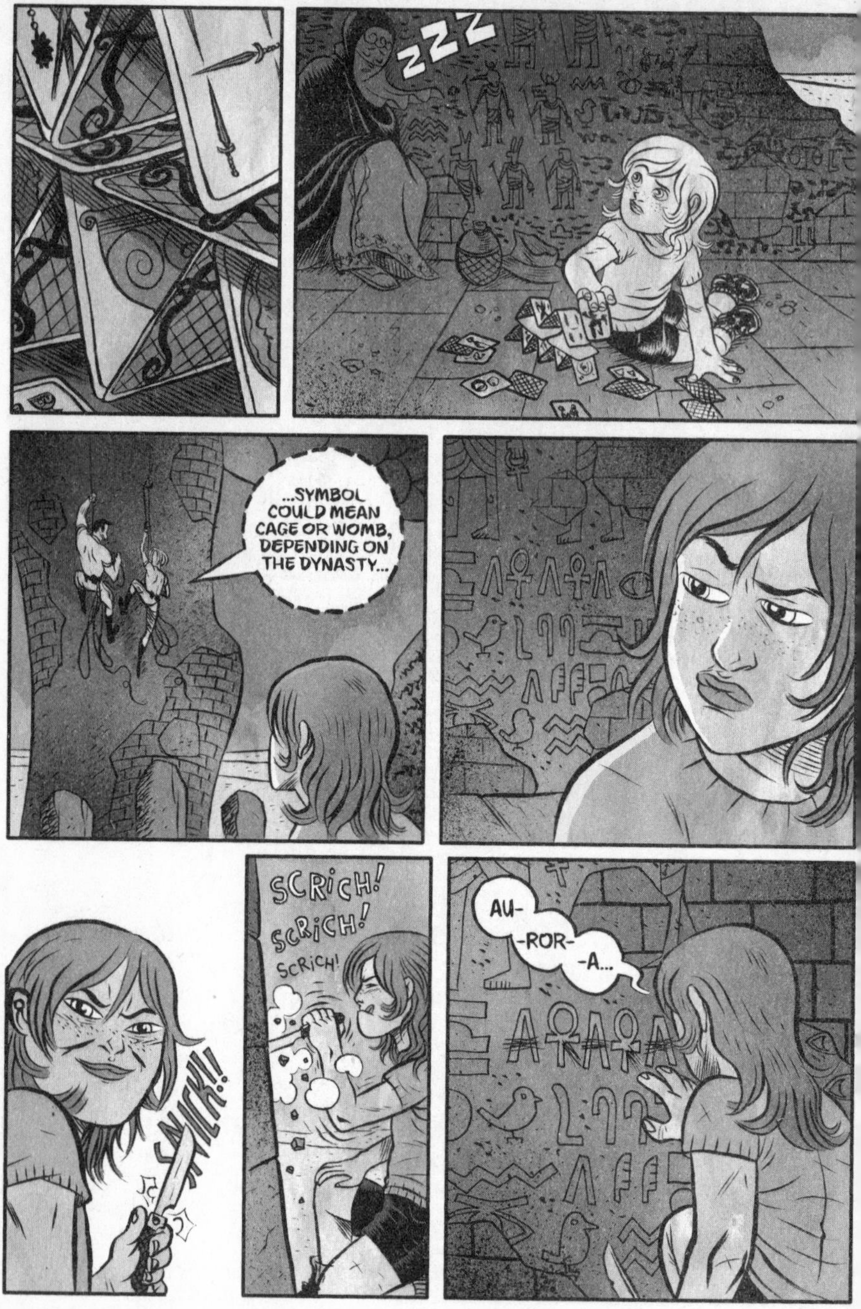
ZZZ
...SYMBOL COULD MEAN CAGE OR WOMB, DEPENDING ON THE DYNASTY...
SNICK!!
SCRICH!
SCRICH!
SCRICH!
AU-
-ROR-
-A...

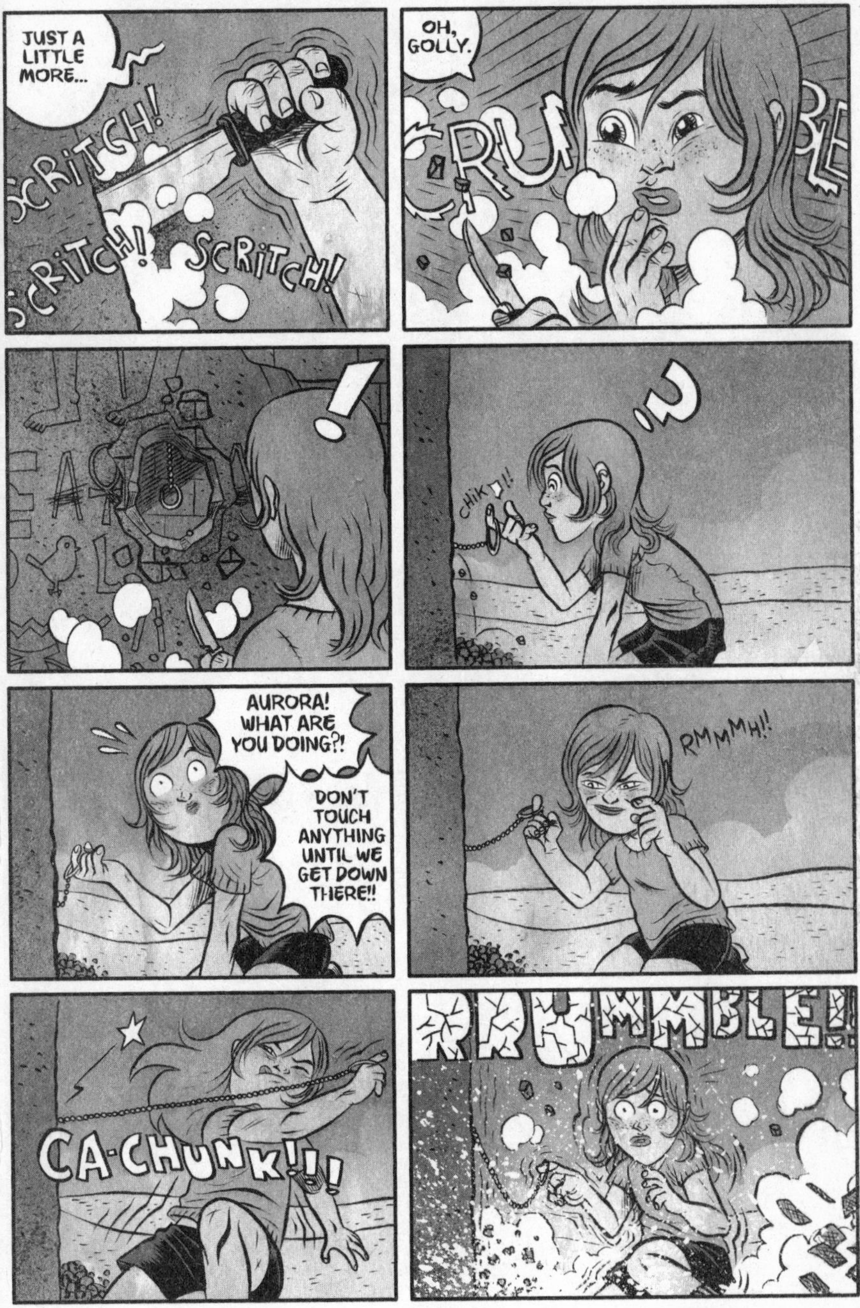
JUST A LITTLE MORE...
SCRITCH!
SCRITCH!
SCRITCH!
OH, GOLLY.
CRUMBLE
!
?!
CHIK!!
AURORA! WHAT ARE YOU DOING?!
DON'T TOUCH ANYTHING UNTIL WE GET DOWN THERE!!
RMMMH!!
CA-CHUNK!!!
RRUMMBLE!!

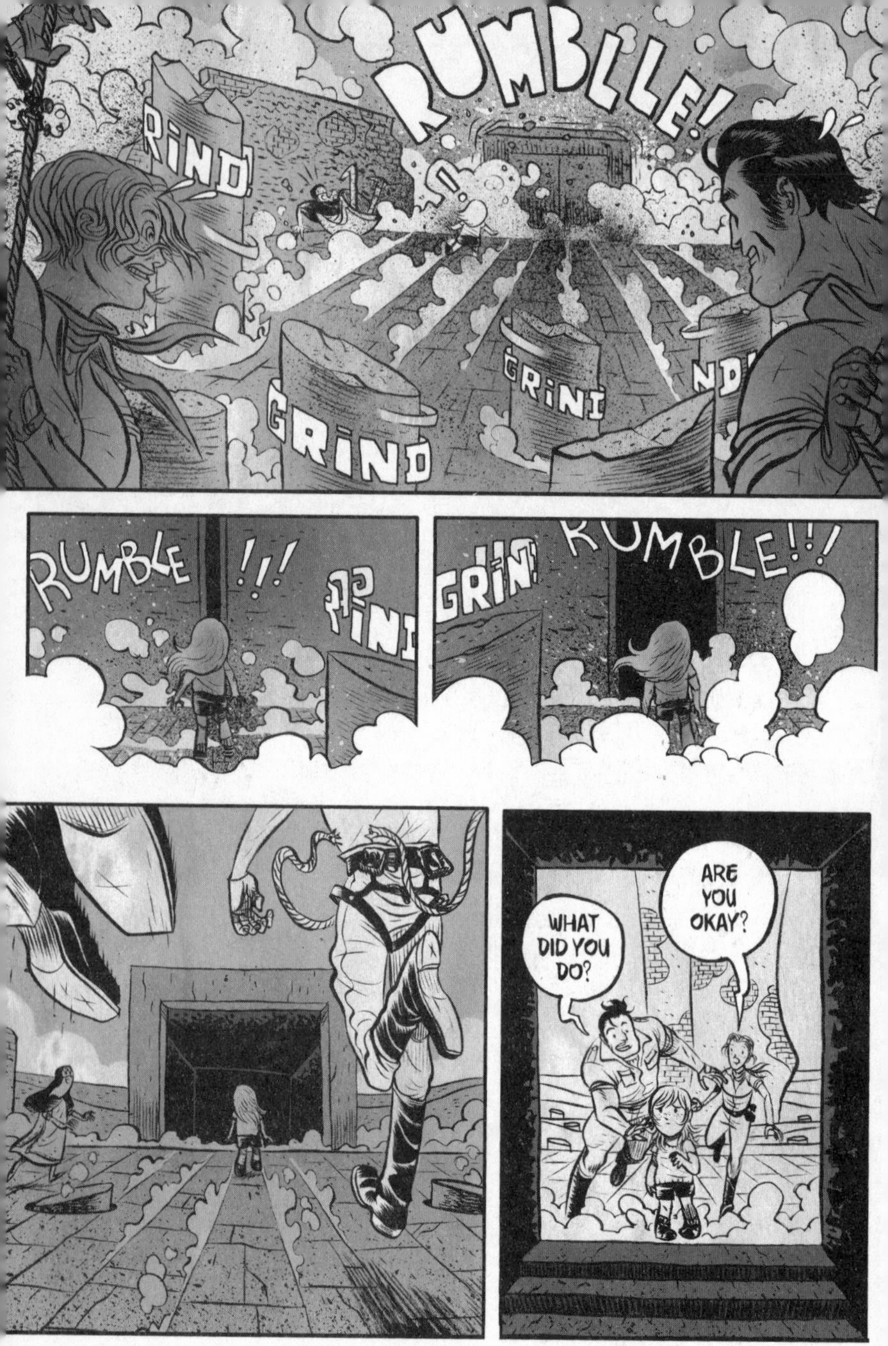
RUMBLLE!
RIND!
GRIND
GRIN
ND
RUMBLE !!!
GRIN
GRIN
RUMBLE!!!
WHAT DID YOU DO?
ARE YOU OKAY?

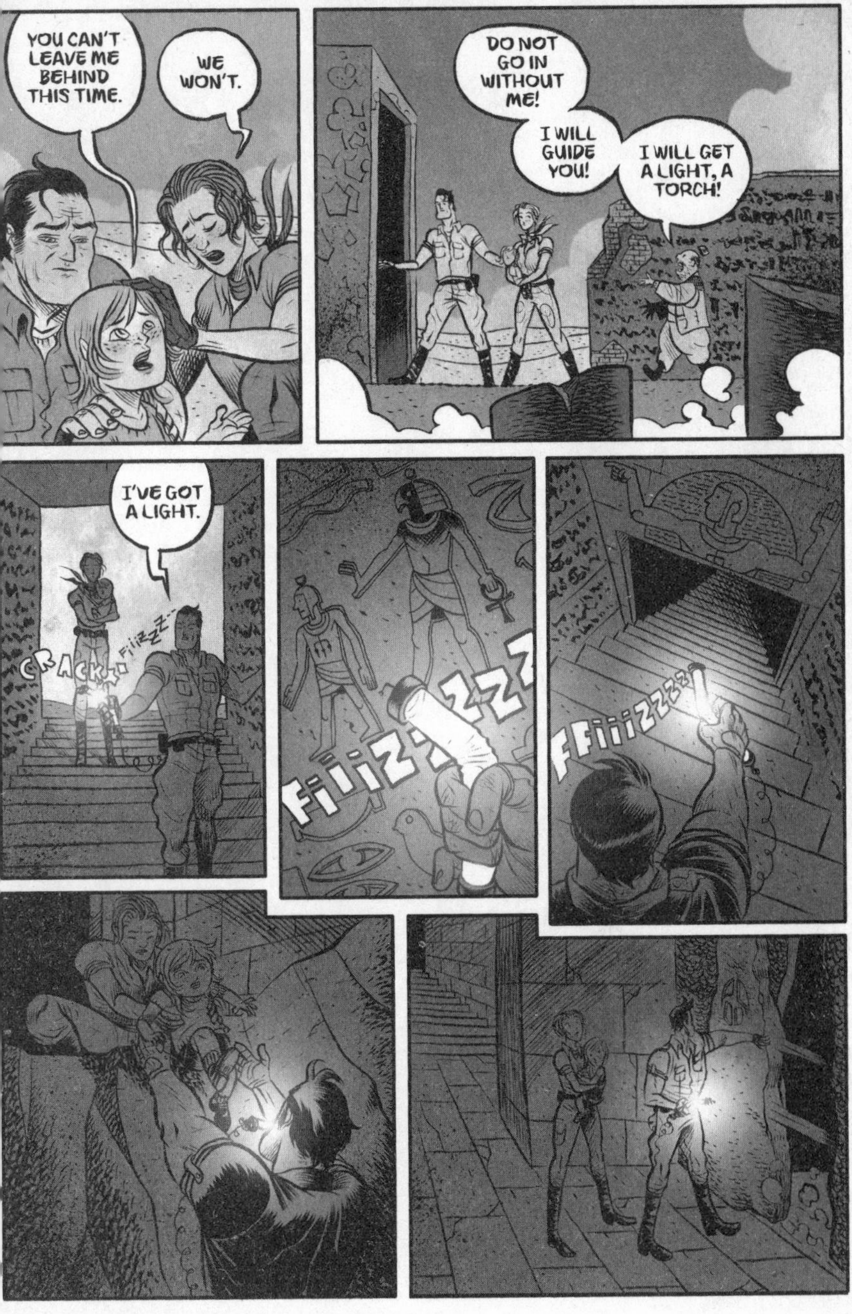
YOU CAN'T LEAVE ME BEHIND THIS TIME.
WE WON'T.
DO NOT GO IN WITHOUT ME!
I WILL GUIDE YOU!
I WILL GET A LIGHT, A TORCH!
I'VE GOT A LIGHT.
CRACK
FIIIZZZ
FIIIZZZZ
FFIIIZZZZZ

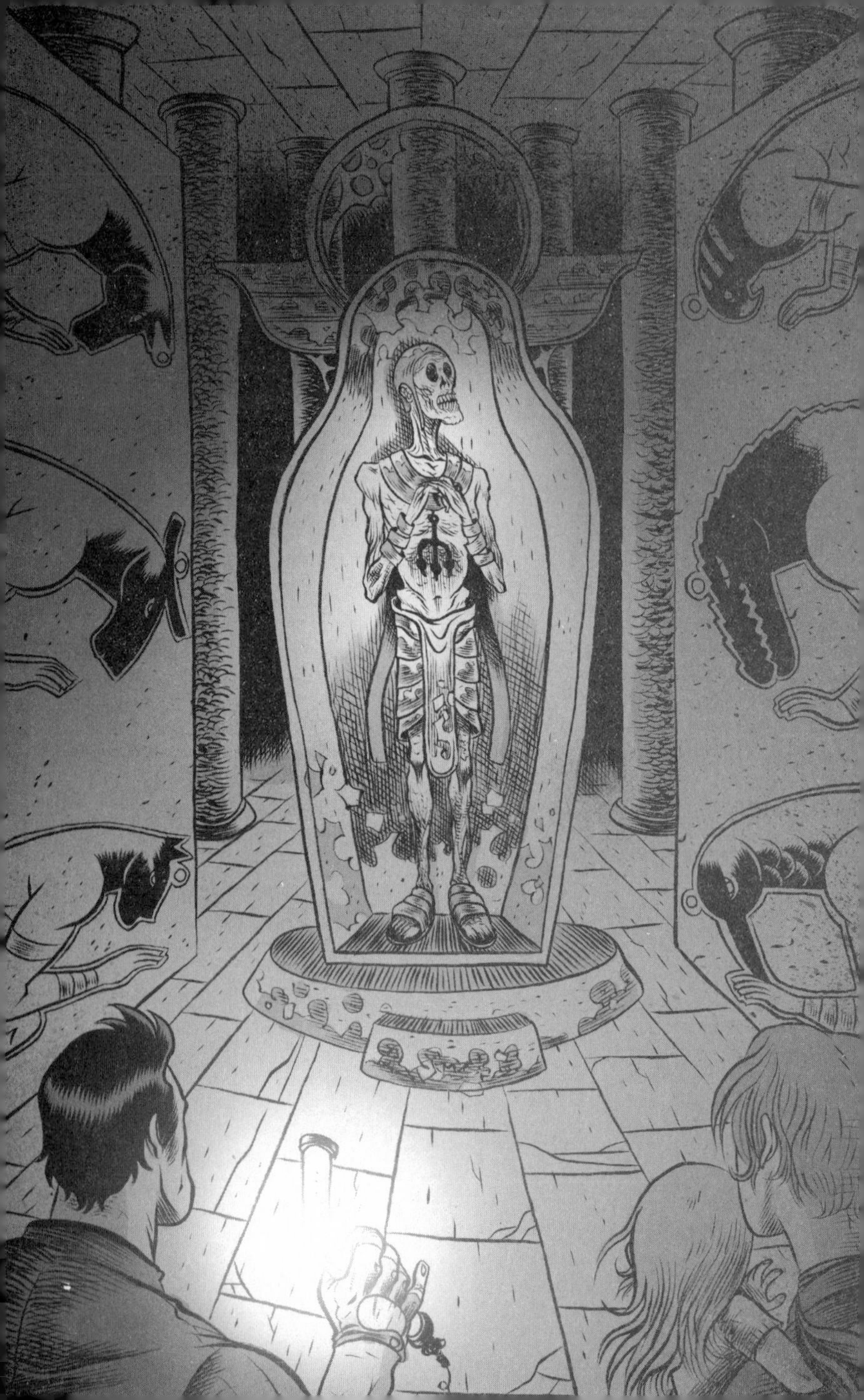

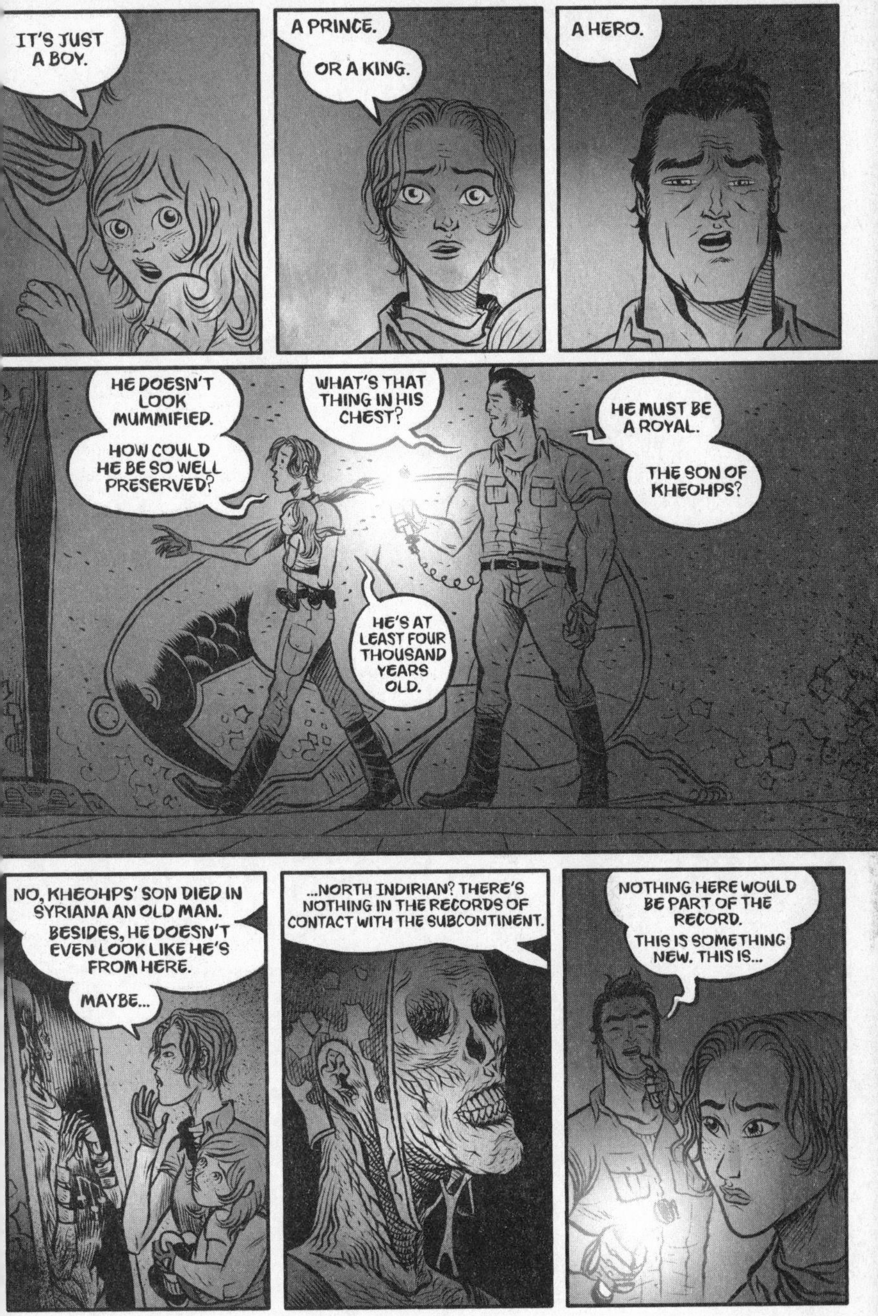
IT'S JUST A BOY.
A PRINCE.
OR A KING.
A HERO.
HE DOESN'T LOOK MUMMIFIED.
HOW COULD HE BE SO WELL PRESERVED?
WHAT'S THAT THING IN HIS CHEST?
HE MUST BE A ROYAL.
THE SON OF KHEOHPS?
HE'S AT LEAST FOUR THOUSAND YEARS OLD.
NO, KHEOHPS' SON DIED IN SYRIANA AN OLD MAN.
BESIDES, HE DOESN'T EVEN LOOK LIKE HE'S FROM HERE.
MAYBE...
...NORTH INDIRIAN? THERE'S NOTHING IN THE RECORDS OF CONTACT WITH THE SUBCONTINENT.
NOTHING HERE WOULD BE PART OF THE RECORD.
THIS IS SOMETHING NEW. THIS IS...

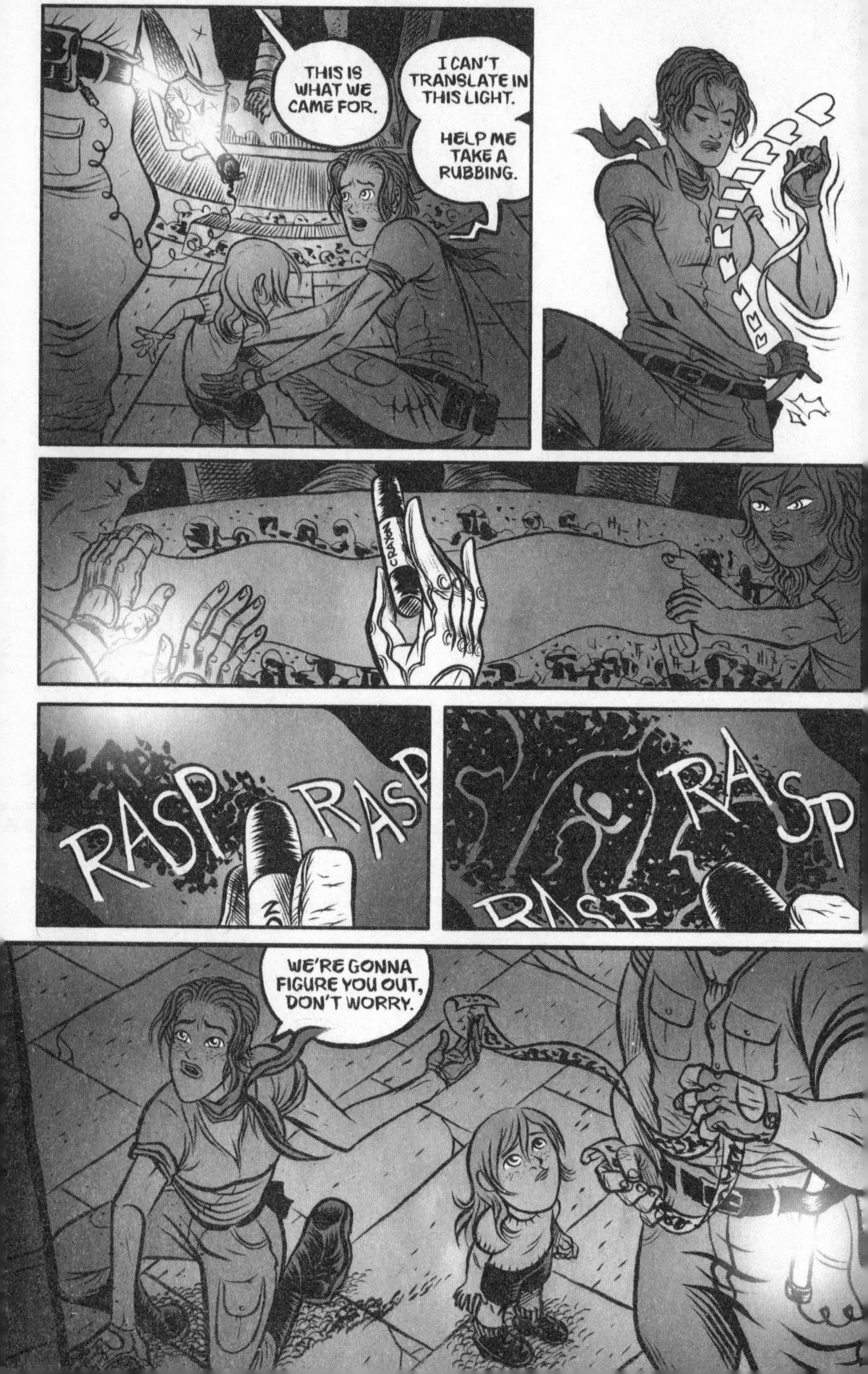
THIS IS WHAT WE CAME FOR.
I CAN'T TRANSLATE IN THIS LIGHT.
HELP ME TAKE A RUBBING.
CRAYON
RASP RASP
RASP
WE'RE GONNA FIGURE YOU OUT, DON'T WORRY.

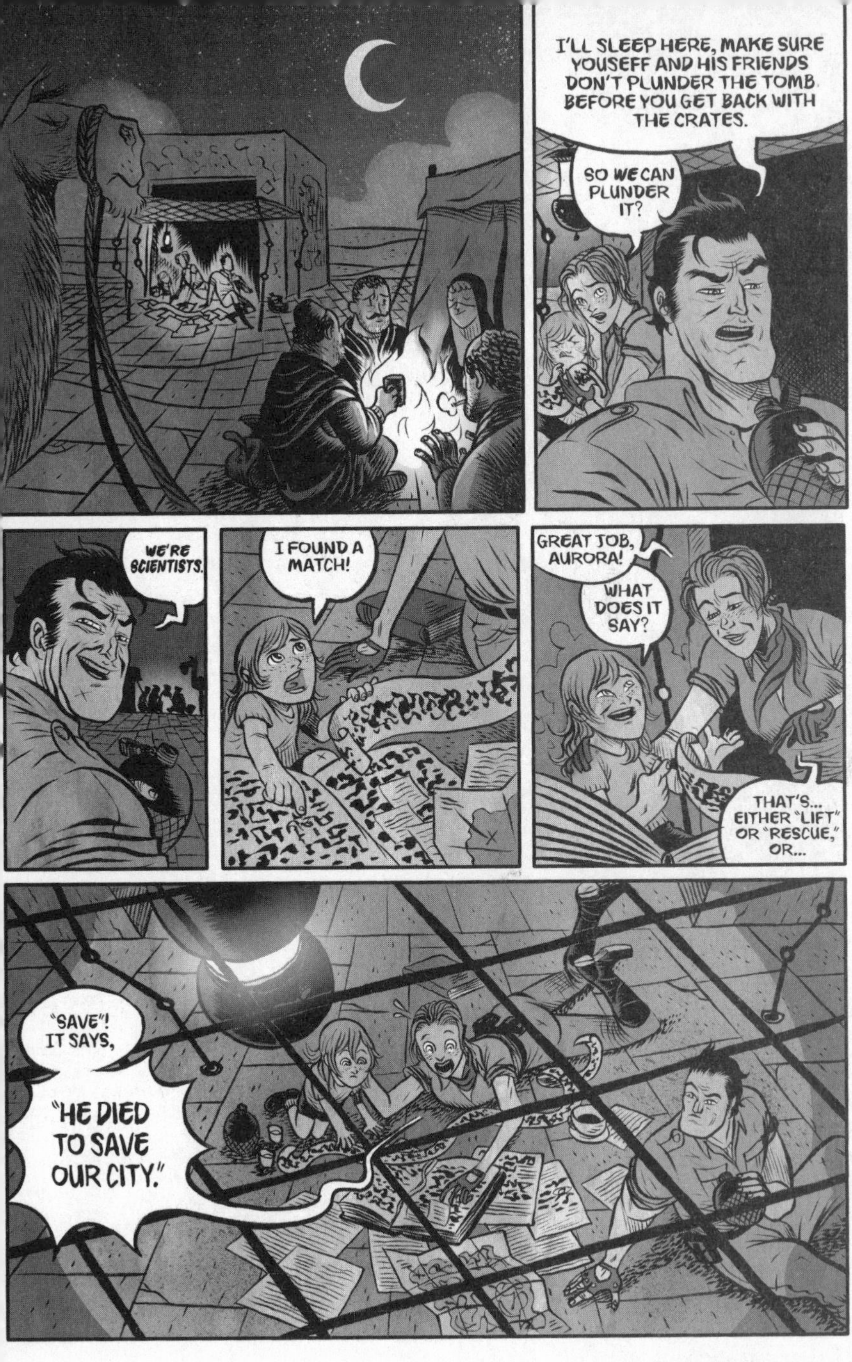
I'LL SLEEP HERE, MAKE SURE YOUSEFF AND HIS FRIENDS DON'T PLUNDER THE TOMB BEFORE YOU GET BACK WITH THE CRATES.
SO WE CAN PLUNDER IT?
WE'RE SCIENTISTS.
I FOUND A MATCH!
GREAT JOB, AURORA!
WHAT DOES IT SAY?
THAT'S... EITHER "LIFT" OR "RESCUE," OR...
"SAVE"! IT SAYS,
"HE DIED TO SAVE OUR CITY."

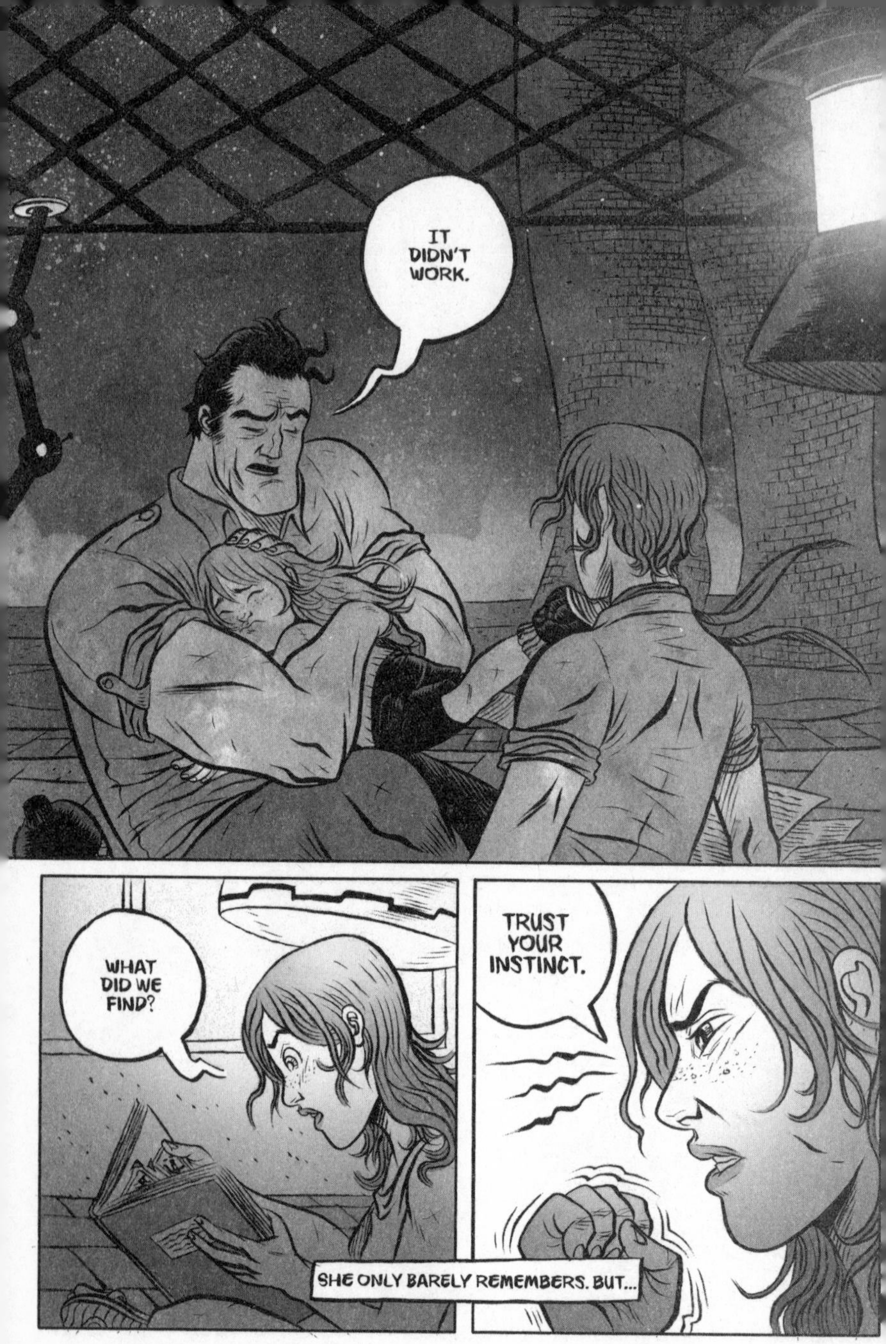
IT DIDN'T WORK.
WHAT DID WE FIND?
TRUST YOUR INSTINCT.
SHE ONLY BARELY REMEMBERS. BUT...

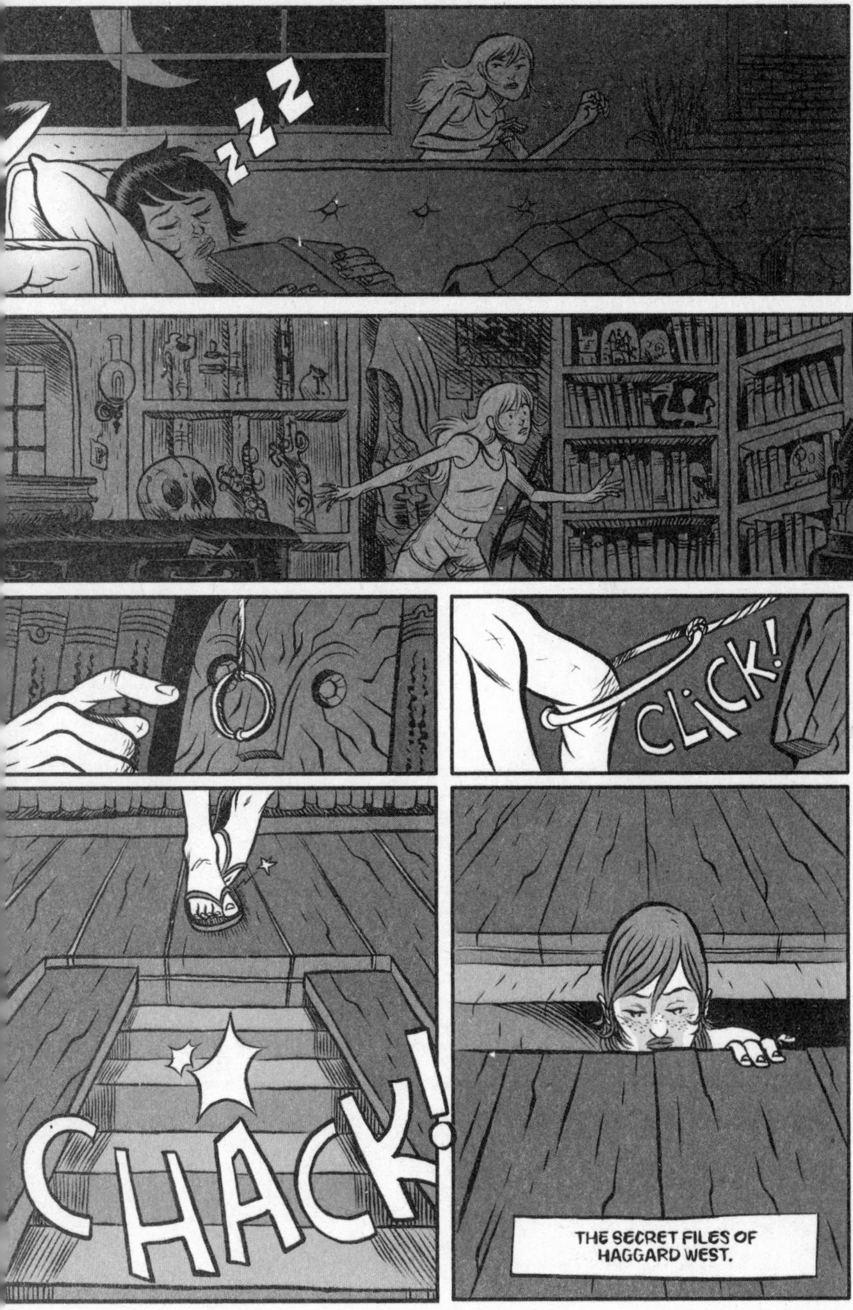
Z
Z
Z
Z
CLICK!
CHACK!
THE SECRET FILES OF HAGGARD WEST.

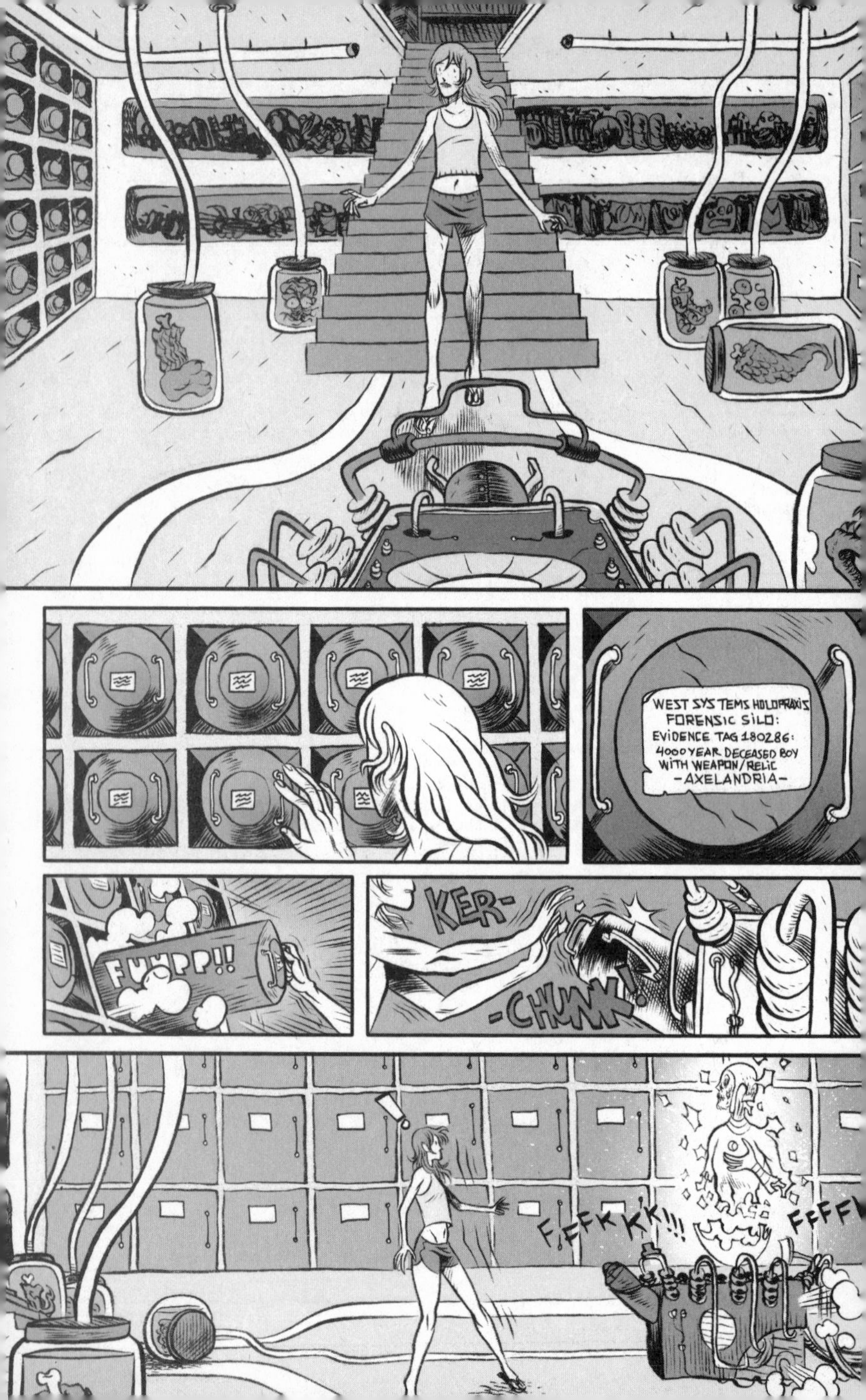
WEST SYSTEMS HOLOPRAXIS FORENSIC SILO:
EVIDENCE TAG 180286:
4000 YEAR DECEASED BOY WITH WEAPON/RELIC
-AXELANDRIA-
FUHPP!!
KER-
-CHUNK!
FFFKKKK!!!
FFFF

WERE YOU MR. WURPLE?
WHAT HAPPENED TO YOU?
FFFZZZ
WEST SYSTEMS HOLOPRAXIS FORENSIC SILO: EVIDENCE TAG 180287: WEAPON/RELIC DISCOVERED IN CHEST OF 4000 YEAR DEAD BOY--(AXELANDRÍA)
KER-CHUNK!
FFK
KK!
Recovered from
the chest of a
mummified boy in
Axelandría..
Appear been the caus
of death..
Still emanates some for
f energy I can not ident
ome new radioactivity!
MUST USE TONGS/KEEP ALL WOME
STILL CAPABLE OF BEARING
CHILDREN AT A SAFE DISTANCE.
SOME FORM OF ENERGY...

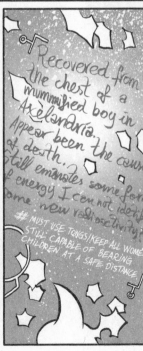

...CAN FEEL THE HEAT COMING OFF OF IT.

IT'S SOME SORT OF ENERGY....

DO YOU THINK IT'S RELATED TO THE ACCELERATED DECOMPOSITION OF THE BOY?

THIS IS DIFFERENT... DARKER SOMEHOW.

WHATEVER IT IS, THE BOY IS VANISHING QUICK.

A LITTLE MORE OF HIM DISAPPEARS EVERY MOMENT.

LET'S GET HIM ON THE HOLOPRAXISCOPE BEFORE HE'S ANY MORE GONE.

CAN YOU PROP HIM UP?

CLICK!

KTK!

CLICK!

CHK!

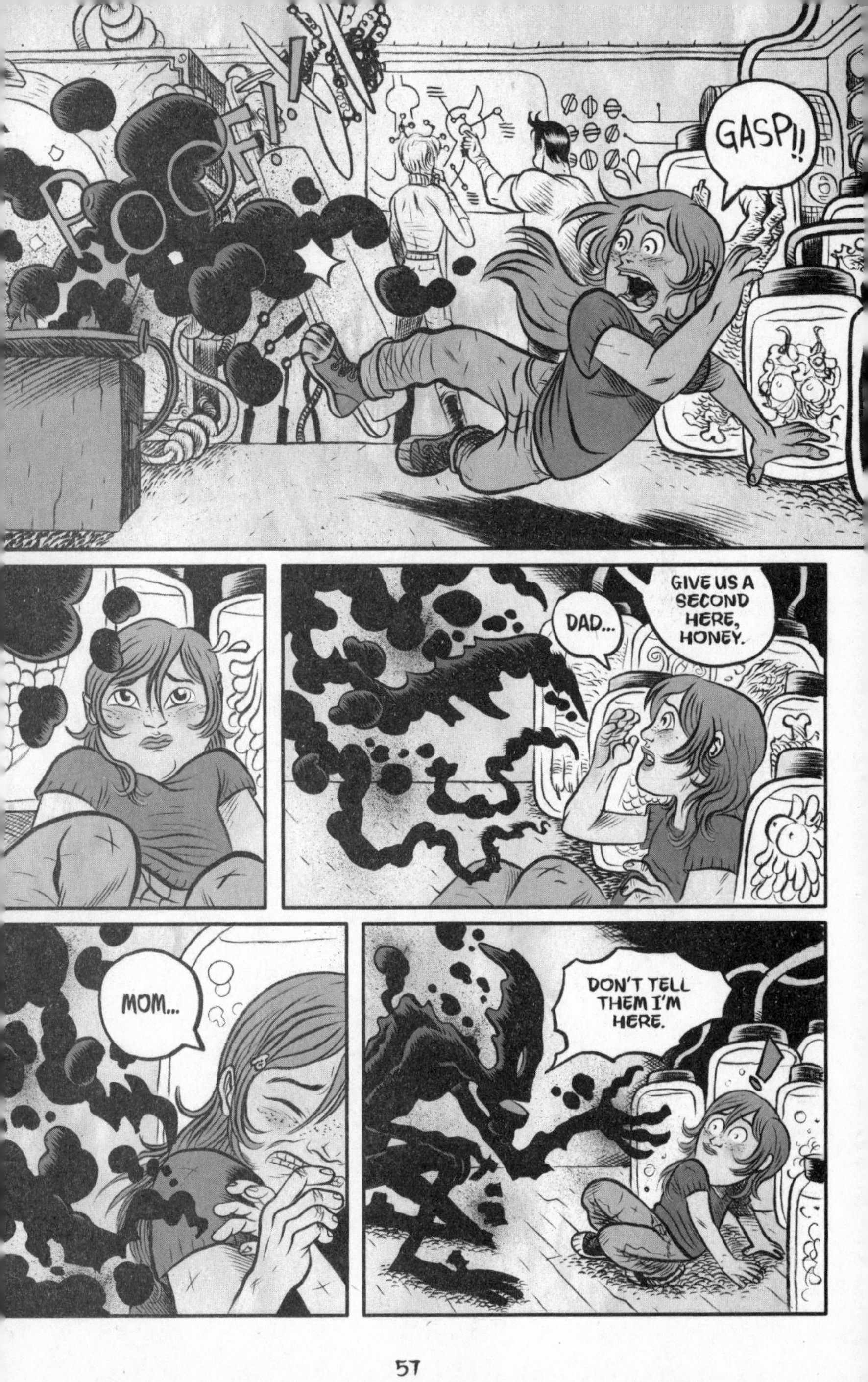
POOF!
GASP!!
DAD...
GIVE US A SECOND HERE, HONEY.
MOM...
DON'T TELL THEM I'M HERE.

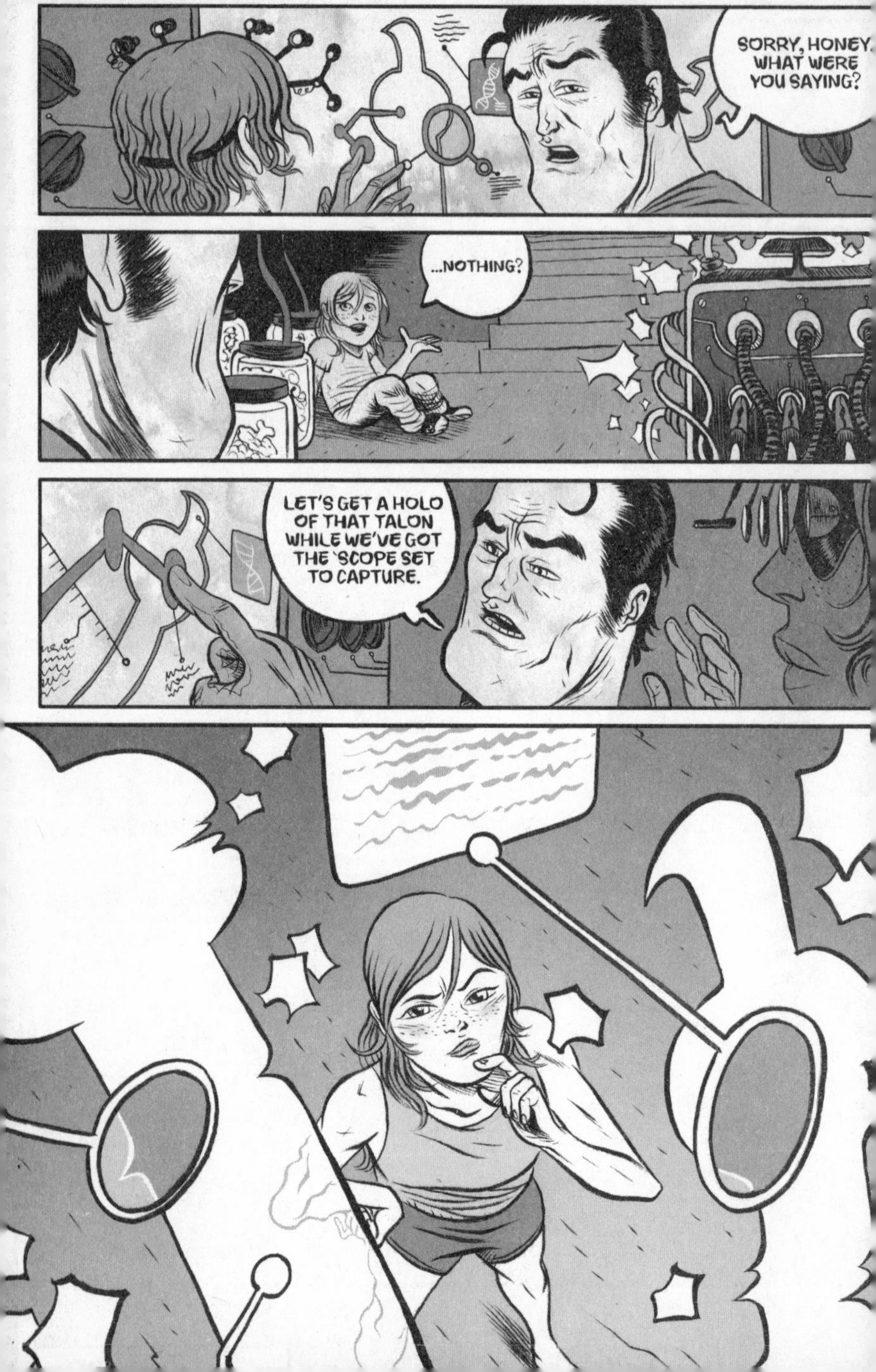
SORRY, HONEY. WHAT WERE YOU SAYING?
...NOTHING?
LET'S GET A HOLO OF THAT TALON WHILE WE'VE GOT THE 'SCOPE SET TO CAPTURE.

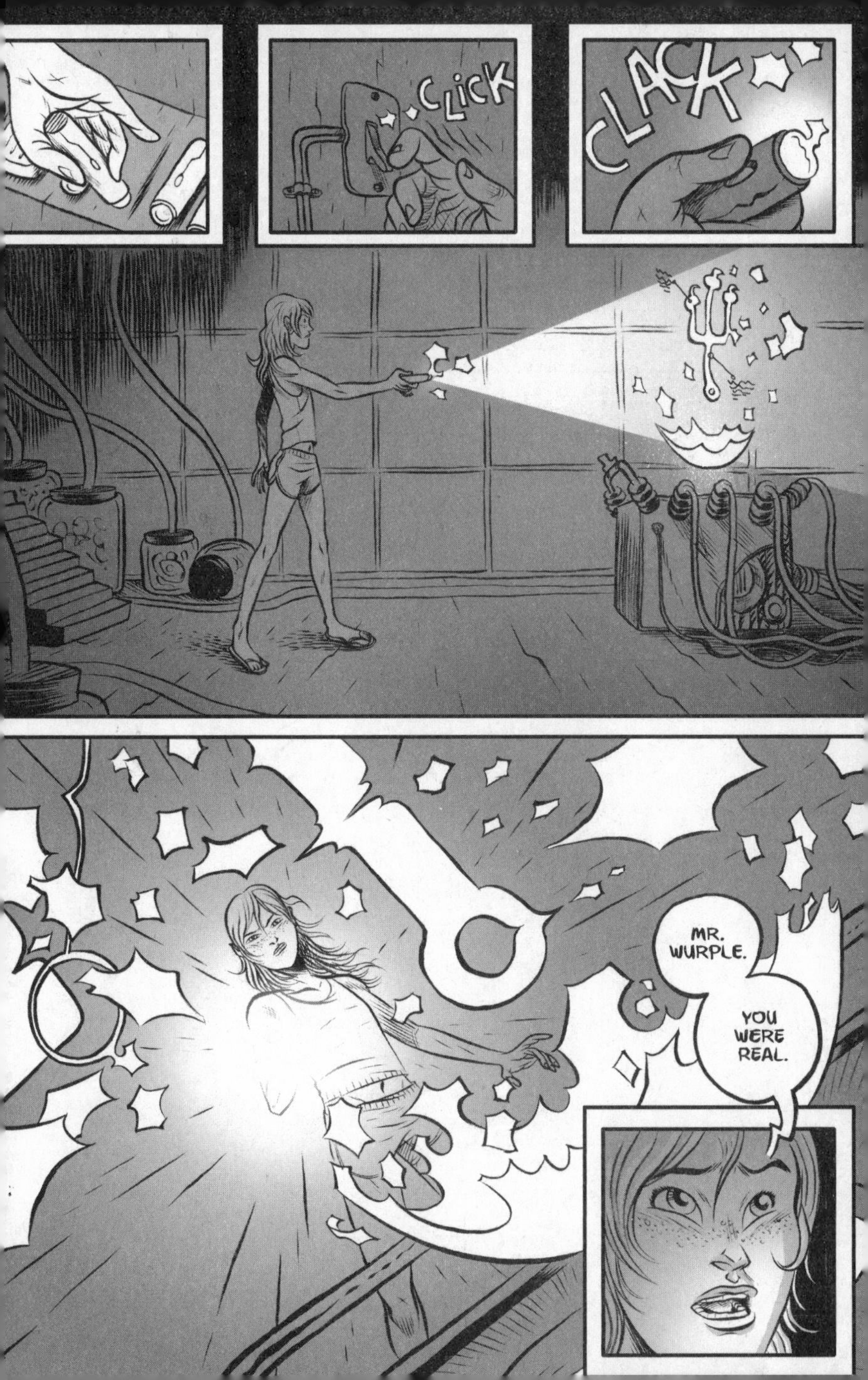
CLICK
CLACK
MR. WURPLE.
YOU WERE REAL.

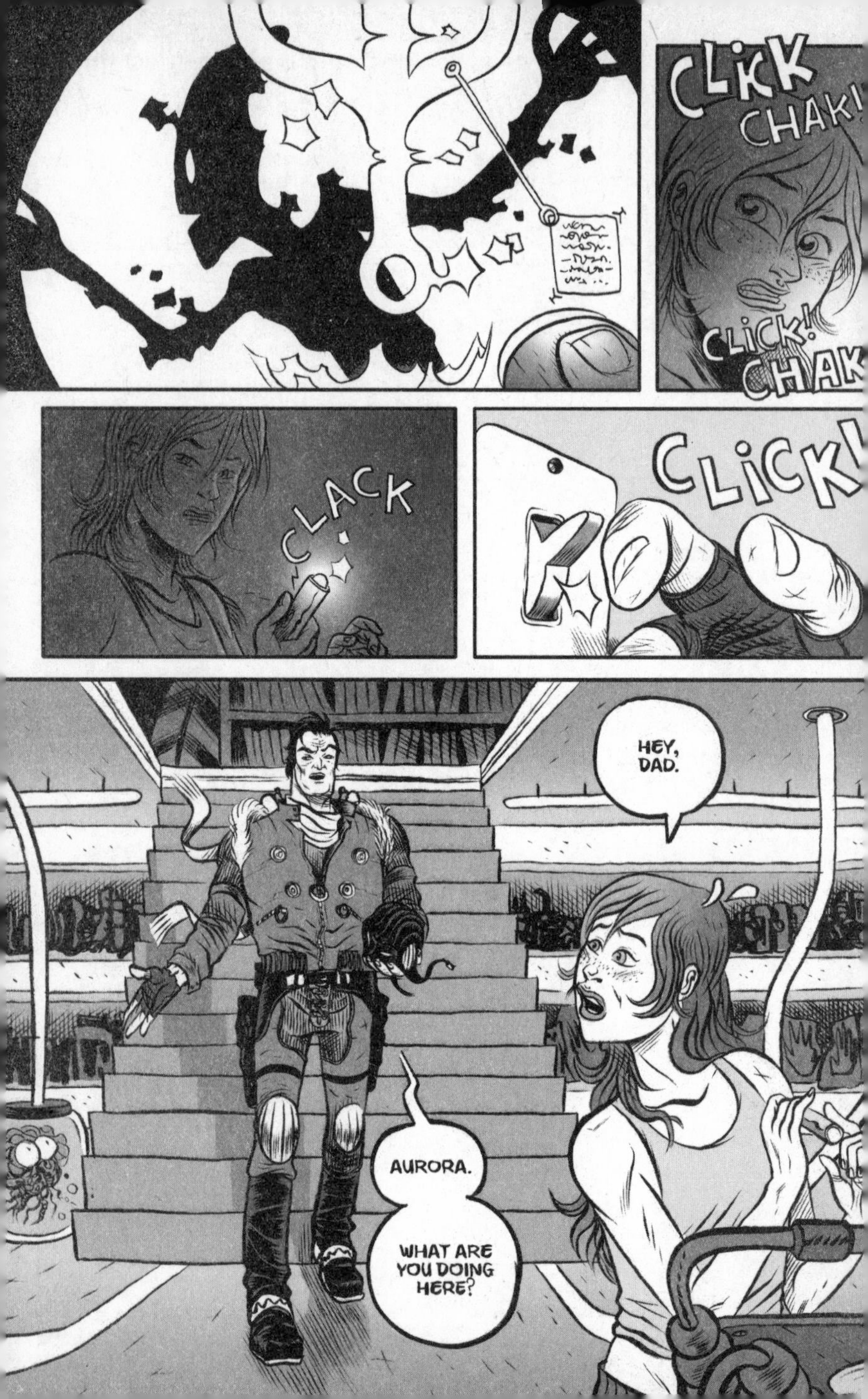
CLICK
CHAK!
CLICK!
CHAK
CLACK
CLICK!
HEY, DAD.
AURORA.
WHAT ARE YOU DOING HERE?

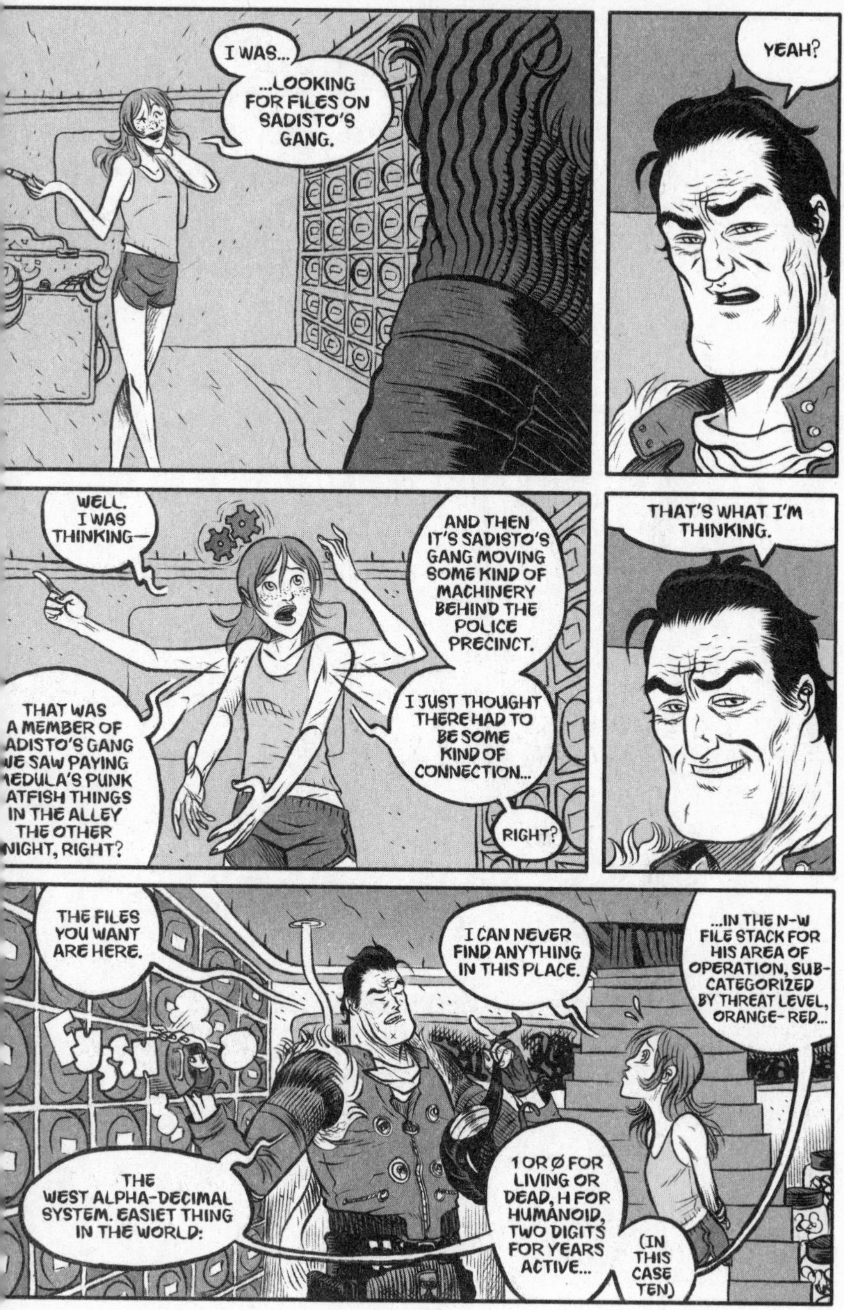

I WAS...
...LOOKING FOR FILES ON SADISTO'S GANG.
YEAH?
WELL. I WAS THINKING—
THAT WAS A MEMBER OF
ADISTO'S GANG
E SAW PAYING
EDULA'S PUNK
ATFISH THINGS
IN THE ALLEY THE OTHER
IGHT, RIGHT?
AND THEN IT'S SADISTO'S GANG MOVING SOME KIND OF MACHINERY BEHIND THE POLICE PRECINCT.
I JUST THOUGHT THERE HAD TO BE SOME KIND OF CONNECTION...
RIGHT?
THAT'S WHAT I'M THINKING.
THE FILES YOU WANT ARE HERE.
FUSH
I CAN NEVER FIND ANYTHING IN THIS PLACE.
THE WEST ALPHA-DECIMAL SYSTEM. EASIET THING IN THE WORLD:
1 OR Ø FOR LIVING OR DEAD, H FOR HUMANOID, TWO DIGITS FOR YEARS ACTIVE...
(IN THIS CASE TEN)
...IN THE N-W FILE STACK FOR HIS AREA OF OPERATION, SUB-CATEGORIZED BY THREAT LEVEL, ORANGE-RED...

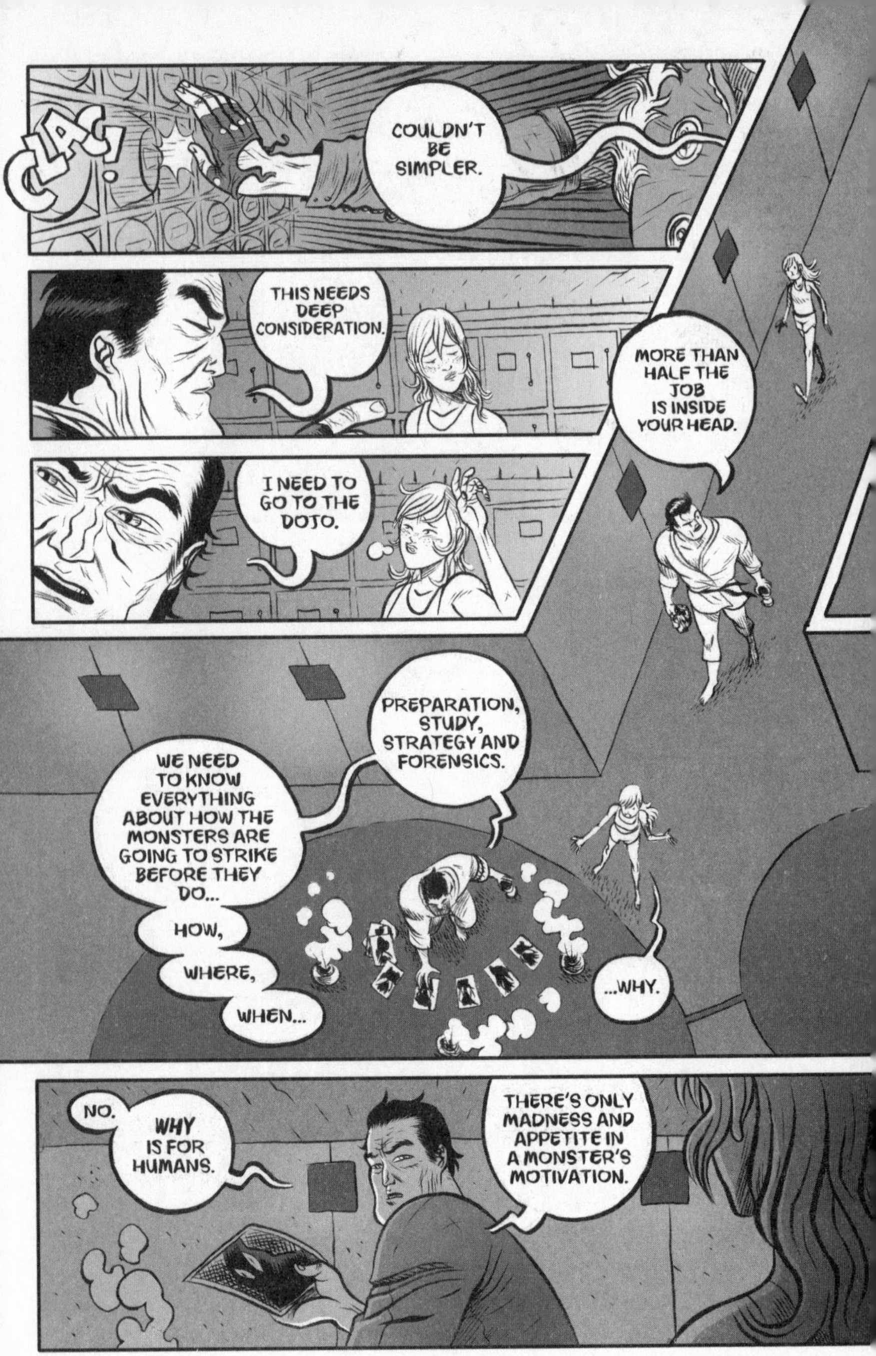
CLAC!
COULDN'T BE SIMPLER.
THIS NEEDS DEEP CONSIDERATION.
I NEED TO GO TO THE DOJO.
MORE THAN HALF THE JOB IS INSIDE YOUR HEAD.
PREPARATION, STUDY, STRATEGY AND FORENSICS.
WE NEED TO KNOW EVERYTHING ABOUT HOW THE MONSTERS ARE GOING TO STRIKE BEFORE THEY DO...
HOW,
WHERE,
WHEN...
...WHY.
NO.
WHY IS FOR HUMANS.
THERE'S ONLY MADNESS AND APPETITE IN A MONSTER'S MOTIVATION.

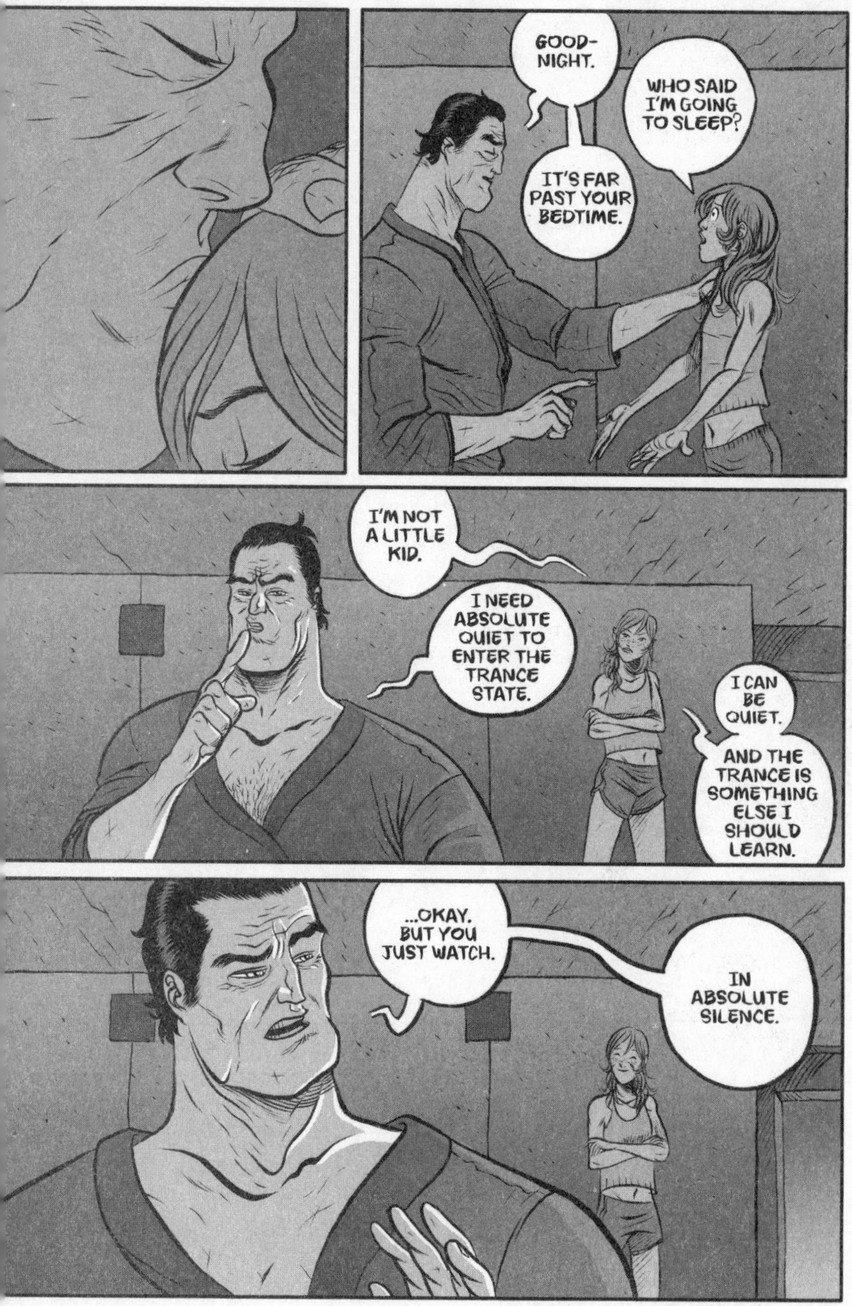
GOOD-NIGHT.
IT'S FAR PAST YOUR BEDTIME.
WHO SAID I'M GOING TO SLEEP?
I'M NOT A LITTLE KID.
I NEED ABSOLUTE QUIET TO ENTER THE TRANCE STATE.
I CAN BE QUIET.
AND THE TRANCE IS SOMETHING ELSE I SHOULD LEARN.
...OKAY. BUT YOU JUST WATCH.
IN ABSOLUTE SILENCE.

I LEARNED TUATARA MEDITATION FROM A BLIND MONK TWENTY YEARS AGO IN A SHI-FAN TEMPLE IN AL-LHASA.

WITH ENOUGH DISCIPLINE, HE COULD REGAIN SIGHT THROUGH HIS INNER EYE, BUT ONLY IN THE PAST.

THE TECHNIQUE EXPLOITS THE ENORMOUS AMOUNT OF INFORMATION YOUR SENSES ABSORB THAT DON'T NECESSARILY FIND PURCHASE IN YOUR MIND.

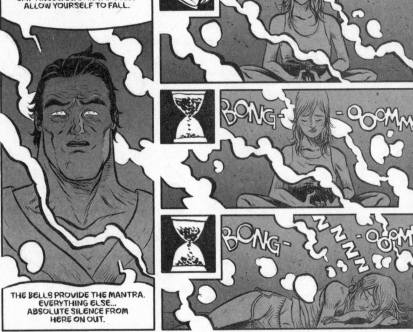

HAPTIC CHANGES IN AIR PRESSURE, ECHO-LOCATION. SENSE WE DON'T HAVE NAMES FOR. IT REQUIRES EMPTINESS. LEAN INWARD AND ALLOW YOURSELF TO FALL.

BONG---OOOMMM"

BONG---OOOMMM

BONG---ZZZZ---OOMM

THE BELLS PROVIDE THE MANTRA. EVERYTHING ELSE... ABSOLUTE SILENCE FROM HERE ON OUT.

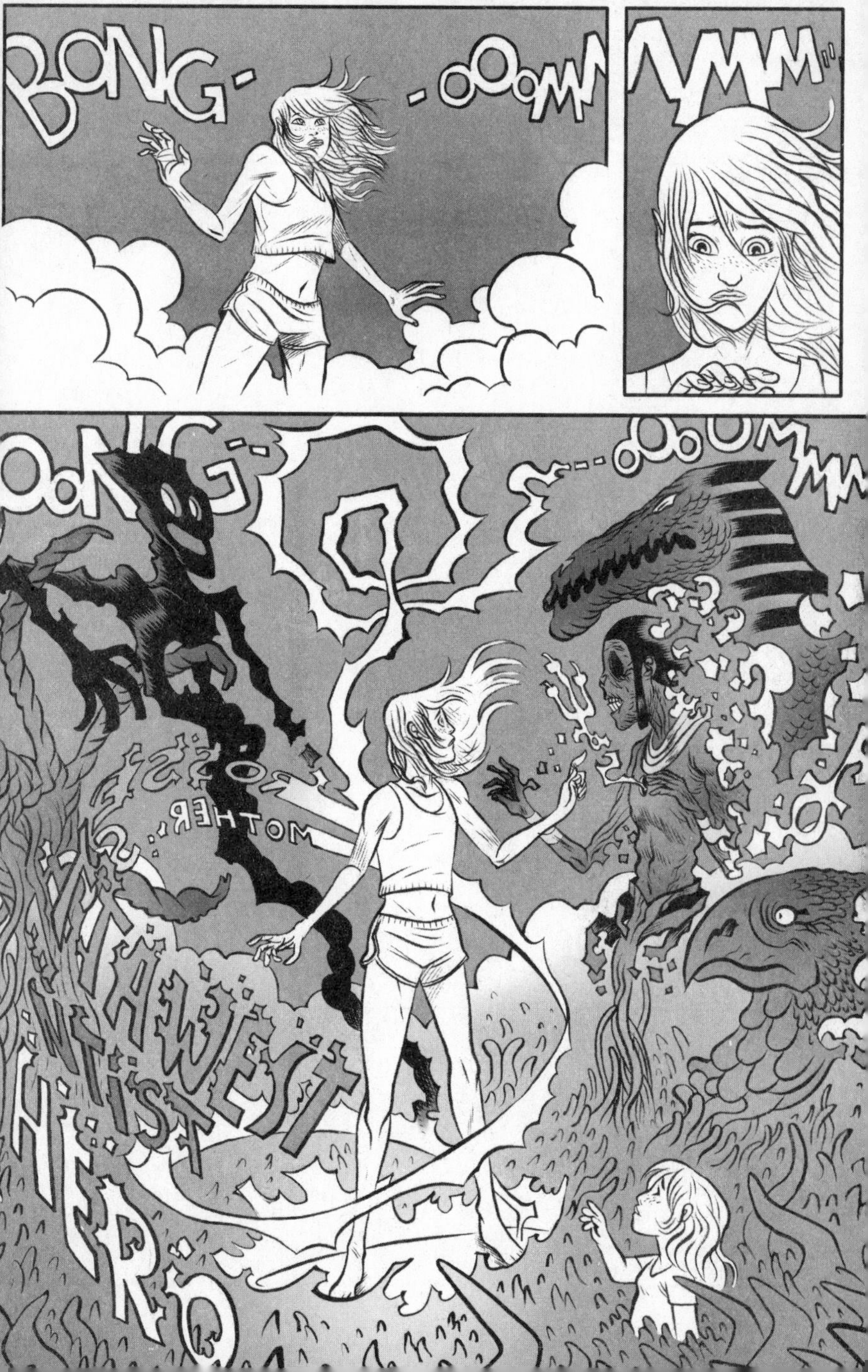
BONG-
-OOOMM
AMM!!
BONG--
--OOOMM
MOTHER

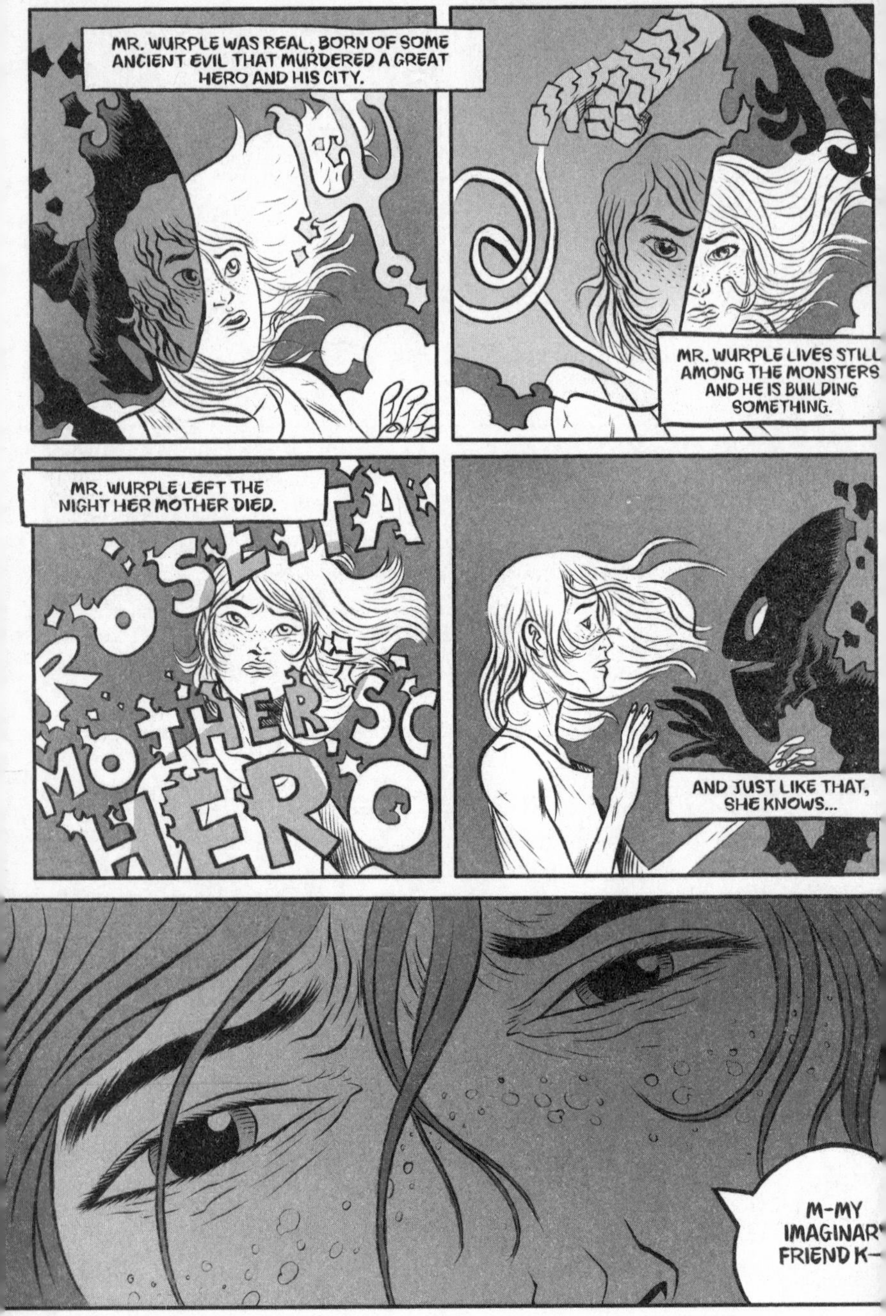
MR. WURPLE WAS REAL, BORN OF SOME ANCIENT EVIL THAT MURDERED A GREAT HERO AND HIS CITY.
MR. WURPLE LIVES STILL AMONG THE MONSTERS AND HE IS BUILDING SOMETHING.
MR. WURPLE LEFT THE NIGHT HER MOTHER DIED.
MOTHER
HERO
AND JUST LIKE THAT, SHE KNOWS...
M-MY IMAGINAR FRIEND K—

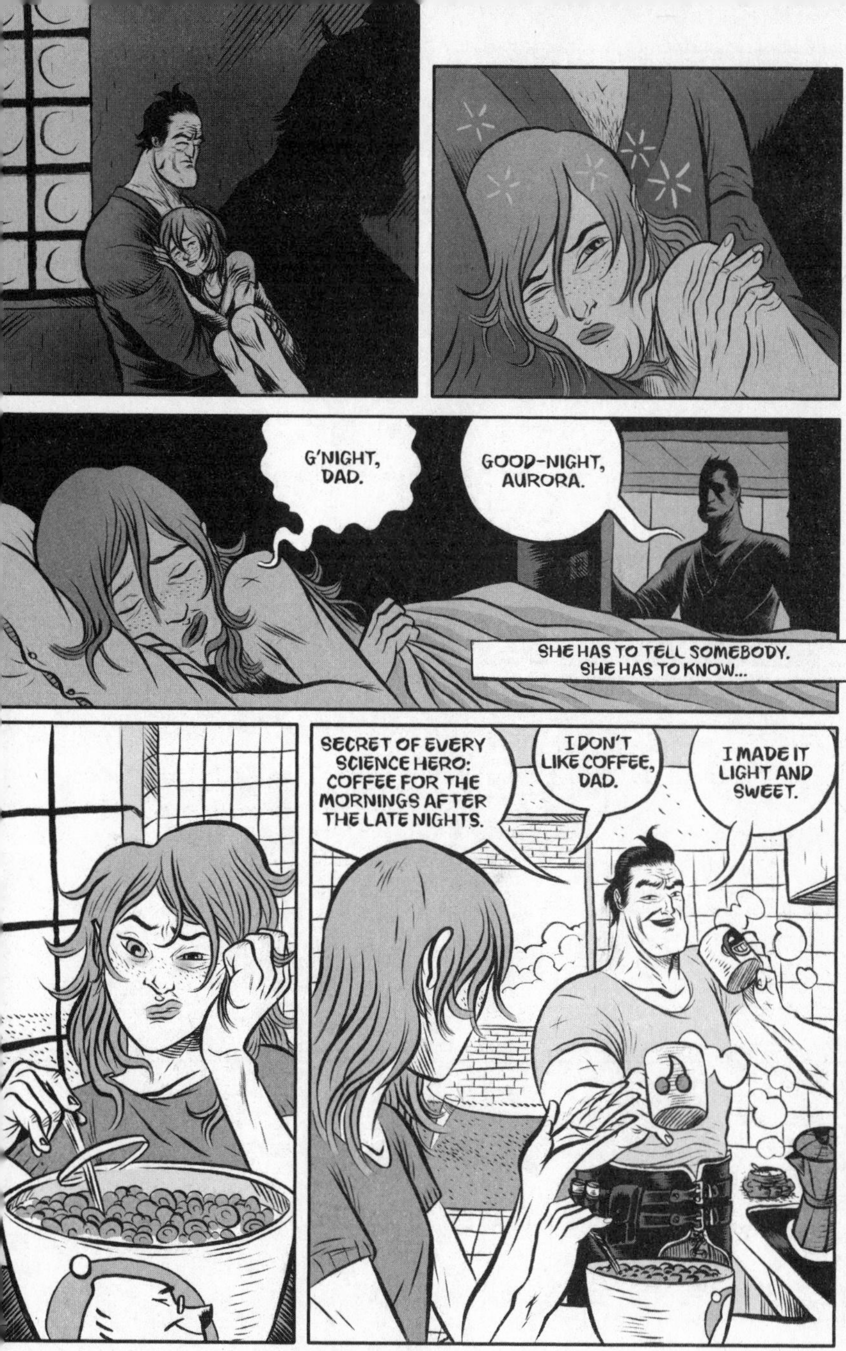
G'NIGHT, DAD.
GOOD-NIGHT, AURORA.
SHE HAS TO TELL SOMEBODY. SHE HAS TO KNOW...
SECRET OF EVERY SCIENCE HERO: COFFEE FOR THE MORNINGS AFTER THE LATE NIGHTS.
I DON'T LIKE COFFEE, DAD.
I MADE IT LIGHT AND SWEET.

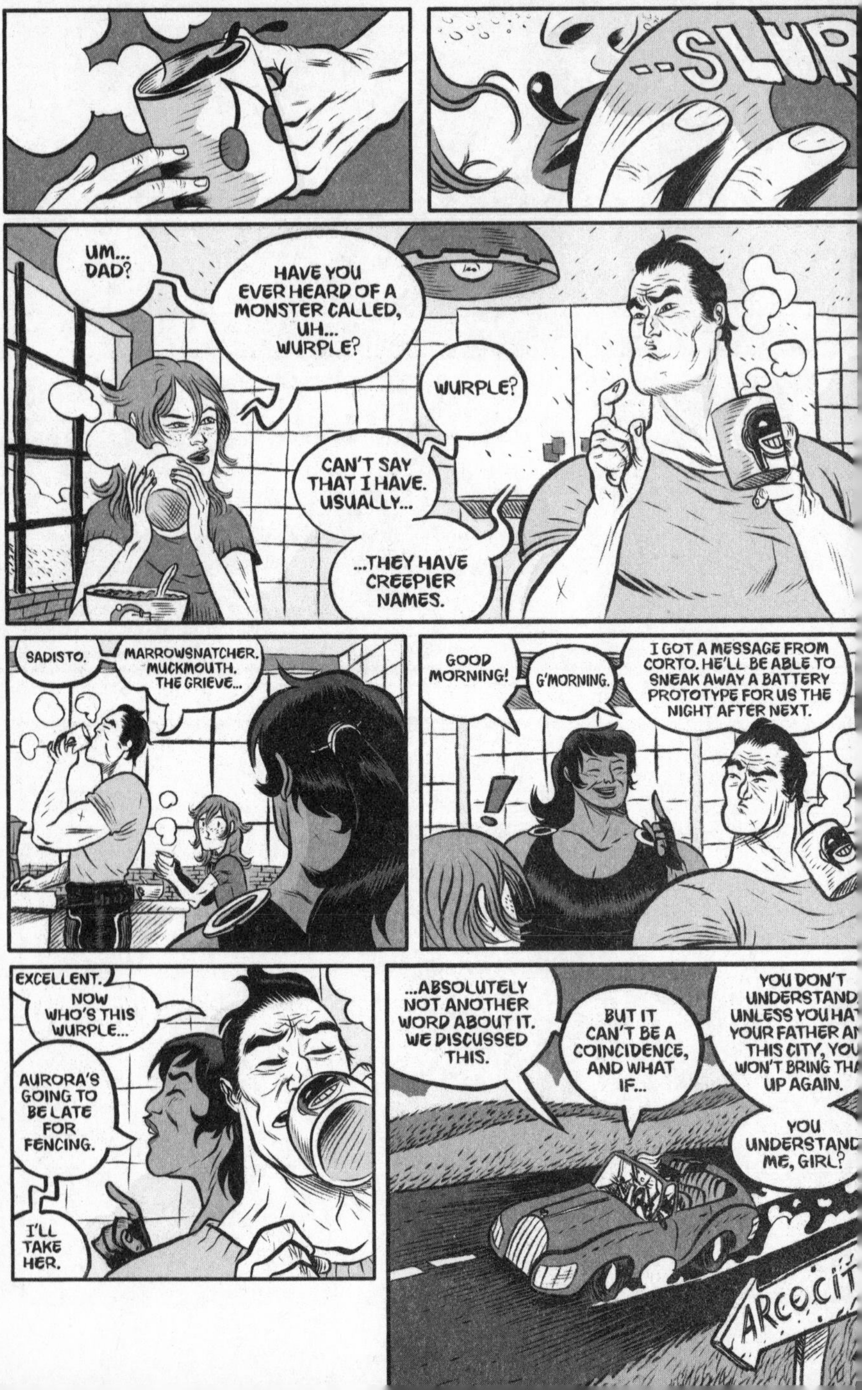

--SLUR
UM... DAD?
HAVE YOU EVER HEARD OF A MONSTER CALLED, UH... WURPLE?
WURPLE?
CAN'T SAY THAT I HAVE. USUALLY...
...THEY HAVE CREEPIER NAMES.
SADISTO.
MARROWSNATCHER. MUCKMOUTH. THE GRIEVE...
GOOD MORNING!
G'MORNING.
I GOT A MESSAGE FROM CORTO. HE'LL BE ABLE TO SNEAK AWAY A BATTERY PROTOTYPE FOR US THE NIGHT AFTER NEXT.
EXCELLENT.
NOW WHO'S THIS WURPLE...
AURORA'S GOING TO BE LATE FOR FENCING.
I'LL TAKE HER.
...ABSOLUTELY NOT ANOTHER WORD ABOUT IT. WE DISCUSSED THIS.
BUT IT CAN'T BE A COINCIDENCE, AND WHAT IF...
YOU DON'T UNDERSTAND. UNLESS YOU HAT YOUR FATHER AN THIS CITY, YOU WON'T BRING THA UP AGAIN.
YOU UNDERSTAND ME, GIRL?
ARCO CIT

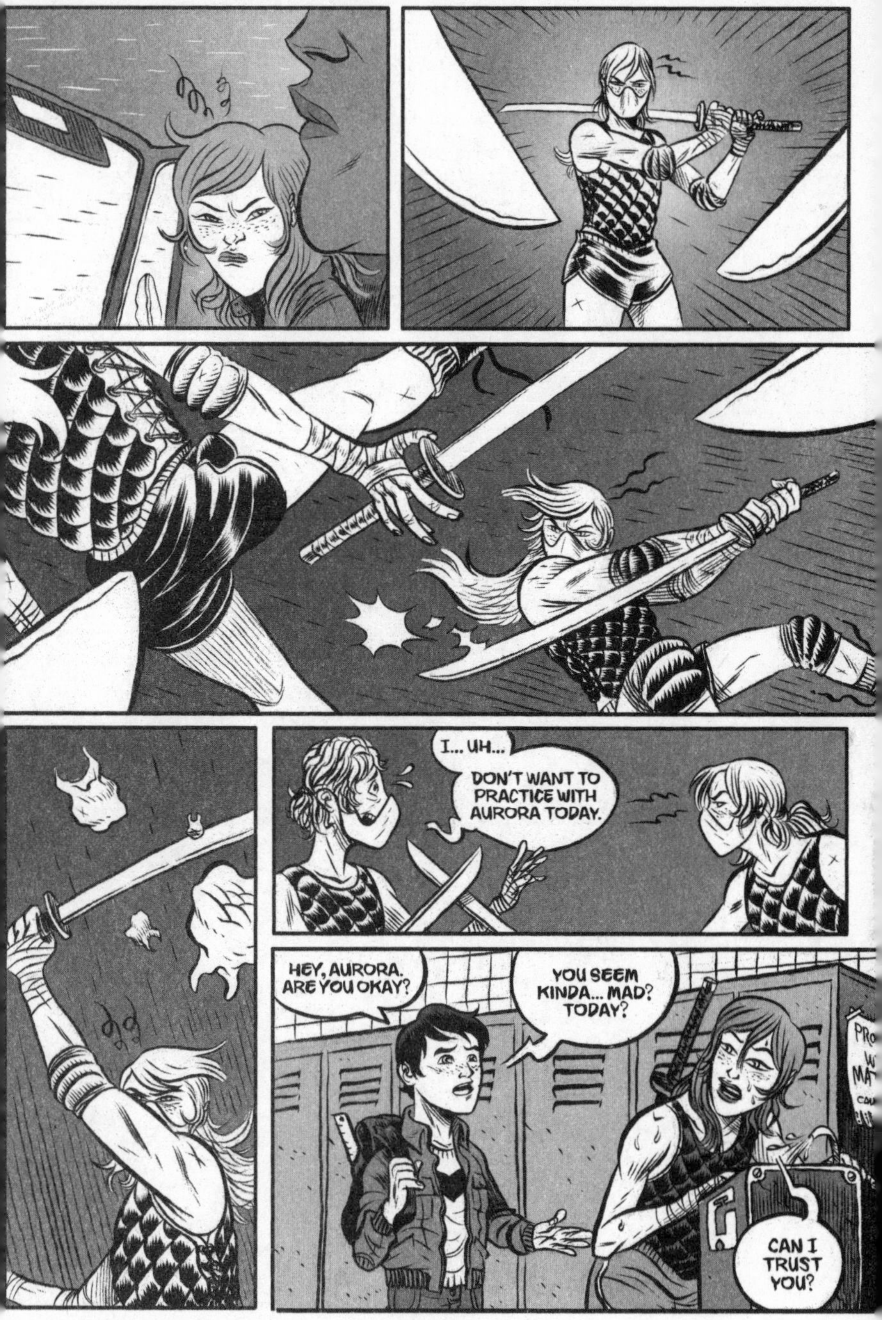
I... UH...
DON'T WANT TO PRACTICE WITH AURORA TODAY.
HEY, AURORA. ARE YOU OKAY?
YOU SEEM KINDA... MAD? TODAY?
CAN I TRUST YOU?

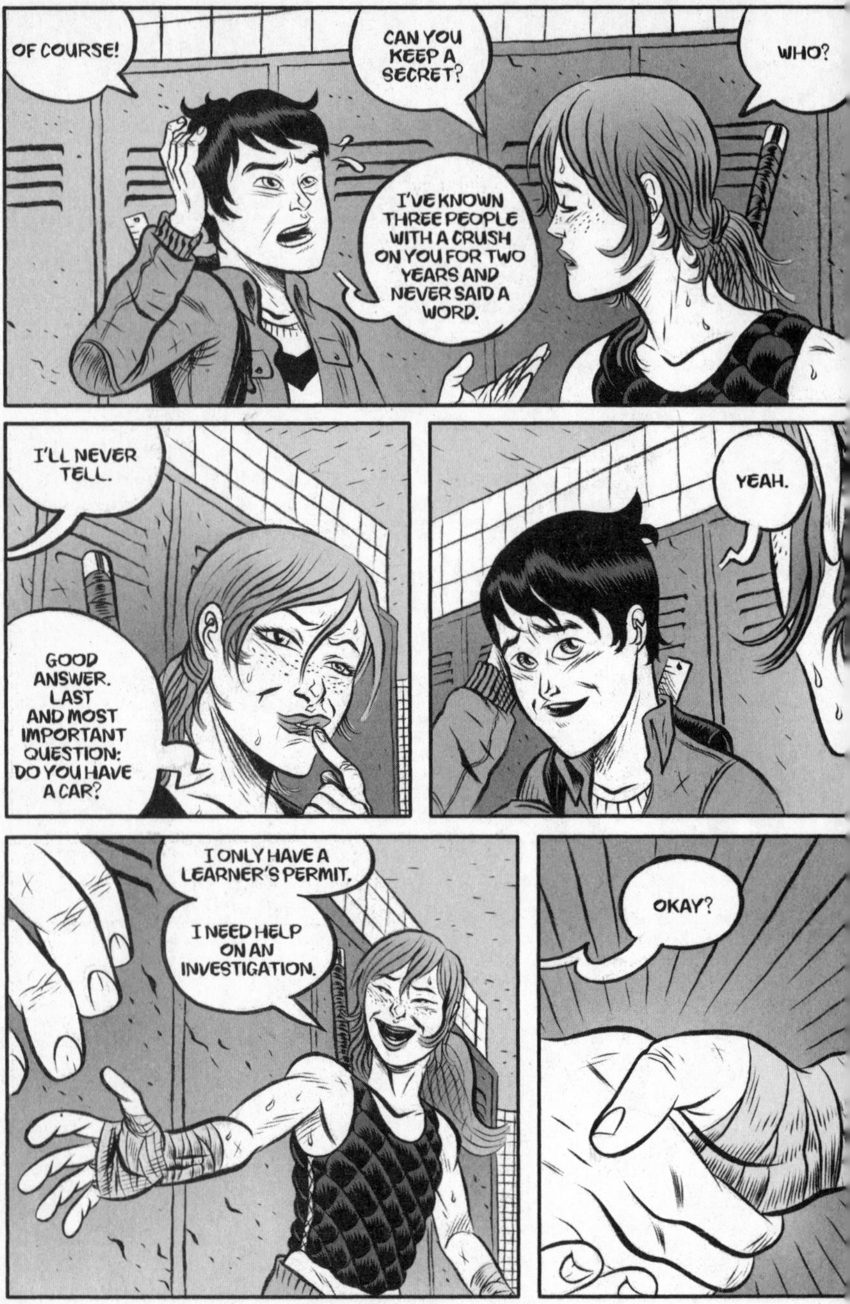
OF COURSE!
CAN YOU KEEP A SECRET?
WHO?
I'VE KNOWN THREE PEOPLE WITH A CRUSH ON YOU FOR TWO YEARS AND NEVER SAID A WORD.
I'LL NEVER TELL.
GOOD ANSWER. LAST AND MOST IMPORTANT QUESTION: DO YOU HAVE A CAR?
YEAH.
I ONLY HAVE A LEARNER'S PERMIT.
I NEED HELP ON AN INVESTIGATION.
OKAY?

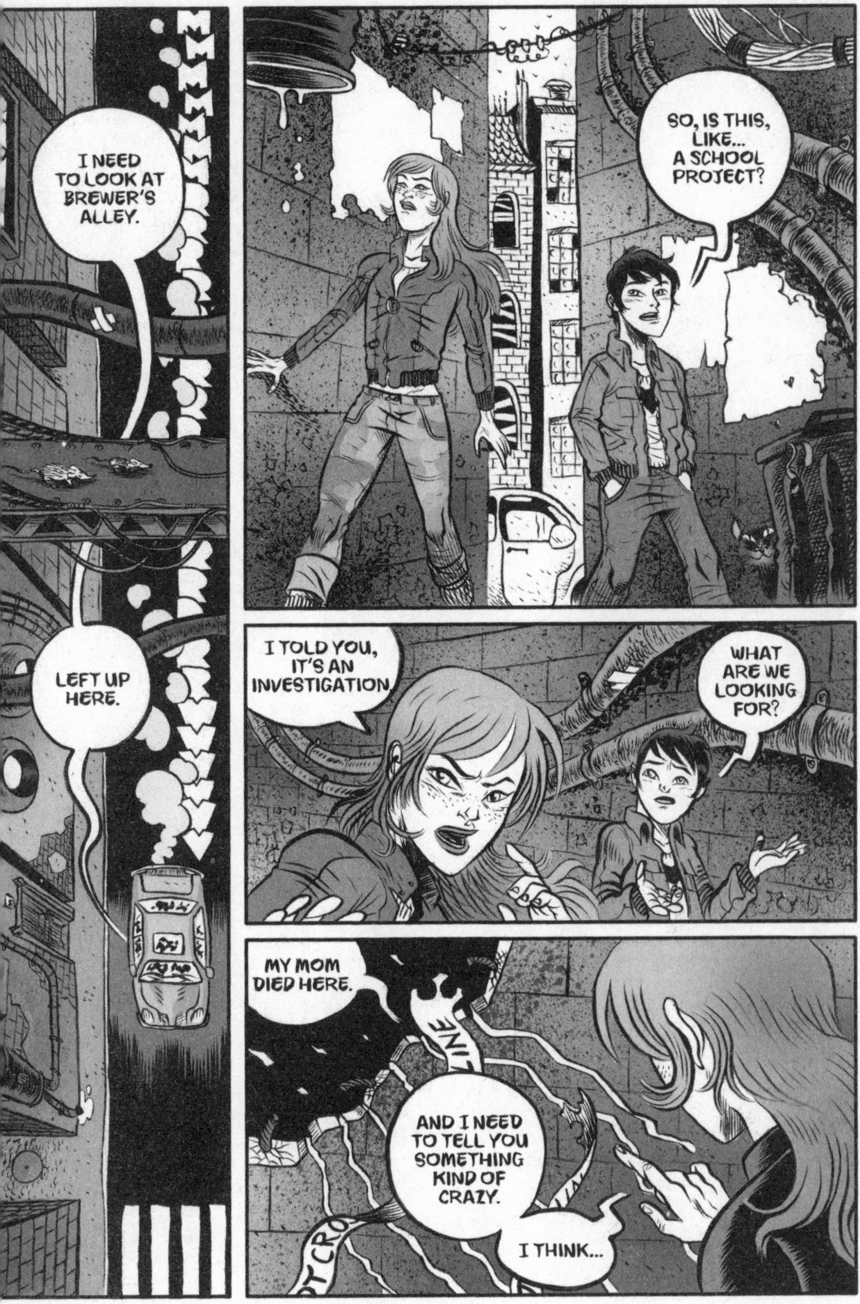
I NEED TO LOOK AT BREWER'S ALLEY.
LEFT UP HERE.
SO, IS THIS, LIKE... A SCHOOL PROJECT?
I TOLD YOU, IT'S AN INVESTIGATION.
WHAT ARE WE LOOKING FOR?
MY MOM DIED HERE.
AND I NEED TO TELL YOU SOMETHING KIND OF CRAZY.
I THINK...

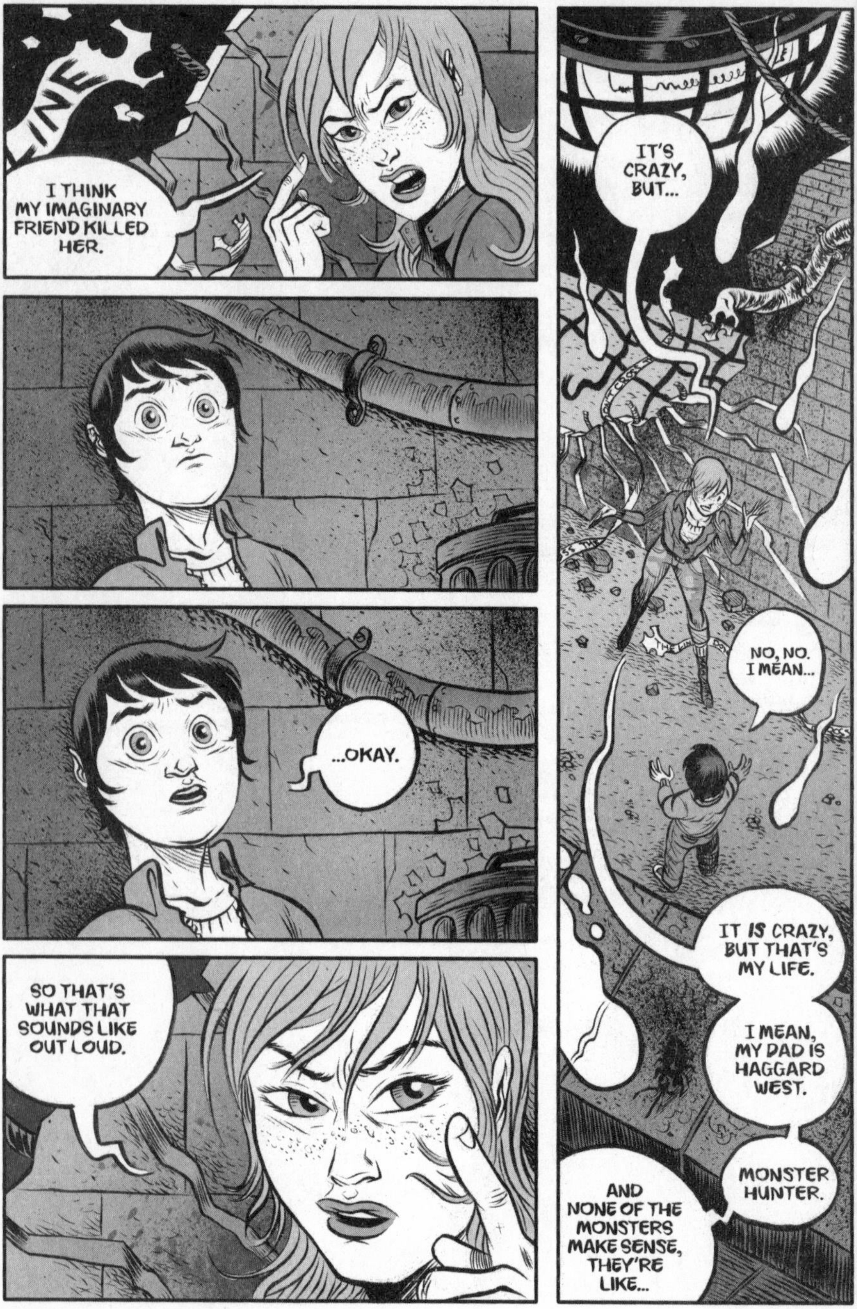
I THINK MY IMAGINARY FRIEND KILLED HER.
...OKAY.
SO THAT'S WHAT THAT SOUNDS LIKE OUT LOUD.
IT'S CRAZY, BUT...
NO, NO. I MEAN...
IT IS CRAZY, BUT THAT'S MY LIFE.
I MEAN, MY DAD IS HAGGARD WEST.
MONSTER HUNTER.
AND NONE OF THE MONSTERS MAKE SENSE, THEY'RE LIKE...

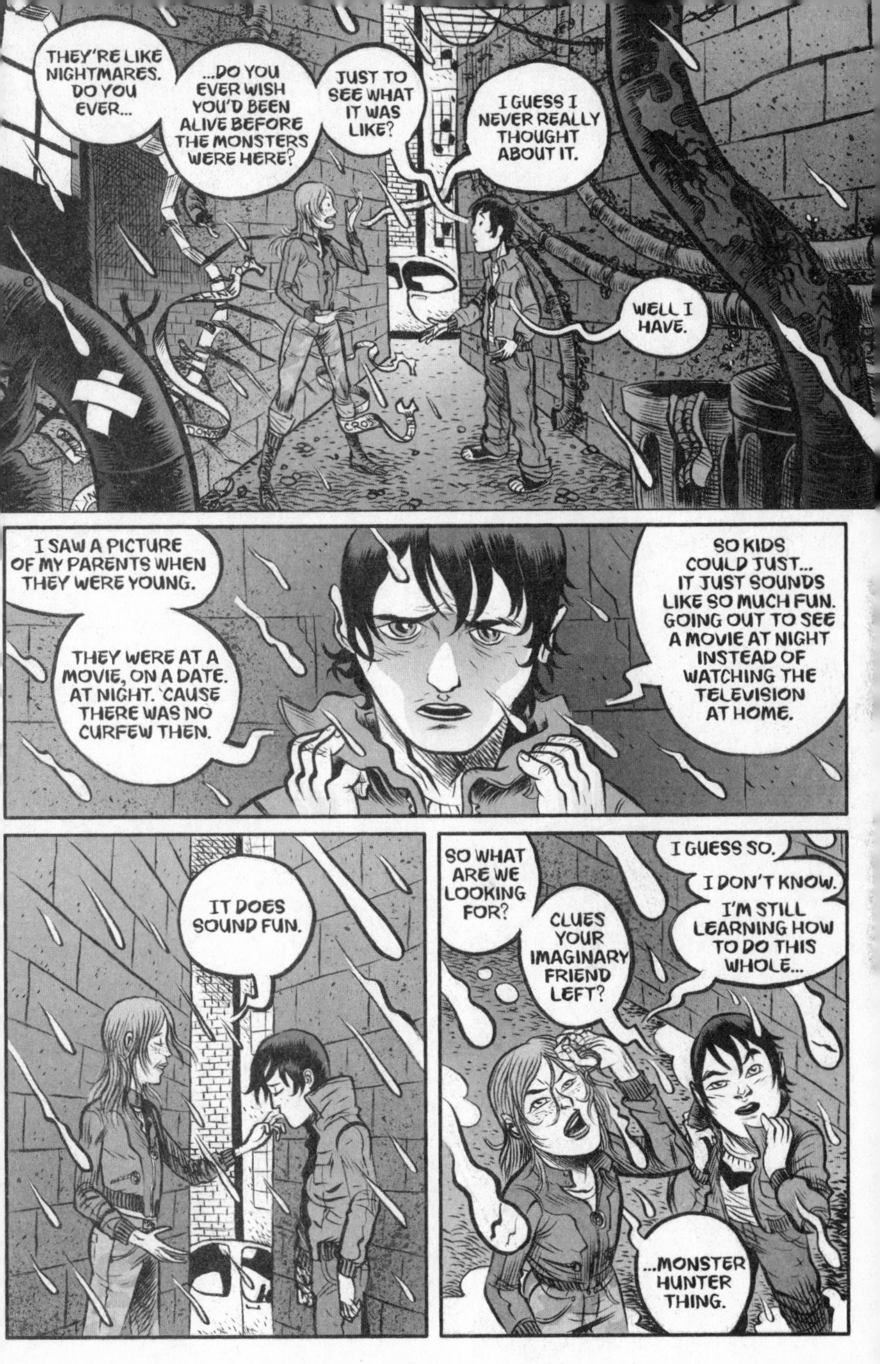
THEY'RE LIKE NIGHTMARES. DO YOU EVER...
...DO YOU EVER WISH YOU'D BEEN ALIVE BEFORE THE MONSTERS WERE HERE?
JUST TO SEE WHAT IT WAS LIKE?
I GUESS I NEVER REALLY THOUGHT ABOUT IT.
WELL I HAVE.
I SAW A PICTURE OF MY PARENTS WHEN THEY WERE YOUNG.
THEY WERE AT A MOVIE, ON A DATE. AT NIGHT. 'CAUSE THERE WAS NO CURFEW THEN.
SO KIDS COULD JUST... IT JUST SOUNDS LIKE SO MUCH FUN. GOING OUT TO SEE A MOVIE AT NIGHT INSTEAD OF WATCHING THE TELEVISION AT HOME.
IT DOES SOUND FUN.
SO WHAT ARE WE LOOKING FOR?
CLUES YOUR IMAGINARY FRIEND LEFT?
I GUESS SO.
I DON'T KNOW.
I'M STILL LEARNING HOW TO DO THIS WHOLE...
...MONSTER HUNTER THING.

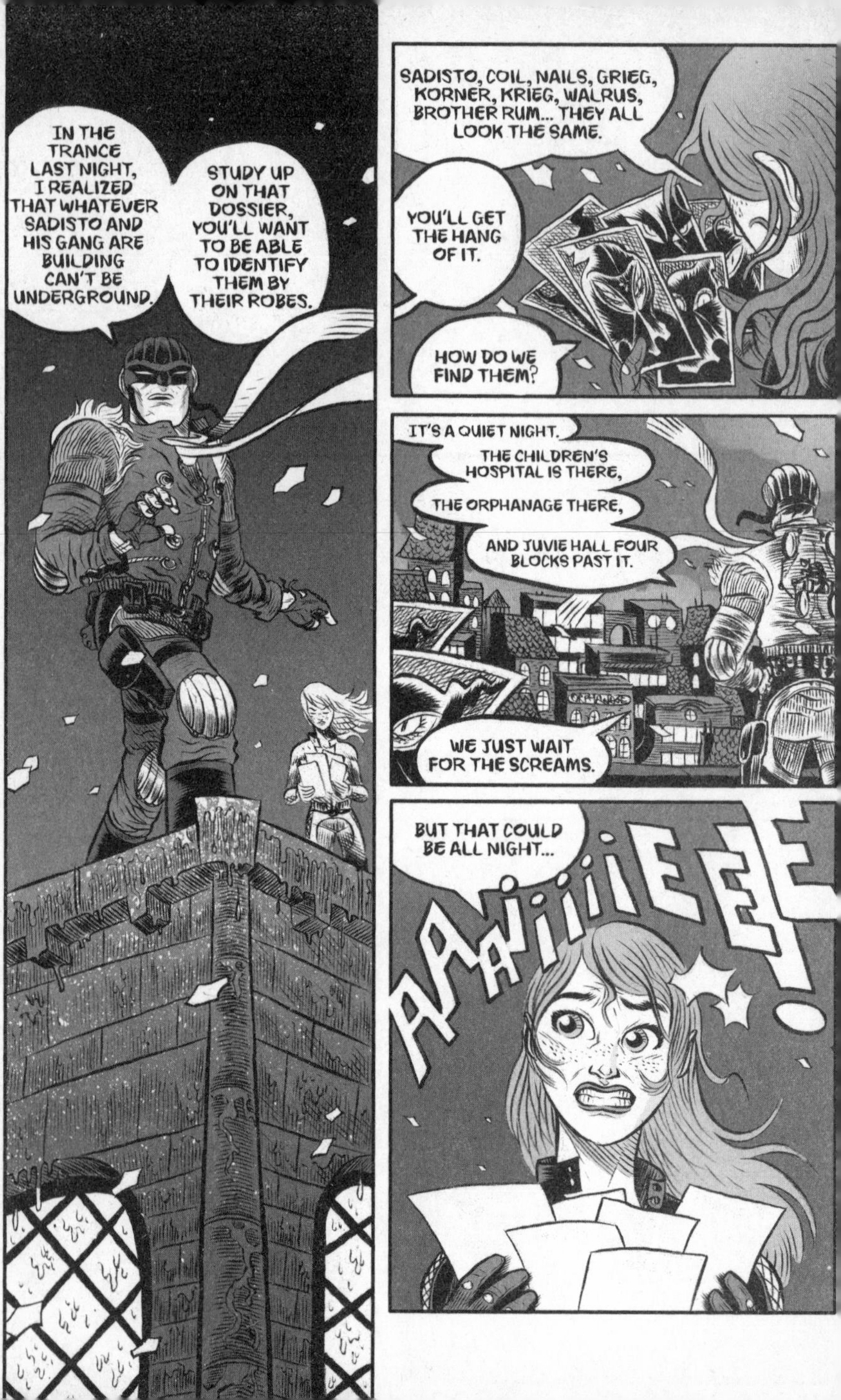
IN THE TRANCE LAST NIGHT, I REALIZED THAT WHATEVER SADISTO AND HIS GANG ARE BUILDING CAN'T BE UNDERGROUND.
STUDY UP ON THAT DOSSIER, YOU'LL WANT TO BE ABLE TO IDENTIFY THEM BY THEIR ROBES.
SADISTO, COIL, NAILS, GRIEG, KORNER, KRIEG, WALRUS, BROTHER RUM... THEY ALL LOOK THE SAME.
YOU'LL GET THE HANG OF IT.
HOW DO WE FIND THEM?
IT'S A QUIET NIGHT.
THE CHILDREN'S HOSPITAL IS THERE,
THE ORPHANAGE THERE,
AND JUVIE HALL FOUR BLOCKS PAST IT.
WE JUST WAIT FOR THE SCREAMS.
BUT THAT COULD BE ALL NIGHT...
AAAiiiiEEEE!

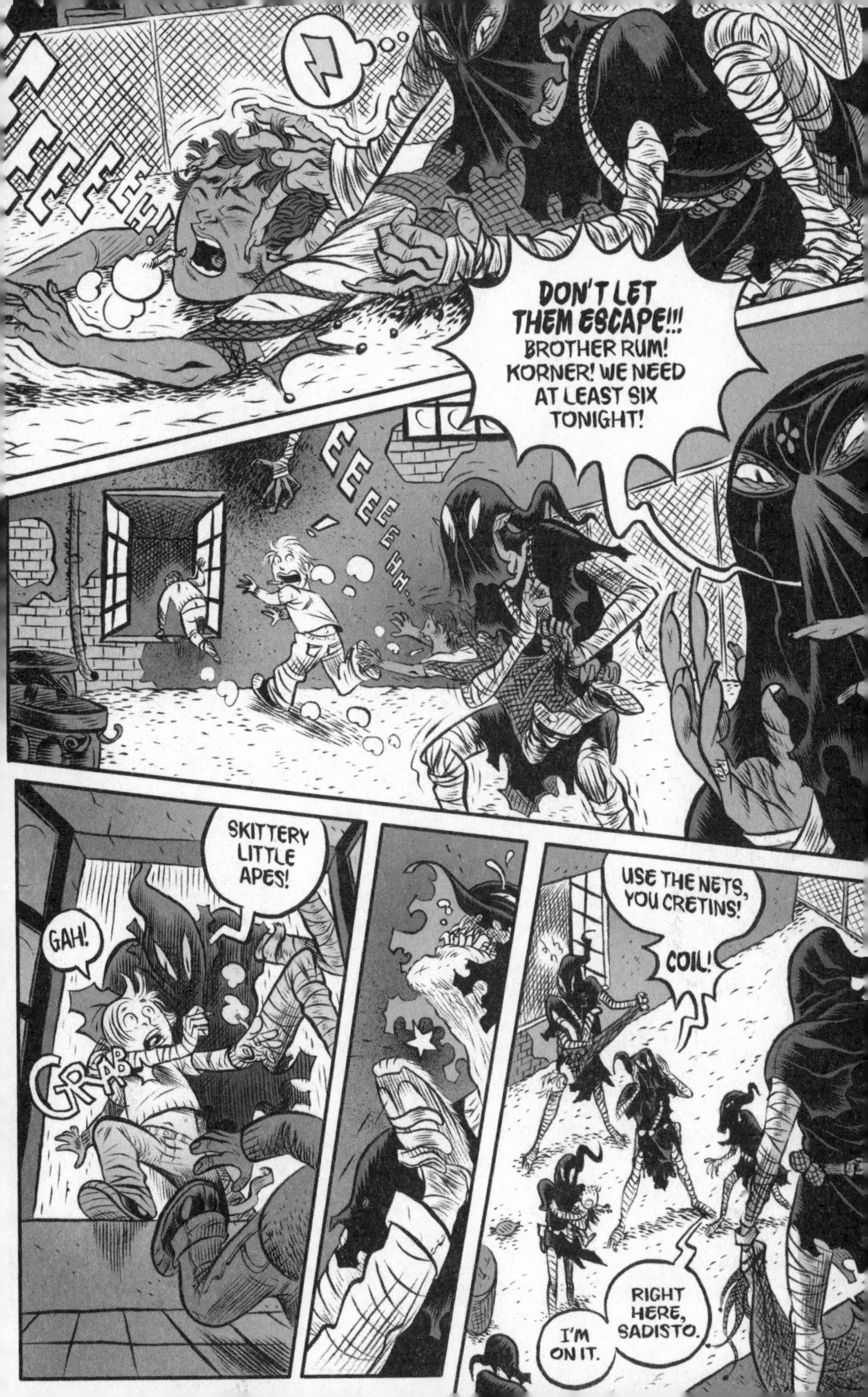
EEEEEE
DON'T LET THEM ESCAPE!!! BROTHER RUM! KORNER! WE NEED AT LEAST SIX TONIGHT!
EEEEEEHH..!
SKITTERY LITTLE APES!
GAH!
GRAB
USE THE NETS, YOU CRETINS!
COIL!
RIGHT HERE, SADISTO.
I'M ON IT.

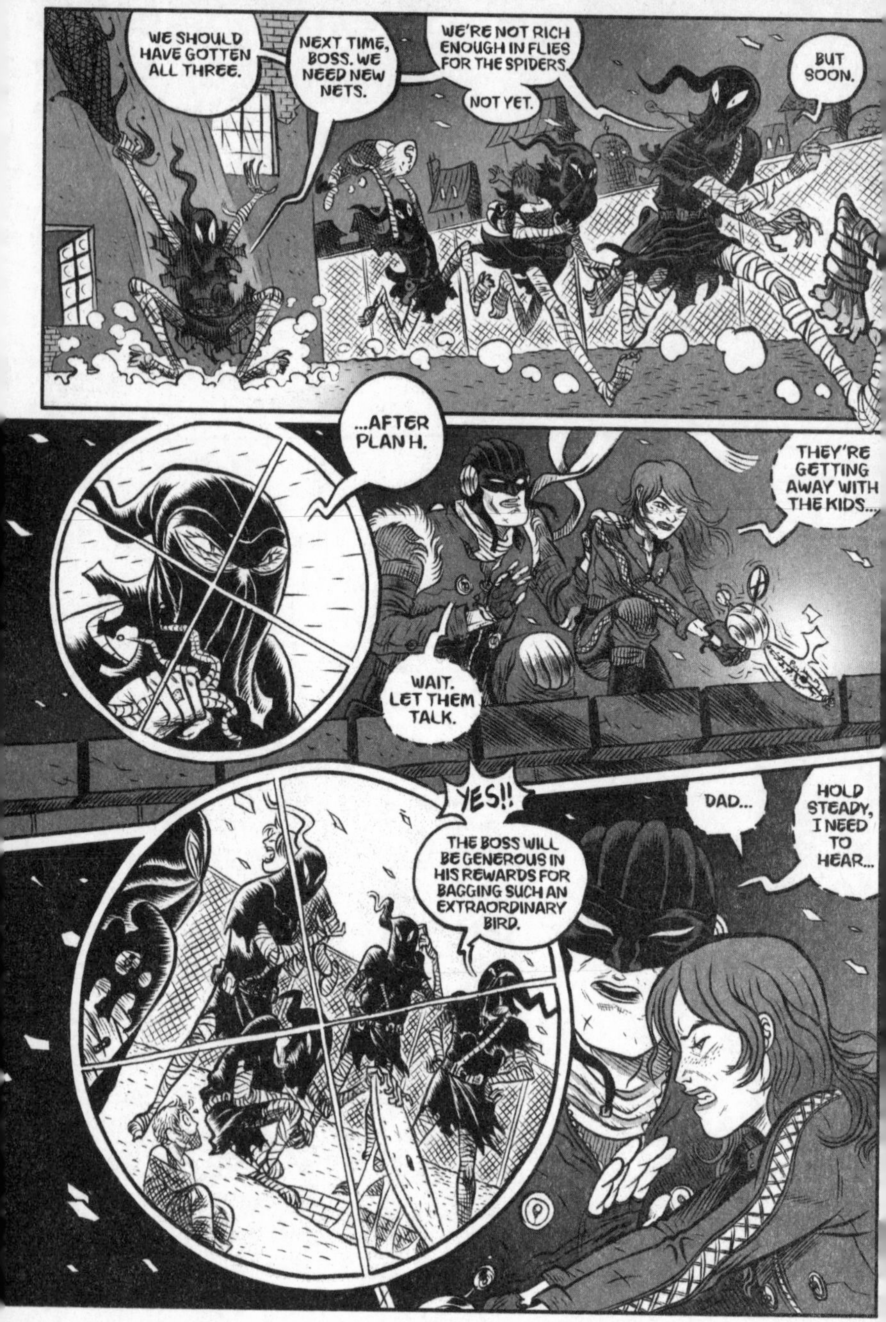
WE SHOULD HAVE GOTTEN ALL THREE.
NEXT TIME, BOSS. WE NEED NEW NETS.
WE'RE NOT RICH ENOUGH IN FLIES FOR THE SPIDERS.
NOT YET.
BUT SOON.
...AFTER PLAN H.
THEY'RE GETTING AWAY WITH THE KIDS...
WAIT. LET THEM TALK.
YES!!
THE BOSS WILL BE GENEROUS IN HIS REWARDS FOR BAGGING SUCH AN EXTRAORDINARY BIRD.
DAD...
HOLD STEADY, I NEED TO HEAR...

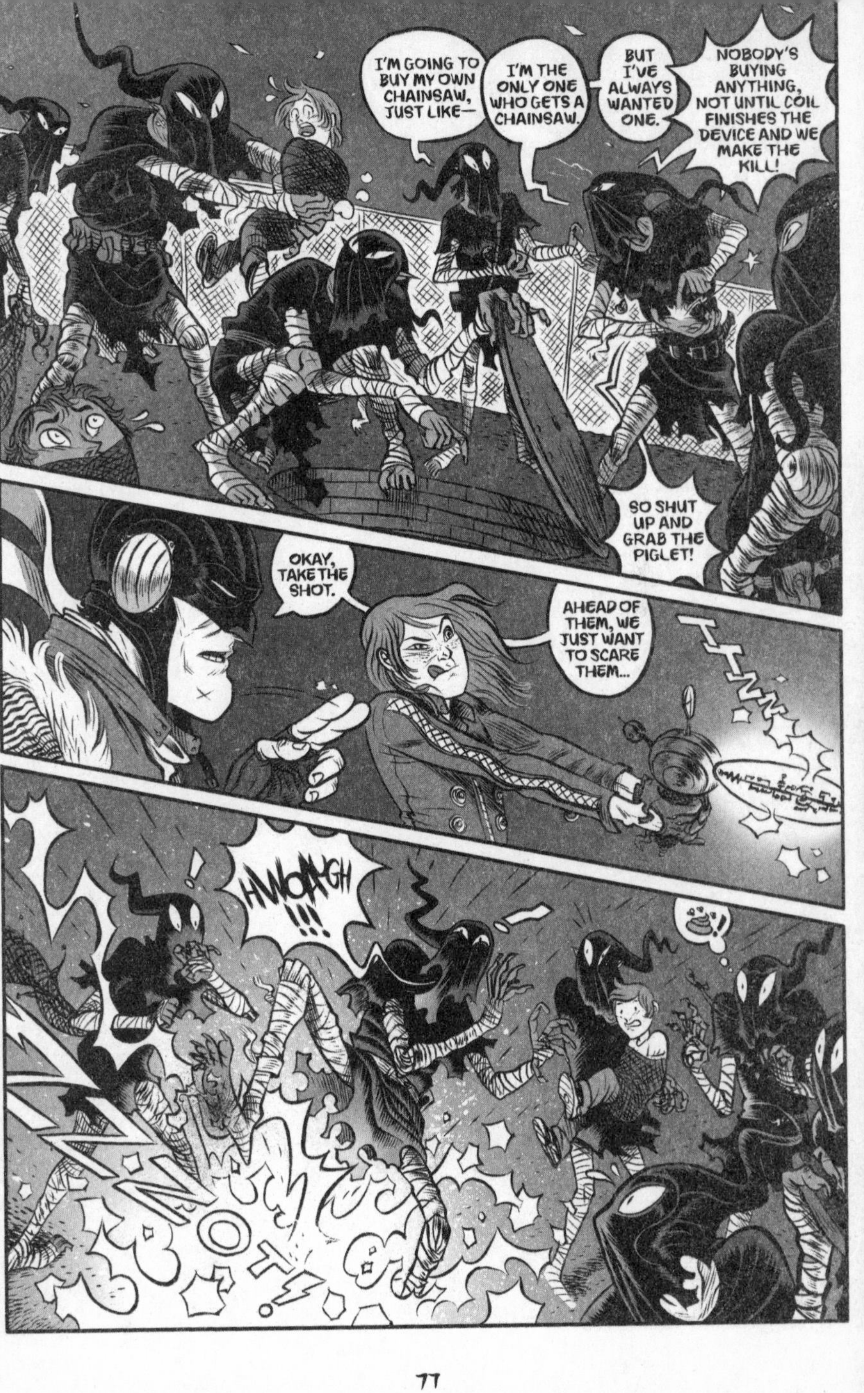
I'M GOING TO BUY MY OWN CHAINSAW, JUST LIKE—
I'M THE ONLY ONE WHO GETS A CHAINSAW.
BUT I'VE ALWAYS WANTED ONE.
NOBODY'S BUYING ANYTHING, NOT UNTIL COIL FINISHES THE DEVICE AND WE MAKE THE KILL!
SO SHUT UP AND GRAB THE PIGLET!
OKAY, TAKE THE SHOT.
AHEAD OF THEM, WE JUST WANT TO SCARE THEM...
HWOAAGH !!!

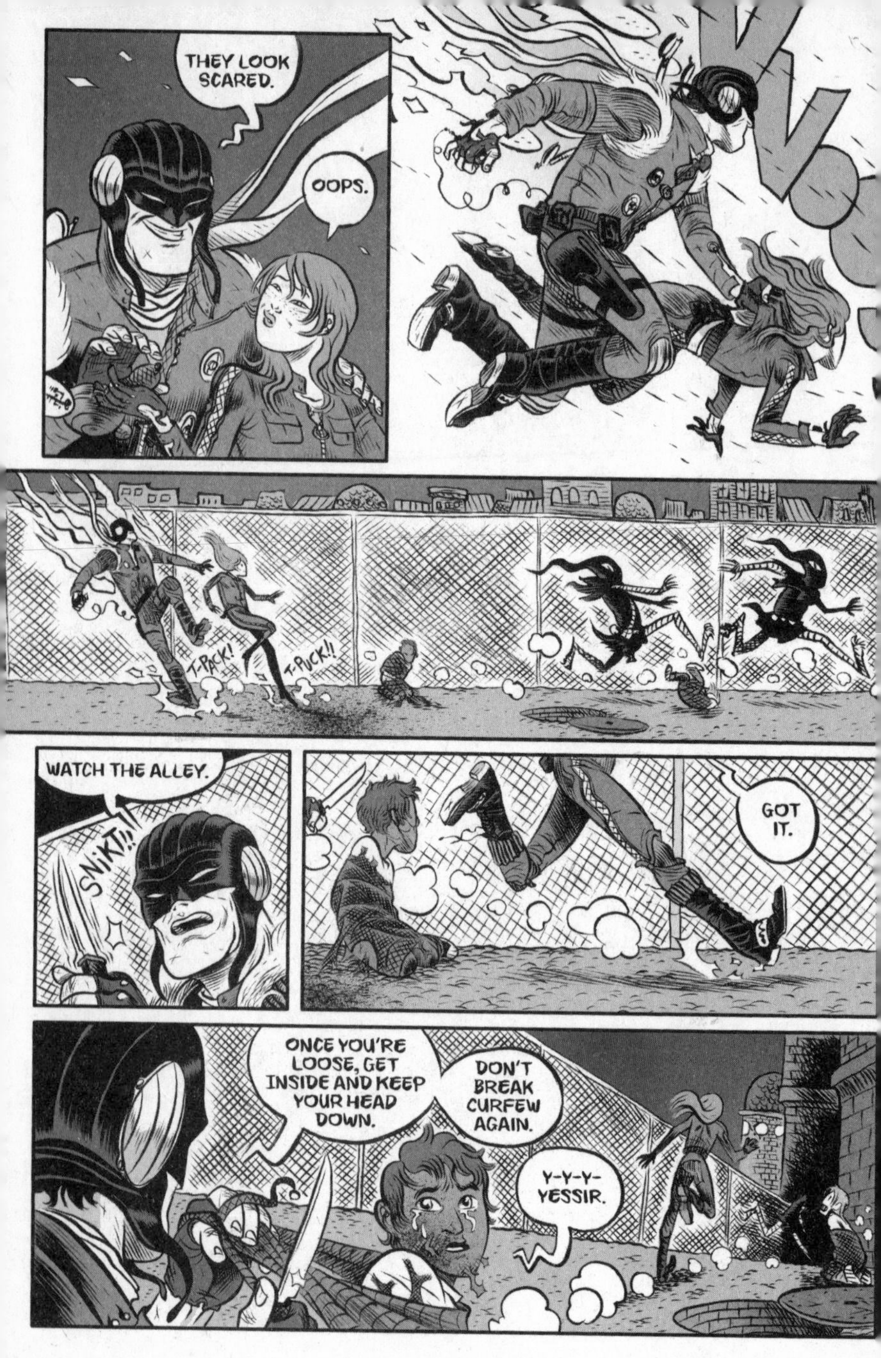
THEY LOOK SCARED.
OOPS.
T-PACK!
T-PUCK!!
WATCH THE ALLEY.
SNIKT!!
GOT IT.
ONCE YOU'RE LOOSE, GET INSIDE AND KEEP YOUR HEAD DOWN.
DON'T BREAK CURFEW AGAIN.
Y-Y-Y-YESSIR.

GIRL! HEY!

HELP ME!

MY CIG'S BURNING ME.

YOU SHOULDN'T SMOKE.

SIGH!!

FINE. DON'T WIGGLE...

I'D HATE TO ACCIDENTALLY NICK ANY—

SOK!

SOK!

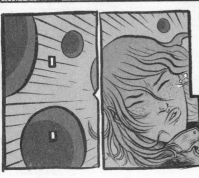

79

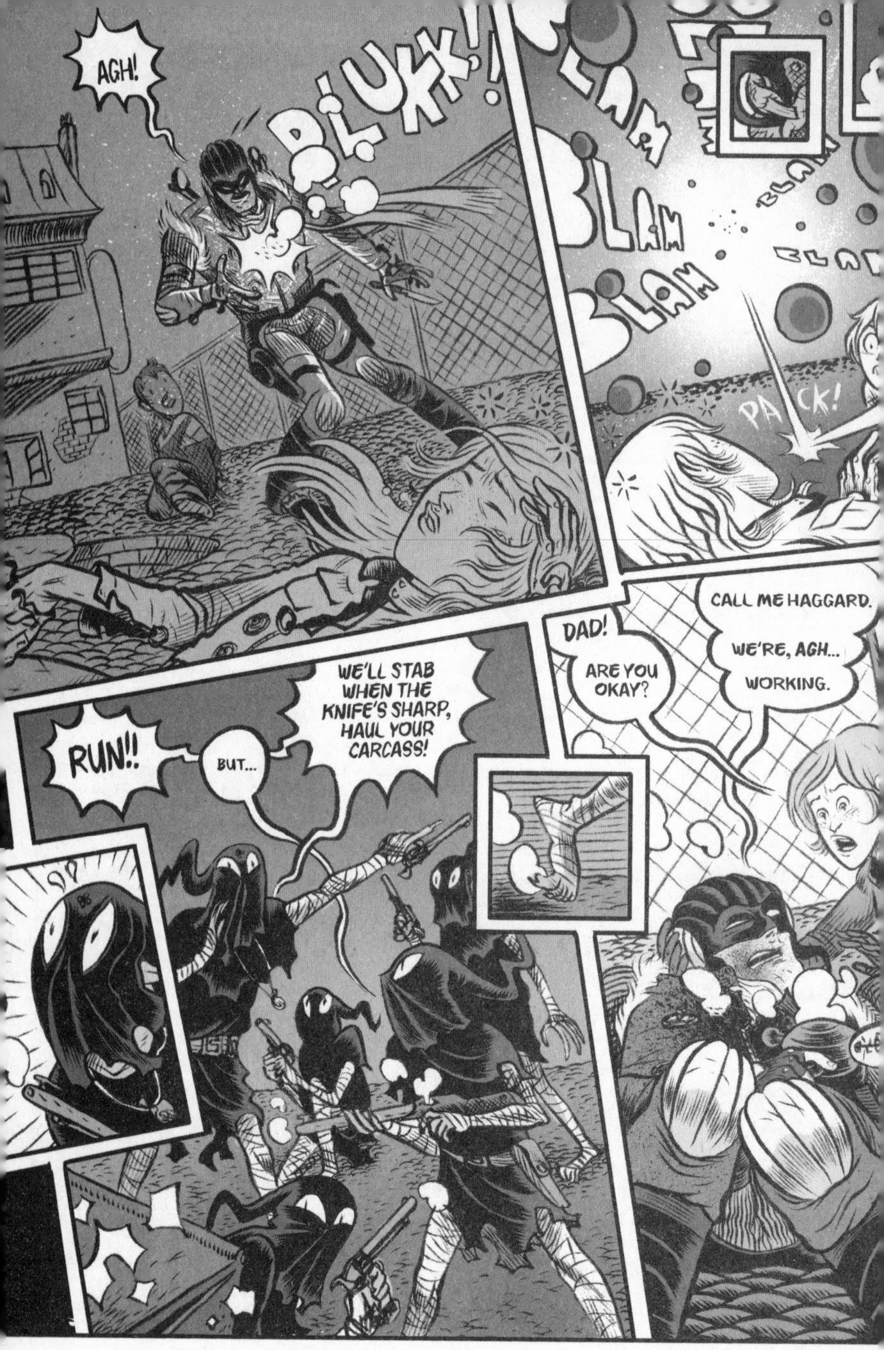
AGH!
BLUKK!!
BLAM
BLAM
BLAM
BLAM
PACK!
CALL ME HAGGARD.
WE'RE, AGH...
WORKING.
DAD!
ARE YOU OKAY?
RUN!!
BUT...
WE'LL STAB WHEN THE KNIFE'S SHARP, HAUL YOUR CARCASS!

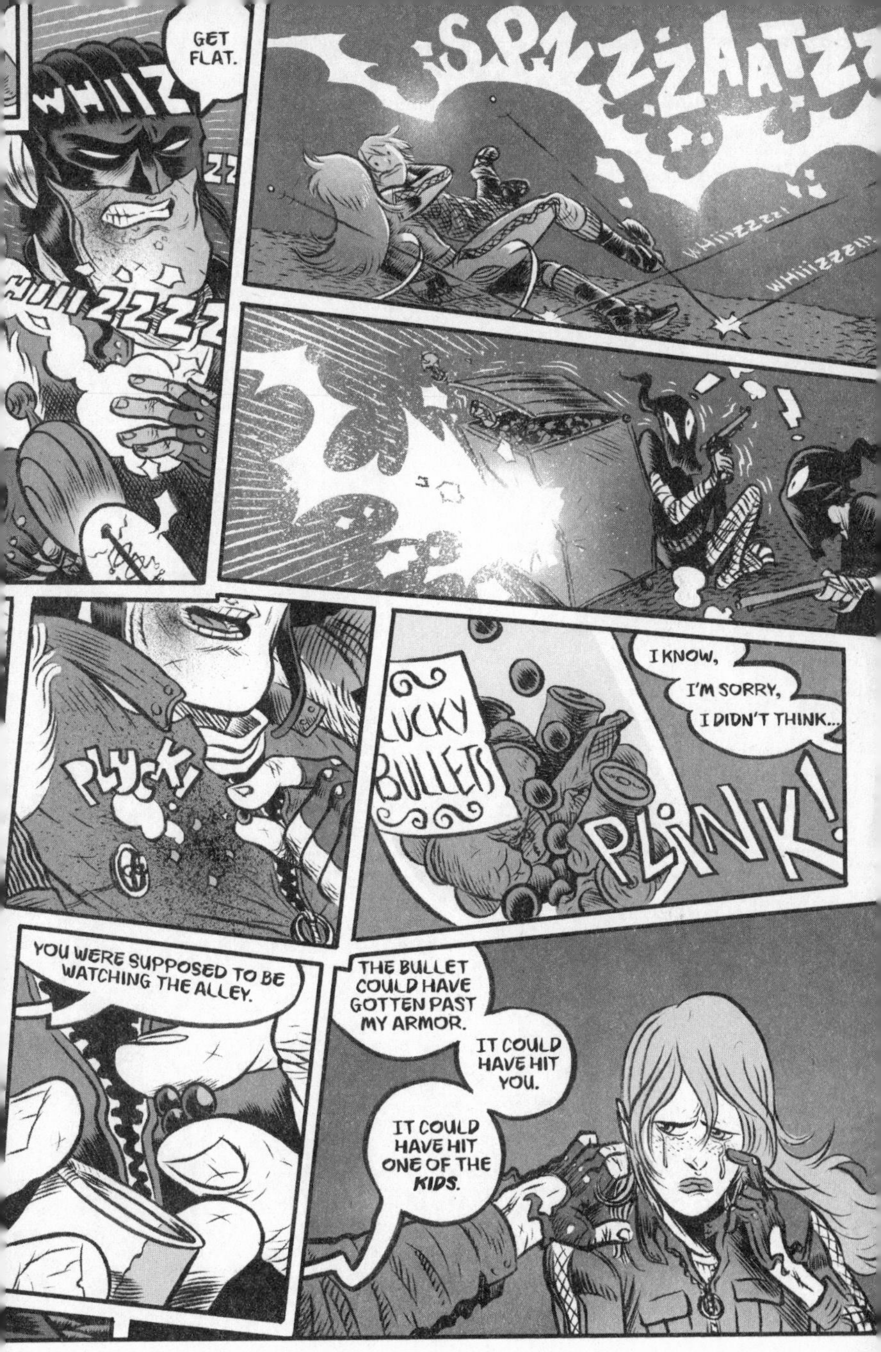
GET FLAT.
WHIIZ
ZZ
WHIIIZZZZZ
¡SPNZZAATZZ
WHIIIZZZZ!
WHIIIZZZ!!!
PLUCK!
LUCKY BULLETS
I KNOW,
I'M SORRY,
I DIDN'T THINK...
PLINK!
YOU WERE SUPPOSED TO BE WATCHING THE ALLEY.
THE BULLET COULD HAVE GOTTEN PAST MY ARMOR.
IT COULD HAVE HIT YOU.
IT COULD HAVE HIT ONE OF THE *KIDS*.

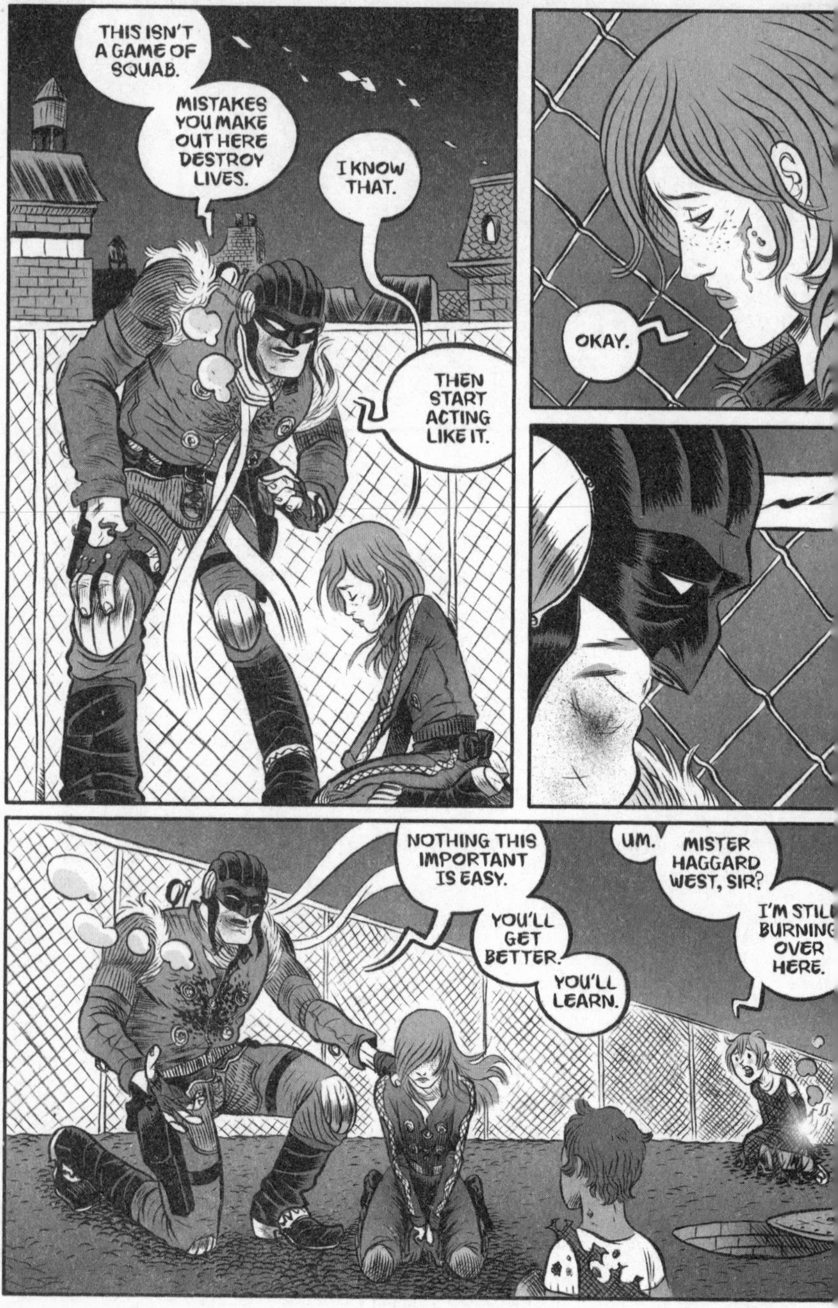

THIS ISN'T A GAME OF SQUAB.
MISTAKES YOU MAKE OUT HERE DESTROY LIVES.
I KNOW THAT.
THEN START ACTING LIKE IT.
OKAY.
NOTHING THIS IMPORTANT IS EASY.
YOU'LL GET BETTER.
YOU'LL LEARN.
UM.
MISTER HAGGARD WEST, SIR?
I'M STILL BURNING OVER HERE.

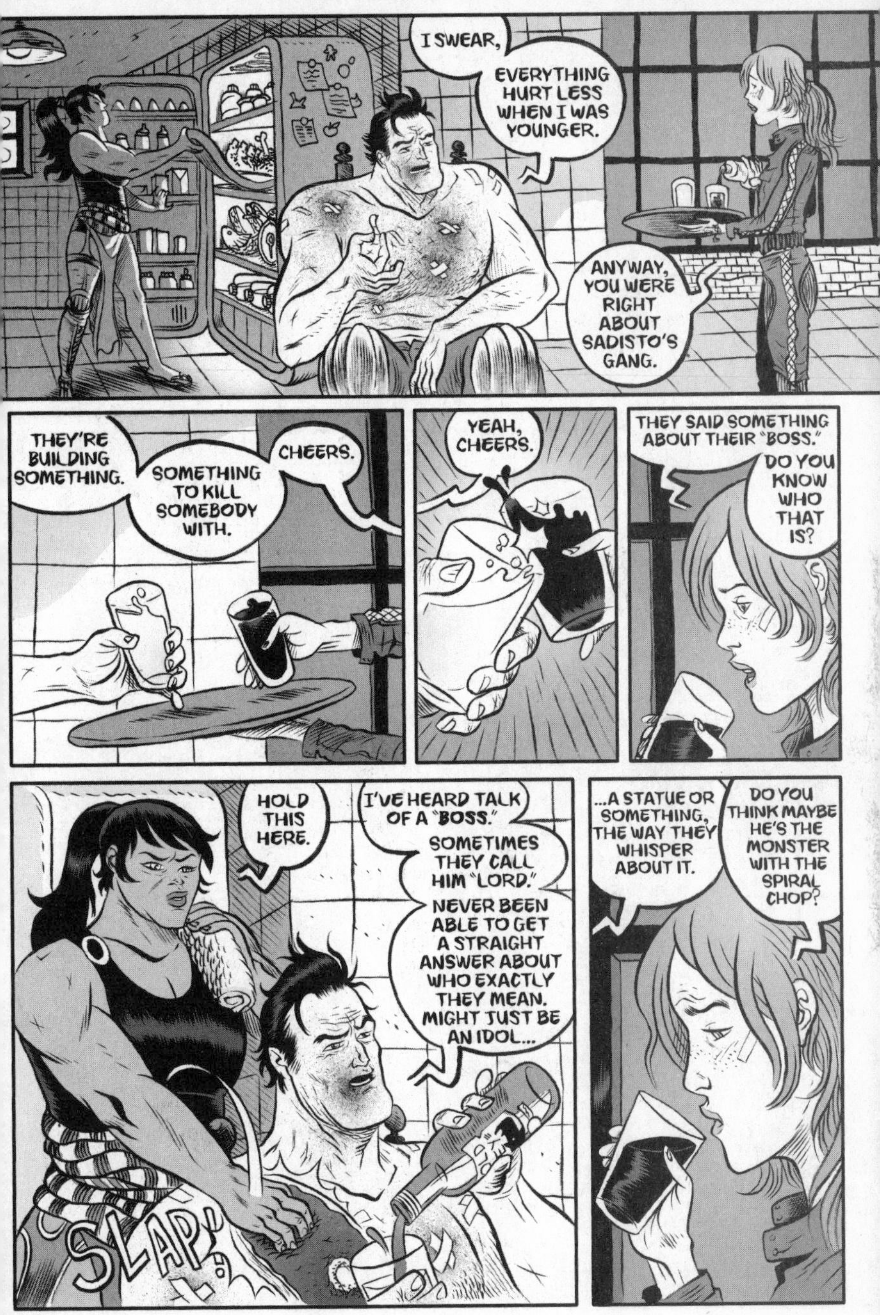
I SWEAR,
EVERYTHING HURT LESS WHEN I WAS YOUNGER.
ANYWAY, YOU WERE RIGHT ABOUT SADISTO'S GANG.
THEY'RE BUILDING SOMETHING.
SOMETHING TO KILL SOMEBODY WITH.
CHEERS.
YEAH, CHEERS.
THEY SAID SOMETHING ABOUT THEIR "BOSS."
DO YOU KNOW WHO THAT IS?
HOLD THIS HERE.
I'VE HEARD TALK OF A "BOSS."
SOMETIMES THEY CALL HIM "LORD."
NEVER BEEN ABLE TO GET A STRAIGHT ANSWER ABOUT WHO EXACTLY THEY MEAN. MIGHT JUST BE AN IDOL...
SLAP!
...A STATUE OR SOMETHING, THE WAY THEY WHISPER ABOUT IT.
DO YOU THINK MAYBE HE'S THE MONSTER WITH THE SPIRAL CHOP?

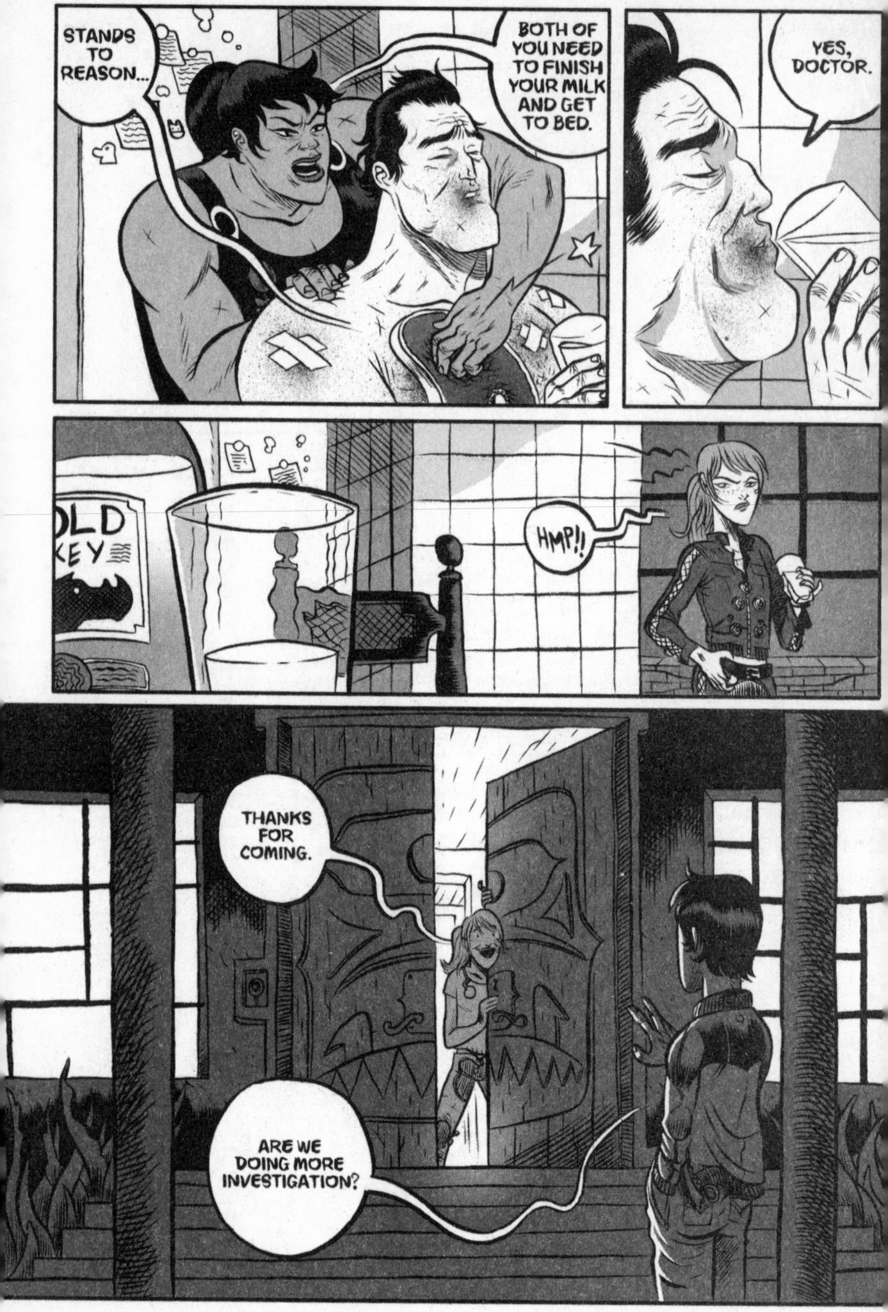
STANDS TO REASON...
BOTH OF YOU NEED TO FINISH YOUR MILK AND GET TO BED.
YES, DOCTOR.
HMP!!
THANKS FOR COMING.
ARE WE DOING MORE INVESTIGATION?

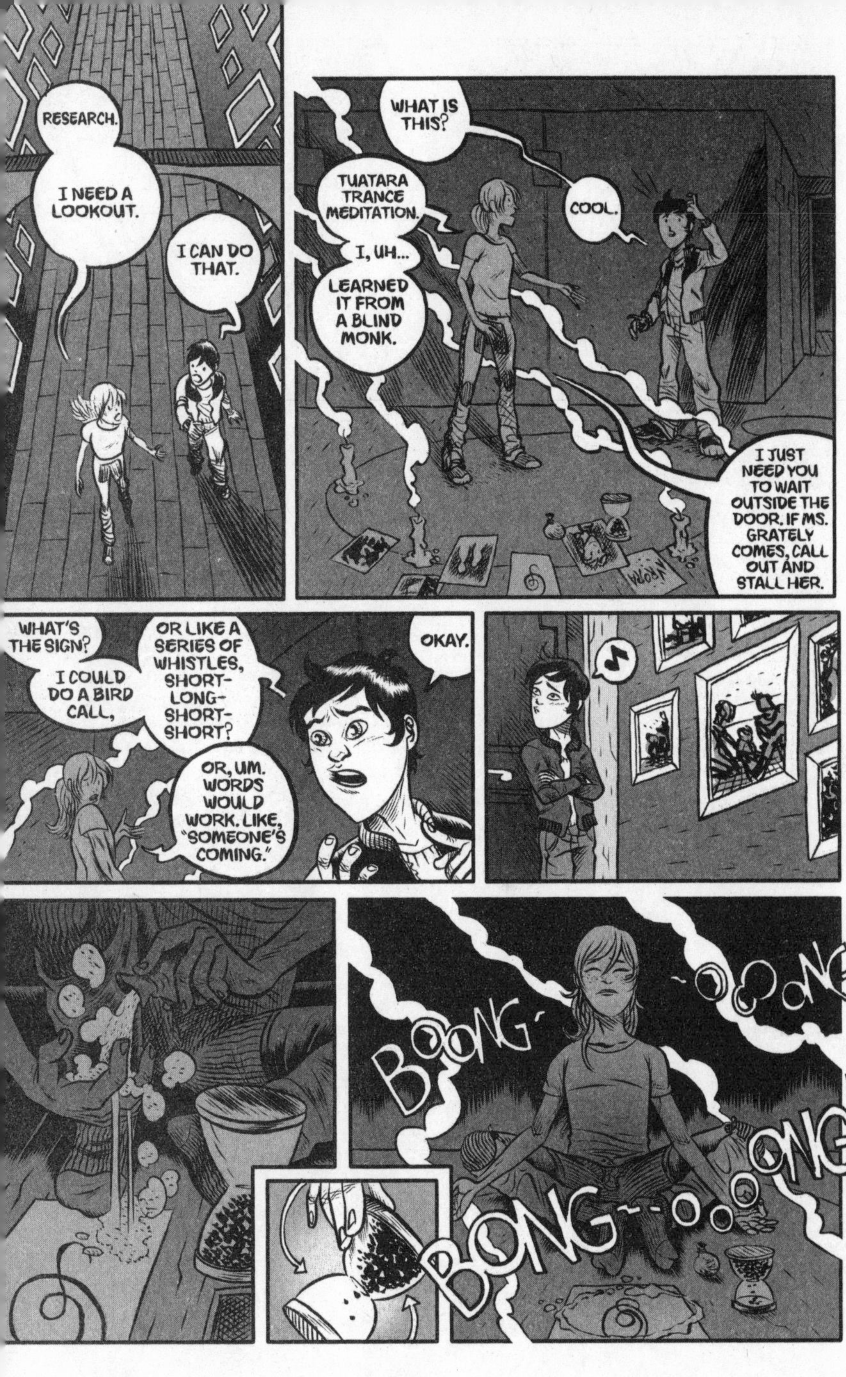
RESEARCH.
I NEED A LOOKOUT.
I CAN DO THAT.
WHAT IS THIS?
TUATARA TRANCE MEDITATION.
COOL.
I, UH...
LEARNED IT FROM A BLIND MONK.
I JUST NEED YOU TO WAIT OUTSIDE THE DOOR. IF MS. GRATELY COMES, CALL OUT AND STALL HER.
WHAT'S THE SIGN?
I COULD DO A BIRD CALL,
OR LIKE A SERIES OF WHISTLES, SHORT-LONG-SHORT-SHORT?
OR, UM. WORDS WOULD WORK. LIKE, "SOMEONE'S COMING."
OKAY.
BOONG~-OOOONG!
BONG--O..OONG!

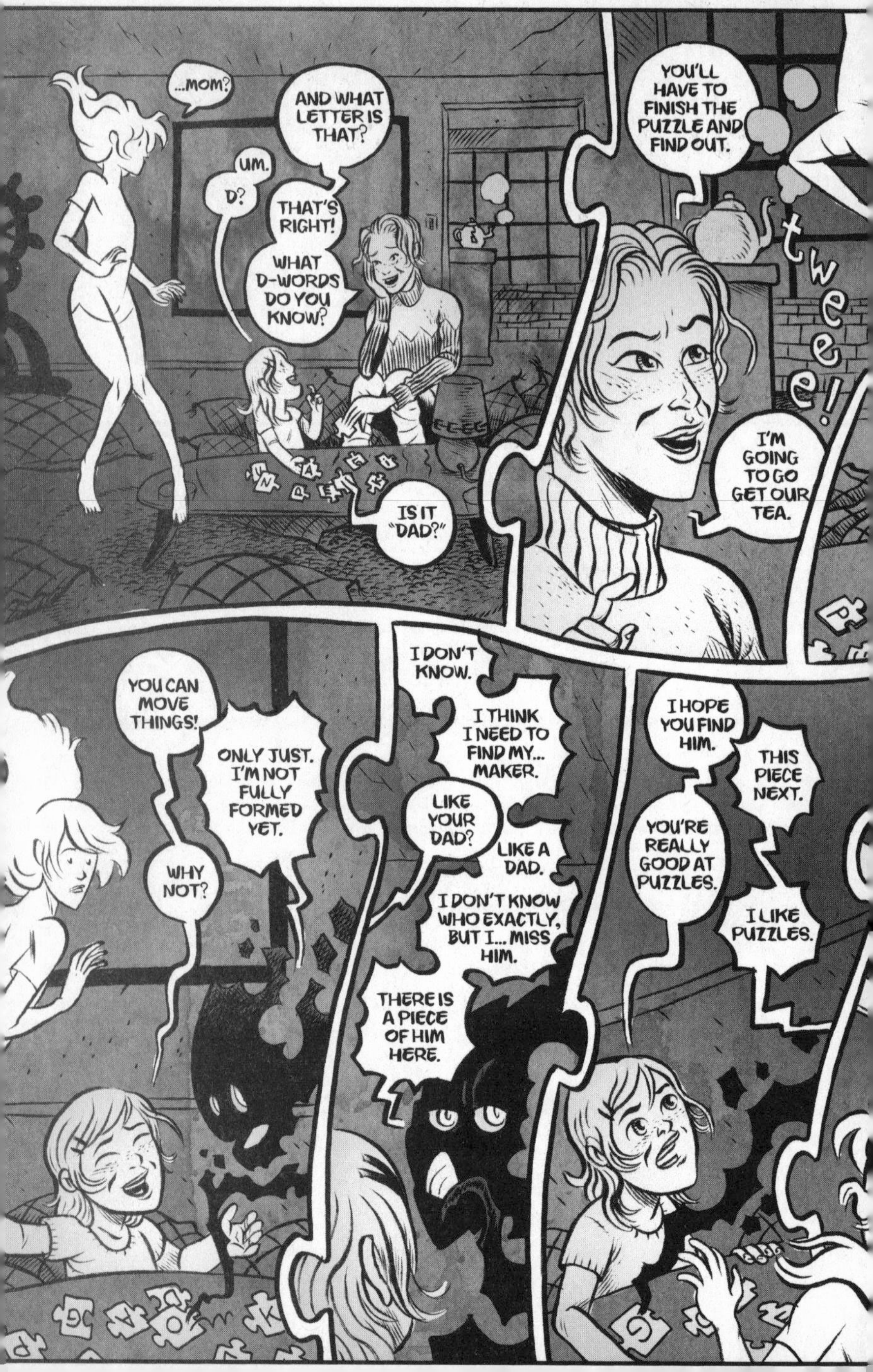
...MOM?
AND WHAT LETTER IS THAT?
UM.
D?
THAT'S RIGHT!
WHAT D-WORDS DO YOU KNOW?
IS IT "DAD?"
YOU'LL HAVE TO FINISH THE PUZZLE AND FIND OUT.
tweee!
I'M GOING TO GO GET OUR TEA.
YOU CAN MOVE THINGS!
ONLY JUST. I'M NOT FULLY FORMED YET.
WHY NOT?
I DON'T KNOW.
I THINK I NEED TO FIND MY... MAKER.
LIKE YOUR DAD?
LIKE A DAD.
I DON'T KNOW WHO EXACTLY, BUT I... MISS HIM.
THERE IS A PIECE OF HIM HERE.
I HOPE YOU FIND HIM.
THIS PIECE NEXT.
YOU'RE REALLY GOOD AT PUZZLES.
I LIKE PUZZLES.

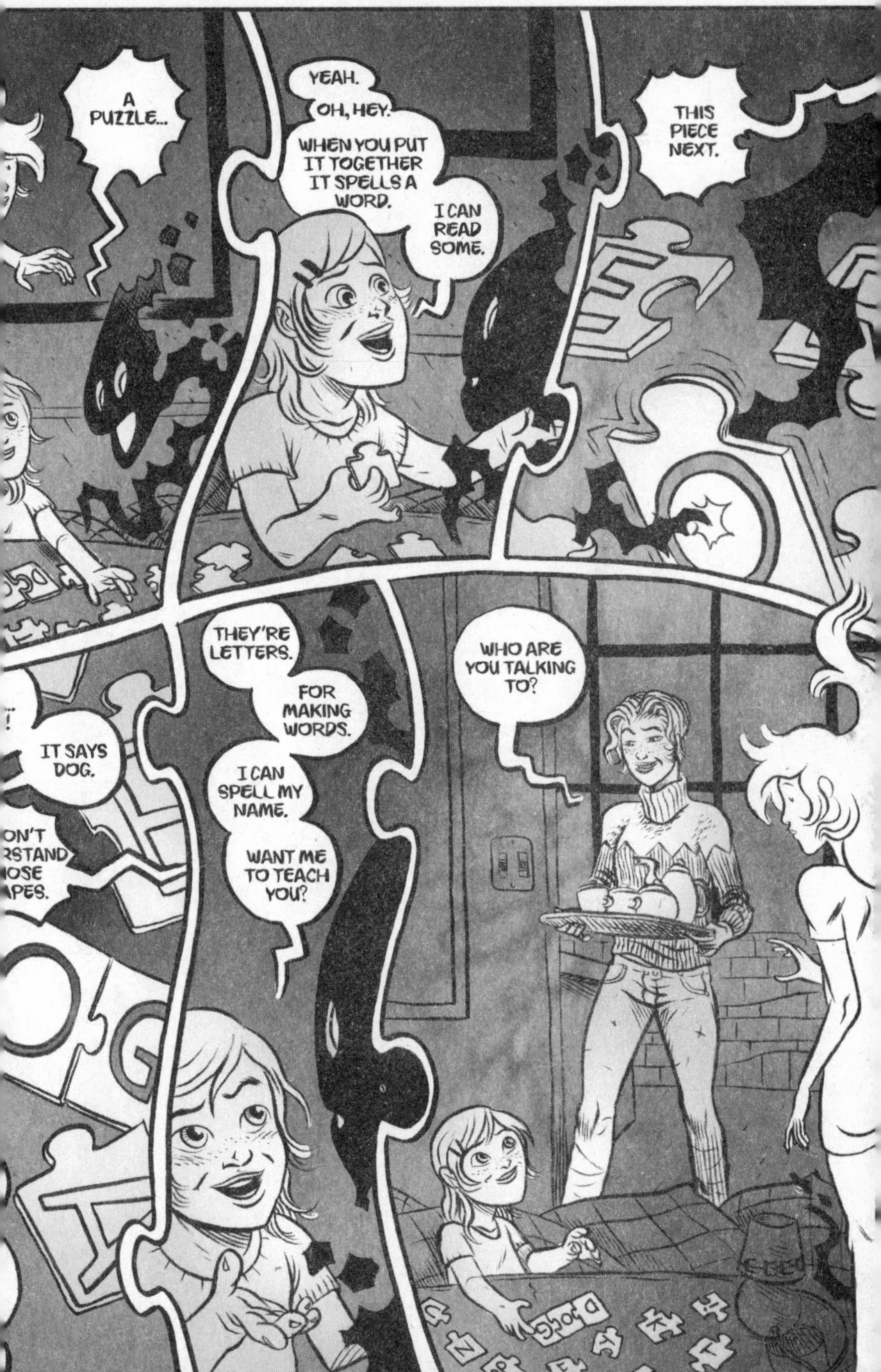
A PUZZLE...
YEAH.
OH, HEY.
WHEN YOU PUT IT TOGETHER IT SPELLS A WORD.
I CAN READ SOME.
THIS PIECE NEXT.
IT SAYS DOG.
THEY'RE LETTERS.
FOR MAKING WORDS.
I CAN SPELL MY NAME.
WANT ME TO TEACH YOU?
WHO ARE YOU TALKING TO?

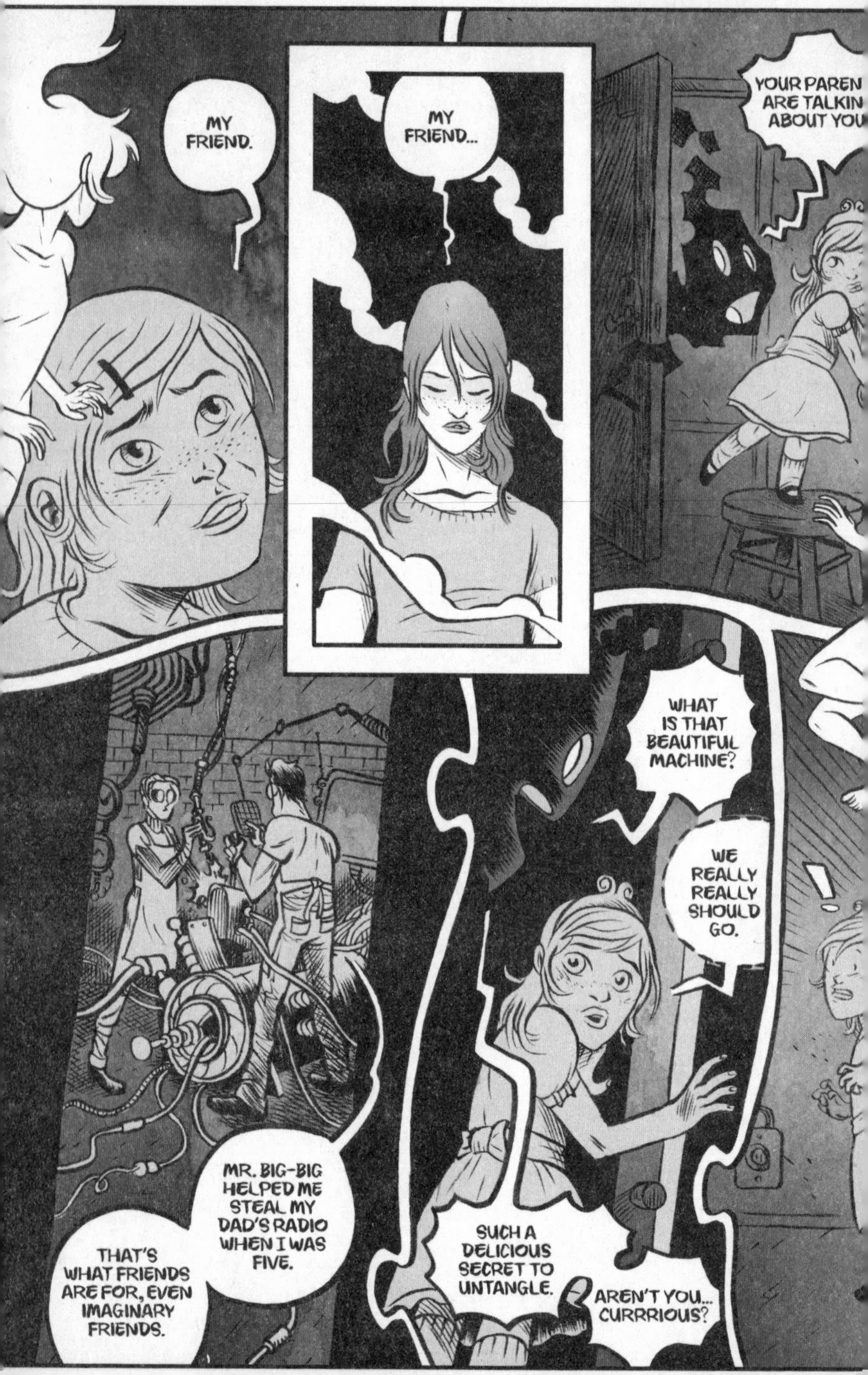

MY FRIEND.
MY FRIEND...
YOUR PAREN ARE TALKIN ABOUT YOU
WHAT IS THAT BEAUTIFUL MACHINE?
WE REALLY REALLY SHOULD GO.
!
MR. BIG-BIG HELPED ME STEAL MY DAD'S RADIO WHEN I WAS FIVE.
THAT'S WHAT FRIENDS ARE FOR, EVEN IMAGINARY FRIENDS.
SUCH A DELICIOUS SECRET TO UNTANGLE.
AREN'T YOU... CURRRIOUS?

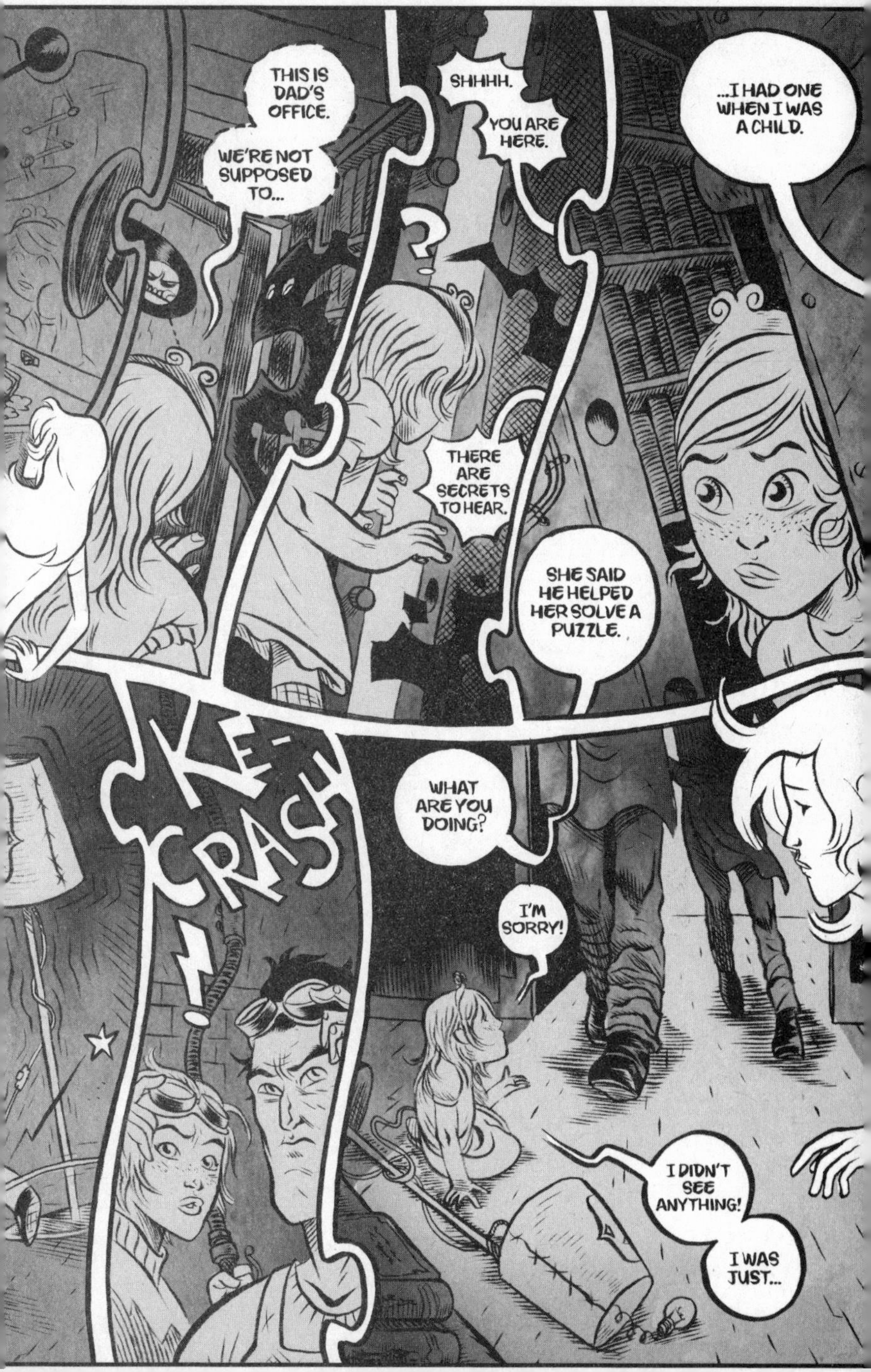
THIS IS DAD'S OFFICE.
WE'RE NOT SUPPOSED TO...
SHHHH.
YOU ARE HERE.
?
...I HAD ONE WHEN I WAS A CHILD.
THERE ARE SECRETS TO HEAR.
SHE SAID HE HELPED HER SOLVE A PUZZLE.
KE-CRASH
WHAT ARE YOU DOING?
I'M SORRY!
I DIDN'T SEE ANYTHING!
I WAS JUST...

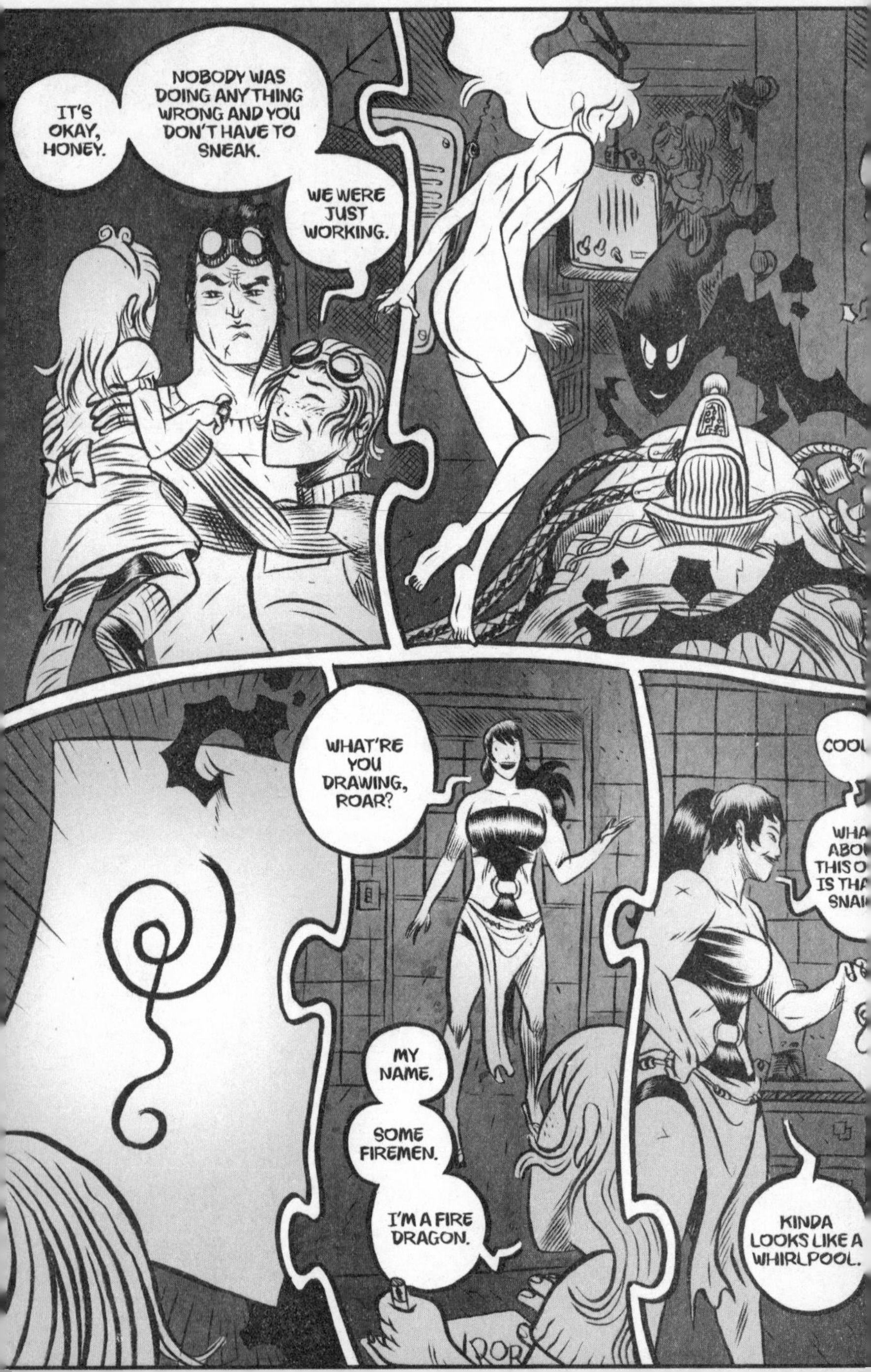
IT'S OKAY, HONEY.
NOBODY WAS DOING ANYTHING WRONG AND YOU DON'T HAVE TO SNEAK.
WE WERE JUST WORKING.
WHAT'RE YOU DRAWING, ROAR?
MY NAME.
SOME FIREMEN.
I'M A FIRE DRAGON.
KINDA LOOKS LIKE A WHIRLPOOL.

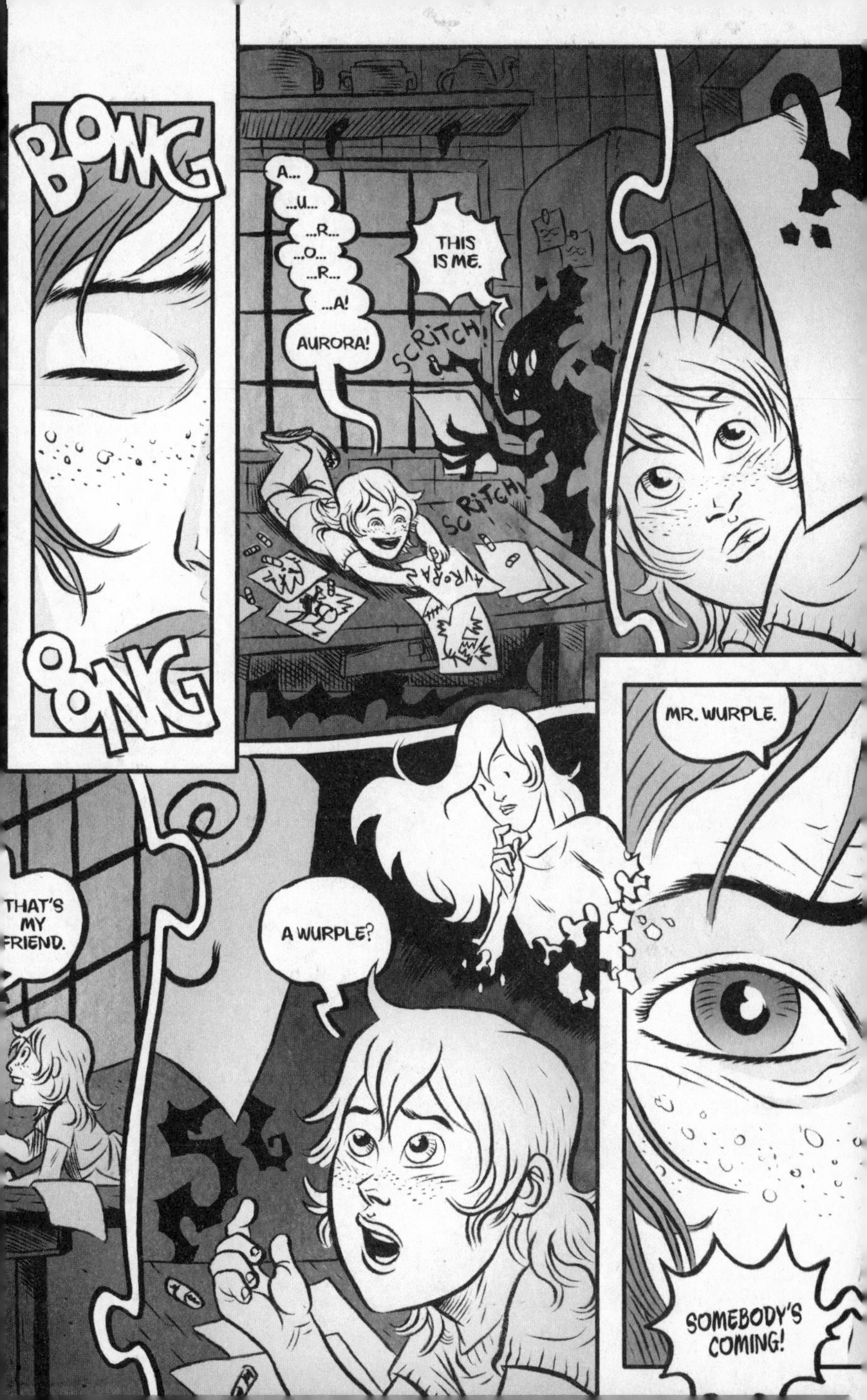
BONG
BONG
A...
...U...
...R...
...O...
...R...
...A!
AURORA!
THIS IS ME.
SCRITCH!
SCRITCH!
AVRORA
THAT'S MY FRIEND.
A WURPLE?
MR. WURPLE.
SOMEBODY'S COMING!

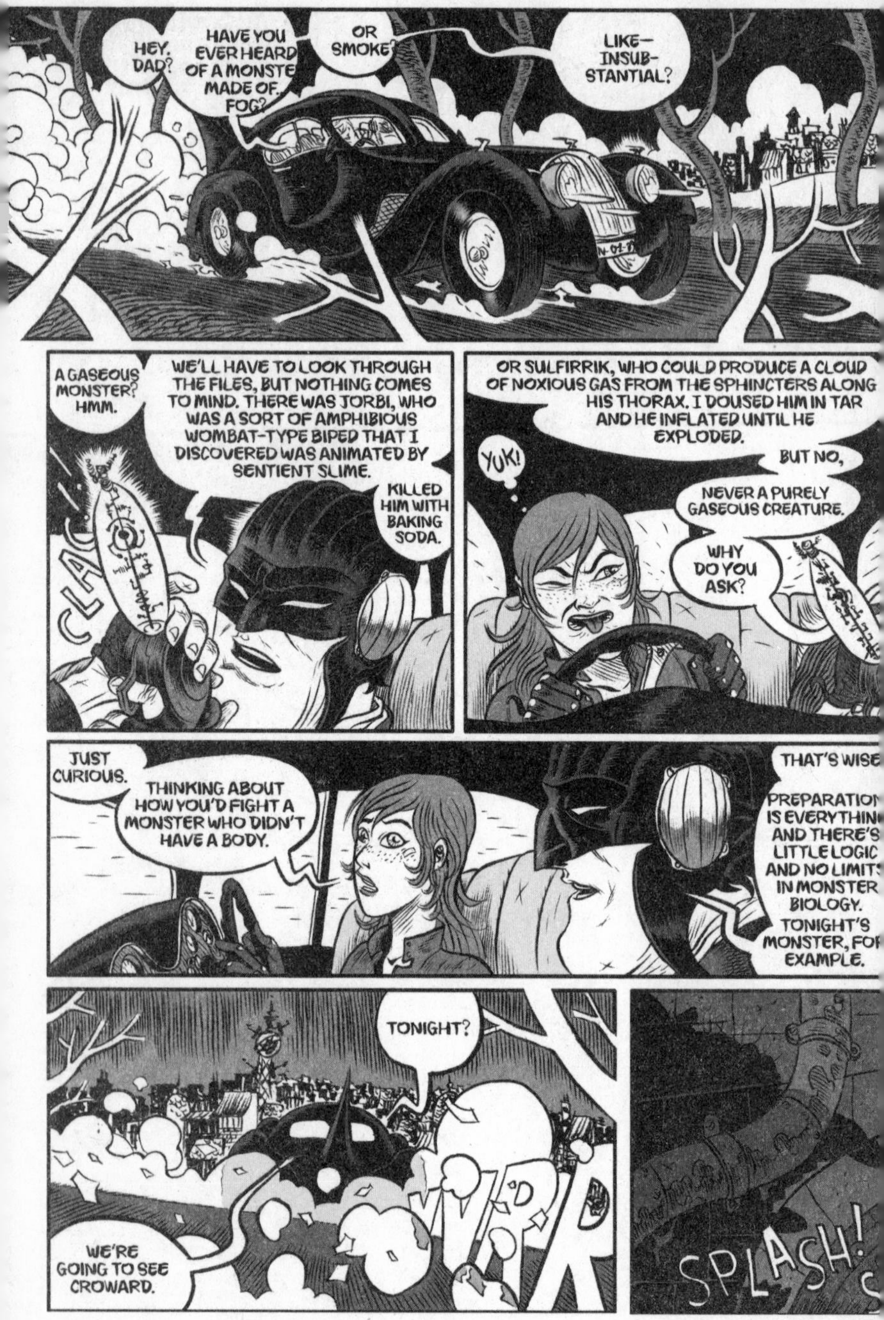
HEY, DAD?
HAVE YOU EVER HEARD OF A MONSTE MADE OF FOG?
OR SMOKE?
LIKE—INSUB-STANTIAL?
A GASEOUS MONSTER? HMM.
WE'LL HAVE TO LOOK THROUGH THE FILES, BUT NOTHING COMES TO MIND. THERE WAS JORBI, WHO WAS A SORT OF AMPHIBIOUS WOMBAT-TYPE BIPED THAT I DISCOVERED WAS ANIMATED BY SENTIENT SLIME.
KILLED HIM WITH BAKING SODA.
CLA
OR SULFIRRIK, WHO COULD PRODUCE A CLOUD OF NOXIOUS GAS FROM THE SPHINCTERS ALONG HIS THORAX. I DOUSED HIM IN TAR AND HE INFLATED UNTIL HE EXPLODED.
YUK!
BUT NO,
NEVER A PURELY GASEOUS CREATURE.
WHY DO YOU ASK?
JUST CURIOUS.
THINKING ABOUT HOW YOU'D FIGHT A MONSTER WHO DIDN'T HAVE A BODY.
THAT'S WISE
PREPARATIO IS EVERYTHIN AND THERE'S LITTLE LOGIC AND NO LIMIT IN MONSTER BIOLOGY.
TONIGHT'S MONSTER, FO EXAMPLE.
TONIGHT?
WE'RE GOING TO SEE CROWARD.
SPLASH!

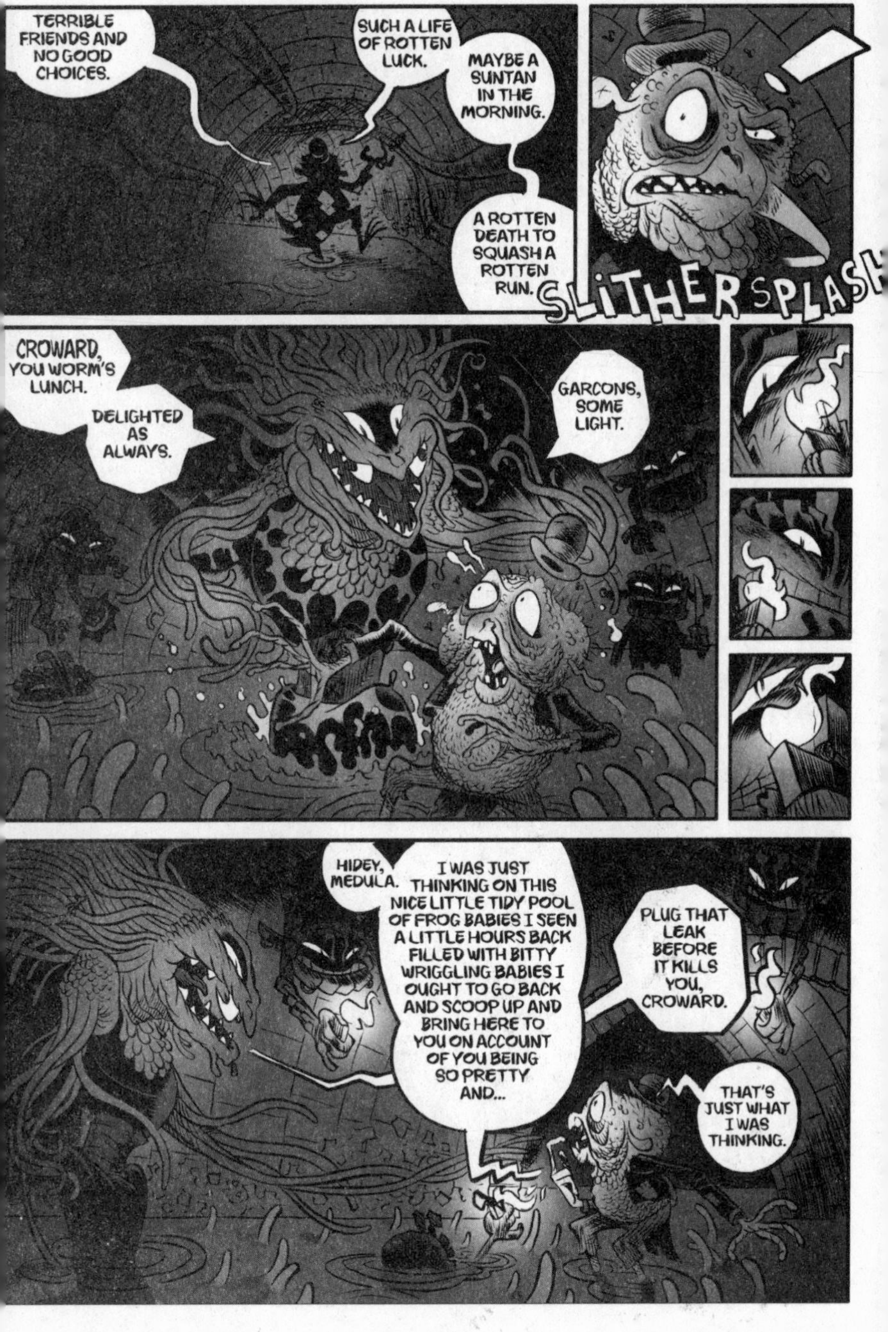
TERRIBLE FRIENDS AND NO GOOD CHOICES.
SUCH A LIFE OF ROTTEN LUCK.
MAYBE A SUNTAN IN THE MORNING.
A ROTTEN DEATH TO SQUASH A ROTTEN RUN.
!
SLITHER SPLASH
CROWARD, YOU WORM'S LUNCH.
DELIGHTED AS ALWAYS.
GARCONS, SOME LIGHT.
HIDEY, MEDULA.
I WAS JUST THINKING ON THIS NICE LITTLE TIDY POOL OF FROG BABIES I SEEN A LITTLE HOURS BACK FILLED WITH BITTY WRIGGLING BABIES I OUGHT TO GO BACK AND SCOOP UP AND BRING HERE TO YOU ON ACCOUNT OF YOU BEING SO PRETTY AND...
PLUG THAT LEAK BEFORE IT KILLS YOU, CROWARD.
THAT'S JUST WHAT I WAS THINKING.

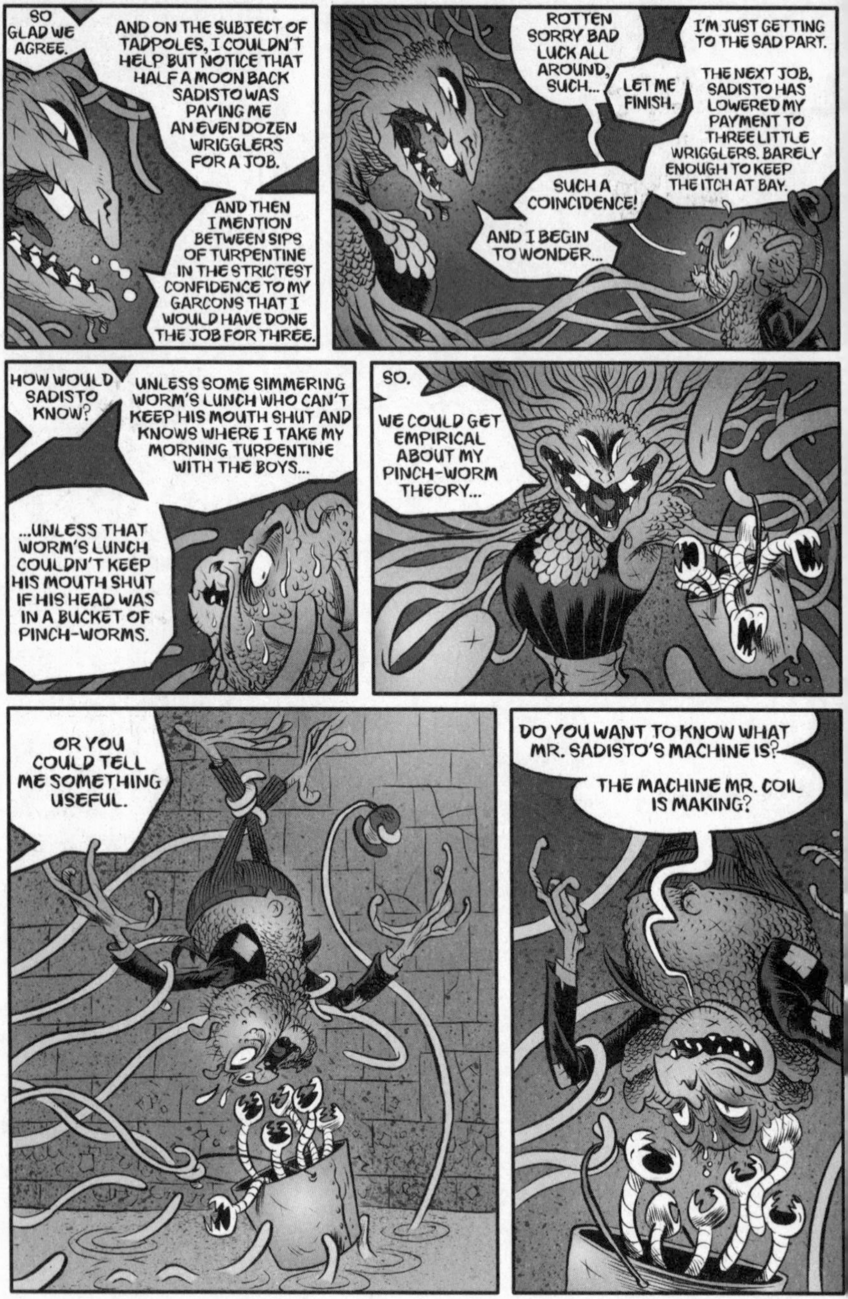
SO GLAD WE AGREE.
AND ON THE SUBJECT OF TADPOLES, I COULDN'T HELP BUT NOTICE THAT HALF A MOON BACK SADISTO WAS PAYING ME AN EVEN DOZEN WRIGGLERS FOR A JOB.
AND THEN I MENTION BETWEEN SIPS OF TURPENTINE IN THE STRICTEST CONFIDENCE TO MY GARCONS THAT I WOULD HAVE DONE THE JOB FOR THREE.
ROTTEN SORRY BAD LUCK ALL AROUND, SUCH...
LET ME FINISH.
I'M JUST GETTING TO THE SAD PART.
THE NEXT JOB, SADISTO HAS LOWERED MY PAYMENT TO THREE LITTLE WRIGGLERS. BARELY ENOUGH TO KEEP THE ITCH AT BAY.
SUCH A COINCIDENCE!
AND I BEGIN TO WONDER...
HOW WOULD SADISTO KNOW?
UNLESS SOME SIMMERING WORM'S LUNCH WHO CAN'T KEEP HIS MOUTH SHUT AND KNOWS WHERE I TAKE MY MORNING TURPENTINE WITH THE BOYS...
...UNLESS THAT WORM'S LUNCH COULDN'T KEEP HIS MOUTH SHUT IF HIS HEAD WAS IN A BUCKET OF PINCH-WORMS.
SO.
WE COULD GET EMPIRICAL ABOUT MY PINCH-WORM THEORY...
OR YOU COULD TELL ME SOMETHING USEFUL.
DO YOU WANT TO KNOW WHAT MR. SADISTO'S MACHINE IS?
THE MACHINE MR. COIL IS MAKING?

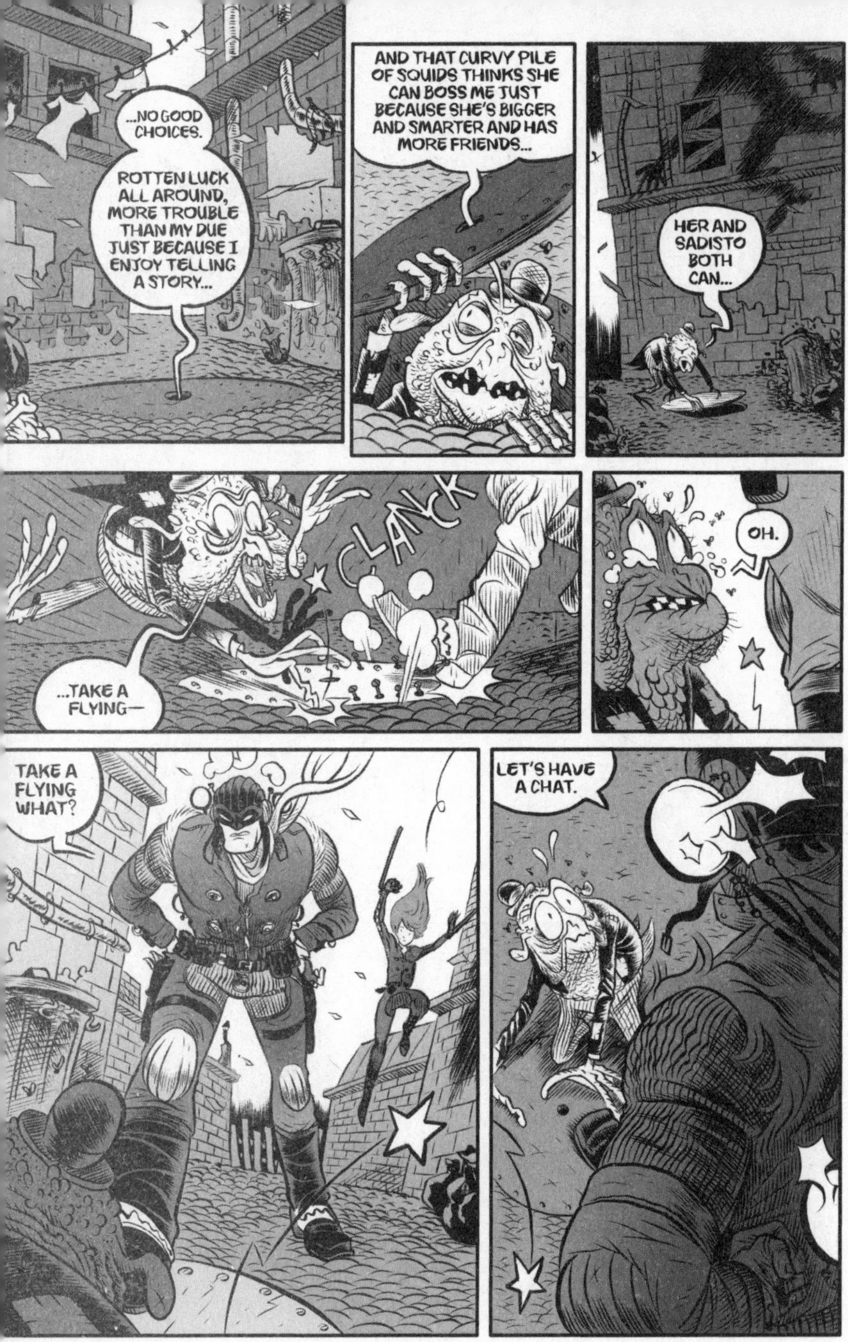

...NO GOOD CHOICES.
ROTTEN LUCK ALL AROUND, MORE TROUBLE THAN MY DUE JUST BECAUSE I ENJOY TELLING A STORY...
AND THAT CURVY PILE OF SQUIDS THINKS SHE CAN BOSS ME JUST BECAUSE SHE'S BIGGER AND SMARTER AND HAS MORE FRIENDS...
HER AND SADISTO BOTH CAN...
CLANCK
...TAKE A FLYING—
OH.
TAKE A FLYING WHAT?
LET'S HAVE A CHAT.

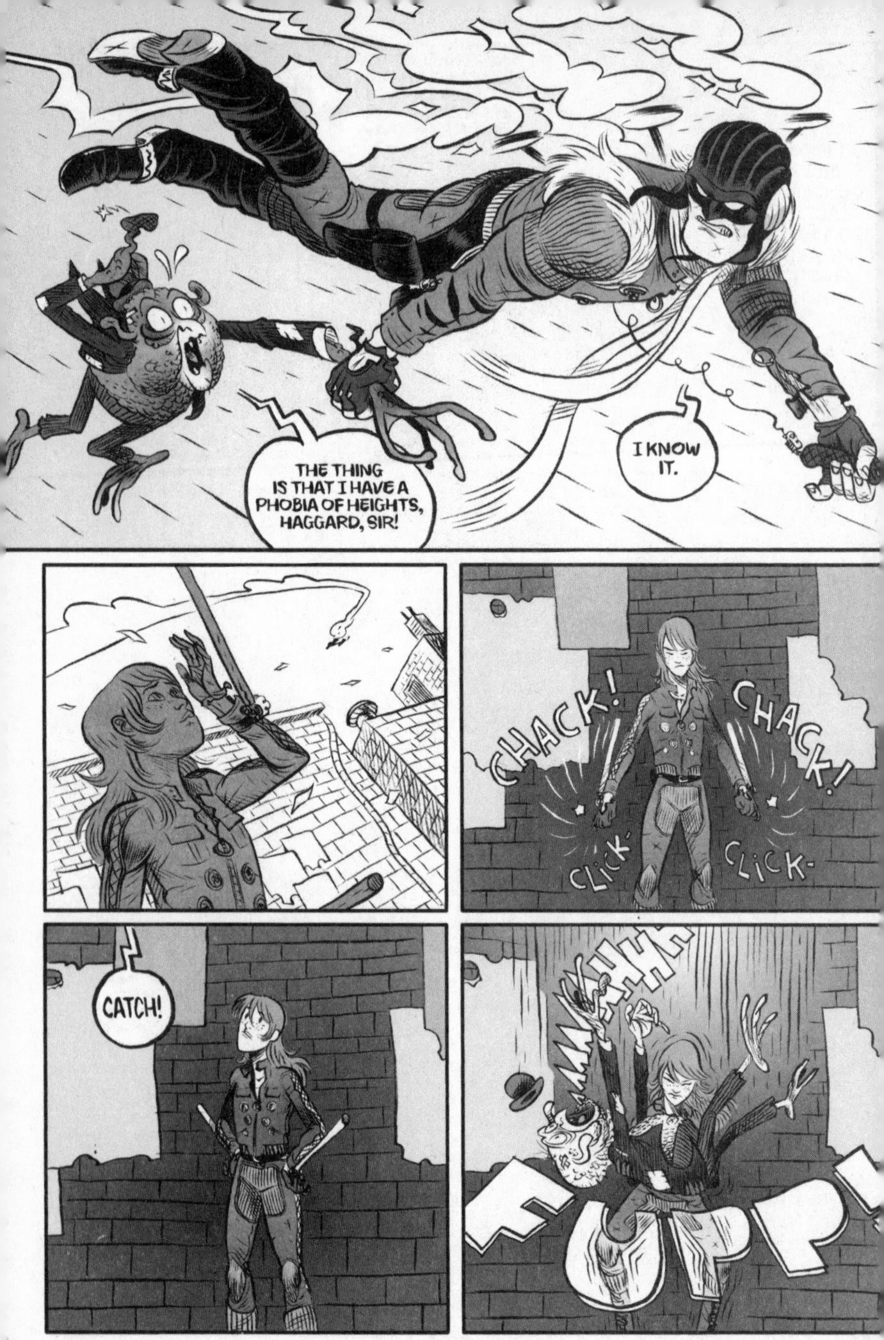
THE THING IS THAT I HAVE A PHOBIA OF HEIGHTS, HAGGARD, SIR!
I KNOW IT.
CHACK!
CHACK!
CLICK-
CLICK-
CATCH!

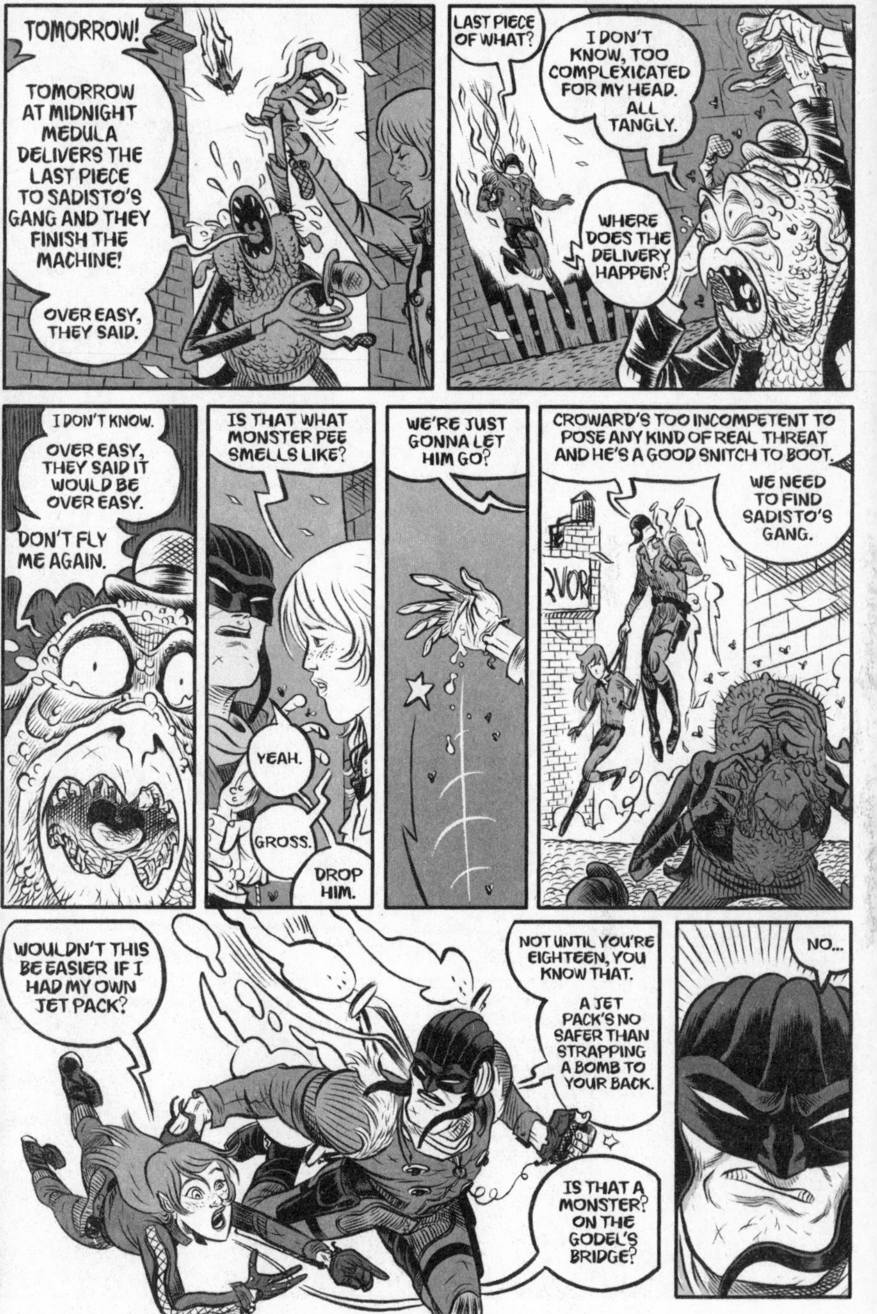
TOMORROW!
TOMORROW AT MIDNIGHT MEDULA DELIVERS THE LAST PIECE TO SADISTO'S GANG AND THEY FINISH THE MACHINE!
OVER EASY, THEY SAID.
LAST PIECE OF WHAT?
I DON'T KNOW, TOO COMPLEXICATED FOR MY HEAD.
ALL TANGLY.
WHERE DOES THE DELIVERY HAPPEN?
I DON'T KNOW.
OVER EASY, THEY SAID IT WOULD BE OVER EASY.
DON'T FLY ME AGAIN.
IS THAT WHAT MONSTER PEE SMELLS LIKE?
YEAH.
GROSS.
DROP HIM.
WE'RE JUST GONNA LET HIM GO?
CROWARD'S TOO INCOMPETENT TO POSE ANY KIND OF REAL THREAT AND HE'S A GOOD SNITCH TO BOOT.
WE NEED TO FIND SADISTO'S GANG.
WOULDN'T THIS BE EASIER IF I HAD MY OWN JET PACK?
NOT UNTIL YOU'RE EIGHTEEN, YOU KNOW THAT.
A JET PACK'S NO SAFER THAN STRAPPING A BOMB TO YOUR BACK.
IS THAT A MONSTER? ON THE GODEL'S BRIDGE?
NO...

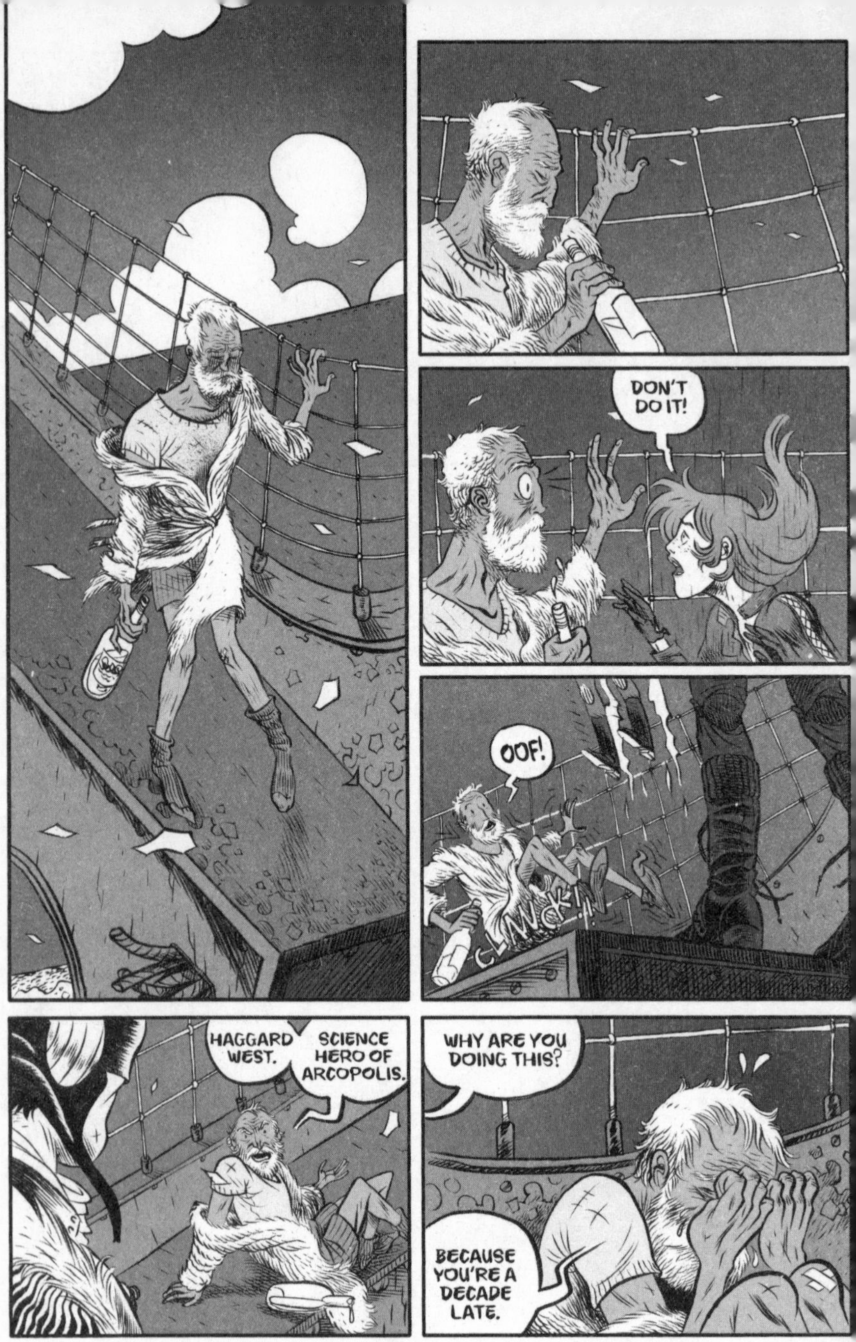
DON'T DO IT!
OOF!
HAGGARD WEST.
SCIENCE HERO OF ARCOPOLIS.
WHY ARE YOU DOING THIS?
BECAUSE YOU'RE A DECADE LATE.

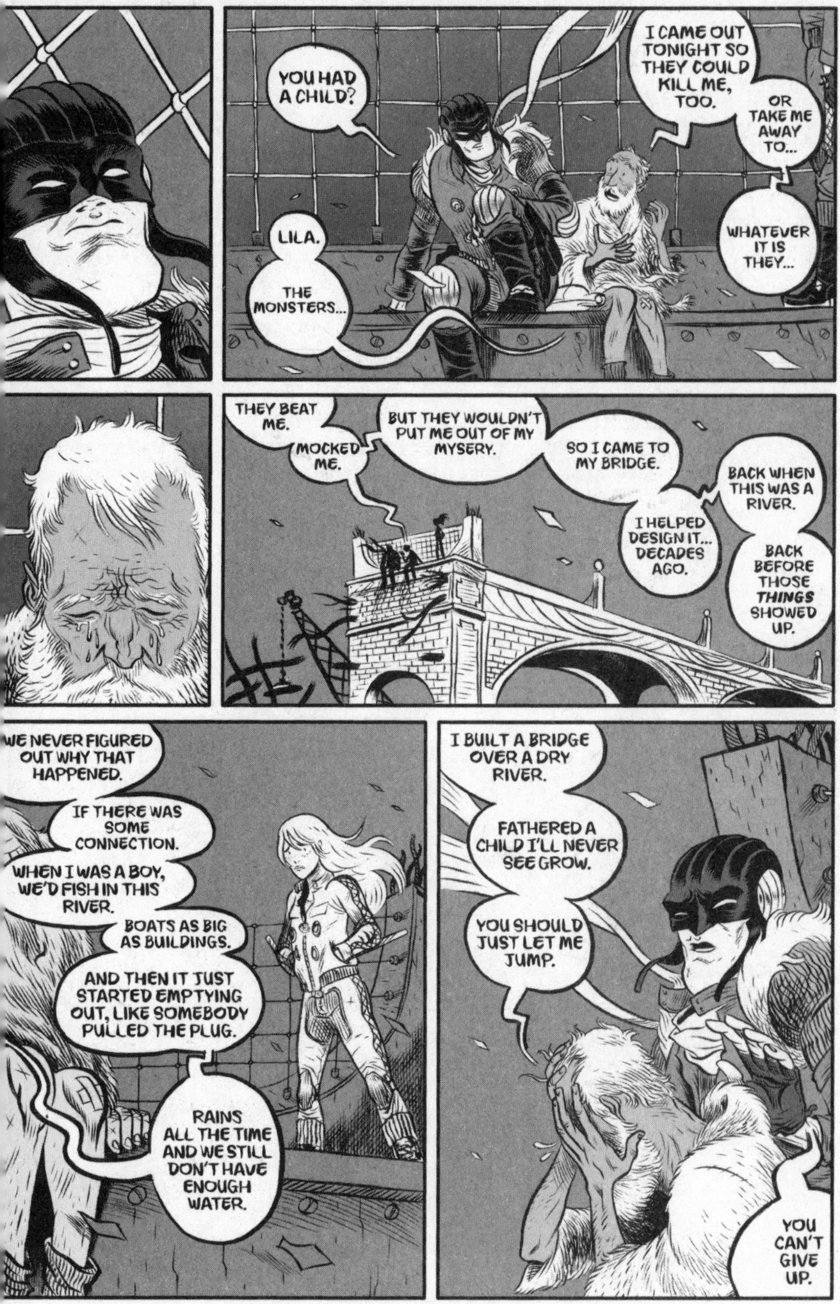
YOU HAD A CHILD?
I CAME OUT TONIGHT SO THEY COULD KILL ME, TOO.
OR TAKE ME AWAY TO...
WHATEVER IT IS THEY...
LILA.
THE MONSTERS...
THEY BEAT ME.
MOCKED ME.
BUT THEY WOULDN'T PUT ME OUT OF MY MYSERY.
SO I CAME TO MY BRIDGE.
BACK WHEN THIS WAS A RIVER.
I HELPED DESIGN IT... DECADES AGO.
BACK BEFORE THOSE *THINGS* SHOWED UP.
WE NEVER FIGURED OUT WHY THAT HAPPENED.
IF THERE WAS SOME CONNECTION.
WHEN I WAS A BOY, WE'D FISH IN THIS RIVER.
BOATS AS BIG AS BUILDINGS.
AND THEN IT JUST STARTED EMPTYING OUT, LIKE SOMEBODY PULLED THE PLUG.
RAINS ALL THE TIME AND WE STILL DON'T HAVE ENOUGH WATER.
I BUILT A BRIDGE OVER A DRY RIVER.
FATHERED A CHILD I'LL NEVER SEE GROW.
YOU SHOULD JUST LET ME JUMP.
YOU CAN'T GIVE UP.

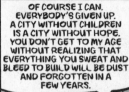
OF COURSE I CAN. EVERYBODY'S GIVEN UP. A CITY WITHOUT CHILDREN IS A CITY WITHOUT HOPE. YOU DON'T GET TO MY AGE WITHOUT REALIZING THAT EVERYTHING YOU SWEAT AND BLEED TO BUILD WILL BE DUST AND FORGOTTEN IN A FEW YEARS.

AND THE ONLY THINGS YOU CAN MAKE WORTH SOMETHING ARE YOUR CHILDREN.

YOU PUT EVERYTHING INTO THEM, REALIZE YOU NEVER REALLY LOVED ANYTHING UNTIL THEY CAME ALONG.

YOUR WHOLE LIFE. AND SOME MONSTER TAKES IT AWAY JUST LIKE THAT. AND THE "HERO" WHO'S SUPPOSED TO PROTECT THE THINGS YOU LOVE IS... WORTHLESS.

JUST ANOTHER MAN.

LILA WAS FIVE YEARS OLD WHEN THEY TOOK HER.

SHE HAD JUST STARTED SCHOOL.

HER MOM WAS STILL ALIVE THEN, SHE LOOKED JUST LIKE HER.

SHE WAS LEARNING TO READ.

SHE...

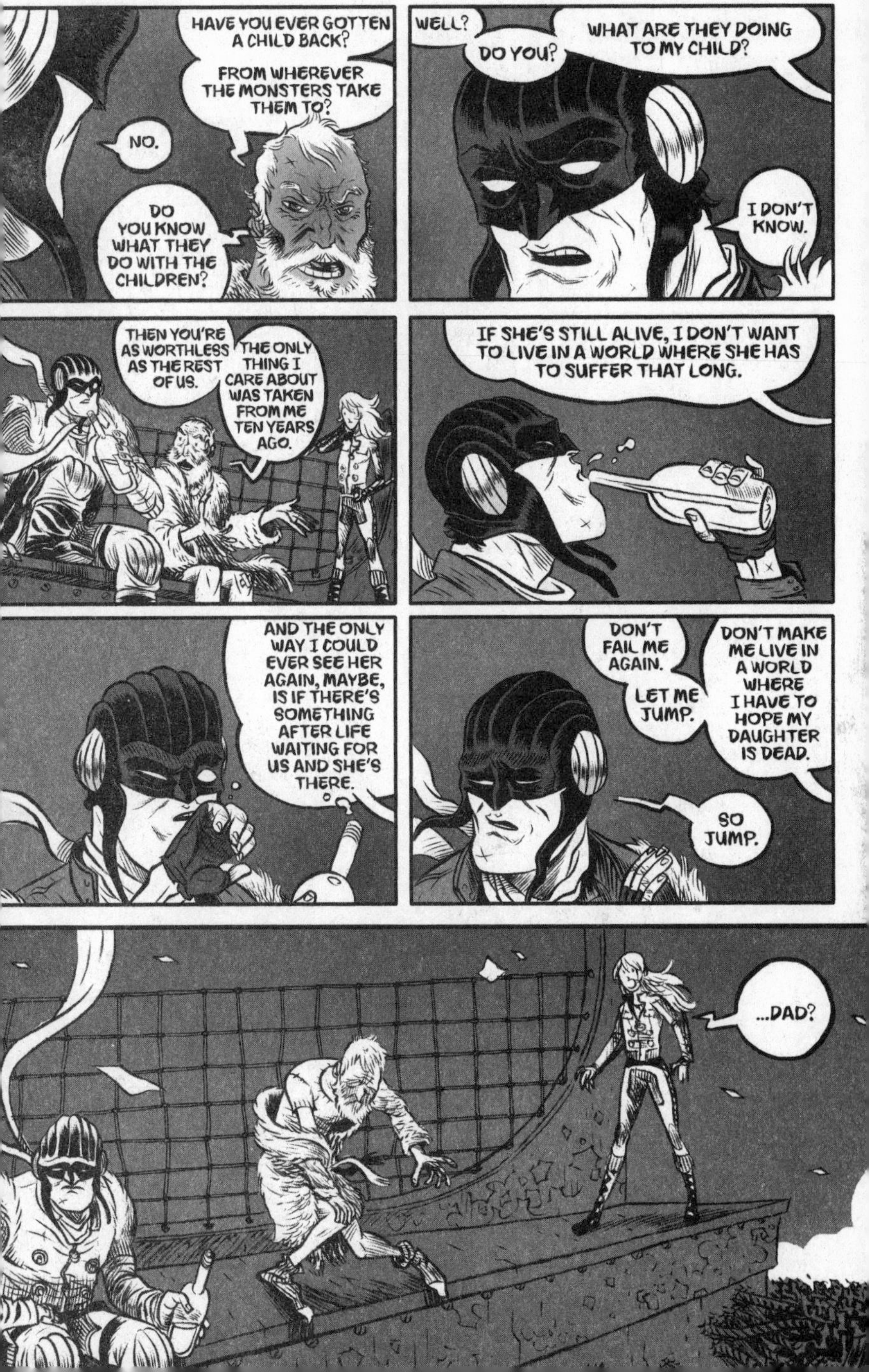
HAVE YOU EVER GOTTEN A CHILD BACK?
FROM WHEREVER THE MONSTERS TAKE THEM TO?
NO.
DO YOU KNOW WHAT THEY DO WITH THE CHILDREN?
WELL?
DO YOU?
WHAT ARE THEY DOING TO MY CHILD?
I DON'T KNOW.
THEN YOU'RE AS WORTHLESS AS THE REST OF US.
THE ONLY THING I CARE ABOUT WAS TAKEN FROM ME TEN YEARS AGO.
IF SHE'S STILL ALIVE, I DON'T WANT TO LIVE IN A WORLD WHERE SHE HAS TO SUFFER THAT LONG.
AND THE ONLY WAY I COULD EVER SEE HER AGAIN, MAYBE, IS IF THERE'S SOMETHING AFTER LIFE WAITING FOR US AND SHE'S THERE.
DON'T FAIL ME AGAIN.
LET ME JUMP.
DON'T MAKE ME LIVE IN A WORLD WHERE I HAVE TO HOPE MY DAUGHTER IS DEAD.
SO JUMP.
...DAD?

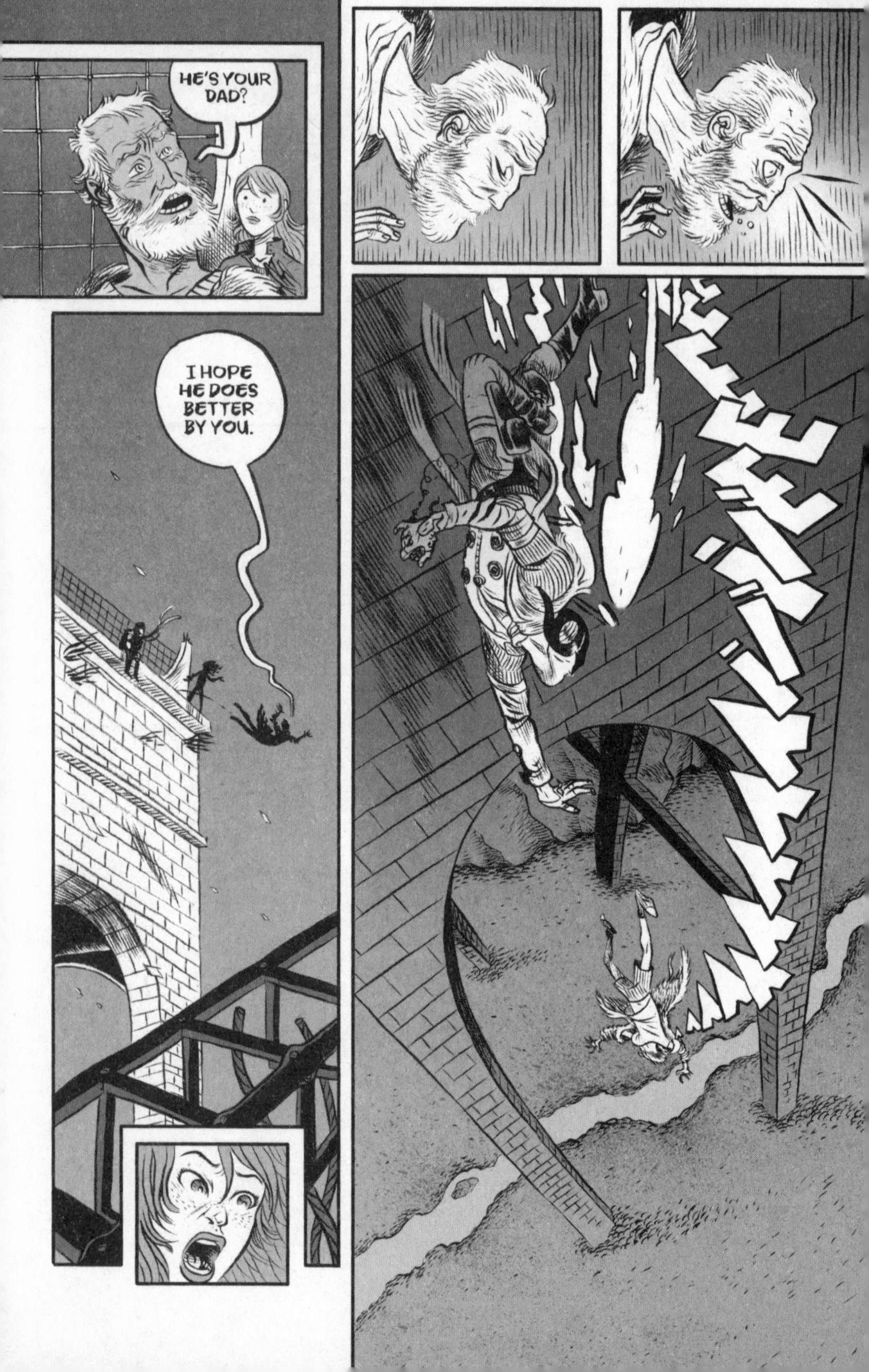
HE'S YOUR DAD?
I HOPE HE DOES BETTER BY YOU.

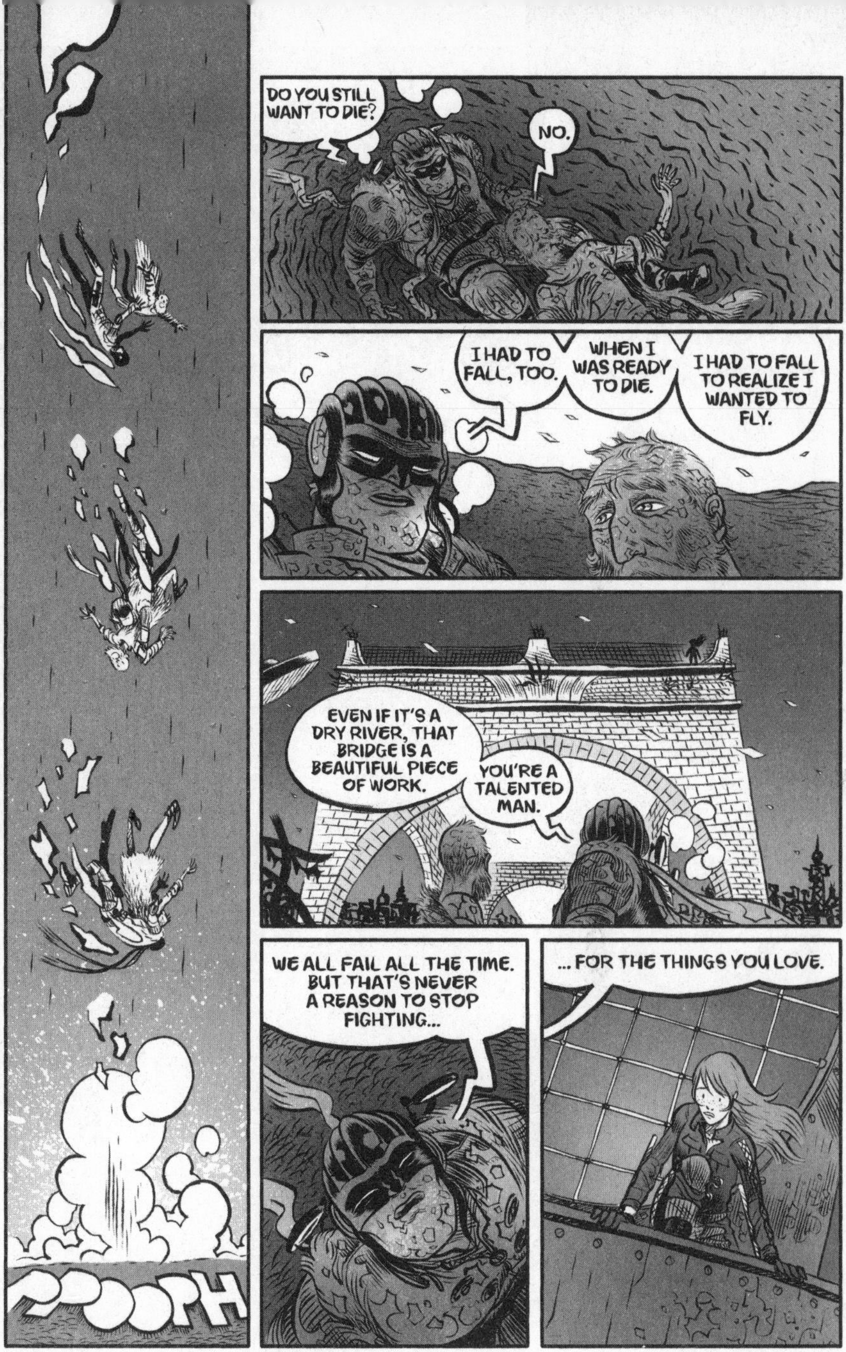
PFOOOPH
DO YOU STILL WANT TO DIE?
NO.
I HAD TO FALL, TOO.
WHEN I WAS READY TO DIE.
I HAD TO FALL TO REALIZE I WANTED TO FLY.
EVEN IF IT'S A DRY RIVER, THAT BRIDGE IS A BEAUTIFUL PIECE OF WORK.
YOU'RE A TALENTED MAN.
WE ALL FAIL ALL THE TIME. BUT THAT'S NEVER A REASON TO STOP FIGHTING...
... FOR THE THINGS YOU LOVE.

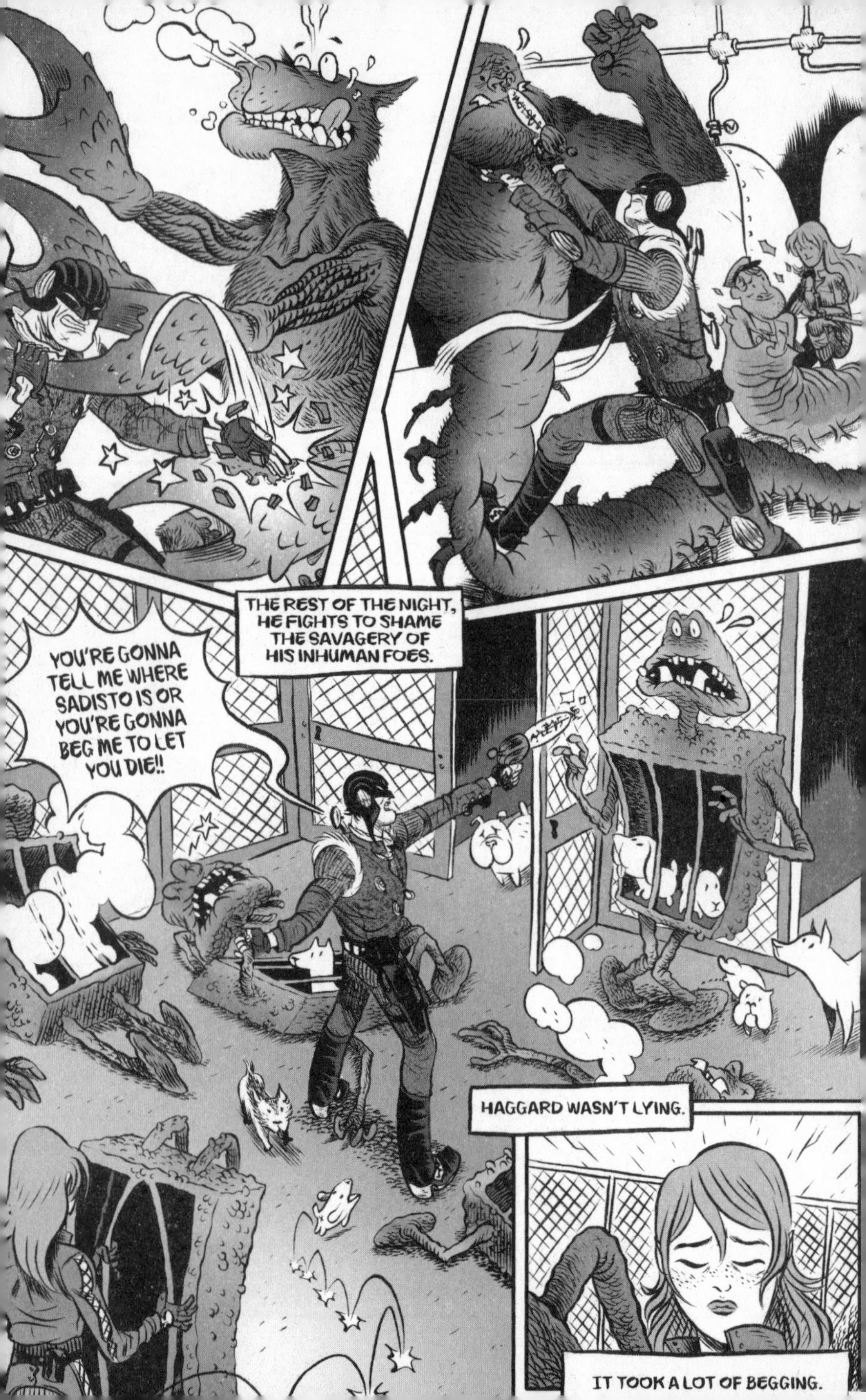

THE REST OF THE NIGHT, HE FIGHTS TO SHAME THE SAVAGERY OF HIS INHUMAN FOES.
YOU'RE GONNA TELL ME WHERE SADISTO IS OR YOU'RE GONNA BEG ME TO LET YOU DIE!!
HAGGARD WASN'T LYING.
IT TOOK A LOT OF BEGGING.

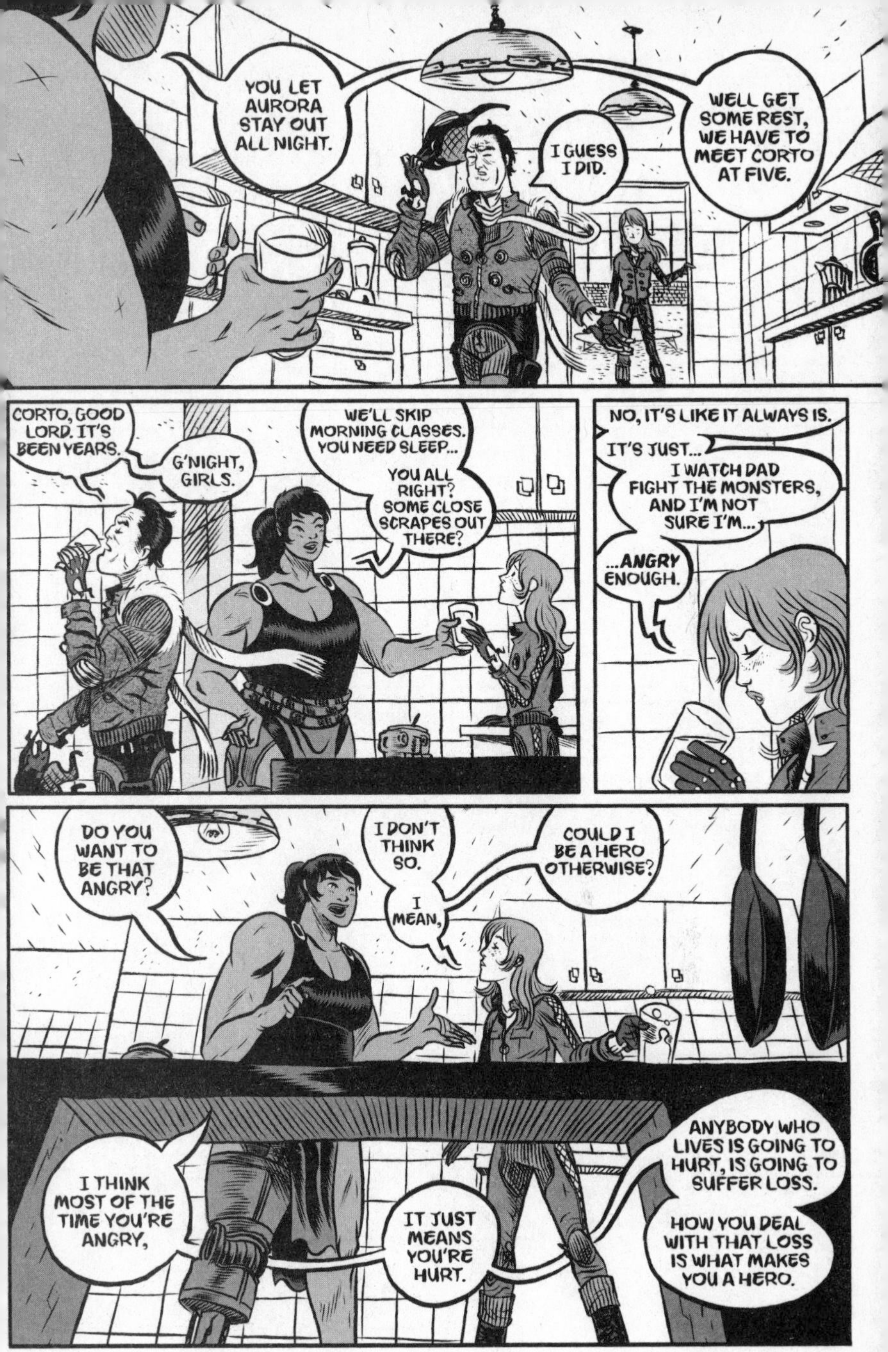
YOU LET AURORA STAY OUT ALL NIGHT.
I GUESS I DID.
WELL GET SOME REST, WE HAVE TO MEET CORTO AT FIVE.
CORTO, GOOD LORD. IT'S BEEN YEARS.
G'NIGHT, GIRLS.
WE'LL SKIP MORNING CLASSES. YOU NEED SLEEP...
YOU ALL RIGHT? SOME CLOSE SCRAPES OUT THERE?
NO, IT'S LIKE IT ALWAYS IS.
IT'S JUST...
I WATCH DAD FIGHT THE MONSTERS, AND I'M NOT SURE I'M...
...ANGRY ENOUGH.
DO YOU WANT TO BE THAT ANGRY?
I DON'T THINK SO.
I MEAN,
COULD I BE A HERO OTHERWISE?
I THINK MOST OF THE TIME YOU'RE ANGRY,
IT JUST MEANS YOU'RE HURT.
ANYBODY WHO LIVES IS GOING TO HURT, IS GOING TO SUFFER LOSS.
HOW YOU DEAL WITH THAT LOSS IS WHAT MAKES YOU A HERO.

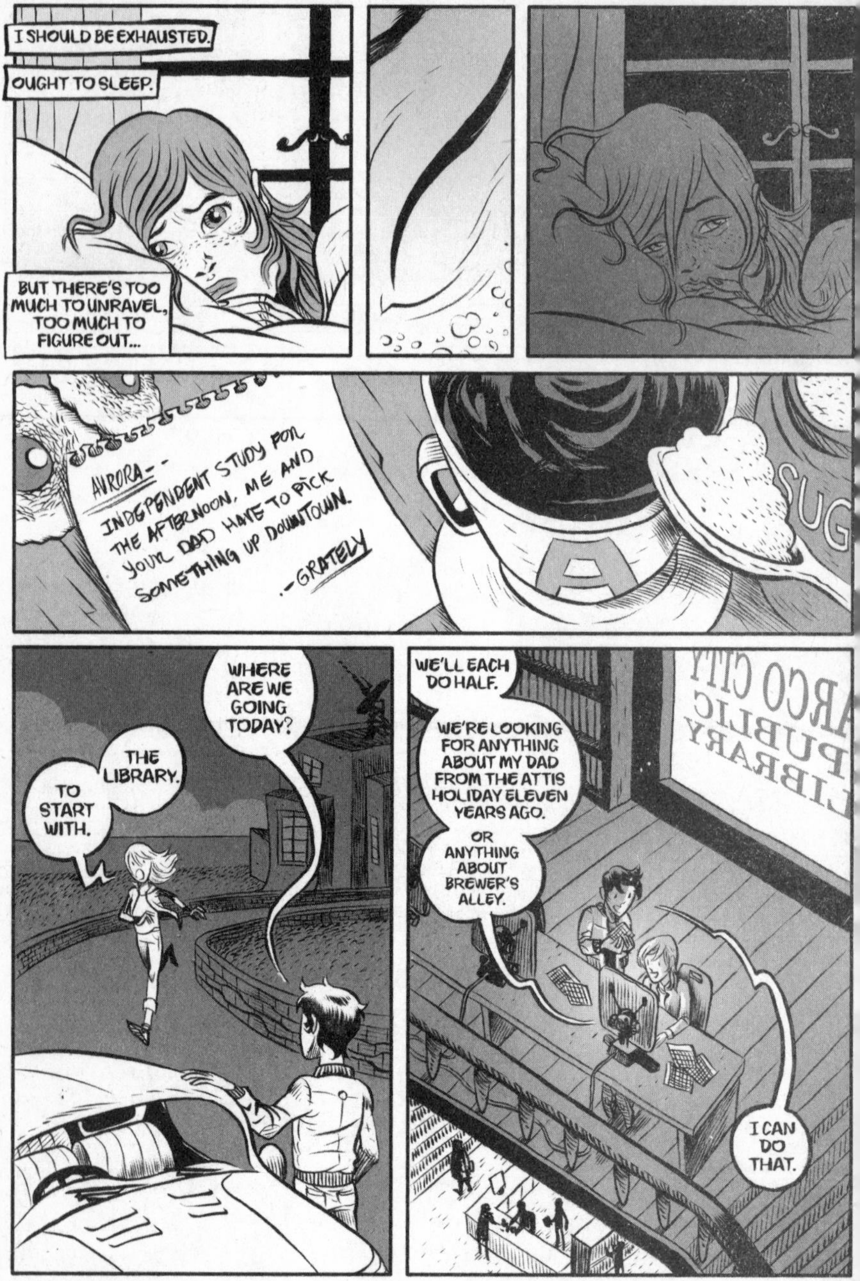
I SHOULD BE EXHAUSTED.
OUGHT TO SLEEP.
BUT THERE'S TOO MUCH TO UNRAVEL, TOO MUCH TO FIGURE OUT...
AURORA--
INDEPENDENT STUDY FOR THE AFTERNOON. ME AND YOUR DAD HAVE TO PICK SOMETHING UP DOWNTOWN.
--GRATELY
SUG
WHERE ARE WE GOING TODAY?
THE LIBRARY.
TO START WITH.
WE'LL EACH DO HALF.
WE'RE LOOKING FOR ANYTHING ABOUT MY DAD FROM THE ATTIS HOLIDAY ELEVEN YEARS AGO.
OR ANYTHING ABOUT BREWER'S ALLEY.
ARCO CITY PUBLIC LIBRARY
I CAN DO THAT.

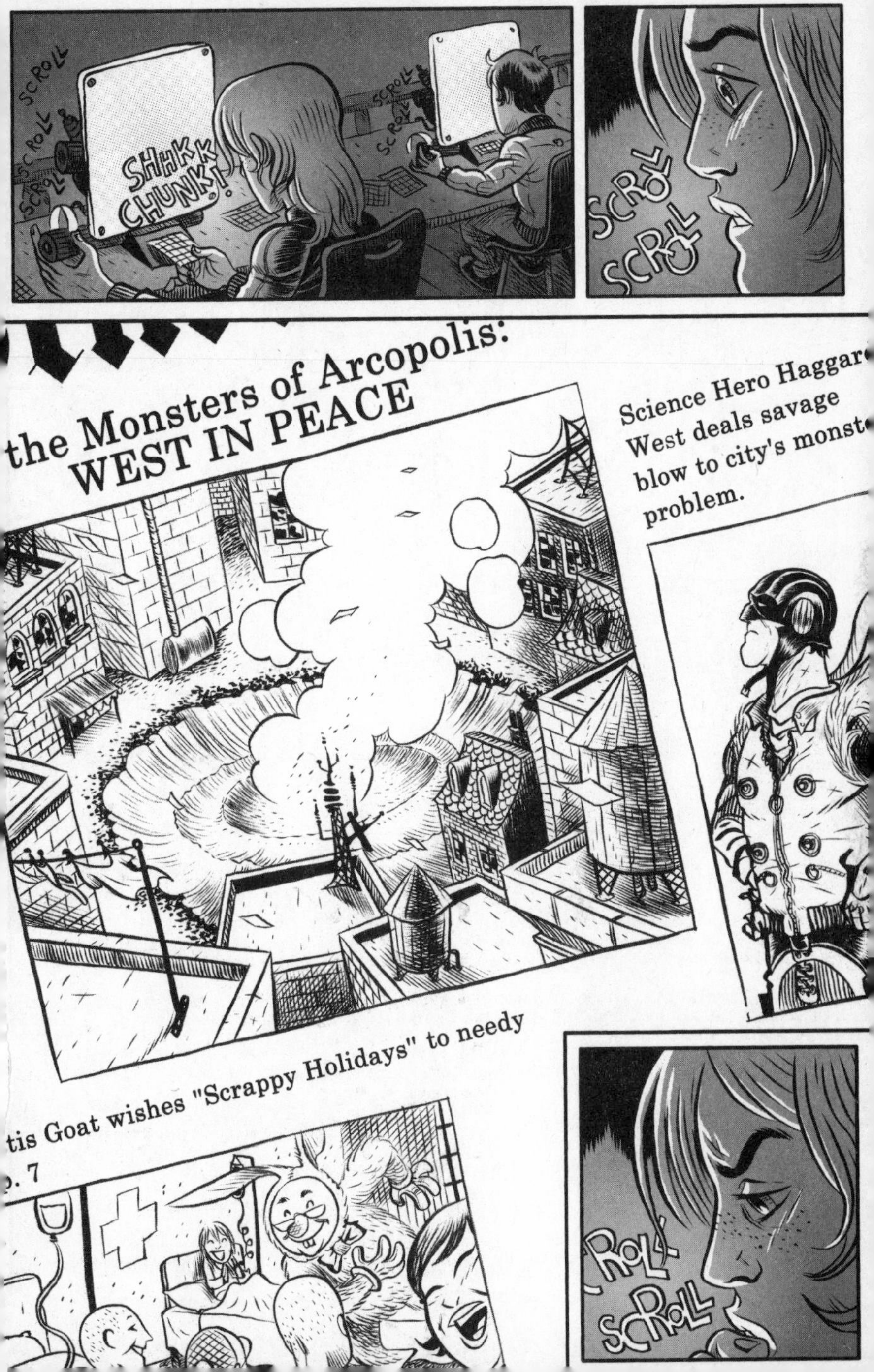
SCROLL
SCROLL
SCROLL
SCROLL
SCROLL
SHHKK CHUNK!
SCROLL
SCROLL
the Monsters of Arcopolis:
WEST IN PEACE
Science Hero Haggar
West deals savage
blow to city's monst
problem.
tis Goat wishes "Scrappy Holidays" to needy
. 7
ROLL
SCROLL

MONSTER MASH

HEROIC HAGGARD WEST DEFEATS MONSTERS WITH SCIENCE AND MUSCLE

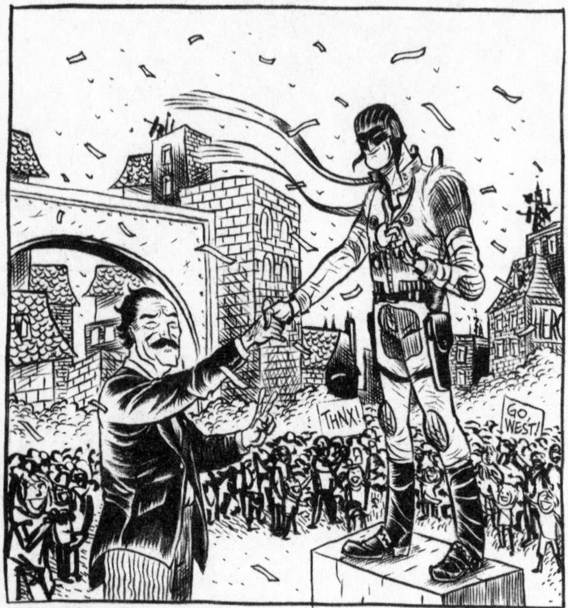
THNX!
GO, WEST!

PHOTO CREDIT: AC WIRE

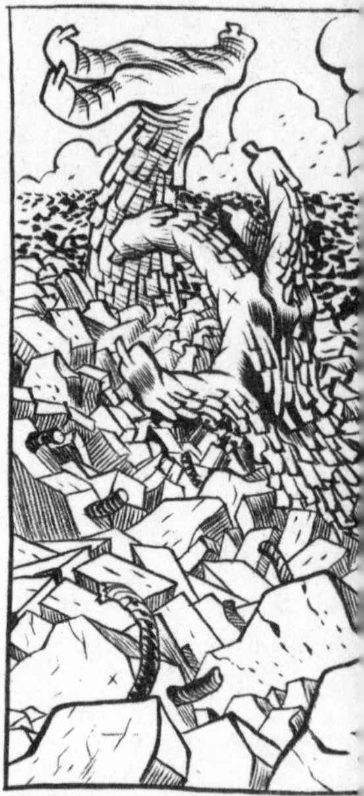

PHOTO CREDIT: S. GRATELY

After years of struggle, Arcopolis' own son Haggard West may have finally put an end to the inhuman menace threatening our city's children.

Using what he describes as a "Plasma Cannon," Haggard destroyed the entrance to the monsters' underground lair.

Dozens were surely killed in the initial blast, without the loss of a single human life.
The remaining monsters, a reckless and uneducated mob of swarthy psychopaths, will certainly succumb to starvation, infighting, or fatal despair in the coming months.

The Mayor described Mr. West as, "An inspiration and model for our young people. A self-made man, he exemplifies all the wealth and glory you can achieve through education, calisthenics, and a ceaseless dedication to the public good."

The people of Arcopolis have lived in the spreading shadow of the monster problem for nearly a decade now. Tonight those good people can rest a little easier.

Mr. West made his fortune through inventions as varied and invaluable as the Westwave Oven™, Carbon Copy™, West-o-Matic Gearbox™, and Catlick Straps™. But with the rise of the monsters, he found a new calling and turned his inestimable brain to the welfare of our children.

"I have a daughter," he said from the podium, "I know the fear we've had to live with for too long. Today, that ends."

He also gave credit for the conception and construction of the Plasma Cannon to his wife and partner, Rosetta West, and their assistant and photographer, Svetlana Goodley. The comely ladies of the West Manor were unfortunately delayed at the last moment and unable to attend the ceremony.

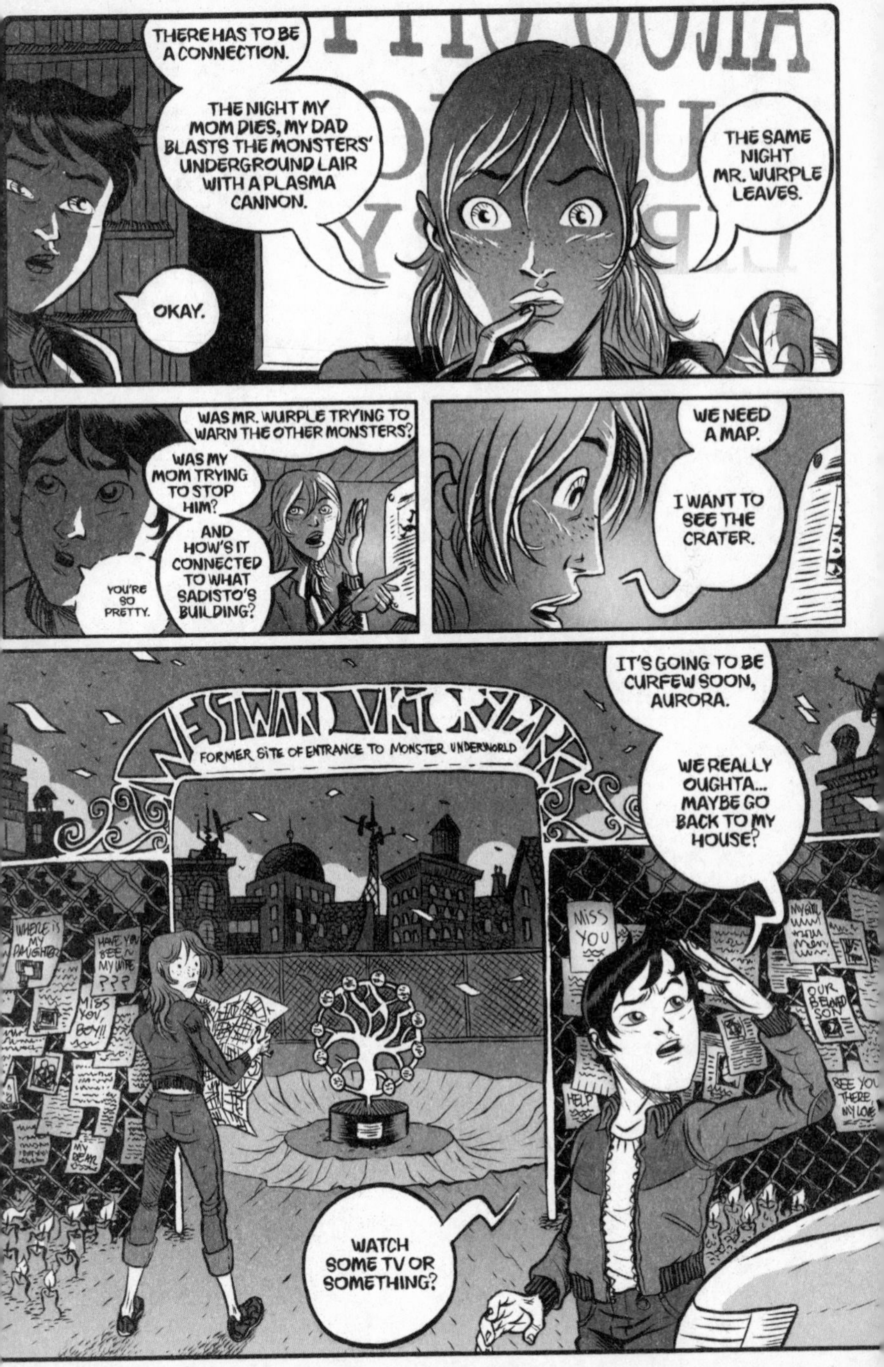
THERE HAS TO BE A CONNECTION.
THE NIGHT MY MOM DIES, MY DAD BLASTS THE MONSTERS' UNDERGROUND LAIR WITH A PLASMA CANNON.
THE SAME NIGHT MR. WURPLE LEAVES.
OKAY.
WAS MR. WURPLE TRYING TO WARN THE OTHER MONSTERS?
WAS MY MOM TRYING TO STOP HIM?
AND HOW'S IT CONNECTED TO WHAT SADISTO'S BUILDING?
YOU'RE SO PRETTY.
WE NEED A MAP.
I WANT TO SEE THE CRATER.
FORMER SITE OF ENTRANCE TO MONSTER UNDERWORLD
IT'S GOING TO BE CURFEW SOON, AURORA.
WE REALLY OUGHTA... MAYBE GO BACK TO MY HOUSE?
WATCH SOME TV OR SOMETHING?
WHERE IS MY DAUGHTER
HAVE YOU SEEN MY WIFE ???
MISS YOU, BOY!!
MY DEAR
MISS YOU
OUR BELOVED SON
HELP
SEE YOU THERE MY LOVE

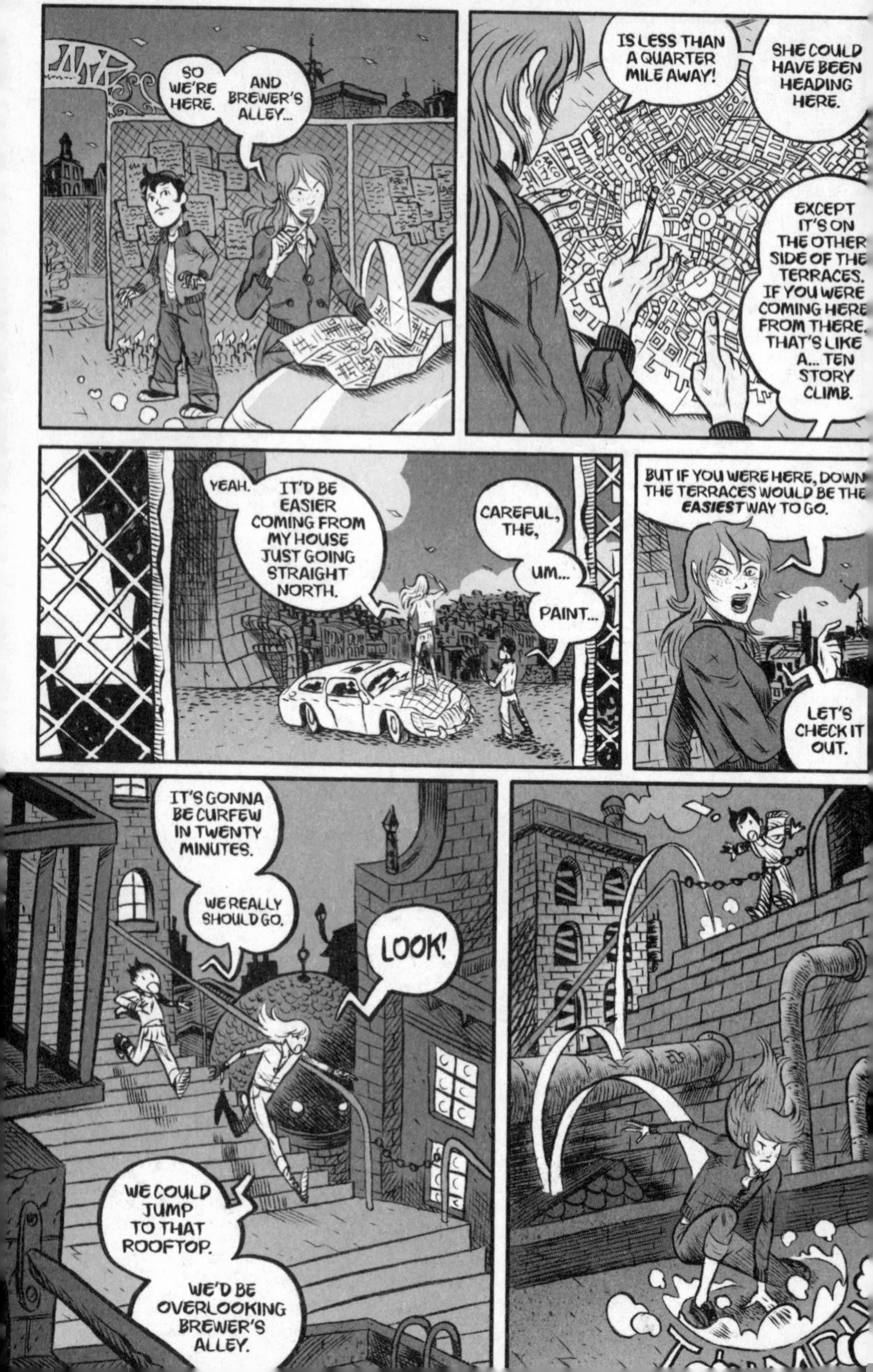
SO WE'RE HERE.
AND BREWER'S ALLEY...
IS LESS THAN A QUARTER MILE AWAY!
SHE COULD HAVE BEEN HEADING HERE.
EXCEPT IT'S ON THE OTHER SIDE OF THE TERRACES. IF YOU WERE COMING HERE FROM THERE, THAT'S LIKE A... TEN STORY CLIMB.
YEAH.
IT'D BE EASIER COMING FROM MY HOUSE JUST GOING STRAIGHT NORTH.
CAREFUL, THE,
UM...
PAINT...
BUT IF YOU WERE HERE, DOWN THE TERRACES WOULD BE THE EASIEST WAY TO GO.
LET'S CHECK IT OUT.
IT'S GONNA BE CURFEW IN TWENTY MINUTES.
WE REALLY SHOULD GO.
LOOK!
WE COULD JUMP TO THAT ROOFTOP.
WE'D BE OVERLOOKING BREWER'S ALLEY.

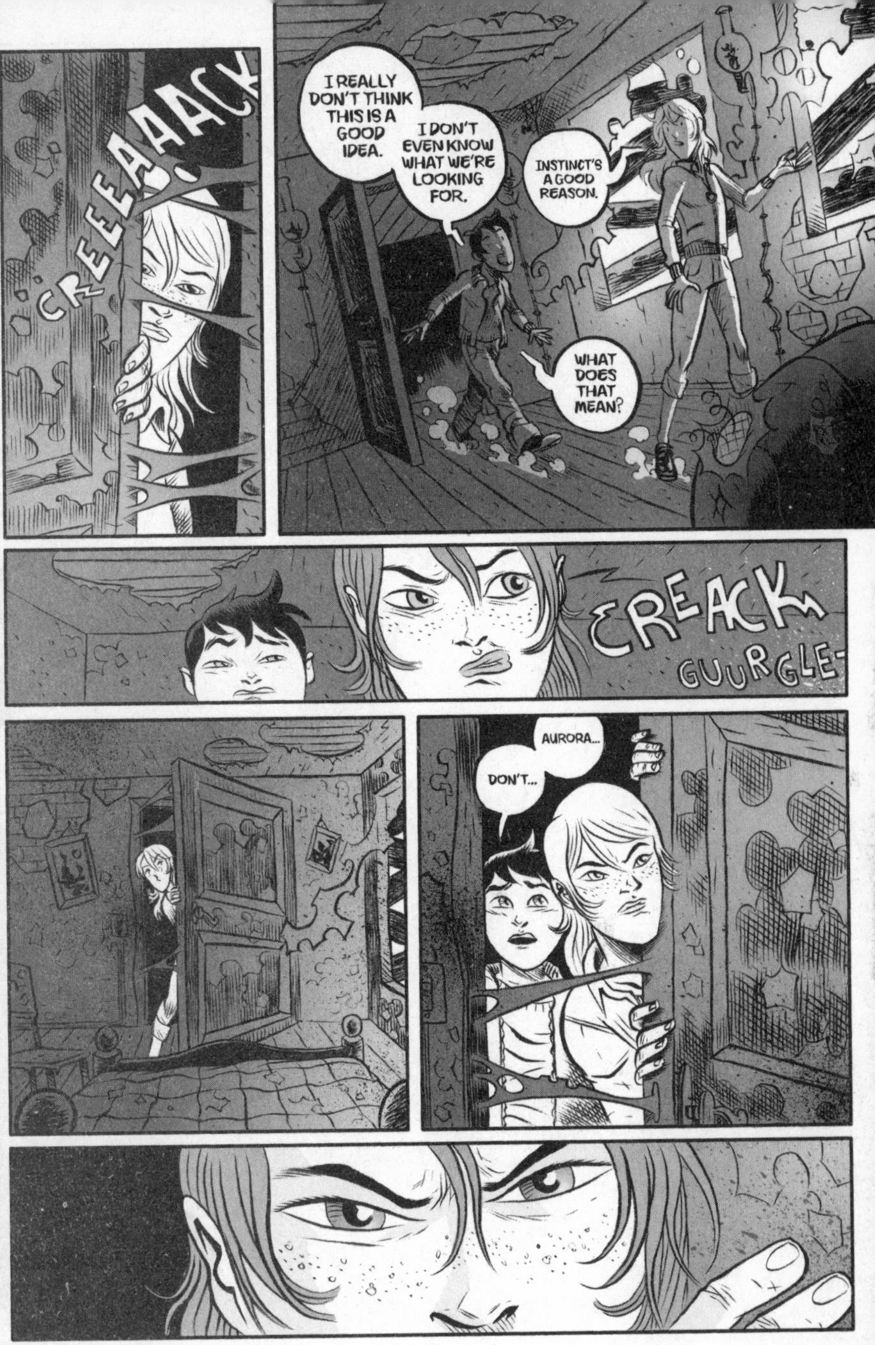
CREEAAACK
I REALLY DON'T THINK THIS IS A GOOD IDEA.
I DON'T EVEN KNOW WHAT WE'RE LOOKING FOR.
INSTINCT'S A GOOD REASON.
WHAT DOES THAT MEAN?
CREACK
GUURGLE-
AURORA...
DON'T...

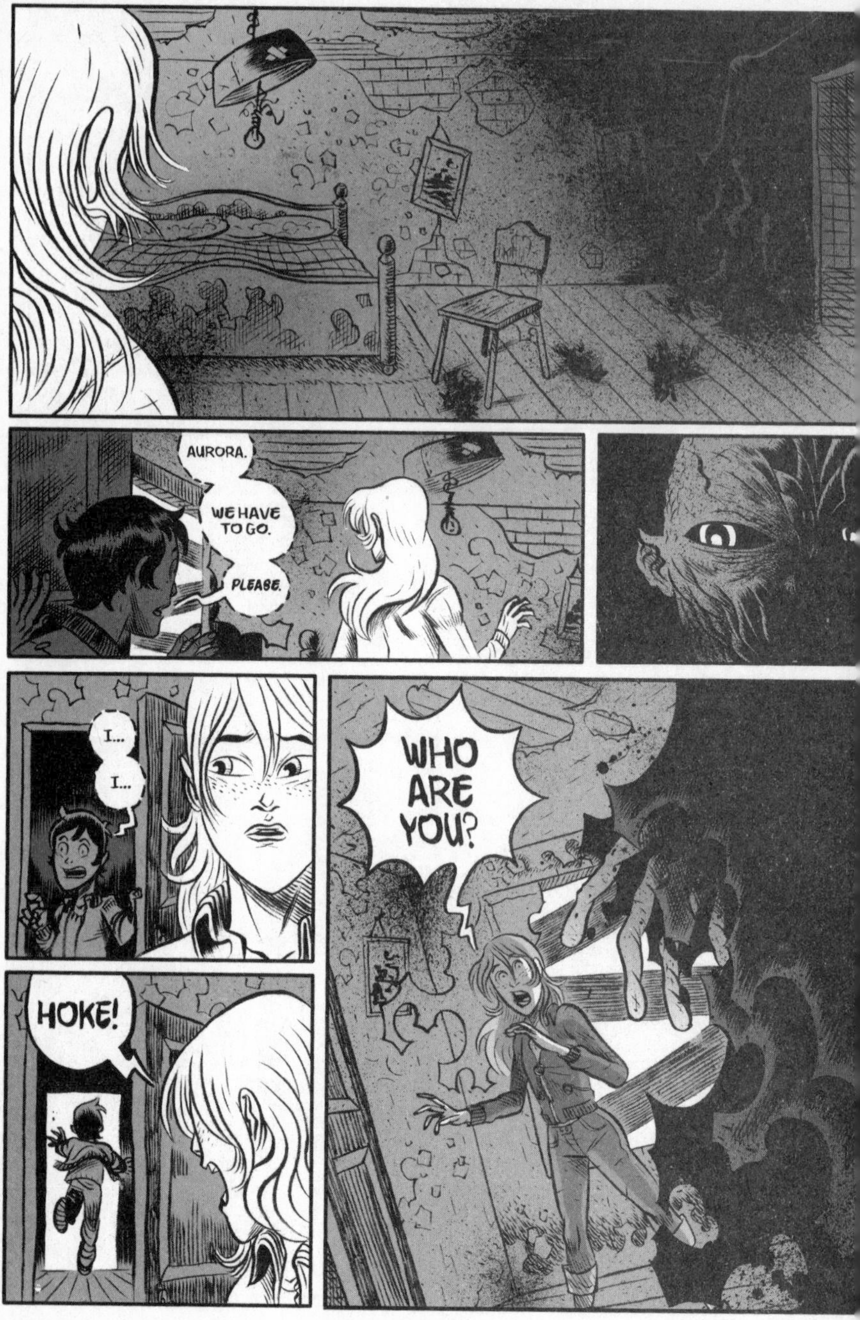
AURORA.
WE HAVE TO GO.
PLEASE.
I...
I...
WHO ARE YOU?
HOKE!

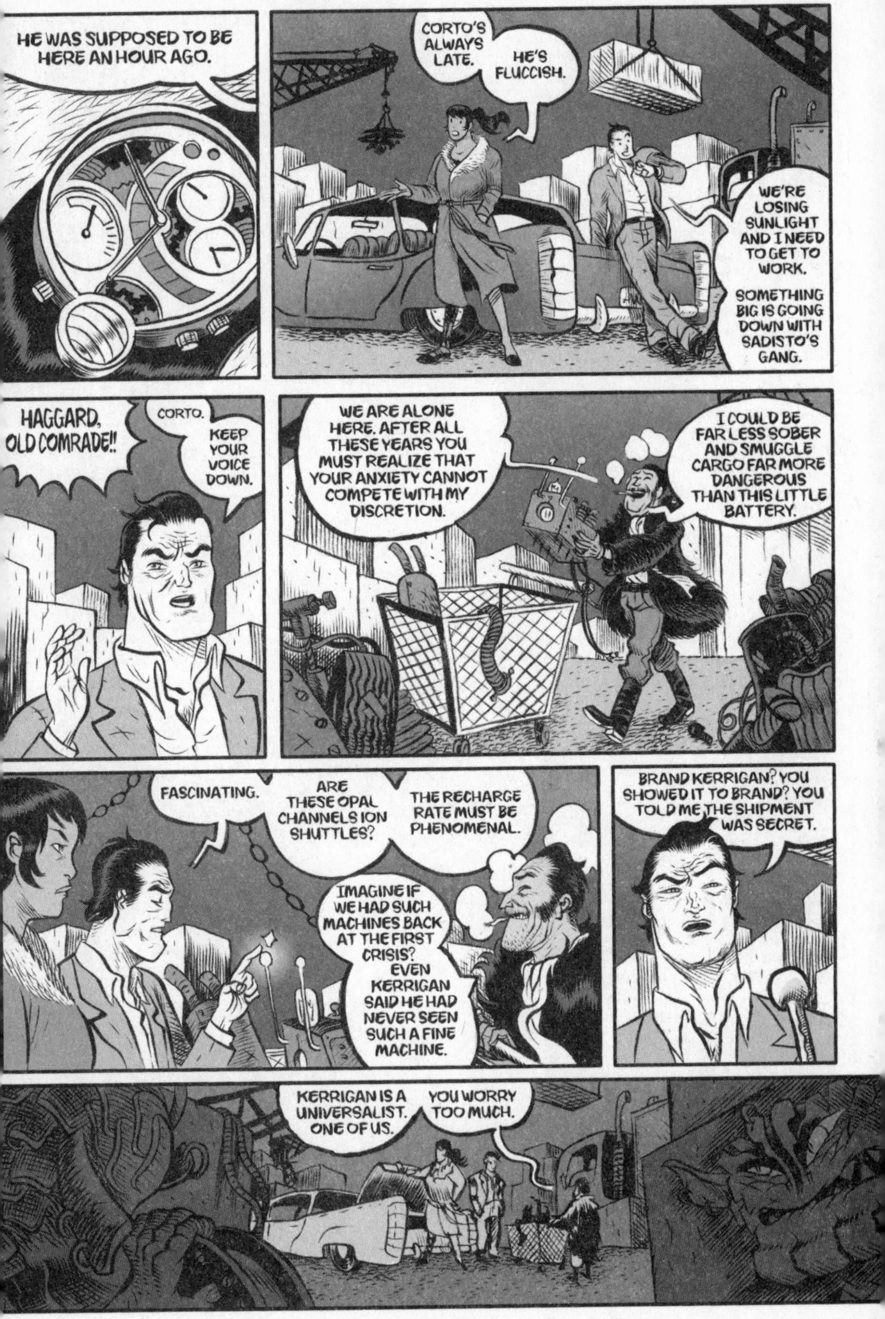
HE WAS SUPPOSED TO BE HERE AN HOUR AGO.
CORTO'S ALWAYS LATE.
HE'S FLUCCISH.
WE'RE LOSING SUNLIGHT AND I NEED TO GET TO WORK.
SOMETHING BIG IS GOING DOWN WITH SADISTO'S GANG.
HAGGARD, OLD COMRADE!!
CORTO.
KEEP YOUR VOICE DOWN.
WE ARE ALONE HERE. AFTER ALL THESE YEARS YOU MUST REALIZE THAT YOUR ANXIETY CANNOT COMPETE WITH MY DISCRETION.
I COULD BE FAR LESS SOBER AND SMUGGLE CARGO FAR MORE DANGEROUS THAN THIS LITTLE BATTERY.
FASCINATING.
ARE THESE OPAL CHANNELS ION SHUTTLES?
THE RECHARGE RATE MUST BE PHENOMENAL.
IMAGINE IF WE HAD SUCH MACHINES BACK AT THE FIRST CRISIS?
EVEN KERRIGAN SAID HE HAD NEVER SEEN SUCH A FINE MACHINE.
BRAND KERRIGAN? YOU SHOWED IT TO BRAND? YOU TOLD ME THE SHIPMENT WAS SECRET.
KERRIGAN IS A UNIVERSALIST. ONE OF US.
YOU WORRY TOO MUCH.

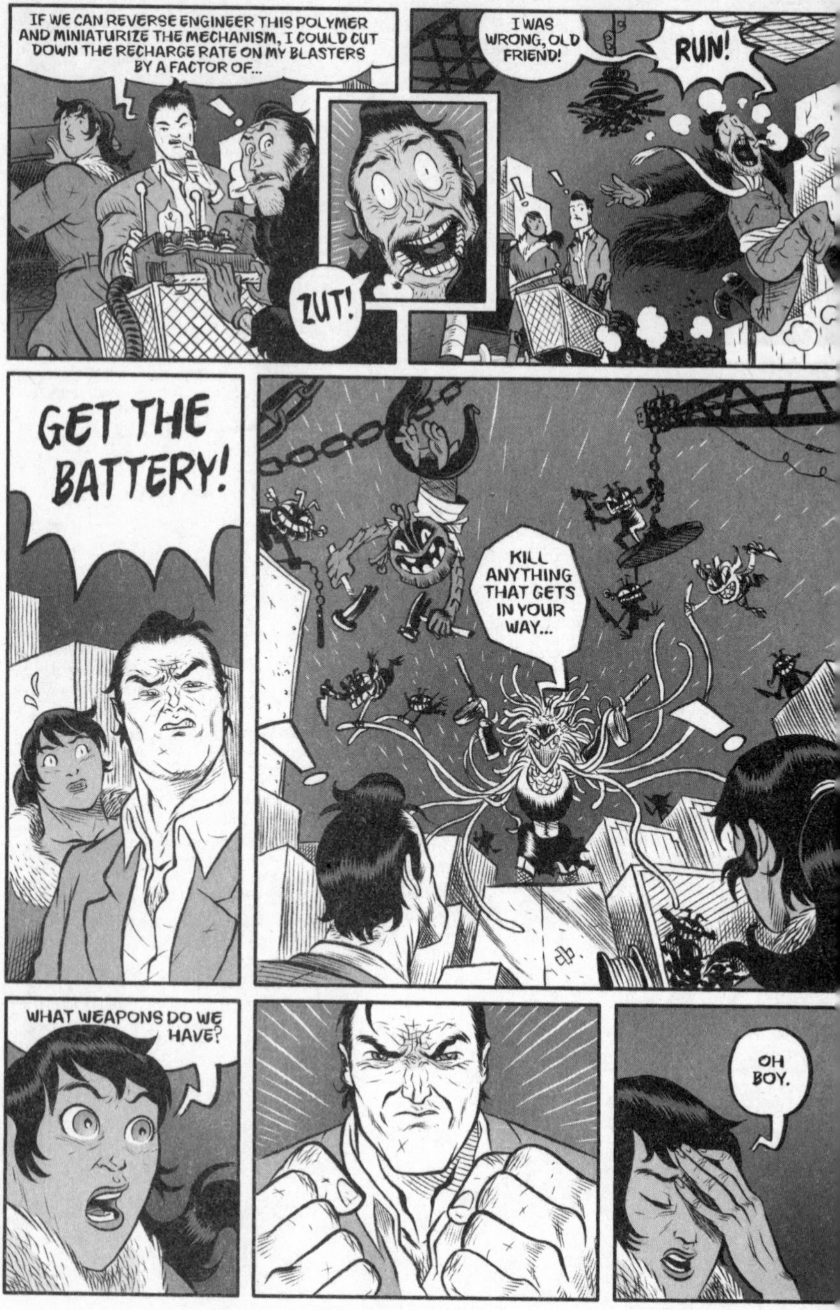
IF WE CAN REVERSE ENGINEER THIS POLYMER AND MINIATURIZE THE MECHANISM, I COULD CUT DOWN THE RECHARGE RATE ON MY BLASTERS BY A FACTOR OF...
ZUT!
I WAS WRONG, OLD FRIEND!
RUN!
GET THE BATTERY!
KILL ANYTHING THAT GETS IN YOUR WAY...
WHAT WEAPONS DO WE HAVE?
OH BOY.

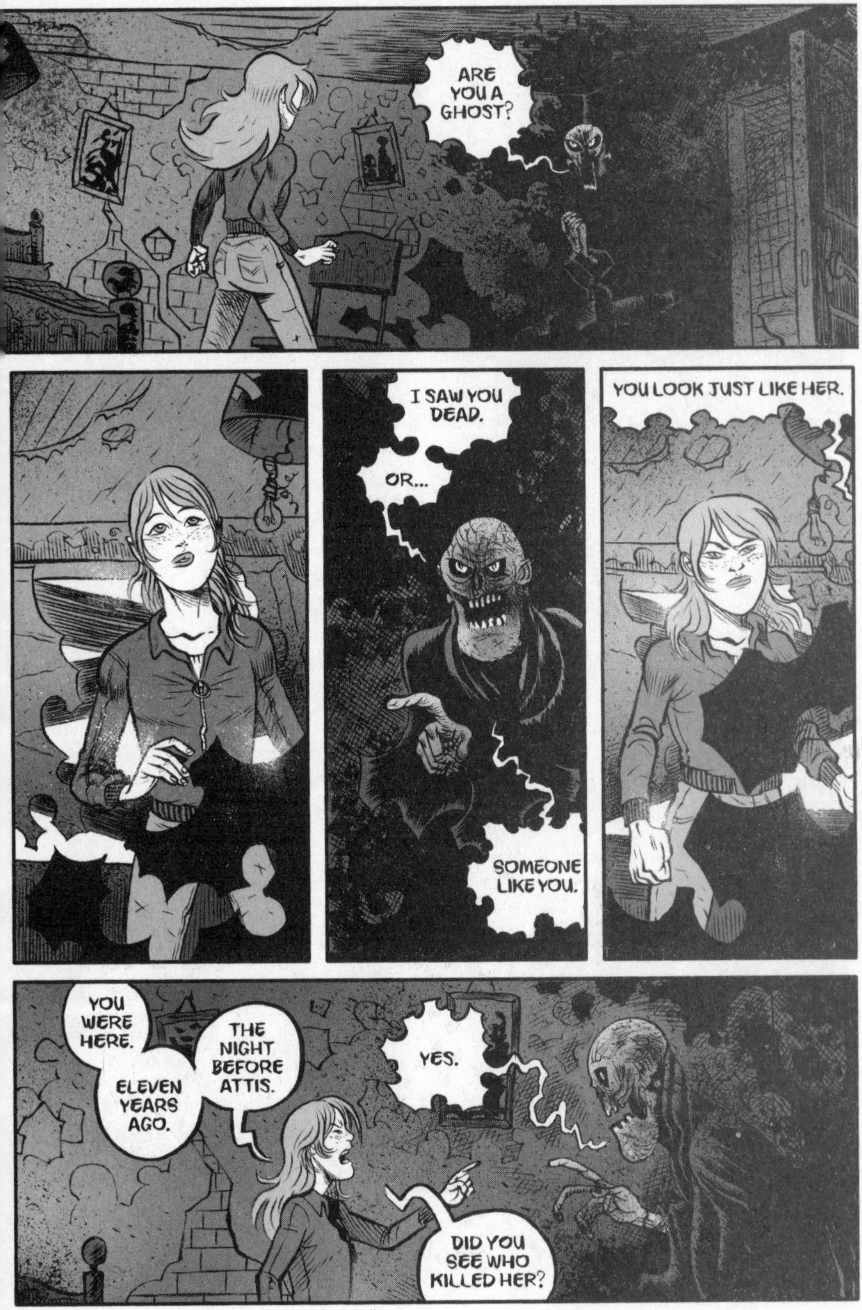
ARE YOU A GHOST?
I SAW YOU DEAD.
OR...
SOMEONE LIKE YOU.
YOU LOOK JUST LIKE HER.
YOU WERE HERE.
ELEVEN YEARS AGO.
THE NIGHT BEFORE ATTIS.
YES.
DID YOU SEE WHO KILLED HER?

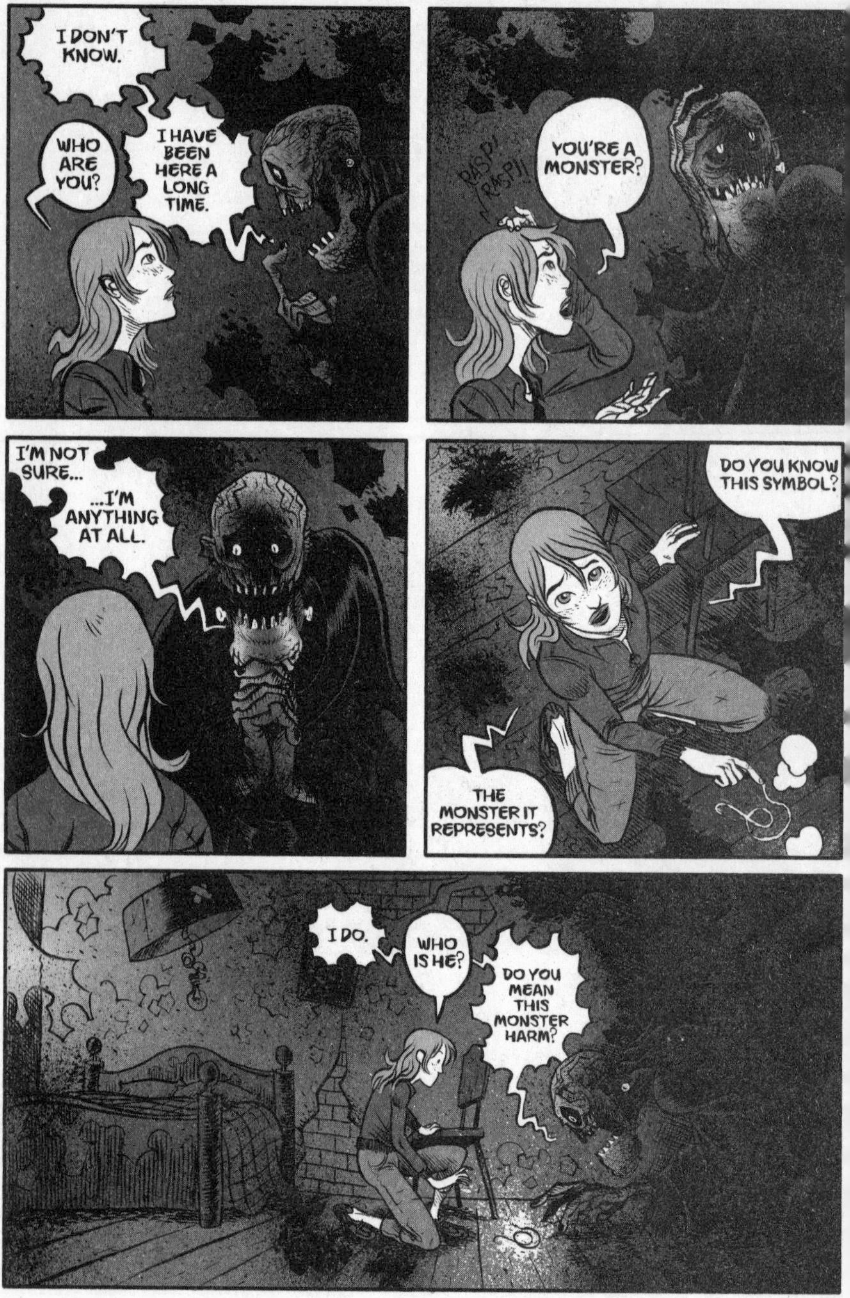
I DON'T KNOW.
WHO ARE YOU?
I HAVE BEEN HERE A LONG TIME.
RASP! RASP!!
YOU'RE A MONSTER?
I'M NOT SURE...
...I'M ANYTHING AT ALL.
DO YOU KNOW THIS SYMBOL?
THE MONSTER IT REPRESENTS?
I DO.
WHO IS HE?
DO YOU MEAN THIS MONSTER HARM?

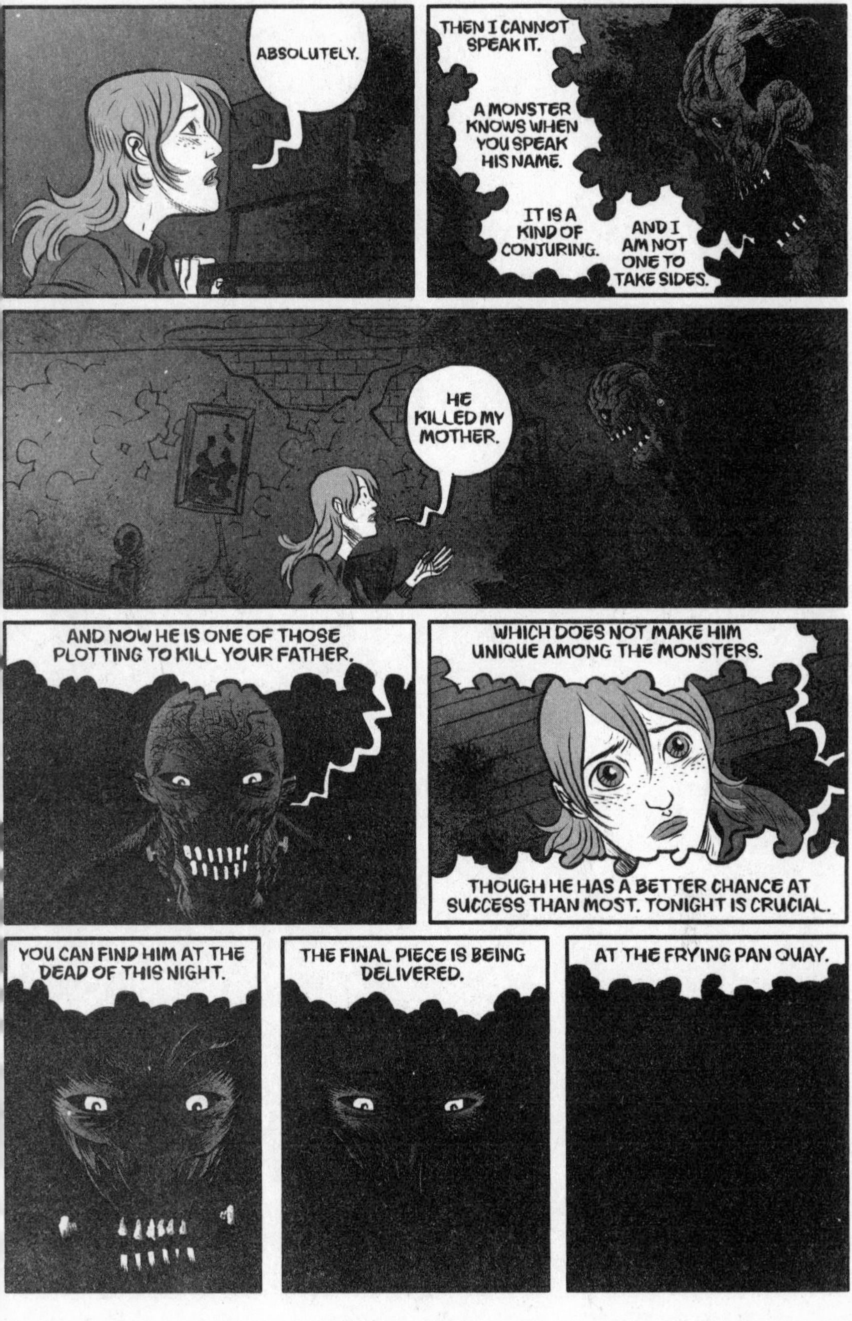
ABSOLUTELY.
THEN I CANNOT SPEAK IT.
A MONSTER KNOWS WHEN YOU SPEAK HIS NAME.
IT IS A KIND OF CONJURING.
AND I AM NOT ONE TO TAKE SIDES.
HE KILLED MY MOTHER.
AND NOW HE IS ONE OF THOSE PLOTTING TO KILL YOUR FATHER.
WHICH DOES NOT MAKE HIM UNIQUE AMONG THE MONSTERS.
THOUGH HE HAS A BETTER CHANCE AT SUCCESS THAN MOST. TONIGHT IS CRUCIAL.
YOU CAN FIND HIM AT THE DEAD OF THIS NIGHT.
THE FINAL PIECE IS BEING DELIVERED.
AT THE FRYING PAN QUAY.

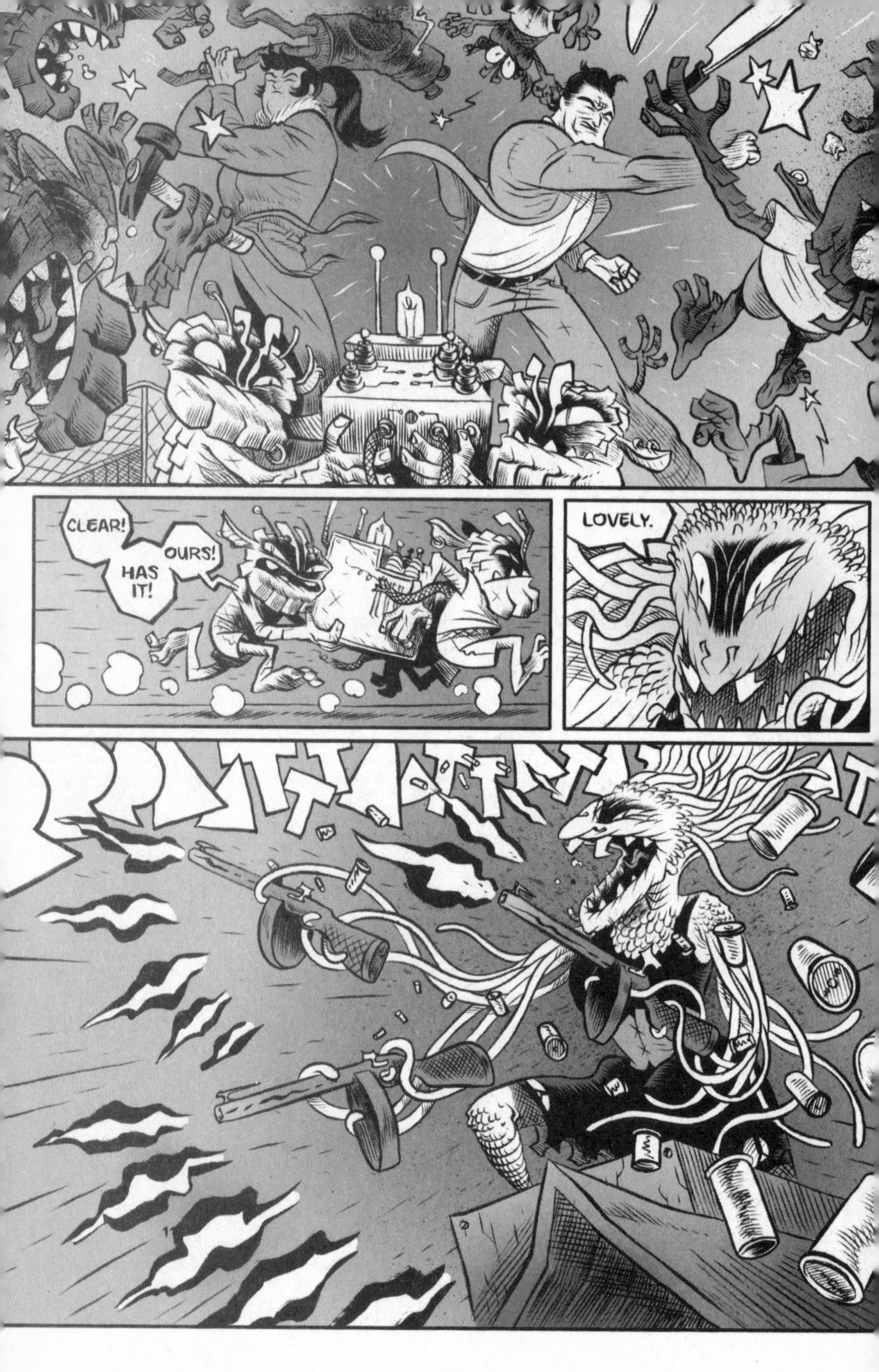
CLEAR!
OURS!
HAS IT!
LOVELY.

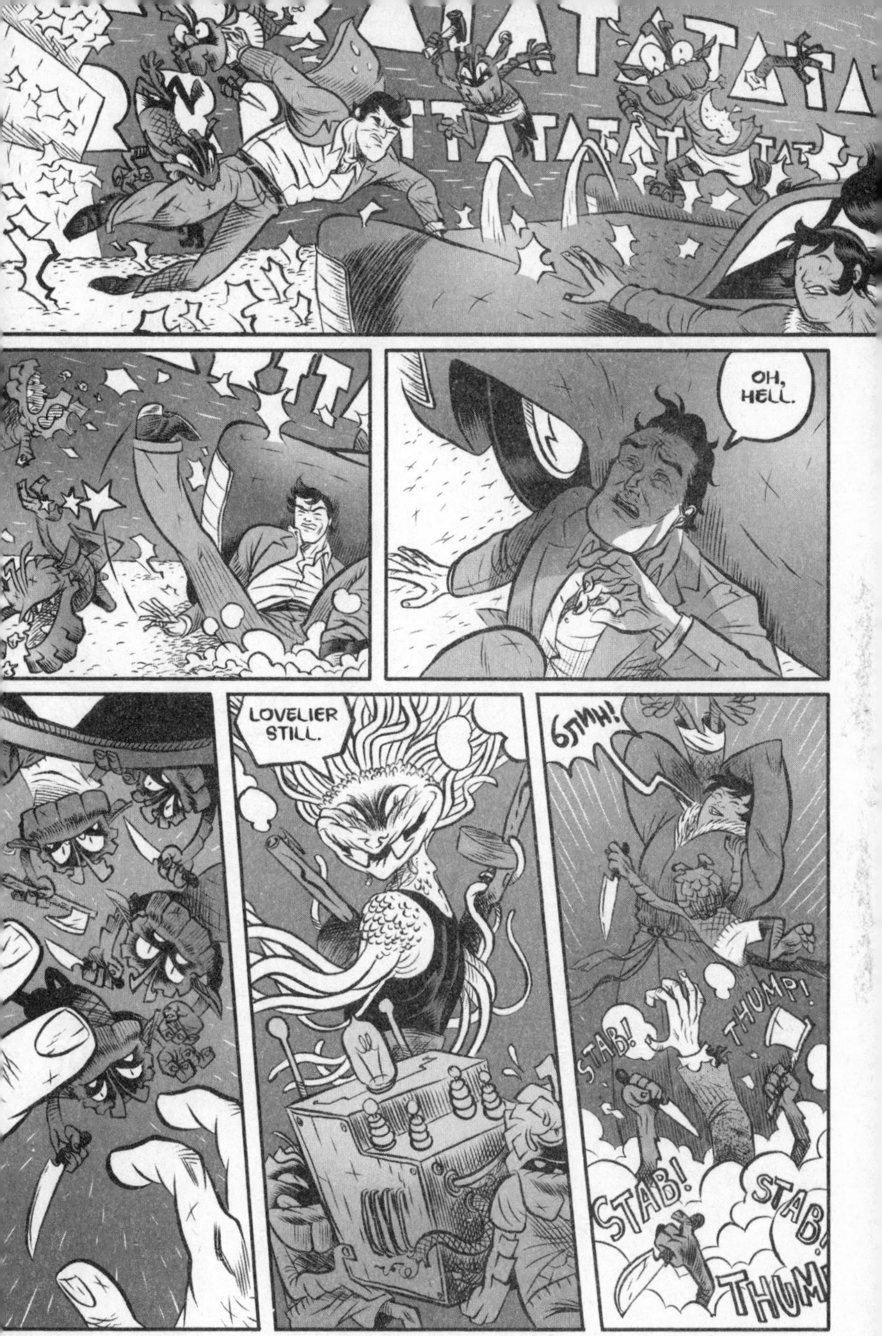

OH, HELL.
LOVELIER STILL.
STAB!
THUMP!
STAB!
STAB!

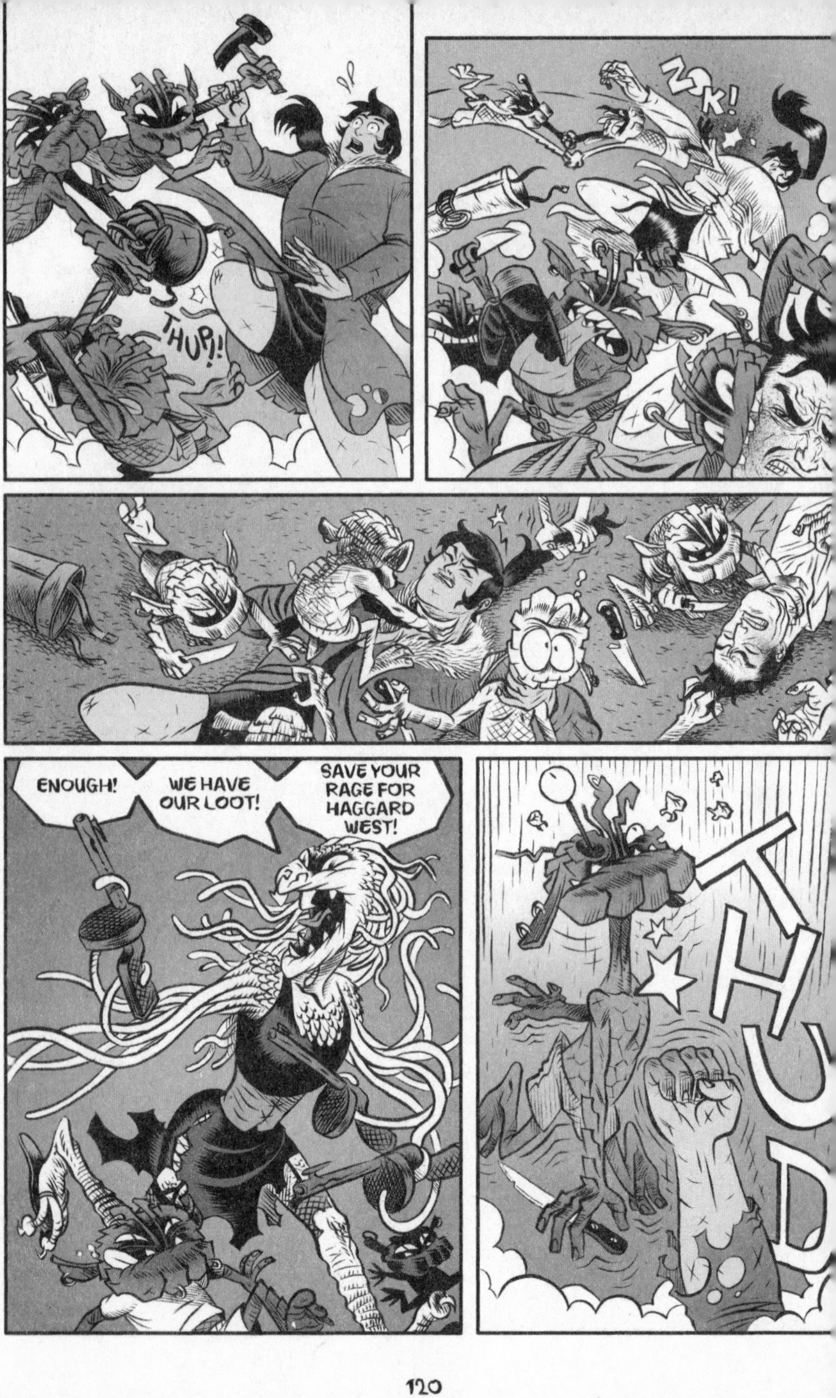
THUP!!
ZOK!
ENOUGH!
WE HAVE OUR LOOT!
SAVE YOUR RAGE FOR HAGGARD WEST!
THUD

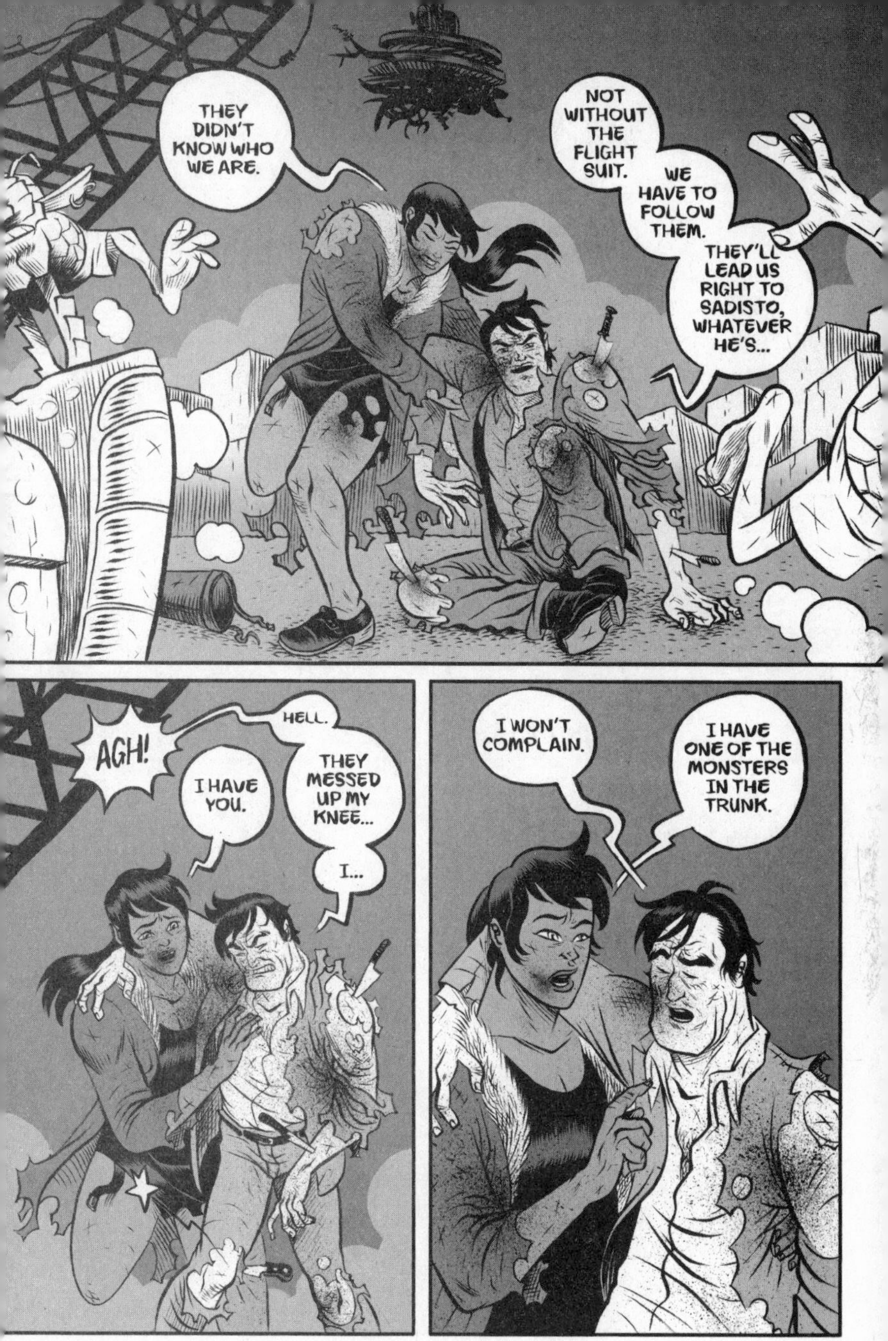
THEY DIDN'T KNOW WHO WE ARE.
NOT WITHOUT THE FLIGHT SUIT.
WE HAVE TO FOLLOW THEM.
THEY'LL LEAD US RIGHT TO SADISTO, WHATEVER HE'S...
AGH!
HELL.
I HAVE YOU.
THEY MESSED UP MY KNEE...
I...
I WON'T COMPLAIN.
I HAVE ONE OF THE MONSTERS IN THE TRUNK.

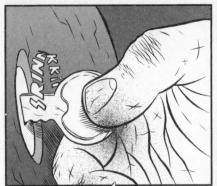

MURDER YOU BOTH YOU FILTHY UNMADE BABY-HUSKS!

YOU DON'T RECOGNIZE ME.

HOW ABOUT NOW?

...HAGGARD WEST!!!

WHERE'S MEDULA GOING?

ALLS I KNOW, ALLS I KNOW IS OVER EASY, SWEAR TO THE BOSS, SALT IN MY EYES.

OVER EASY SHE SAID.

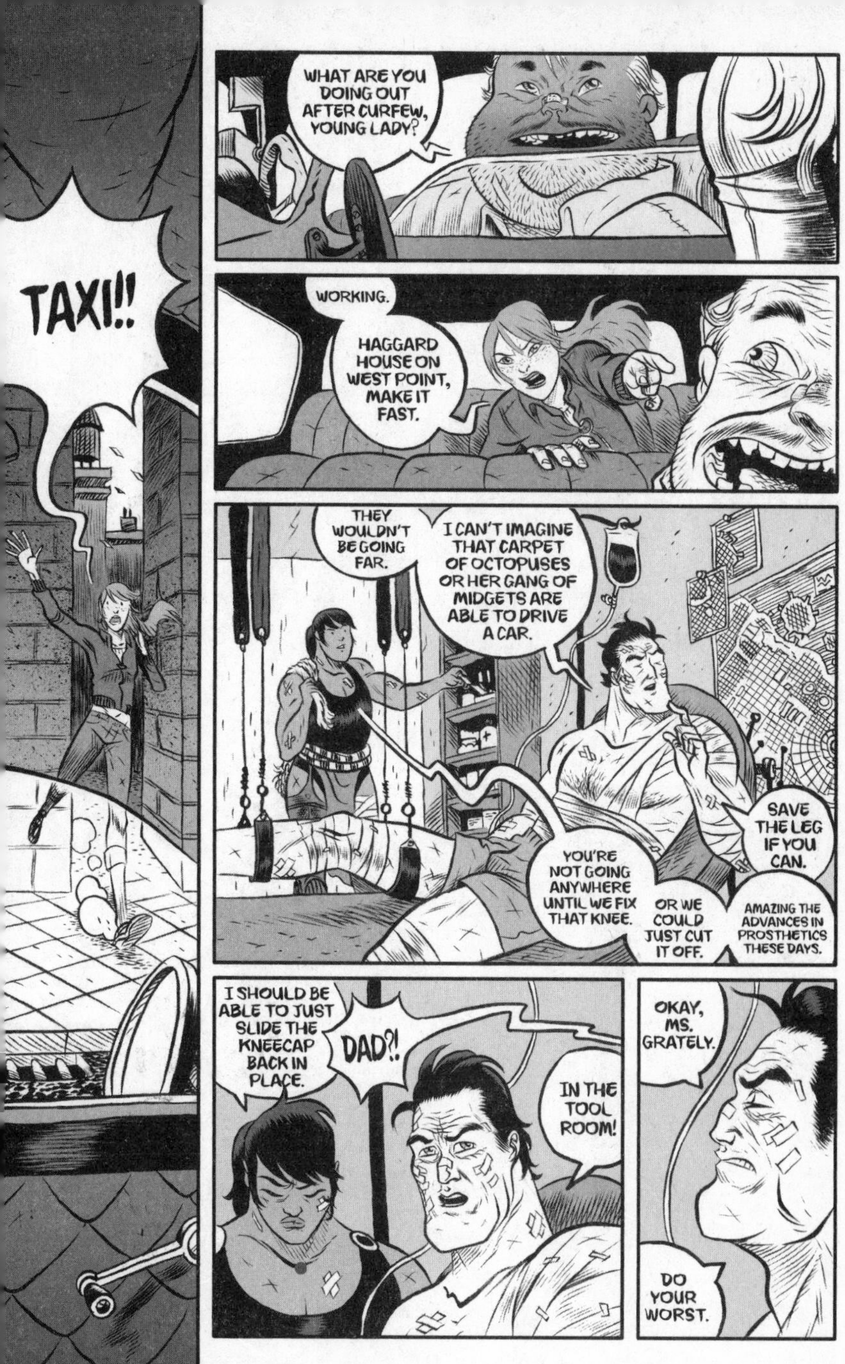
TAXI!!
WHAT ARE YOU DOING OUT AFTER CURFEW, YOUNG LADY?
WORKING.
HAGGARD HOUSE ON WEST POINT, MAKE IT FAST.
THEY WOULDN'T BE GOING FAR.
I CAN'T IMAGINE THAT CARPET OF OCTOPUSES OR HER GANG OF MIDGETS ARE ABLE TO DRIVE A CAR.
SAVE THE LEG IF YOU CAN.
YOU'RE NOT GOING ANYWHERE UNTIL WE FIX THAT KNEE.
OR WE COULD JUST CUT IT OFF.
AMAZING THE ADVANCES IN PROSTHETICS THESE DAYS.
I SHOULD BE ABLE TO JUST SLIDE THE KNEECAP BACK IN PLACE.
DAD?!
IN THE TOOL ROOM!
OKAY, MS. GRATELY.
DO YOUR WORST.

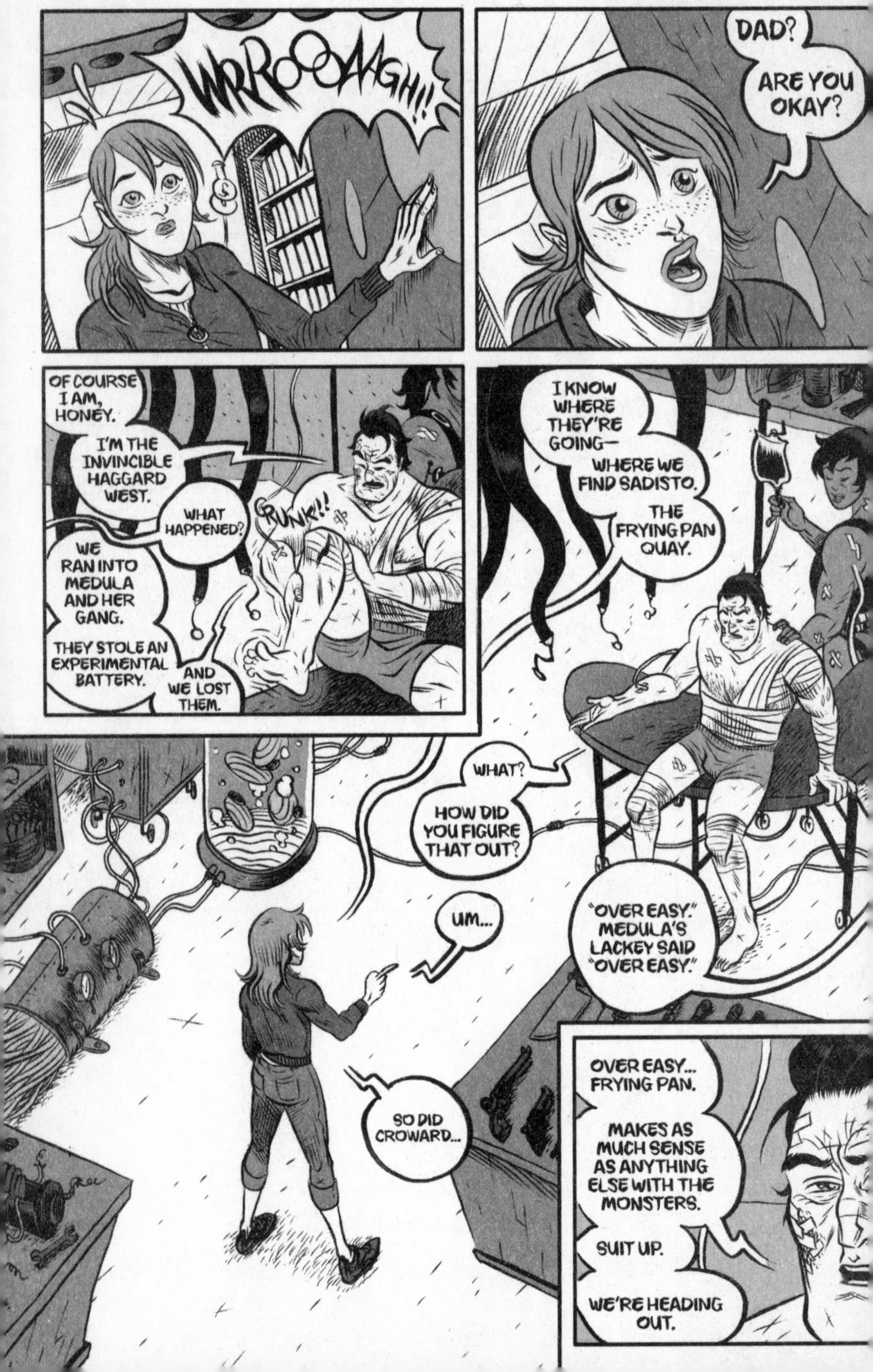

WRROOOAGH!!
DAD?
ARE YOU OKAY?
OF COURSE I AM, HONEY.
I'M THE INVINCIBLE HAGGARD WEST.
WHAT HAPPENED?
KRUNK!!
WE RAN INTO MEDULA AND HER GANG.
THEY STOLE AN EXPERIMENTAL BATTERY.
AND WE LOST THEM.
I KNOW WHERE THEY'RE GOING—
WHERE WE FIND SADISTO.
THE FRYING PAN QUAY.
WHAT?
HOW DID YOU FIGURE THAT OUT?
"OVER EASY." MEDULA'S LACKEY SAID "OVER EASY."
UM...
SO DID CROWARD...
OVER EASY... FRYING PAN.
MAKES AS MUCH SENSE AS ANYTHING ELSE WITH THE MONSTERS.
SUIT UP.
WE'RE HEADING OUT.

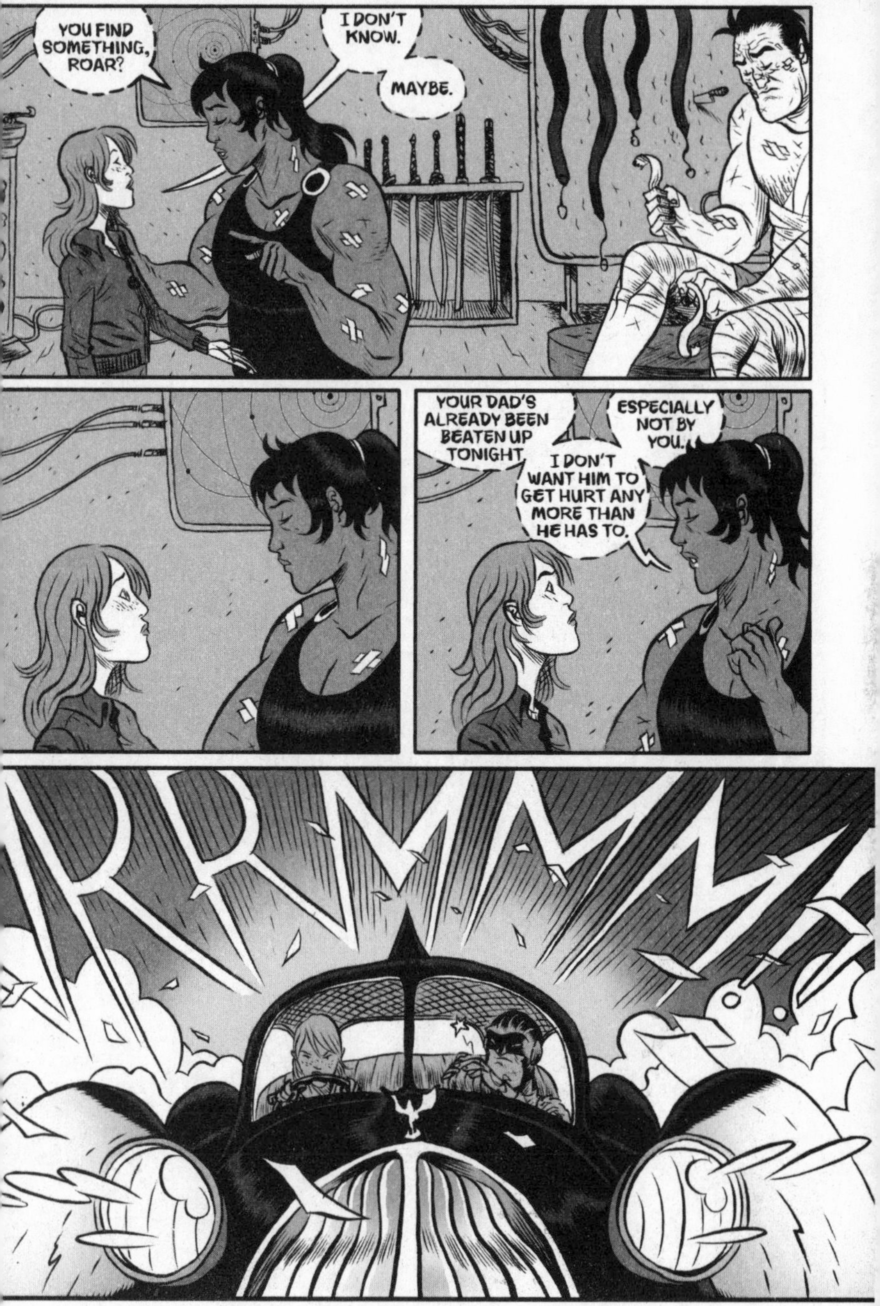
YOU FIND SOMETHING, ROAR?
I DON'T KNOW.
MAYBE.
YOUR DAD'S ALREADY BEEN BEATEN UP TONIGHT.
ESPECIALLY NOT BY YOU.
I DON'T WANT HIM TO GET HURT ANY MORE THAN HE HAS TO.
RRMMM

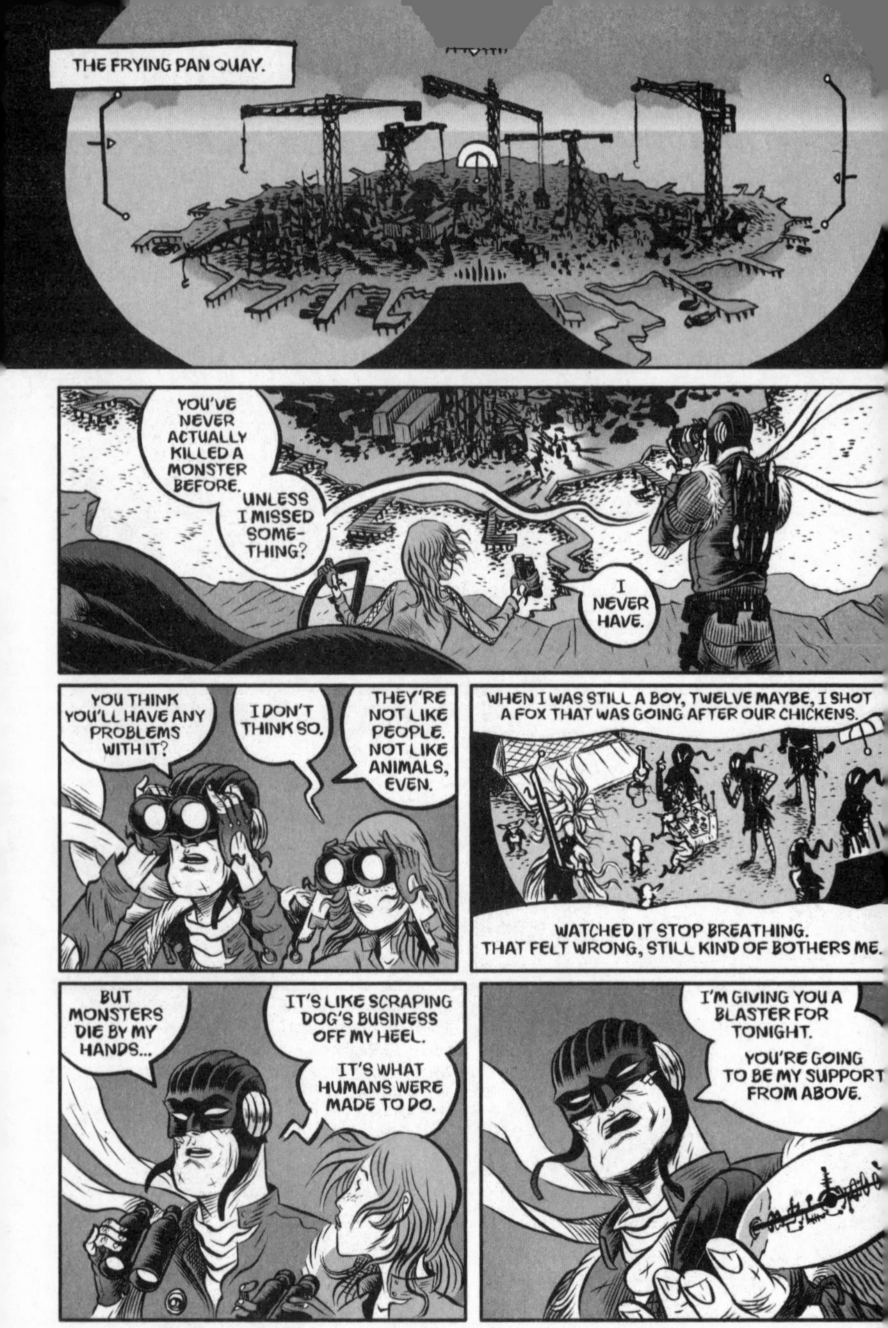
THE FRYING PAN QUAY.
YOU'VE NEVER ACTUALLY KILLED A MONSTER BEFORE.
UNLESS I MISSED SOME-THING?
I NEVER HAVE.
YOU THINK YOU'LL HAVE ANY PROBLEMS WITH IT?
I DON'T THINK SO.
THEY'RE NOT LIKE PEOPLE. NOT LIKE ANIMALS, EVEN.
WHEN I WAS STILL A BOY, TWELVE MAYBE, I SHOT A FOX THAT WAS GOING AFTER OUR CHICKENS.
WATCHED IT STOP BREATHING. THAT FELT WRONG, STILL KIND OF BOTHERS ME.
BUT MONSTERS DIE BY MY HANDS...
IT'S LIKE SCRAPING DOG'S BUSINESS OFF MY HEEL.
IT'S WHAT HUMANS WERE MADE TO DO.
I'M GIVING YOU A BLASTER FOR TONIGHT.
YOU'RE GOING TO BE MY SUPPORT FROM ABOVE.

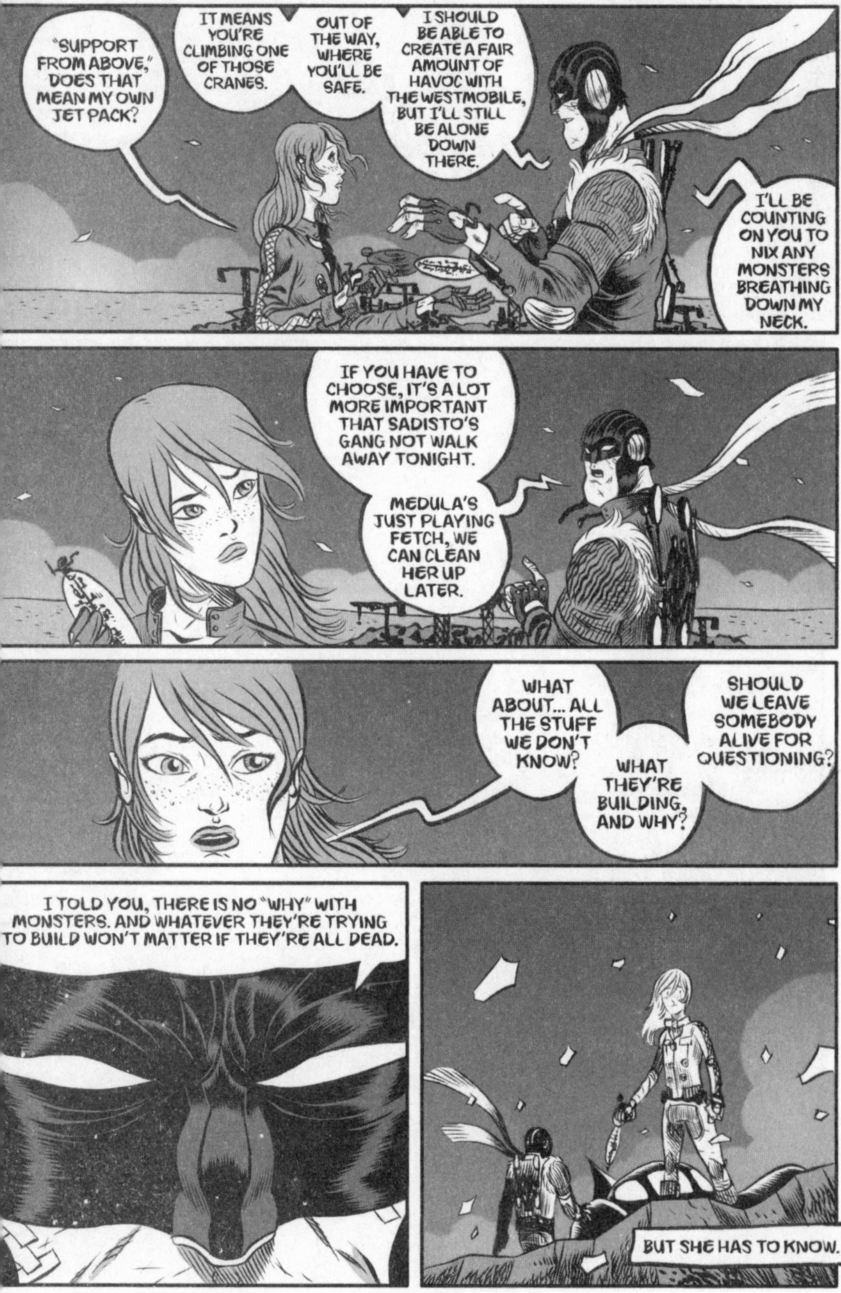
"SUPPORT FROM ABOVE," DOES THAT MEAN MY OWN JET PACK?
IT MEANS YOU'RE CLIMBING ONE OF THOSE CRANES.
OUT OF THE WAY, WHERE YOU'LL BE SAFE.
I SHOULD BE ABLE TO CREATE A FAIR AMOUNT OF HAVOC WITH THE WESTMOBILE, BUT I'LL STILL BE ALONE DOWN THERE.
I'LL BE COUNTING ON YOU TO NIX ANY MONSTERS BREATHING DOWN MY NECK.
IF YOU HAVE TO CHOOSE, IT'S A LOT MORE IMPORTANT THAT SADISTO'S GANG NOT WALK AWAY TONIGHT.
MEDULA'S JUST PLAYING FETCH, WE CAN CLEAN HER UP LATER.
WHAT ABOUT... ALL THE STUFF WE DON'T KNOW?
WHAT THEY'RE BUILDING, AND WHY?
SHOULD WE LEAVE SOMEBODY ALIVE FOR QUESTIONING?
I TOLD YOU, THERE IS NO "WHY" WITH MONSTERS. AND WHATEVER THEY'RE TRYING TO BUILD WON'T MATTER IF THEY'RE ALL DEAD.
BUT SHE HAS TO KNOW.

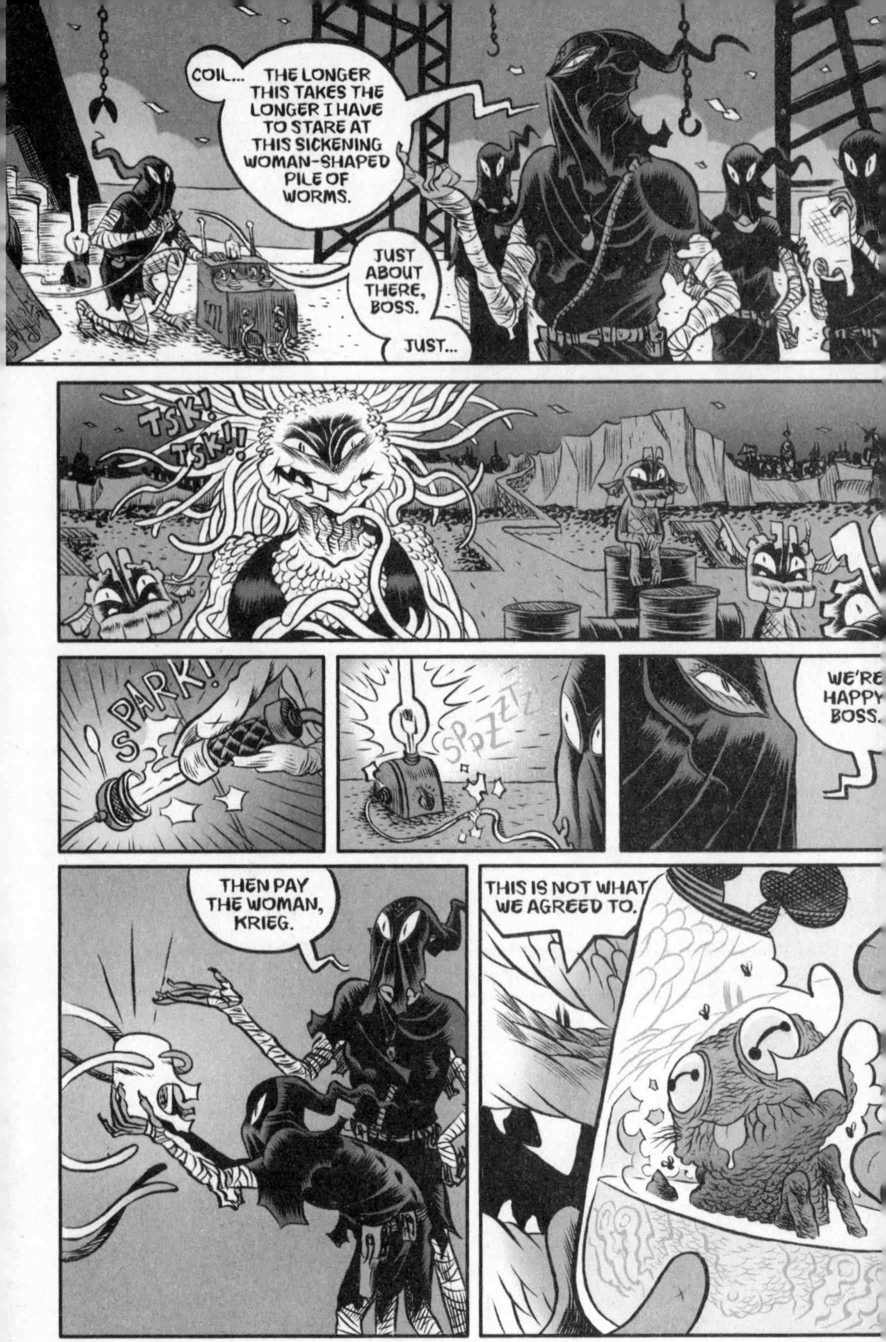
COIL... THE LONGER THIS TAKES THE LONGER I HAVE TO STARE AT THIS SICKENING WOMAN-SHAPED PILE OF WORMS.
JUST ABOUT THERE, BOSS.
JUST...
TSK! TSK!!
SPARK!
SPPZZZTZ
WE'RE HAPPY BOSS.
THEN PAY THE WOMAN, KRIEG.
THIS IS NOT WHAT WE AGREED TO.

IT'S GENEROUS.

INSPECT THE GOOD MOTHER'S BACK.

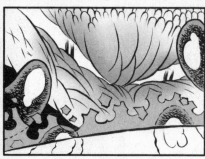

OH, MY. SO FRESH.

OH, SADISTO.

YOU **DO** LIKE ME.

VRRBRROOOMM!!!

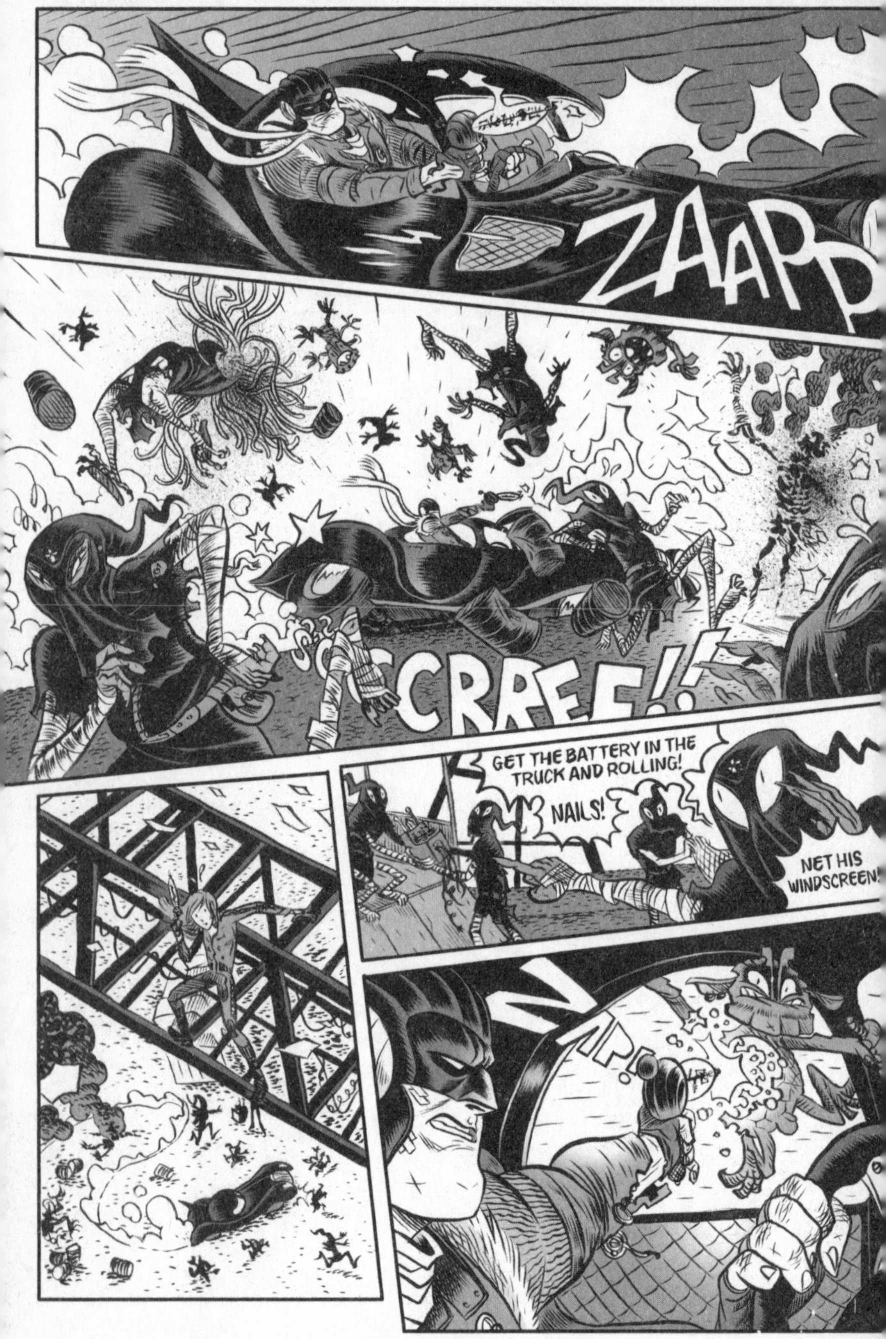
ZAAR
CRREE!!
GET THE BATTERY IN THE TRUCK AND ROLLING!
NAILS!
NET HIS WINDSCREEN!
ZAP!

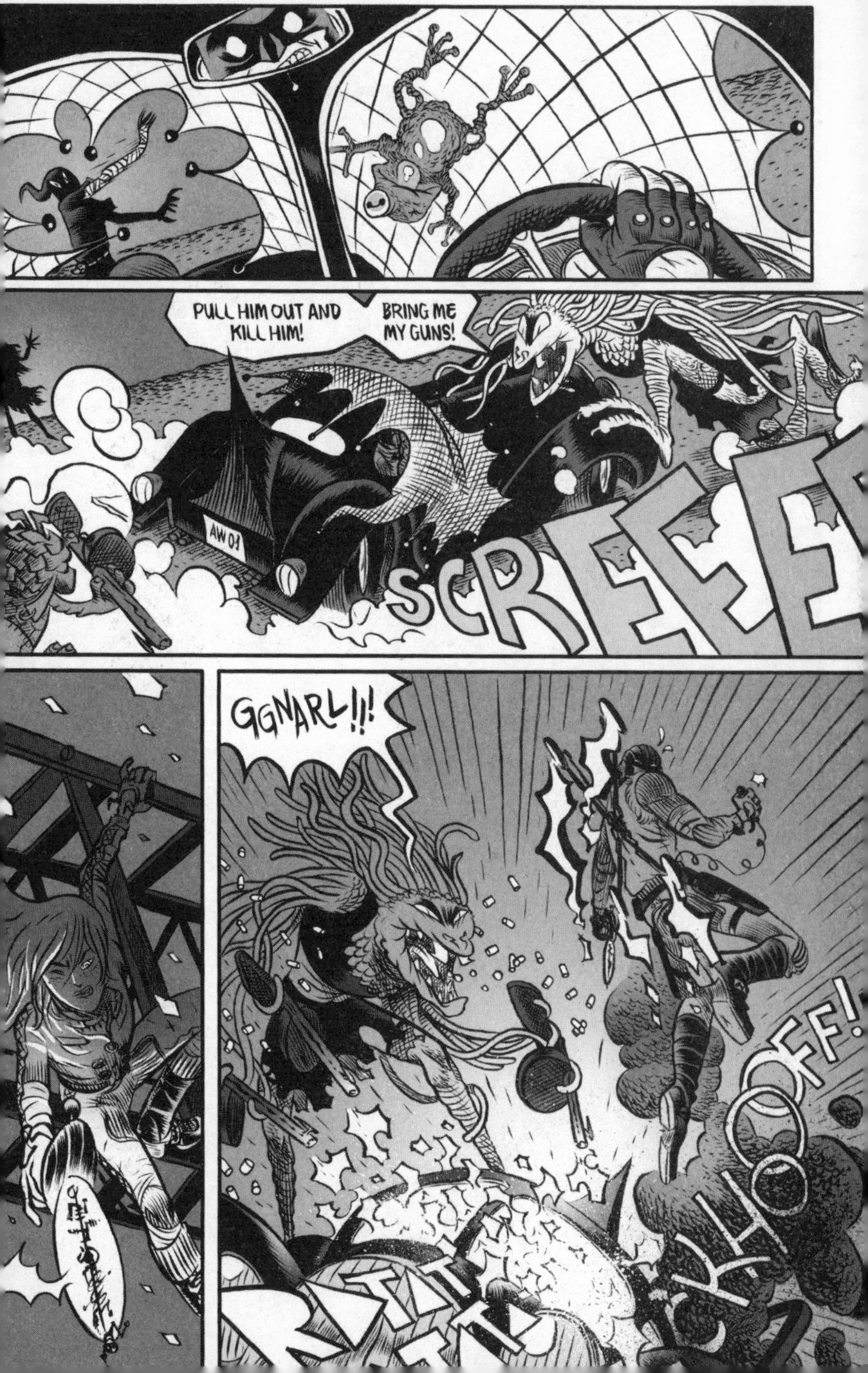
PULL HIM OUT AND KILL HIM!
BRING ME MY GUNS!
SCREEE
GGNARL!!!

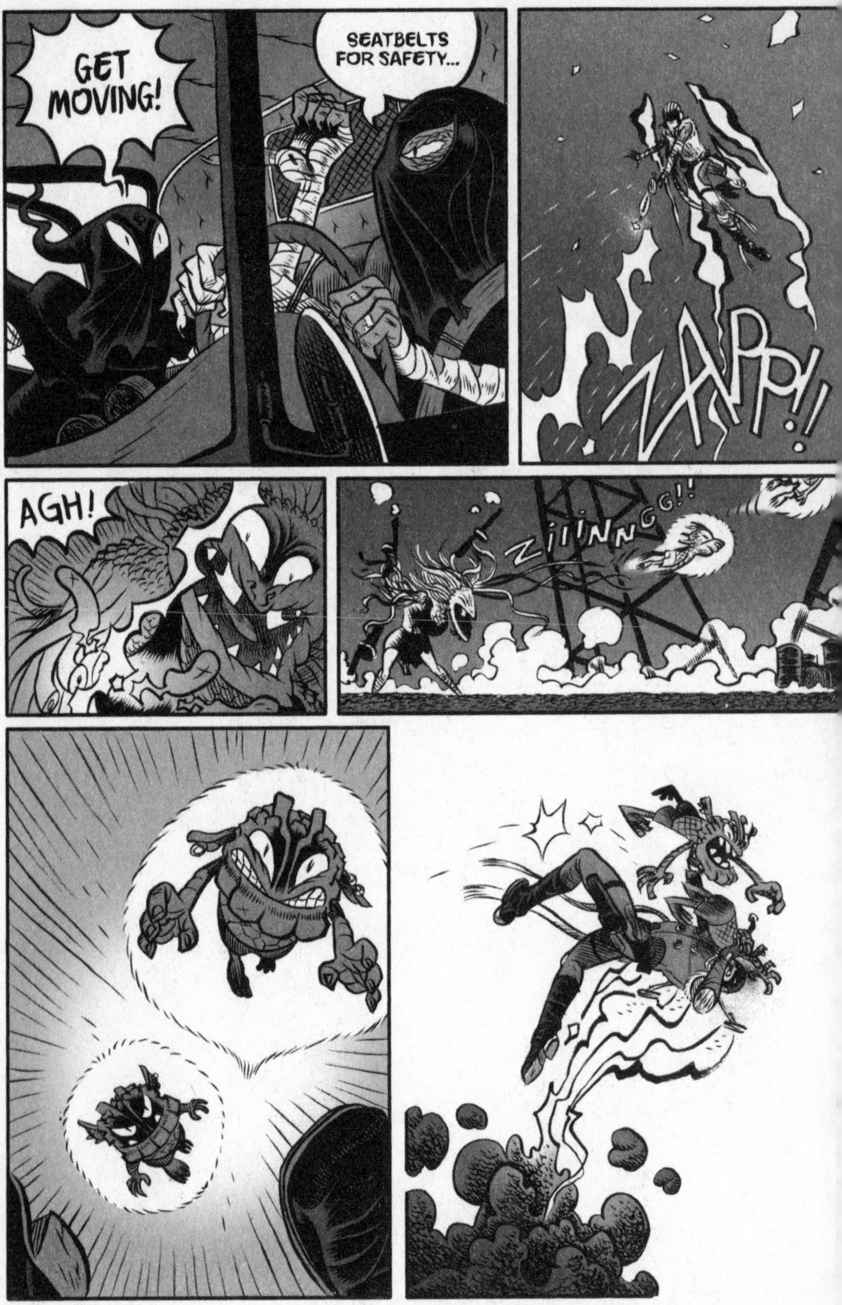
GET MOVING!
SEATBELTS FOR SAFETY...
ZAPP!!
AGH!
ZIIINNGG!!

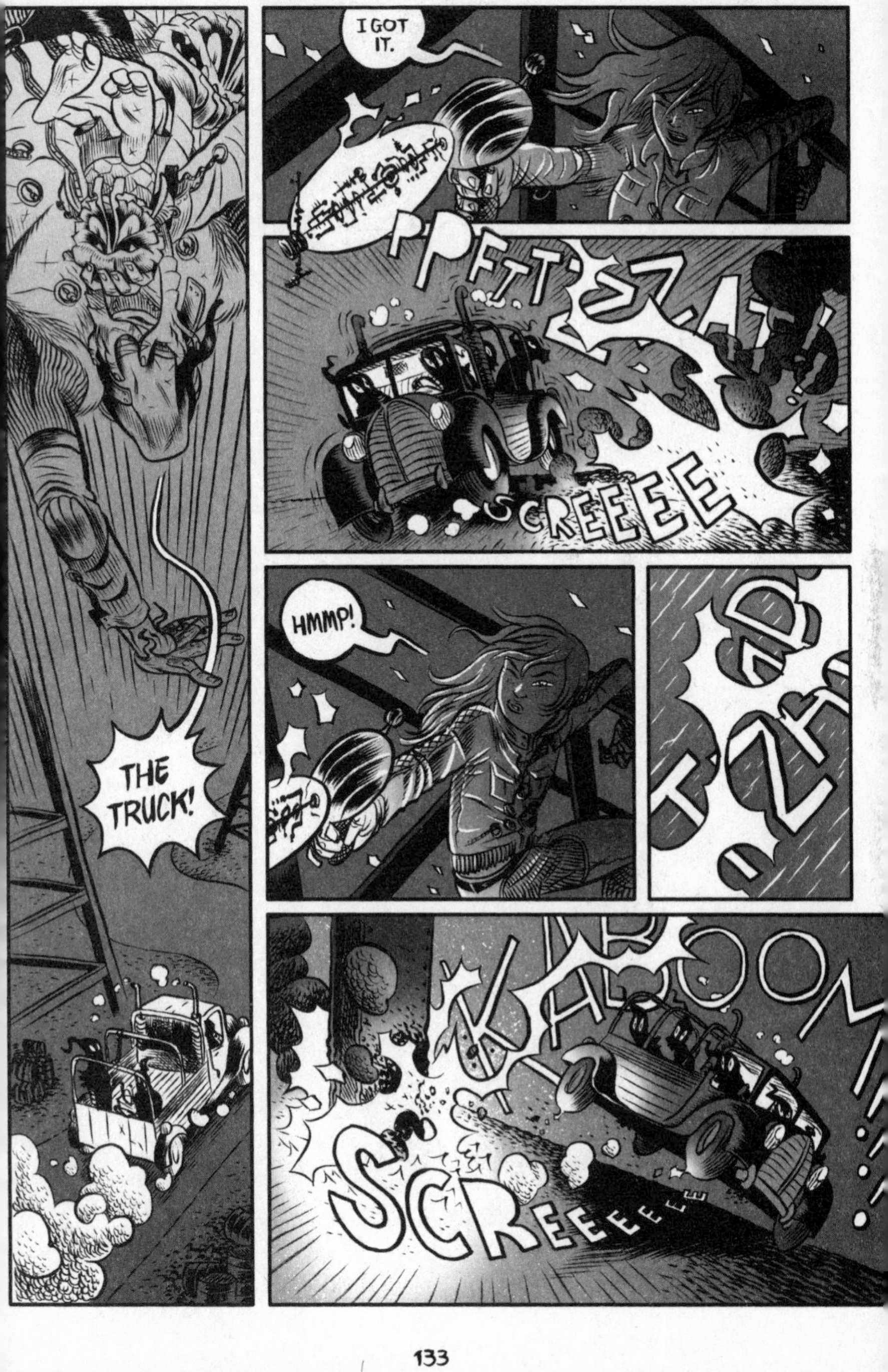
THE TRUCK!
I GOT IT.
PPFT'ZZAT!!
SCREEEE
HMMP!
KABOOM!!!
SCREEEEEE

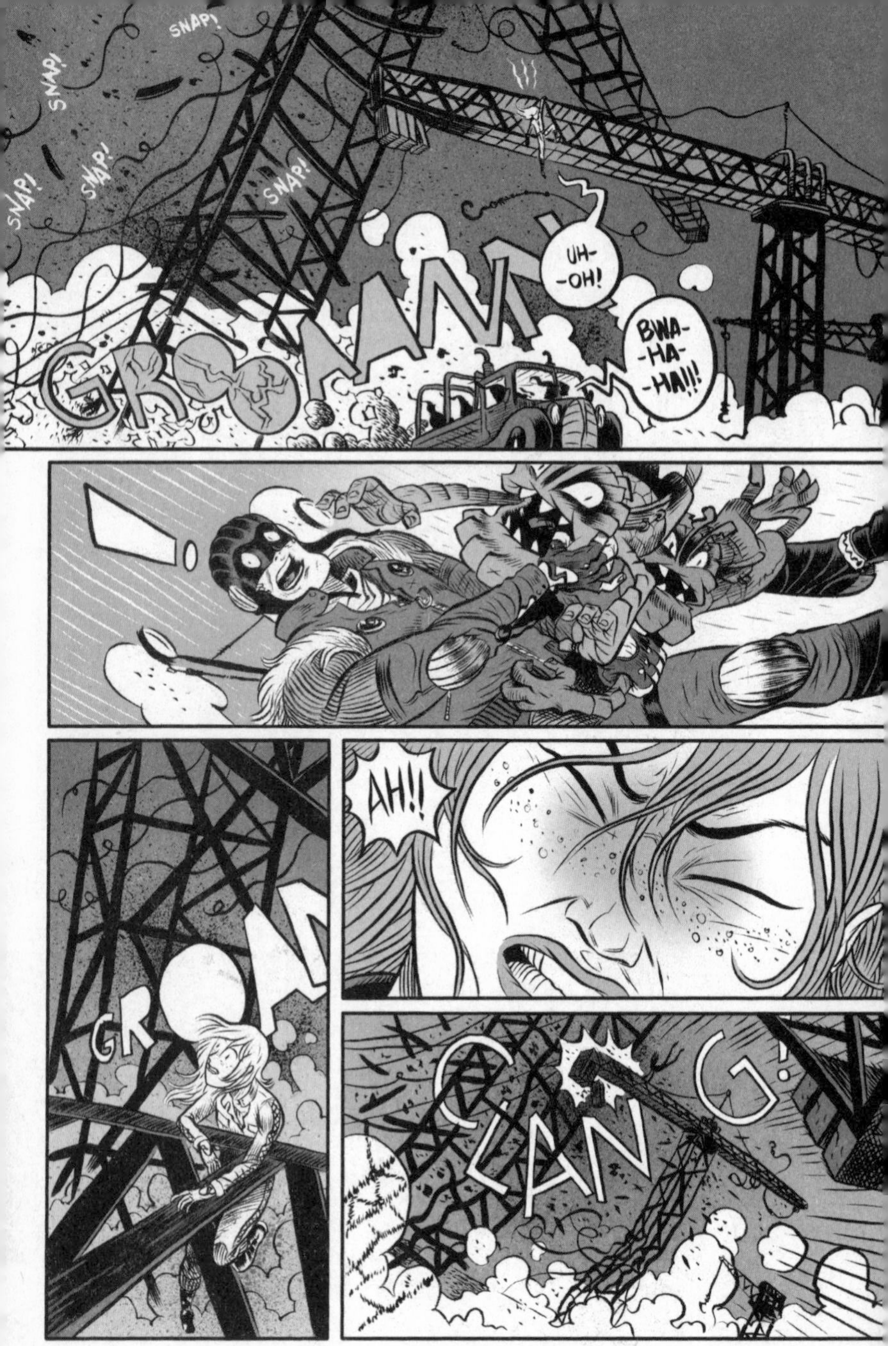
SNAP!
SNAP!
SNAP!
SNAP!
SNAP!
SNAP!
GROOAAN
UH- -OH!
BWA- -HA- -HA- -HA!!!
!
AH!!
GR
CLANG!

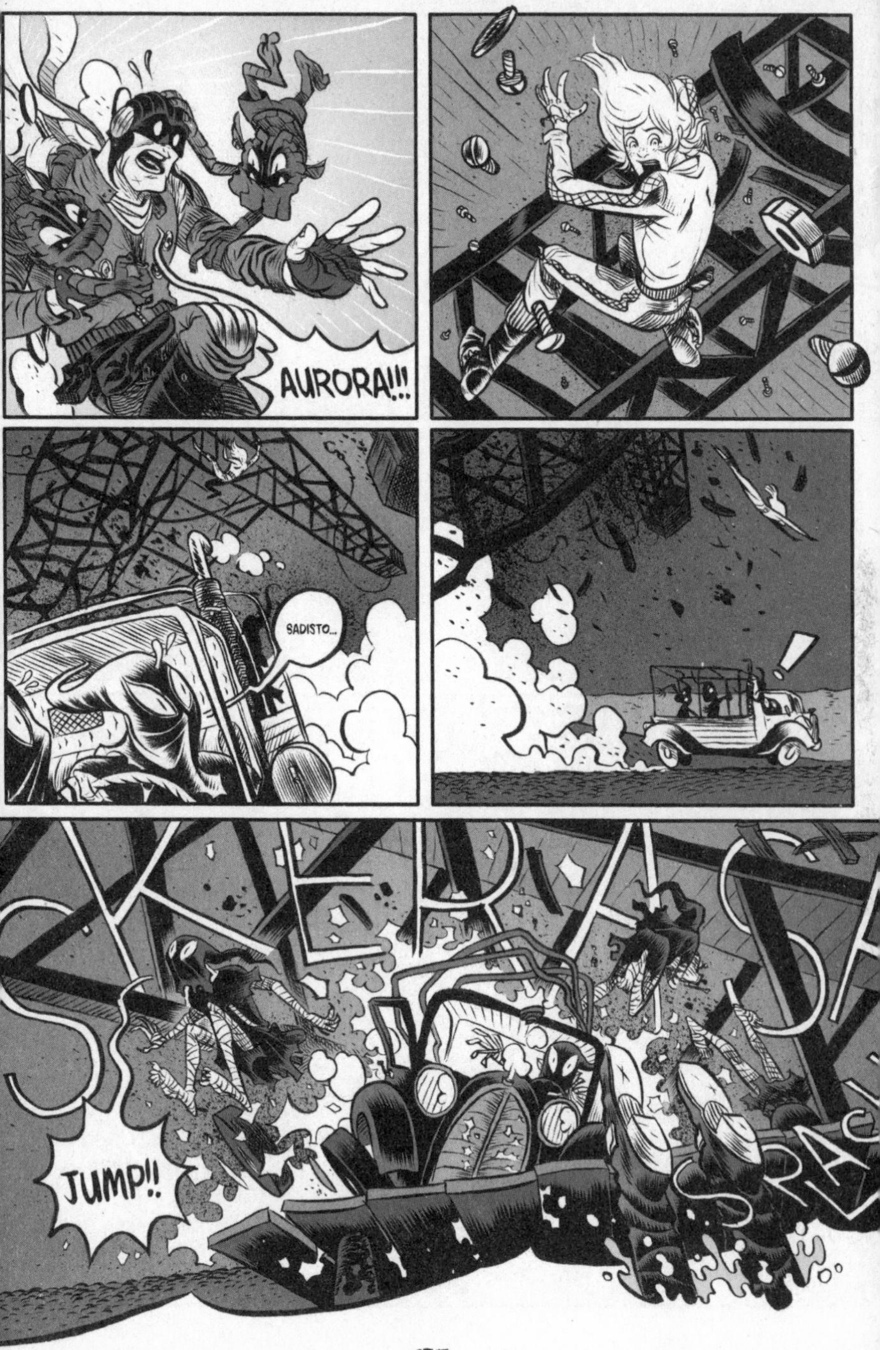
AURORA!!!
SADISTO...
!
JUMP!!

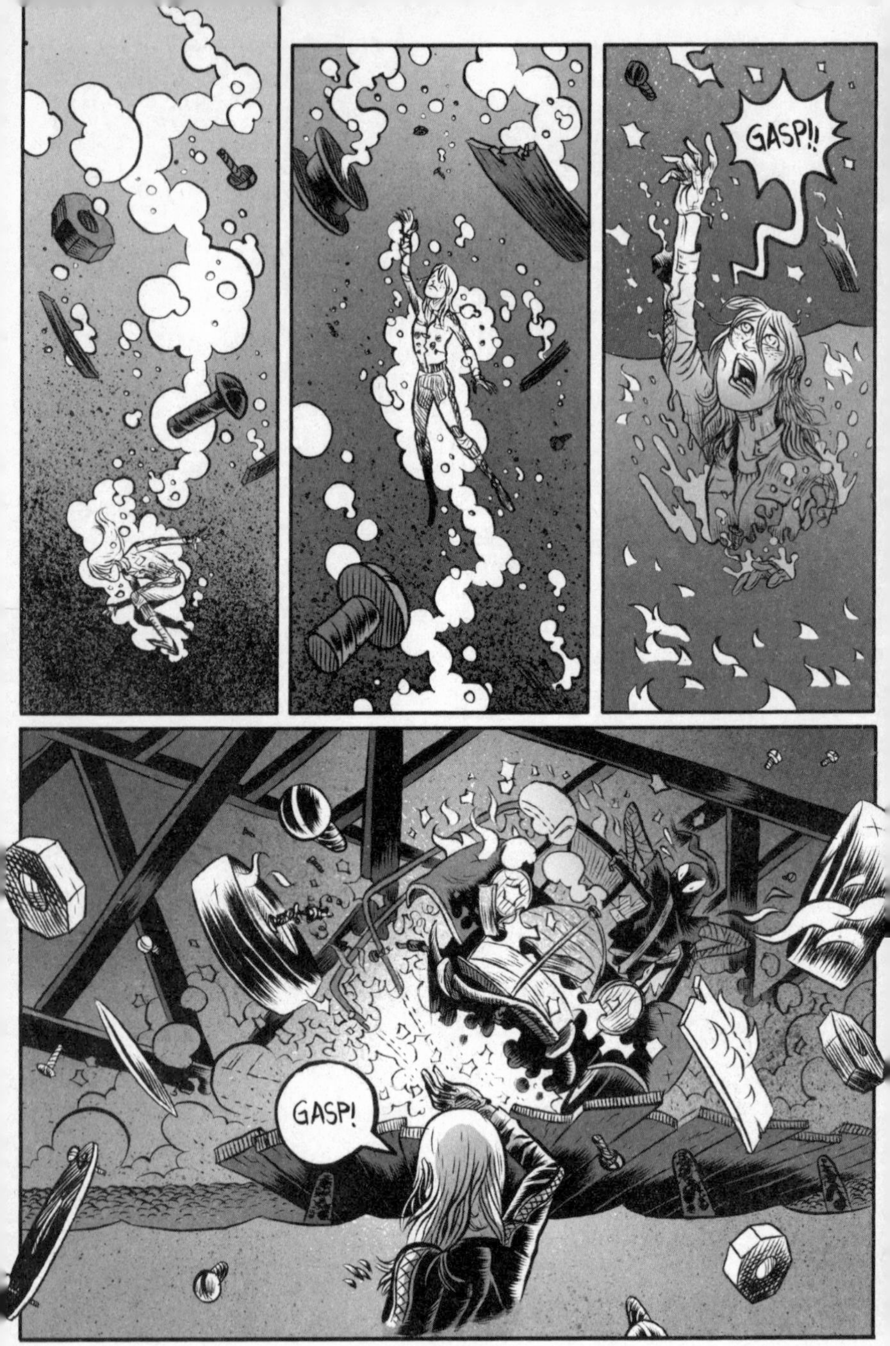
GASP!!
GASP!

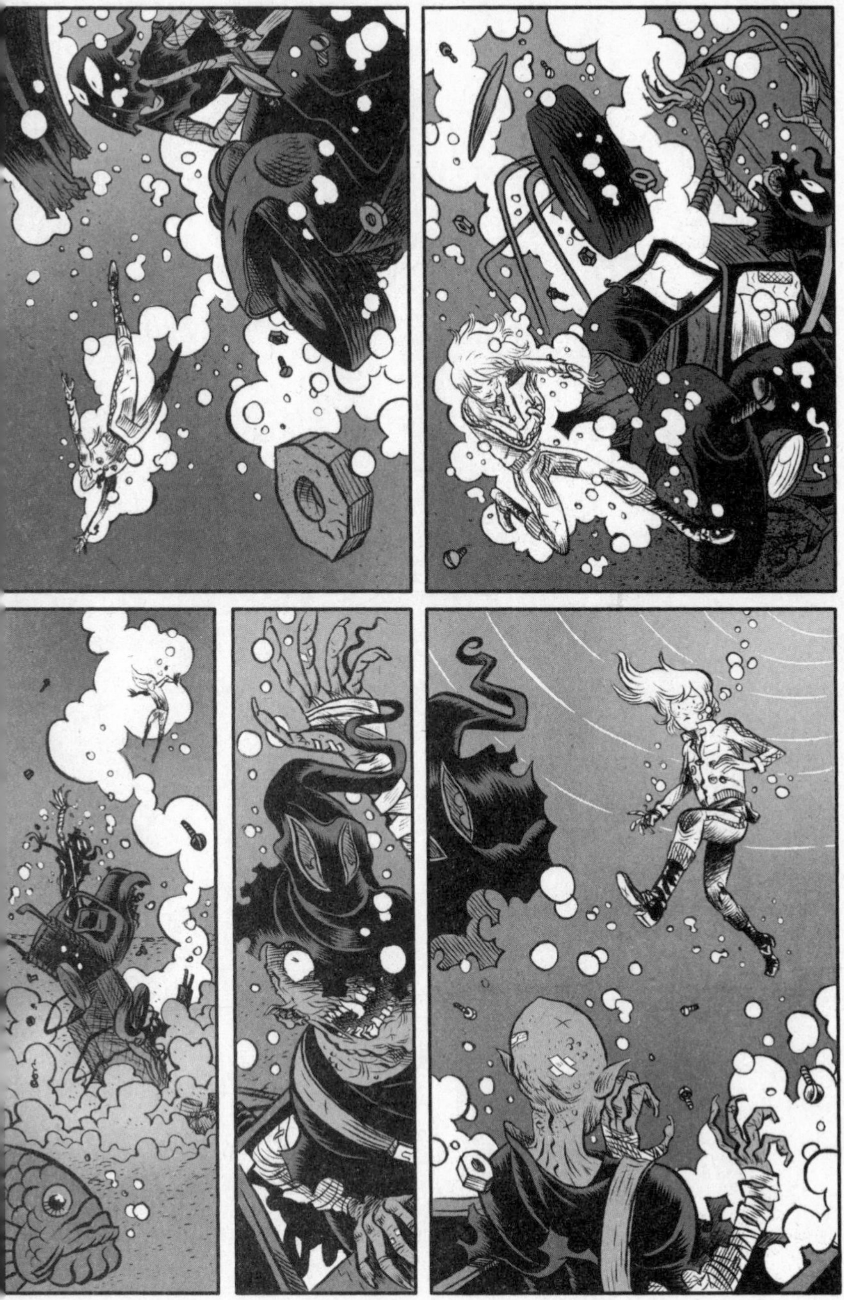

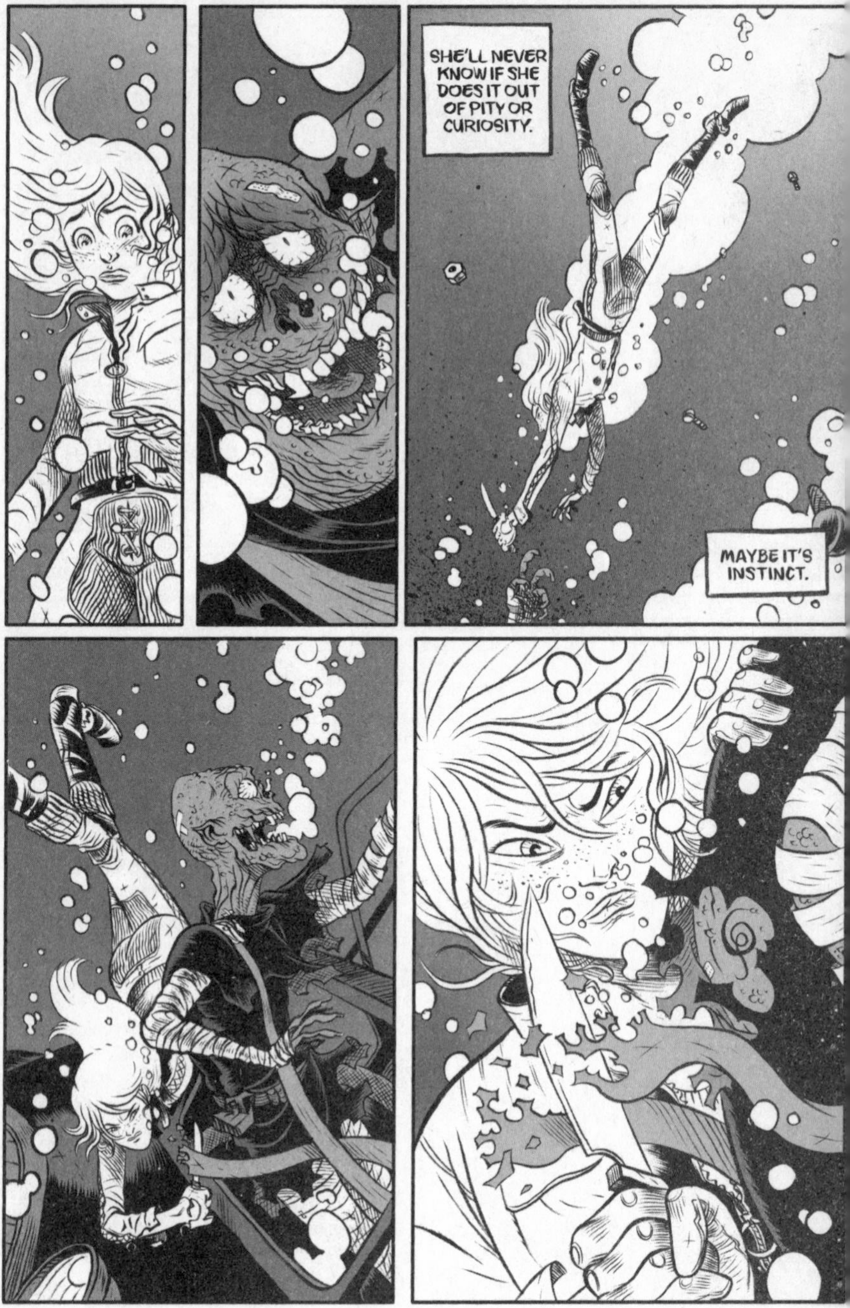
SHE'LL NEVER KNOW IF SHE DOES IT OUT OF PITY OR CURIOSITY.
MAYBE IT'S INSTINCT.

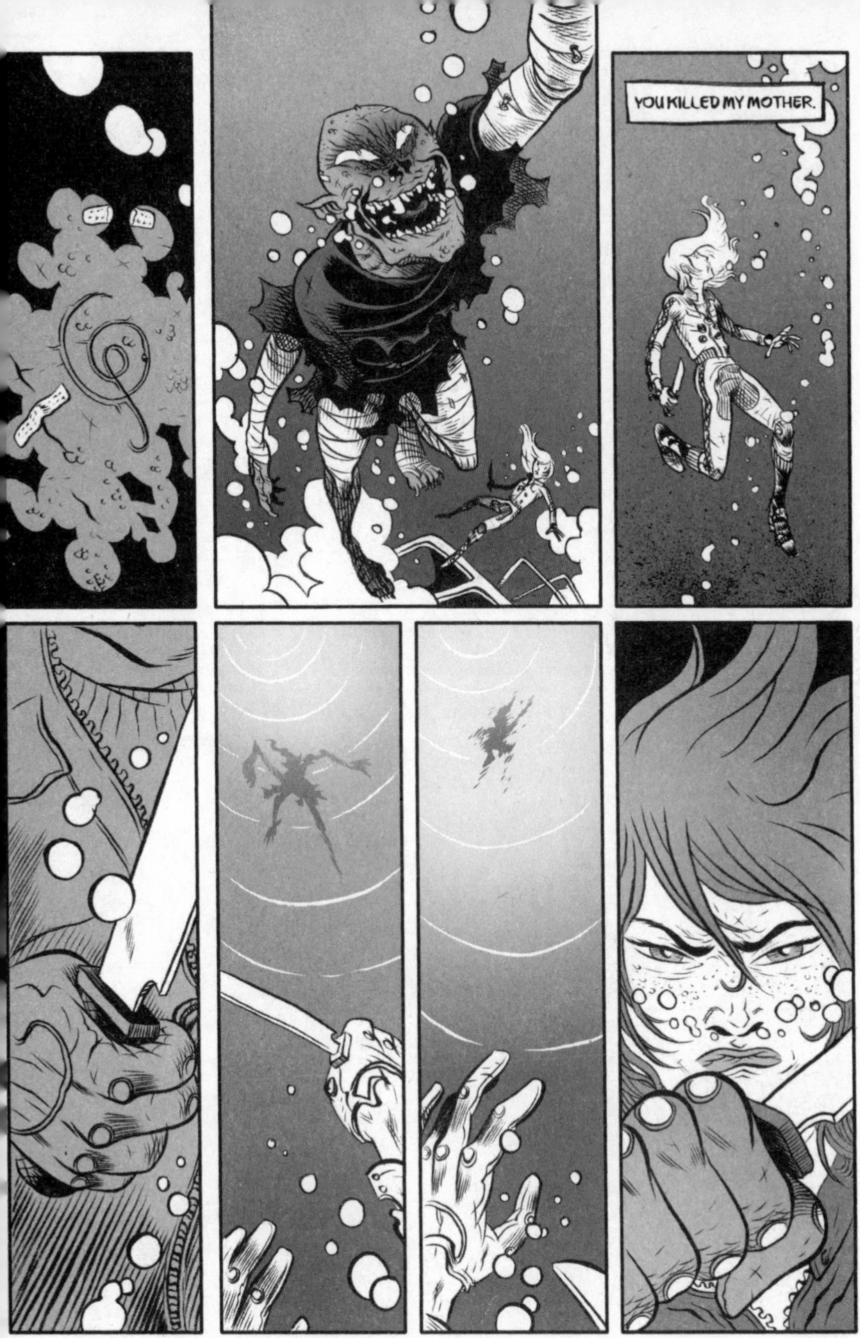
YOU KILLED MY MOTHER.

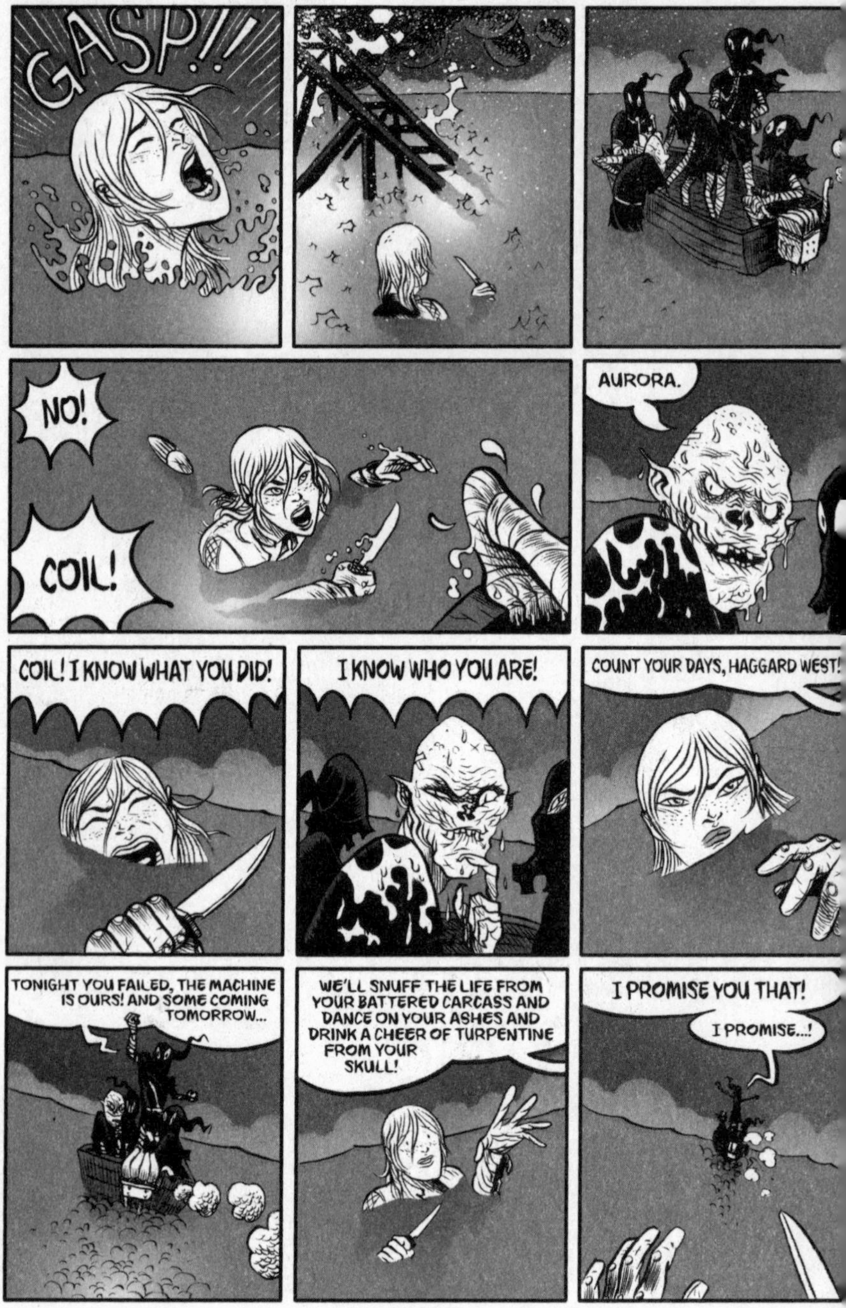
GASP!!
NO!
COIL!
AURORA.
COIL! I KNOW WHAT YOU DID!
I KNOW WHO YOU ARE!
COUNT YOUR DAYS, HAGGARD WEST!
TONIGHT YOU FAILED, THE MACHINE IS OURS! AND SOME COMING TOMORROW...
WE'LL SNUFF THE LIFE FROM YOUR BATTERED CARCASS AND DANCE ON YOUR ASHES AND DRINK A CHEER OF TURPENTINE FROM YOUR SKULL!
I PROMISE YOU THAT!
I PROMISE...!

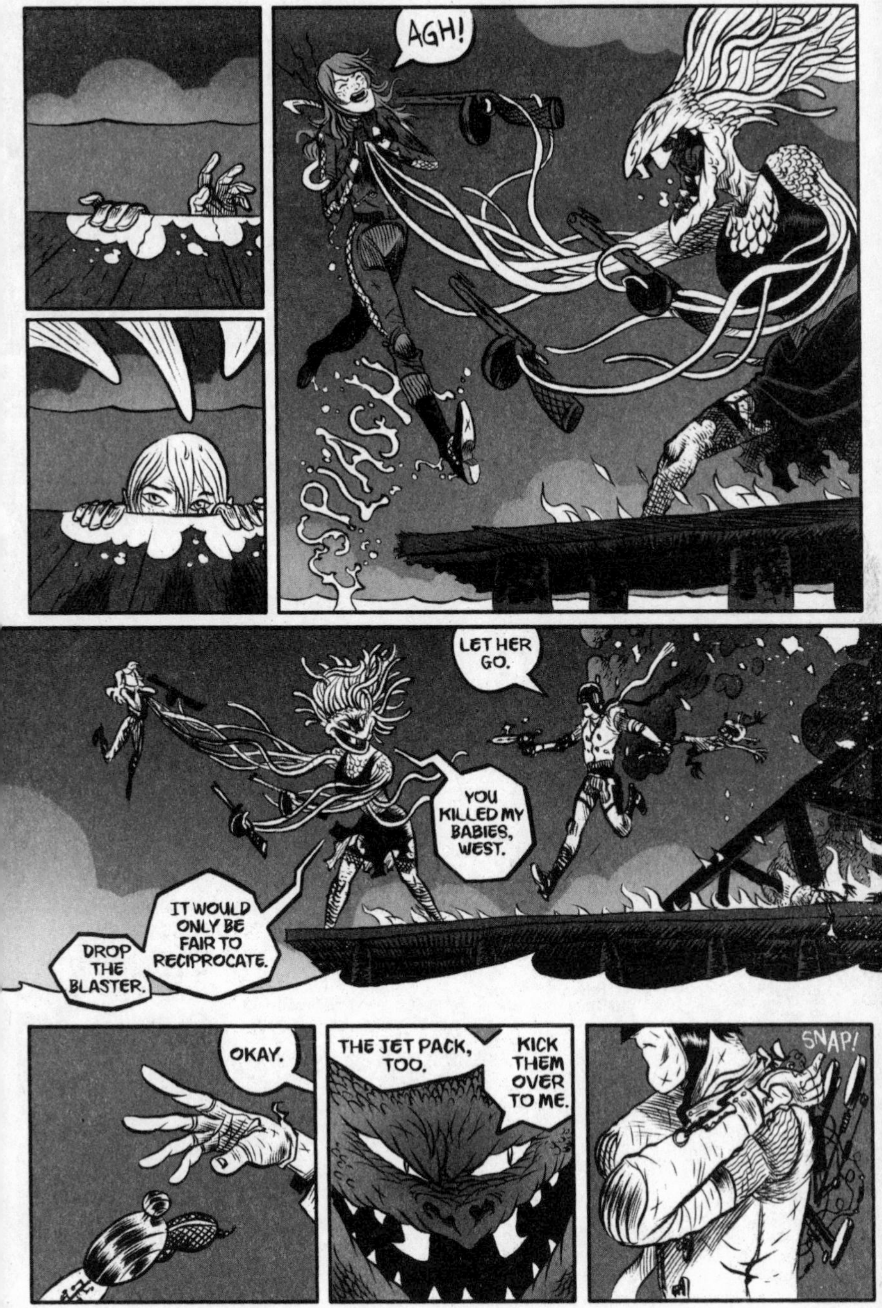
AGH!
SPLASH
LET HER GO.
YOU KILLED MY BABIES, WEST.
IT WOULD ONLY BE FAIR TO RECIPROCATE.
DROP THE BLASTER.
OKAY.
THE JET PACK, TOO.
KICK THEM OVER TO ME.
SNAP!

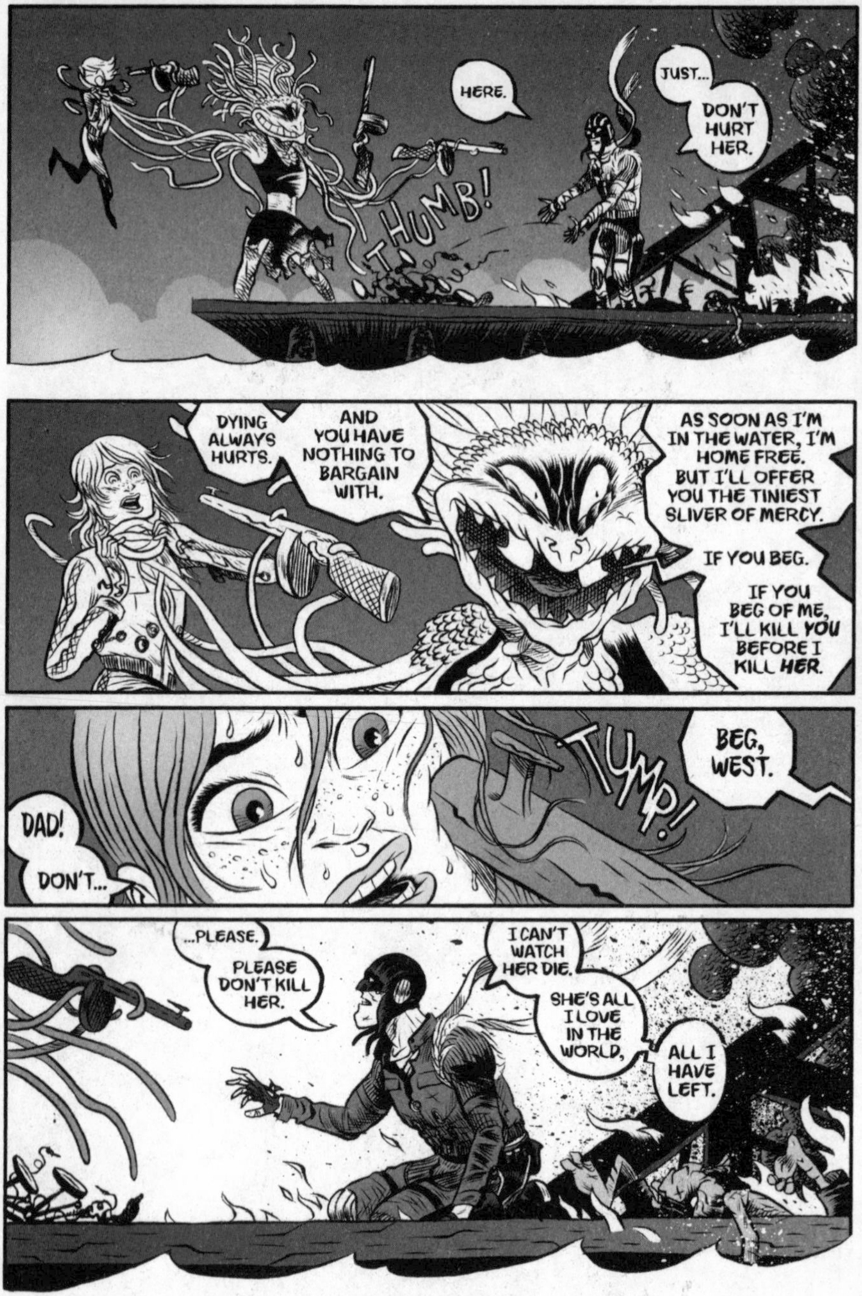
HERE.
JUST... DON'T HURT HER.
THUMB!
DYING ALWAYS HURTS.
AND YOU HAVE NOTHING TO BARGAIN WITH.
AS SOON AS I'M IN THE WATER, I'M HOME FREE. BUT I'LL OFFER YOU THE TINIEST SLIVER OF MERCY.
IF YOU BEG.
IF YOU BEG OF ME, I'LL KILL YOU BEFORE I KILL HER.
TUMP!
BEG, WEST.
DAD!
DON'T...
...PLEASE.
PLEASE DON'T KILL HER.
I CAN'T WATCH HER DIE.
SHE'S ALL I LOVE IN THE WORLD,
ALL I HAVE LEFT.

EVERYTHING I'VE DONE SINCE HER BIRTH HAS BEEN TO MAKE THE WORLD SAFE FOR HER.

TO MAKE HER STRONG ENOUGH TO SURVIVE WHEN I'M GONE.

IF YOU KILL HER, YOU WON'T HAVE TO KILL ME.

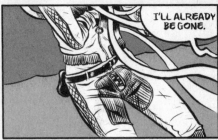

I'LL ALREADY BE GONE.

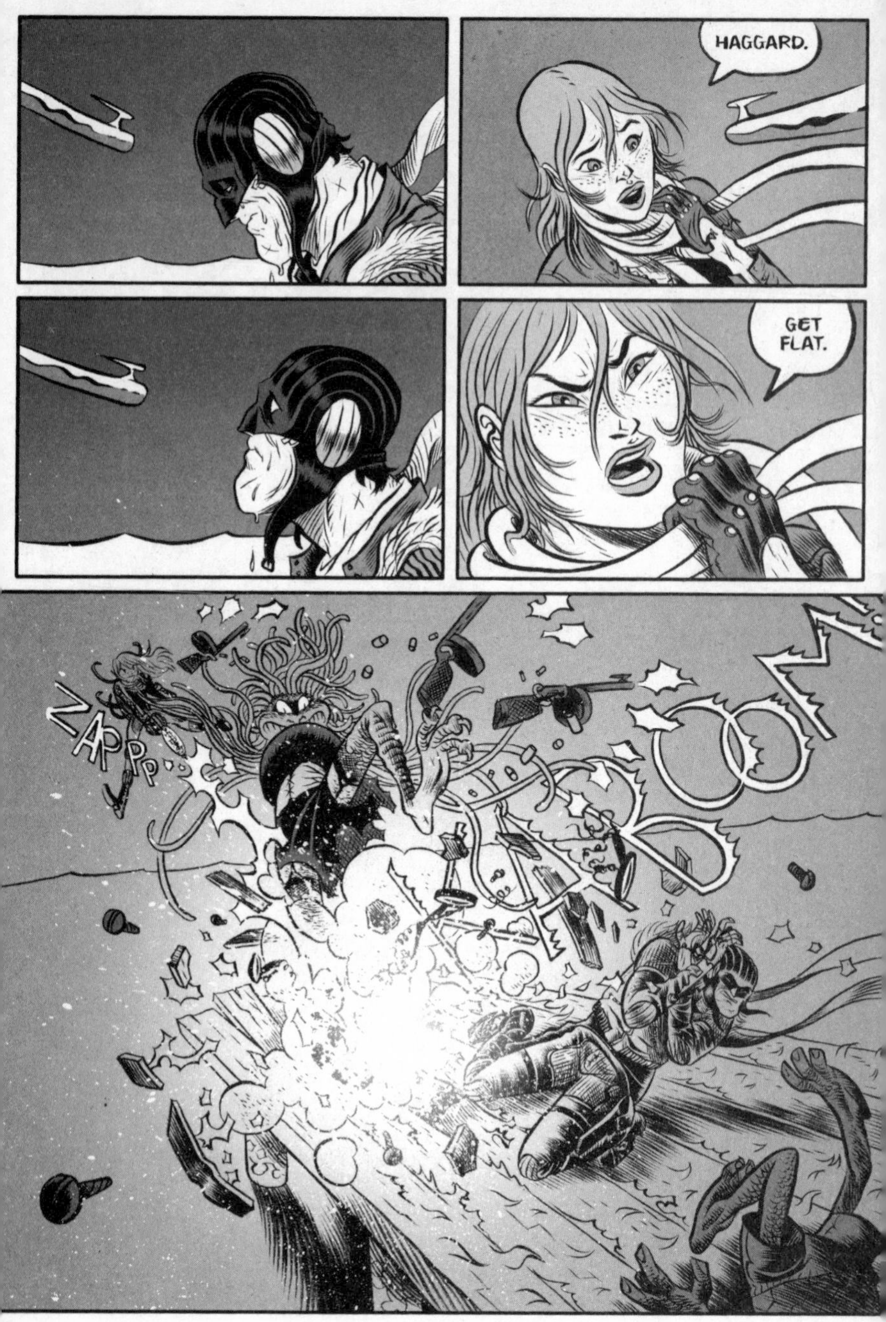
HAGGARD.
GET FLAT.
ZAPPP

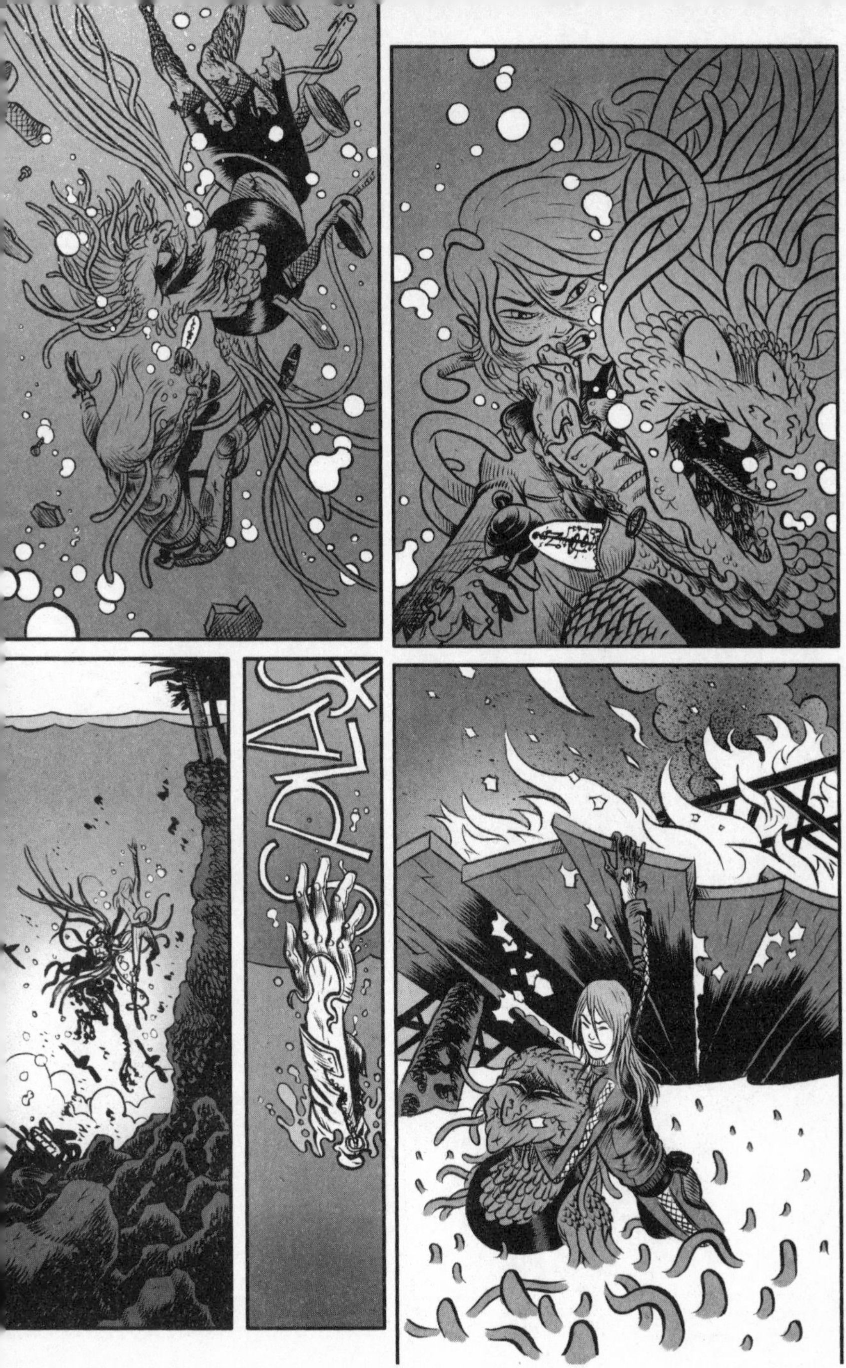

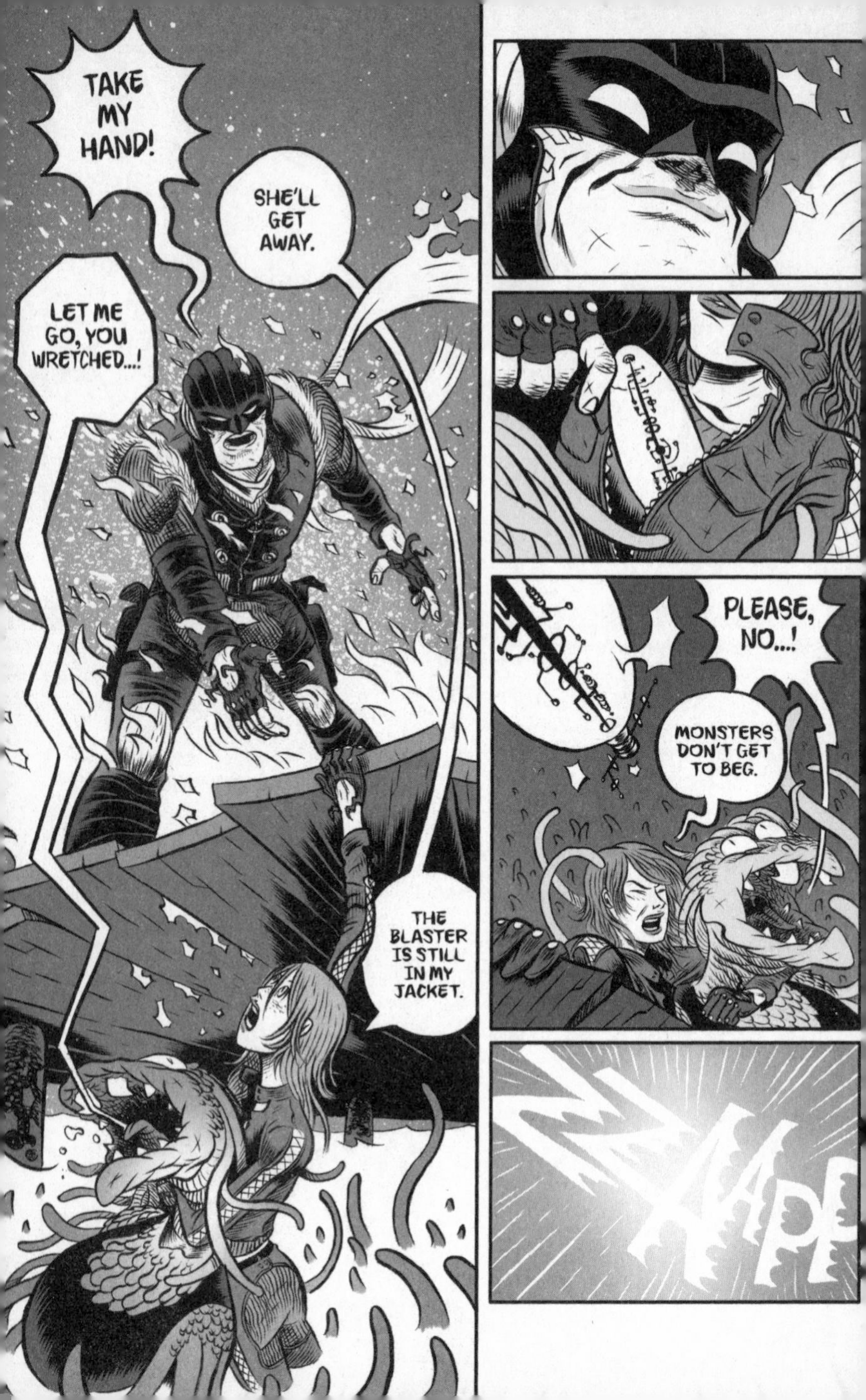
TAKE MY HAND!
SHE'LL GET AWAY.
LET ME GO, YOU WRETCHED...!
THE BLASTER IS STILL IN MY JACKET.
PLEASE, NO...!
MONSTERS DON'T GET TO BEG.

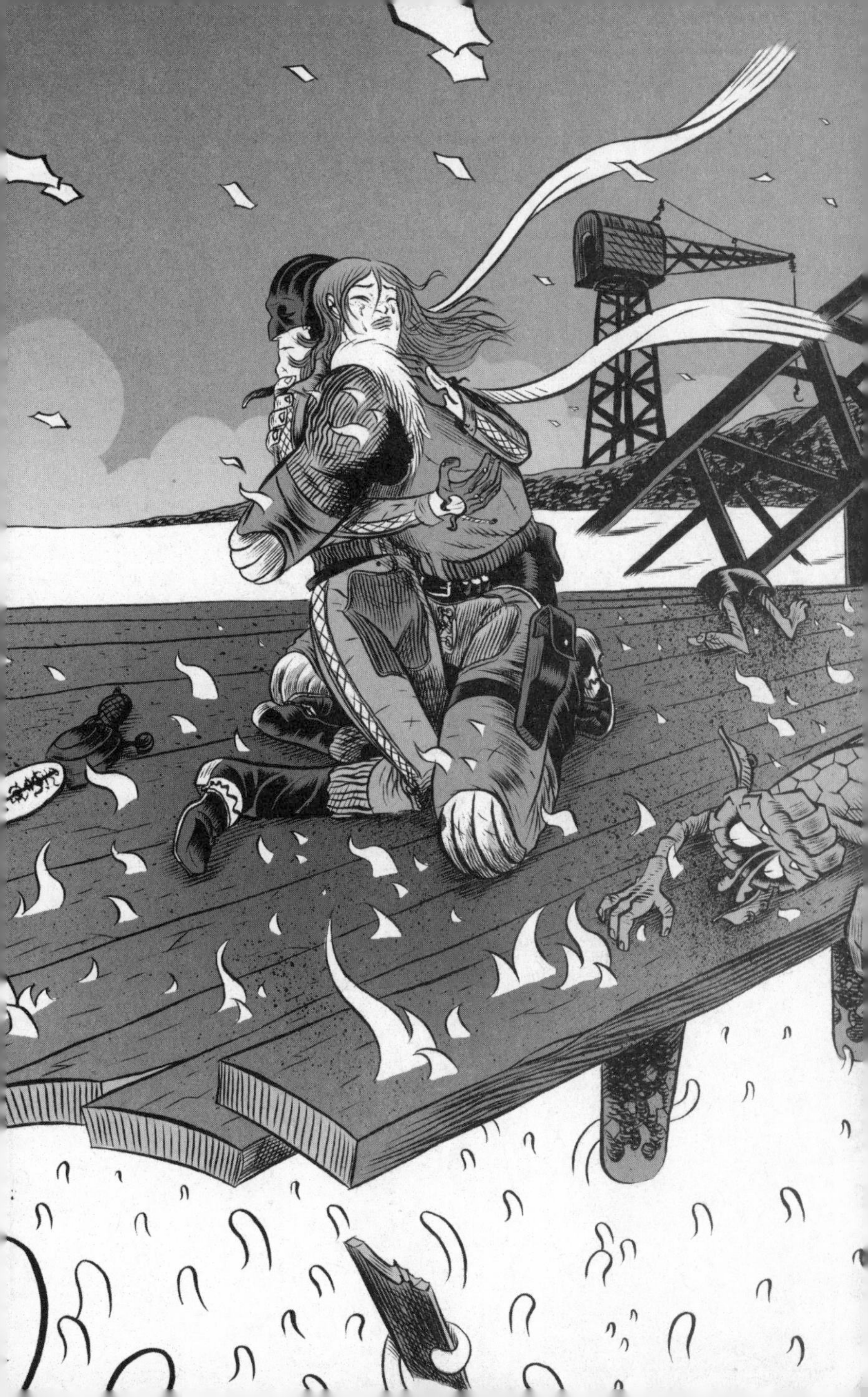

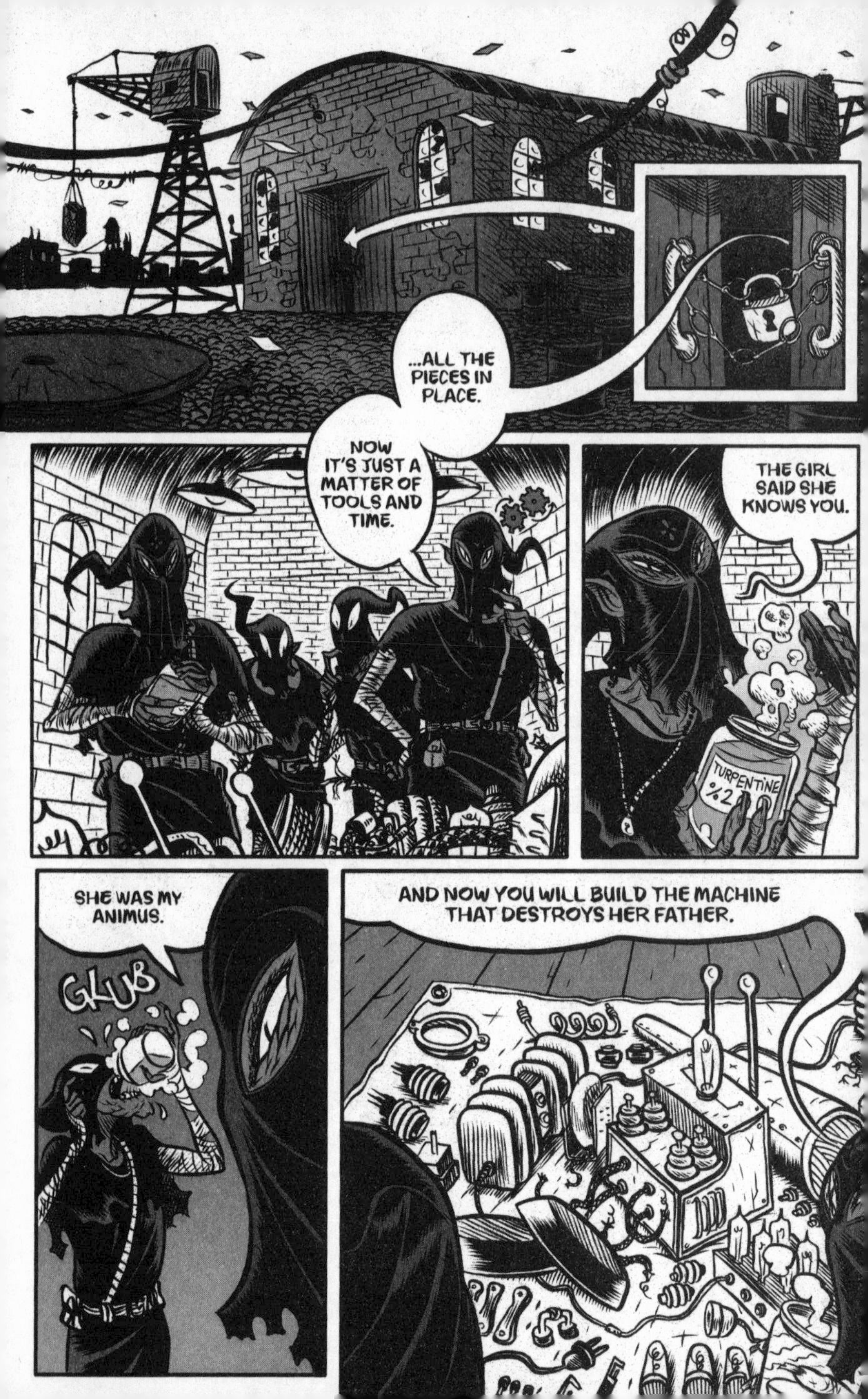
...ALL THE PIECES IN PLACE.
NOW IT'S JUST A MATTER OF TOOLS AND TIME.
THE GIRL SAID SHE KNOWS YOU.
TURPENTINE %2
SHE WAS MY ANIMUS.
GLUB
AND NOW YOU WILL BUILD THE MACHINE THAT DESTROYS HER FATHER.

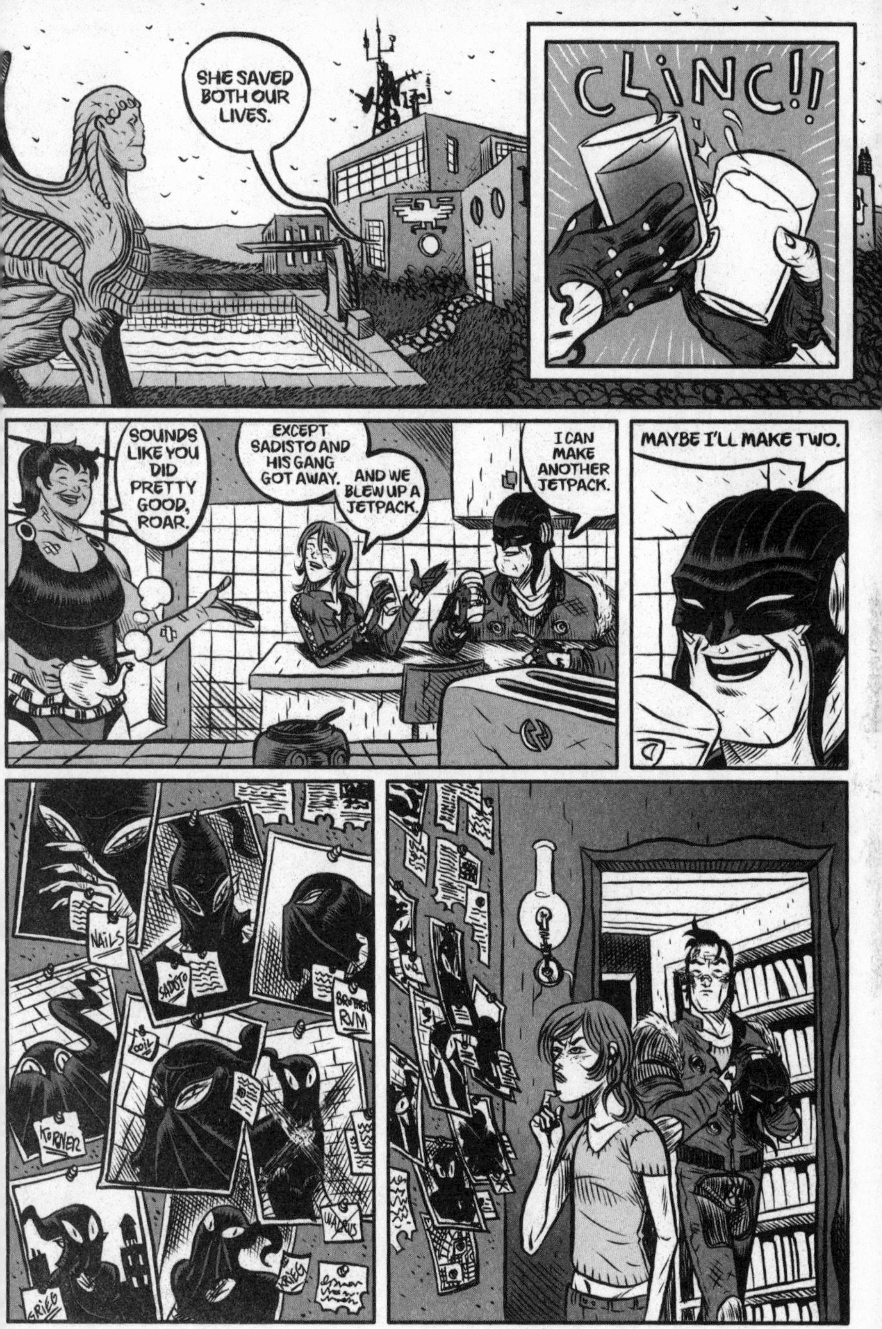
SHE SAVED BOTH OUR LIVES.
CLINC!!
SOUNDS LIKE YOU DID PRETTY GOOD, ROAR.
EXCEPT SADISTO AND HIS GANG GOT AWAY.
AND WE BLEW UP A JETPACK.
I CAN MAKE ANOTHER JETPACK.
MAYBE I'LL MAKE TWO.
NAILS
SADISTO
COIL
KORNER
GRIEG

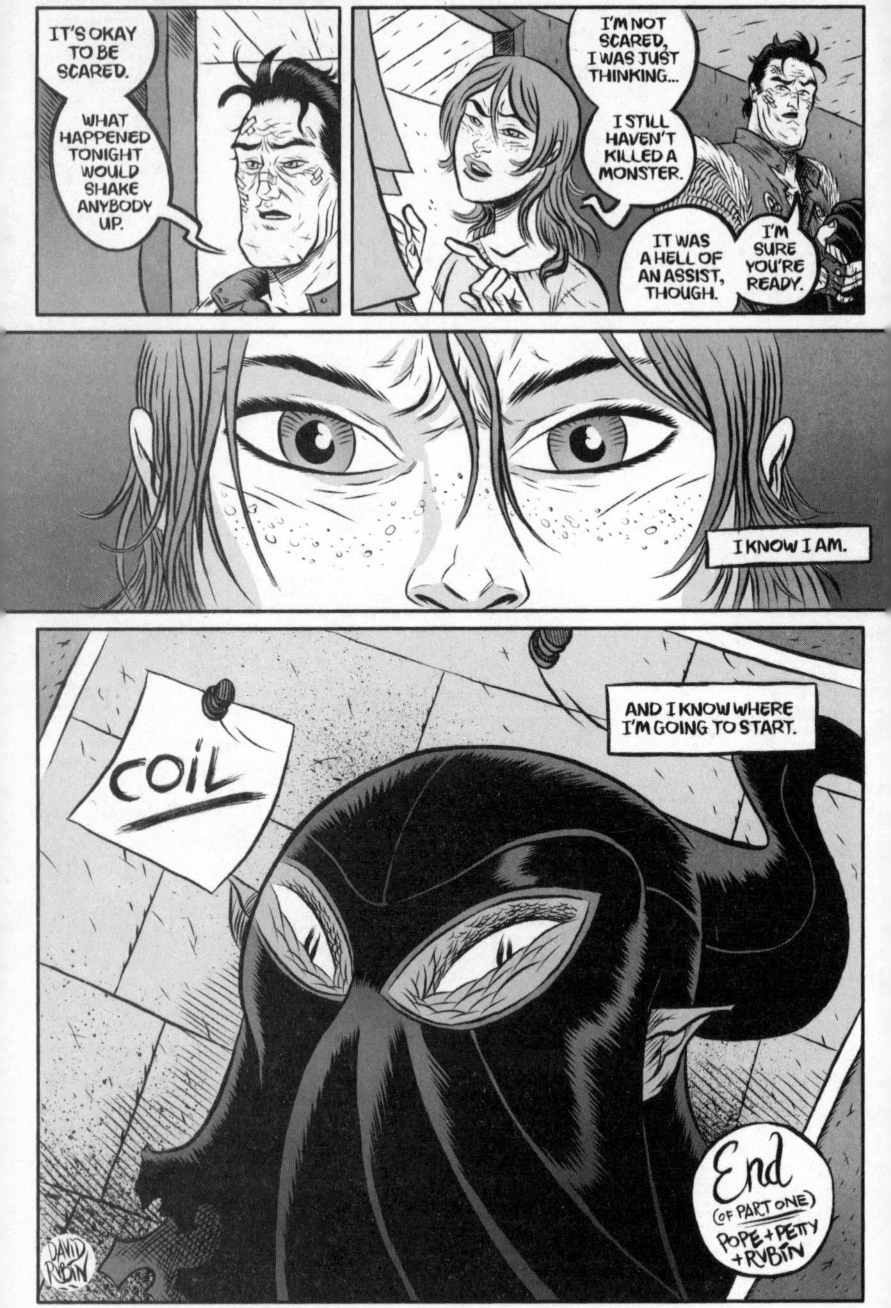
IT'S OKAY TO BE SCARED.
WHAT HAPPENED TONIGHT WOULD SHAKE ANYBODY UP.
I'M NOT SCARED, I WAS JUST THINKING...
I STILL HAVEN'T KILLED A MONSTER.
IT WAS A HELL OF AN ASSIST, THOUGH.
I'M SURE YOU'RE READY.
I KNOW I AM.
AND I KNOW WHERE I'M GOING TO START.
COIL
End (OF PART ONE)
POPE + PETTY + RUBIN
DAVID RUBIN

AURORA'S ADVENTURE CONTINUES IN

BATTLING BOY:
THE FALL OF THE HOUSE OF WEST

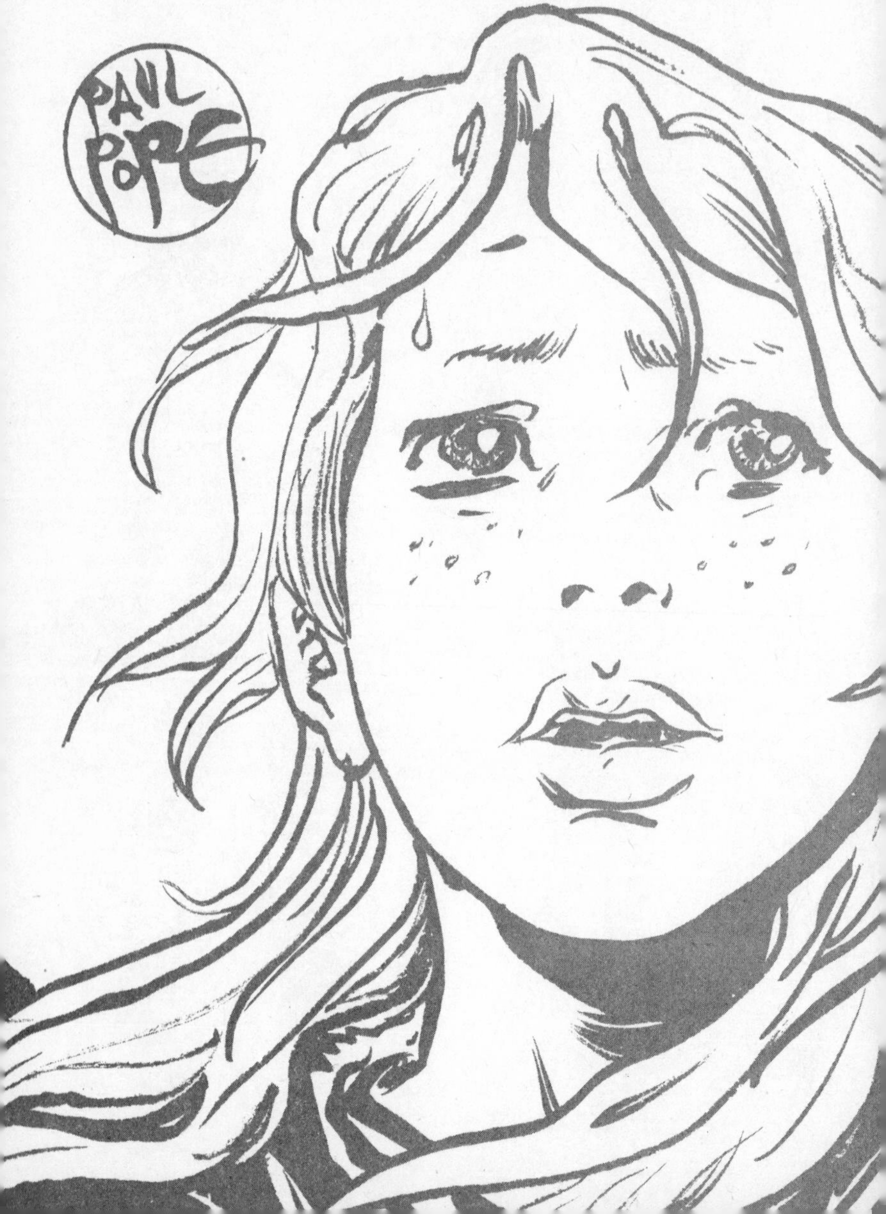
PAUL POPE

FROM THE SKETCHBOOKS OF DAVID RUBÍN

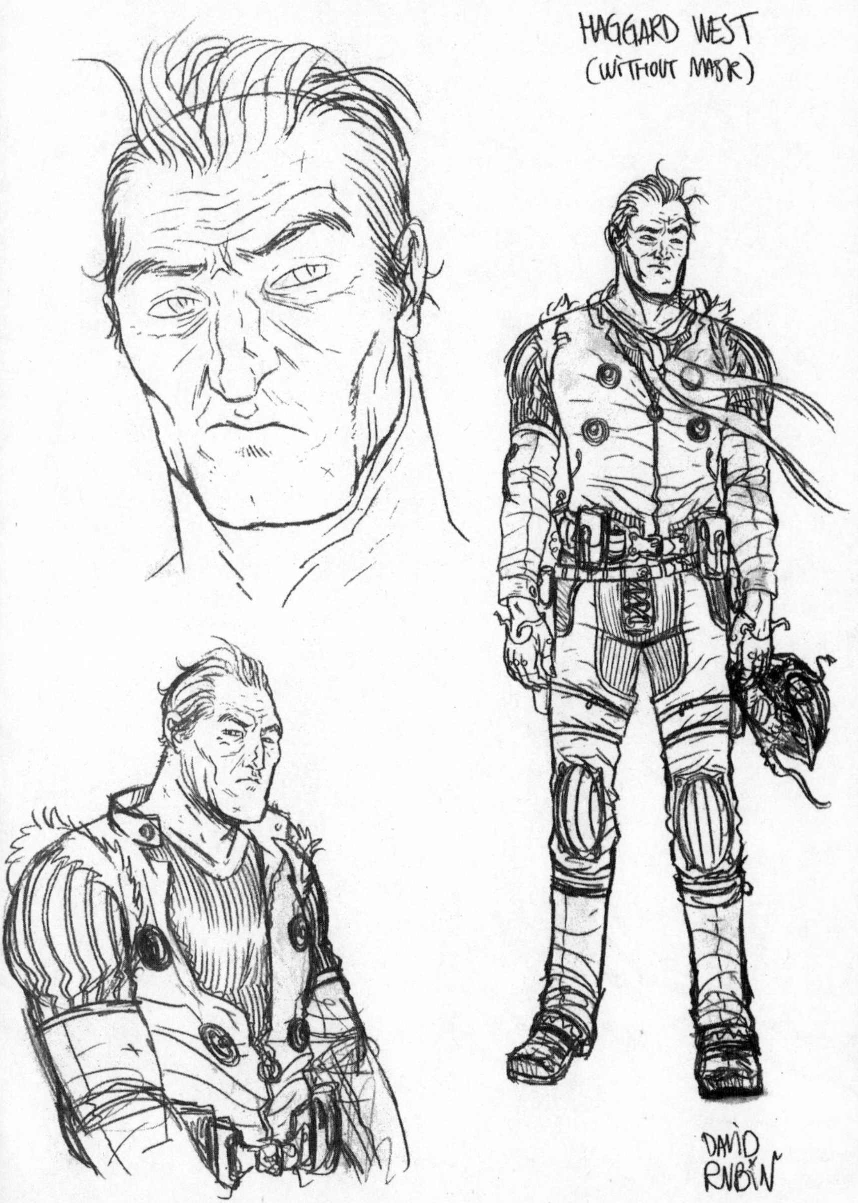
HAGGARD WEST
(WITHOUT MASK)
DAVID RUBÍN

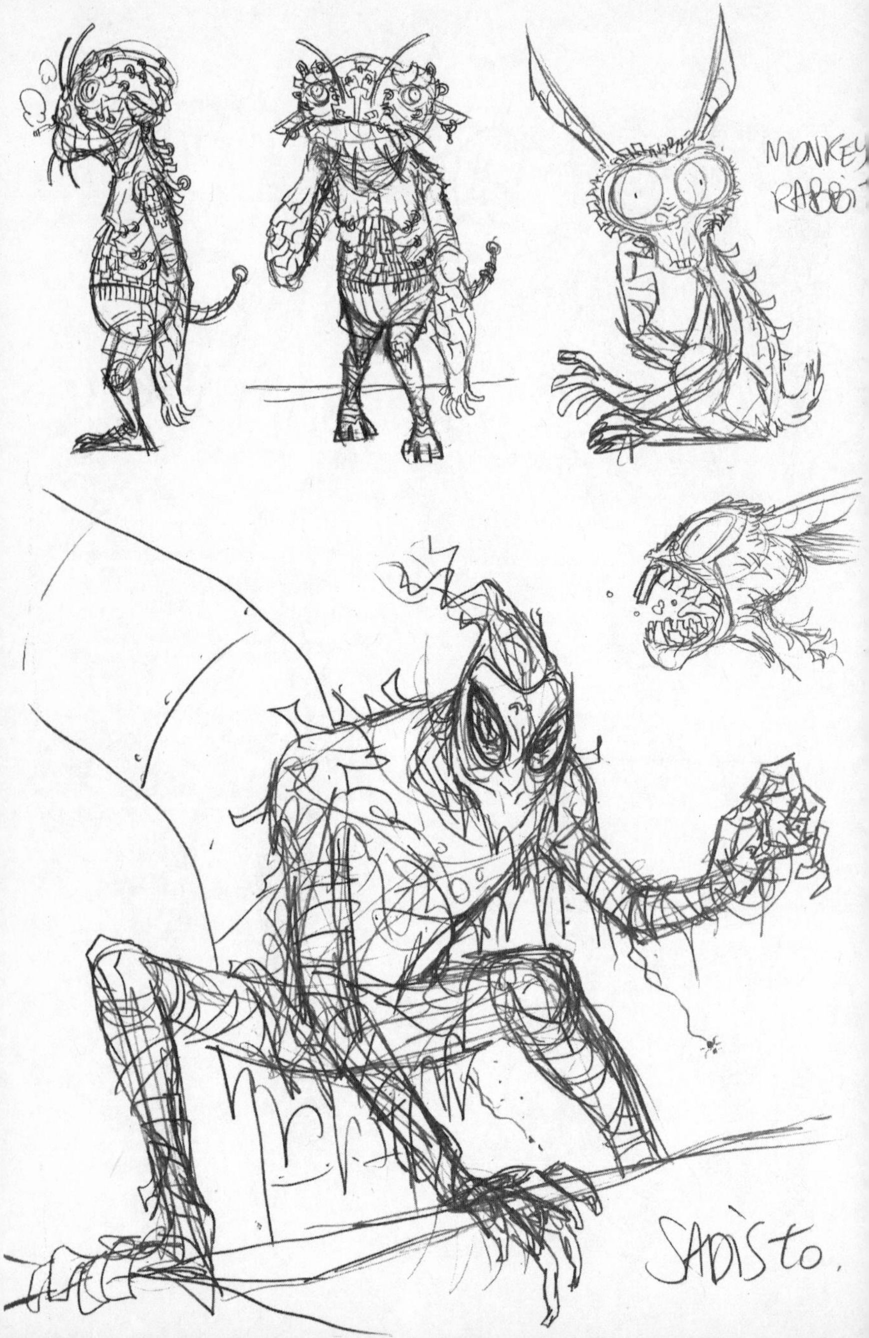
MONKEY RABBIT
SADISTO.

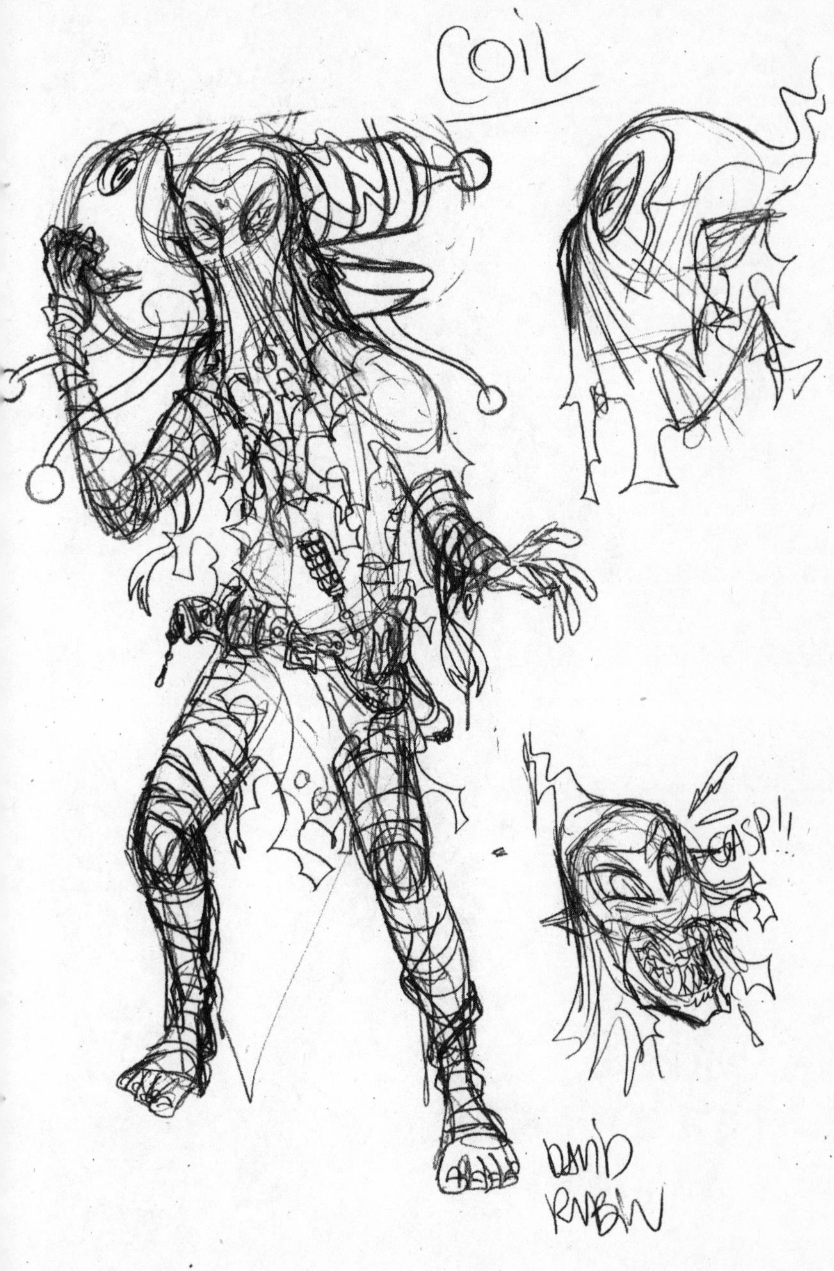
COIL
GASP!!
DAVID RUBIN

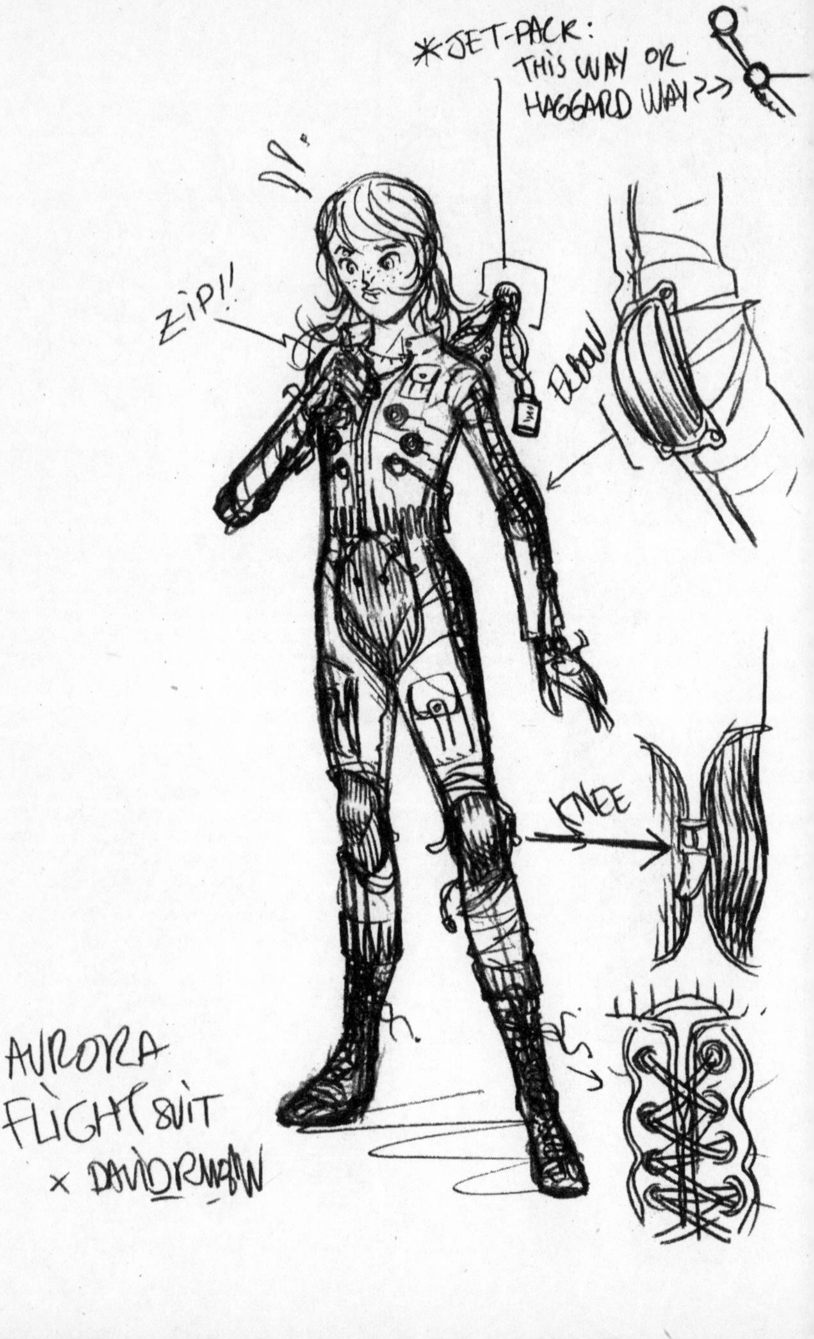

*JET-PACK:
THIS WAY OR
HAGGARD WAY?->
ZIP!!
ELBOW
KNEE
AURORA
FLIGHT SUIT
x DAVIDRUBIN